Praise for Craig Robertson

'Craig Robertson has surpassed himself with *Witness the Dead*, a **perfectly constructed** police procedural with real psychological depth' crimefictionlover.com

'A thoroughly satisfying, **thrilling and chilling ride** through the cold and dark streets of Glasgow' Keith B Walters

'Powerful and resolute and at times sensitive and compassionate . . . with a well thought out plot and **INTELLIGENT** narrative' Miles Orchard

'What you get is a good solid police procedural underpinned by an adept feeling for the realm of human relationships and the darker recesses of the human psyche' Jackie Farrant

'The story itself is **GRIPPING** and . . . [if] you like **GRITTY** crime fiction and don't mind a splash of gore, then this is a book you should read' Sue Gunnee

'**One of the best** crime writers in Scotland, if not Britain' Matt Craig

During his 20-year career in Glasgow with a Scottish Sunday newspaper, Craig Robertson interviewed three recent Prime Ministers, attended major stories including 9/11, Dunblane, the Omagh bombing and the disappearance of Madeleine McCann. He was pilloried on breakfast television, beat Oprah Winfrey to a major scoop, spent time on Death Row in the USA and dispensed polio drops in the backstreets of India. His debut novel, *Random*, was shortlisted for the CWA New Blood Dagger and was a *Sunday Times* bestseller

Also by Craig Robertson

Cold Grave
Snapshot
Random

WITNESS THE DEAD

CRAIG ROBERTSON

**SIMON &
SCHUSTER**

London · New York · Sydney · Toronto · New Delhi

A CBS COMPANY

First published in Great Britain by Simon & Schuster UK Ltd, 2013
This paperback edition published, 2013
A CBS COMPANY

1 3 5 7 9 10 8 6 4 2

Simon & Schuster UK Ltd
1st Floor
222 Gray's Inn Road
London WC1X 8HB

www.simonandschuster.co.uk

Simon & Schuster Australia, Sydney
Simon & Schuster India, New Delhi

A CIP catalogue record for this book
is available from the British Library

Paperback ISBN 978-0-85720-420-2
Ebook ISBN 978-0-85720-421-9

Typeset by M Rules
Printed and bound by CPI Group (UK) Ltd, Croydon, CR0 4YY

To Isaac Paul Berman,
born 2nd February 2013.

Chapter 1

Early Saturday morning

They called it the City of the Dead. The sprawling Gothic landscape that perched over Glasgow and contained the remains of fifty thousand lost souls. Now it held fifty thousand and one.

The flash from Tony Winter's camera lit up the Necropolis and threw fleeting shadows across the nearby gravestones and the twisted figure of the young woman who lay broken below them.

Along with the dark-blonde hair that was wetly plastered across her ashen face was a look of terror fitting for someone seeing their last in a Victorian graveyard. Winter shut out the angry buzz from the throng around him and saw only the girl, her skirt pulled obscenely above her waist, her arms and legs splayed wide across the flat top of the raised gravestone that she had been laid out on.

Her bare feet, streaked with dirt, hung stiffly from either side of the tomb and were being tickled by rogue blades of grass that grew tall by the grave's edge. But the grass couldn't cause her to shiver any more than the dank morning air or the chill wind that whirled and whistled round the Necropolis. She was as cold as the stone slab she lay on.

Under the make-up she could have been anything from eighteen to thirty, but Winter took her to be in her early twenties, Saturday-night glam turned Sunday-morning grim. Her steel-silver skirt had been short enough before her attacker left it high and, to all extents and purposes, absent. Her knickers were minimal, designed more for show than to be practical, and now lay on the grass below her. Her sparkly black top was cut low and set off by the ornate silver necklace that was now wound tightly round her throat. Its sharp edges were biting her skin and had persuaded a dry slither of burgundy to trail towards her cleavage.

Winter focused on the necklace, his lens picking out its flashy knots and the sharp tips that now met the girl's torn flesh. He photographed her hands, placed palm up as if in supplication, the pale pink fingernails, which showed no obvious signs of having clawed at an assailant. Her skin was tanned.

Her light-blue eyes were now staring into some hell beyond her worst nightmare. Her mouth, its pink lipstick smeared, was locked in mid-scream. Winter circled her, patiently, diligently, capturing her from every angle, seizing scale, perspective and horror. Finally, he stood back and took a full-length shot, encapsulating the dignity that had been stolen from her along with her life.

Words from behind him began to invade his focus, distracting him from the job he had to do. *Raped. Strangled. Ritualistic. Barbaric.*

Winter realised it was probably the first time he had truly taken in what anyone else was saying from the moment that he and DI Derek Addison had crossed the Bridge of Sighs into the Necropolis itself. As soon as they had got out of Addison's car, he knew that his *sgriob*, that tingle of anticipation at the prospect of photographing what lay ahead, was flaring furiously. He'd itched to see what lay on top of the hill that loomed darkly before them and it tingled again when he'd seen the faint glow of light behind the summit that signalled where the others had already gathered.

He'd been almost in a dream as Addison led him through the knot of people gathered around the girl. As they'd parted to reveal the brutal sight on top of the tomb, Winter was struck as much with the guilty pang of an undeclared pleasure as with revulsion. Photographing the dead, particularly those so horrifically murdered, gave him an inexcusable thrill that he didn't dare try to explain, far less justify, even to himself.

They stood almost reverentially and watched while he worked, their own disgust largely subsumed by professionalism. It was Addison's words that finally broke his focus.

'So where are her shoes?' the DI muttered. Then, louder, 'Where are her fucking shoes?'

'We've looked within a forty-yard circle of the grave, sir,' piped up Sandy Murray, the first of the uniformed constables at the scene. 'But we haven't seen anything. We'll do a wider search once the sun is up properly.'

Addison nodded but one of the new DCs, Fraser Toshney, interrupted him before he could reply.

'Maybe they turned back into something else at midnight.'

He grinned blackly. 'Along with her pumpkin coach and ball gown made from rags.'

The rest of the team held their collective breaths as Addison fixed Toshney with a furious stare.

'Son, you're new round here, and I'll give you the benefit of the doubt that that was a nervous mistake. But if the phrase Cinderella Killer appears in any fucking newspaper, then I'm holding you personally responsible. Do you understand me?'

Toshney reddened and stammered an apology.

'Yes, boss. I was only ... Sorry. Sorry.'

'Don't be sorry. Just go and find me a witness from some of the scumbags here in the middle of the night. Anyway, the slippers don't turn back into anything. They were given to her by her Fairy Godmother, you ignorant bastard. Now piss off.'

Addison knew that the breathing part-time residents of the Necropolis, the neds and drunks with their bottles of Buckfast, sleeping bags and discarded needles, had doubtless scattered at the first sign of the approaching plods. Even if Toshney was able to find any of them, it would most likely achieve the square root of hee-haw in terms of useful information. The DC knew it too but wasn't stupid enough to annoy Addison further, so disappeared over the hill with a nod to one of the uniforms to follow him.

'Okay,' Addison barked as Toshney left. 'Now that we are one fuckwit less, let's continue. Her handbag is just off the path, money in it but no ID. Not a robbery, then, as if we hadn't already guessed. And any ID that was in there was probably taken to slow us down. Constable Murray, you and your troops search on the perimeter for places he might have dumped it.'

The cop nodded without much enthusiasm.

'Mr Baxter,' Addison continued, 'if you could examine any ground that hasn't been trampled all over and see if you can tell me if she was wearing shoes on her way up here. Presuming that she did walk here, that is.'

Campbell Baxter, the rotund, grey-bearded crime-scene manager, frowned at being told how to do his job but acquiesced grimly.

For the first time, Winter looked across the gravestone and saw DS Rachel Narey looking back at him. It was barely a month since they, or more accurately she, had agreed it would be better if they split up, and here they were, staring at each other across the cold of an early Glasgow morning, a body between them. Their relationship had always been a secret from everyone else and now its ending was similarly wrapped in silence.

He saw her seek his eyes above the mêlée, a shared moment, nothing more than a raising of eyebrows, but it said everything. This was bad.

They watched Addison crouch by the girl's body, slowly working his way round the tombstone, his head at times uncomfortably close to the girl's semi-naked body. Narey's expression flashed distaste.

Addison finished his circumnavigation and stood, his eyes briefly closing over and exhaling hard. Even for a flippant, war-weary soldier like him, it was harder going than he wished to admit.

He finally turned to Cat Fitzpatrick, the pathologist at the scene, and gestured for her to join him.

'External signs would suggest she's had sex recently,' he said to her. 'Agreed?'

Fitzpatrick nodded her accord.

'So, Ms Fitzpatrick,' Addison continued, 'I would be grateful if you could tell me two things. One, was she raped? Two, was she alive when it happened?'

Fitzpatrick sighed.

'We'll need to get her back to base to give you a definitive answer, but I'll give you an opinion before we get off this hill. Although I'll give you an opinion on something else for nothing. The bastard who did this needs his bollocks cut off.'

'No argument here,' Addison said softly.

As Fitzpatrick went to work, Addison went over to Narey to get her take on the night's events, leaving Winter to quietly take shots of the small but busy crowd of cops and forensics gathered in the gloom above the city. He reeled off as many scene-setting pictures as he could despite the risk of the flashgun alerting his subjects to what he was up to. He caught the look of compassion on Cat Fitzpatrick's face as she worked her way up from the dead girl's shoeless feet. He framed the solemn discussion between Addison and Narey, his best mate and his former girlfriend, the pair charged with the heavy responsibility of finding out who had done this. He also photographed a young WPC standing on the edge of the group, looking lost and frightened, her damp eyes always returning to the body on the slab. Moving back six feet, he changed his angle and managed to position a seated angel behind the girl, the sculpture's shadowy head turned away as if the pain of looking was all too much. It was all he needed.

As he lowered his camera and walked towards Addison and Rachel, he slowly tuned into their terse conversation.

'Is this place not supposed to be locked up at night?' she was asking him.

'It is, but there's always a way in,' he replied. 'You can't keep people out of a place like this if they're determined enough.'

'Yes, but surely they can be kept out if they're carrying a body,' Narey countered. 'I don't see how he could have slipped through or over railings if he had to carry her as well.'

'The same thing occurred to me,' Addison agreed. 'Unless she walked in here alive.'

Narey shook her head.

'You're thinking like a man. I don't scare easy but I don't think I'd be in a hurry to go into the creepiest place in Glasgow in the middle of the night. Not with someone capable of murder.'

Addison shrugged. 'Well, maybe some girls are a bit more adventurous,' he answered, a sly smile playing across his lips. 'But you're probably right. I have a fair bit of experience of persuading young ladies to do odd things but I can't think of too many who'd be keen on coming in here in the dark.'

A sudden voice from behind them cut off Narey's sarcastic response.

'Detective Inspector?'

Cat Fitzpatrick had turned to face them.

'You better see this.'

As they looked, the pathologist began to slowly ease up the young woman's top, exposing the pale flesh of her midriff. As Fitzpatrick pulled up the material, the other cops crowded in to see what she had discovered.

Inch by inch, she revealed daubs of bright red on the

woman's stomach and it slowly dawned on them that the scarlet marks were forming words.

With an unconscious flourish, Fitzpatrick stood back to let them see properly, one gloved hand still holding the top just below the girl's chest.

Some of the cops muttered darkly, someone let out a gasp, Addison swore and Winter lifted his camera.

Written in a heavy hand was a single word.

SIN

Chapter 2

Winter pushed his way silently past Addison and Narey. Fitzpatrick continued to hold the young woman's top above the lurid red lettering and he zoomed in on the wording, seeing clearly that it had been written in lipstick, its waxy swathe standing starkly against her pasty skin. Winter could see the anger that the thick block capitals had been written in. The lipstick had been pressed hard, furiously even, onto the girl's flesh, the wording thick and smudged where the material had clung to it.

Winter stood back, then smartly to the side to cut off Addison, who was attempting to get a closer look. Winter raised his camera again and rattled off a number of full-length shots, the lettering appearing darkly, almost comically Gothic, on the granite canvas of the gravestone.

Instinctively, he stepped forward again, filled the frame with the word and snapped. Winter knew this photograph was going straight onto his wall. Just three letters, one colour, no blood, no broken bones, but it would hang there with the best and worst of them because it hit every mark.

'Fucking great,' Addison was muttering softly. 'As if this wasn't bad enough already.'

Narey turned to look at Addison.

'Worse? A girl is murdered and left draped across a gravestone and you think it can get worse?'

'You know what I mean,' he snapped back at her. '*That*' – he gestured broadly towards the girl – 'is murder. But *that*' – he pointed directly at the lettering – '*that* is frightening. It's psycho stuff. *That* worries me.'

Narey didn't respond beyond a shrug that suggested she wasn't entirely convinced. Murder was as bad as it got in her book. She edged past Addison and took Winter's place standing over the body. Almost unconsciously, she traced the shape of the letters in the air with her index finger.

'What shade of lipstick is that?' Addison asked behind her.

An amused look flashed between Narey and Fitzpatrick.

'Rimmel's Autumn Red?' the DS suggested.

'I'd say almost definitely,' the pathologist replied.

'Great. But how can you be sure th—' Addison spotted the grins on the women's faces. 'Are you two taking the piss?'

'Um, yes, sir. It could be a thousand shades and a hundred manufacturers. There's no way we could tell by looking at it.'

'Aye, very funny. I haven't got time for you two—'

'There's tests we can run that will tell us what it is,' Fitzpatrick said, quickly interrupting him, attempting to soothe the savage beast. 'But it will take a while.'

'Yeah? Well get it done quicker than that. And, seeing as

you two are such experts, one of you explain to me why the lipstick she's wearing is a different colour to the one that's been used to write this on her stomach.'

Winter turned to see Narey and Fitzpatrick exchange more wry glances.

'Women aren't usually that good at organising their hand-bags,' Fitzpatrick explained. 'If we wear a lipstick for one night out, then we'll probably still be carrying it around the next time we go out, even though we've put something else on.'

'Or the killer brought this one with him?' Addison asked them.

'It's possible,' Narey conceded.

'Well, find out. It's obviously women's work, so you two sort it. And, while you're at it, find if the bastard that wrote this is right or left-handed. Same goes for the way the chain's been pulled round her neck.'

'No problem, guvnor,' Narey mocked. 'It's a privilege for us wee women even to be given the opportunity to work. God bless Emmeline Pankhurst.'

'Just do it,' Addison grouched. 'Cat, get on with examining the rest of her. Tony, you come with me. Murray says the guy who found her is at the bottom of the hill.'

Winter fell into line behind Addison with an apologetic shrug to the two women as soon as the DI's back was turned. The cop and the photographer walked back onto the gravel path, dodging the puddles that had formed on the rutted surface, and headed back down the hill. Addison paused at the top of the bend and looked at the city waking up below them.

A mist was lifting like steam rising from a pot left to boil too long, the city emerging beneath it, half asleep and half awake, lights on and lights off. High-rises and office blocks, shops, homes and factories, all stretching and scratching and reaching for the first cigarette of the day. The Necropolis overlooked it all, untouched and another world away. Winter quickly reached into his bag and changed the lens on his camera so that he could photograph the emerging cityscape, noting how it was cast in its own sepia tones without the need for fancy filters or Photoshop.

'Used to come here when I was a kid,' he told Addison. 'My pals and I knew the place like the backs of our hands. We even camped out here one night for a dare. It's based on the Père Lachaise, you know?'

'The what?'

'The Père Lachaise, ya heathen. It's the cemetery in Paris where Jim Morrison's buried.'

'Did he no' used to play for Dunfermline?'

'Piss off. Anyway, why am I going with you to see a witness? I'm guessing you don't want me to photograph him.'

'Well, I do hear he's a picture, but no. I just wanted some company and those women were doing my head in. Anyway, if I leave Narey up there, then we get finished sooner, and the sooner we get finished—'

'The sooner you can get breakfast.' Winter finished for him. 'You ever think with anything other than your stomach? Actually, don't answer that. I know the answer.'

Addison grinned.

'I'm thinking the King's Café on Elmbank Street,' he said dreamily. 'Two rolls, bacon and black pudding on each. Mind you, they do the best chips-and-cheese in the city. You know the secret? They double-deck the cheese. Above *and* below the chips. Amazing.'

'It's a miracle of anatomy that you aren't a fat bastard, Addy,' Winter chided him.

Addison was a lanky six foot four, carrying barely an ounce of fat despite his unrelentingly patriotic diet of stodge.

'It's the truth,' the DI admitted. 'But it would be rude not to take advantage of it. So let's go interview our star witness so I can get fed.'

The man was waiting nervously for them at the foot of the hill, standing between the Bridge of Sighs and the menacing doors of the Façade – the entrance to a tunnel that was to have been built into the heart of the hill to contain catacombs but now protected nothing more than a collection of lawn-mowers. Addison was right, Winter thought: the guy was a picture all right.

In his late fifties, he was wearing a navy-and-white-striped dressing gown over pale-blue pyjamas and black slippers. A couple of days of grey grizzle adorned his face and thick locks of dark hair were pushed back on his head. Most strikingly, though, was the ginger cat that he was holding at the end of a leash.

'It's a well-known fact that most dead bodies are found by people taking their dog for a walk,' Addison murmured to Winter as they neared the man. 'But this is a first for me.'

Winter stifled a laugh as well as the urge to take the man's photograph.

'Mr Gibson? I'm DI Addison. I understand you found the deceased.'

The man looked up, startled, and began nodding fiercely.

'Yes, yes. Yes. I was just telling this officer. It ... I was so ... I mean, this is just so ...'

Addison sighed, not exactly famed for his patience.

'Take your time, Mr Gibson. I'm sure it was very upsetting, but please start from the beginning and just tell me what happened.'

The man nodded, less fiercely this time.

'Well, I had to take Lulu outside for her ablutions. She'd had sardines, you see. It's my fault, really, because, although she loves them, I know they don't always agree with her. It's the oil. The vet says she's just being a madam, but she's a sensitive soul, her breeding, you see. She's very—'

'So you had to take her out,' Addison interrupted.

'Yes, yes. Sorry. Yes. She just won't *go* inside the flat. She's very particular that way. Just too ... respectful for that. Well bred, you see. Anyway, we normally go for a walk when we go outside for her business. She expects it and is rather partial to a tour round the Necropolis.'

'She is or you are?' asked Addison, failing to keep the note of scorn out of his voice, knowing full well the Necropolis's reputation as a late-night meeting place for men.

'*She* is,' Gibson replied indignantly.

'Even though the cemetery gates are locked at night?' the DI queried.

The man had the good grace to look embarrassed.

'I just live over there,' he said by way of explanation. 'I know where the gaps in the fence are.'

'Do you, now?' Addison asked pointedly.

Gibson ignored the question and continued.

'Lulu and I went up the hill and she did her business near

the big tombstone of Corlinda Lee. You know? Queen of the Gypsies? She read Queen Victoria's palm at a Gypsy ball in Dunbar. No?'

Addison shook his head brusquely and Winter knew he was bitterly regretting asking Gibson to start at the beginning.

'Anyway,' the man continued blithely, 'we did our stuff near Corlinda and continued up the hill. I think Lulu must have sensed something. Cats are very perceptive that way – the well-bred ones are at any rate. She led me there. Better than a bloodhound, I'd say. I couldn't see what it was at first but I knew there was something wrong. Her hair was standing on end and she was hissing something terrible. And then we saw her, the girl.'

'What time was this, Mr Gibson?'

'About five. It was still pitch black and when I shone my torch on her ... well, I just couldn't ... I mean, I'd never seen anything like it in my life.'

Neither Addison nor Winter doubted that.

'Did you touch her, Mr Gibson?' asked Addison.

'No!' the man shrieked crossly. 'I am a great fan of crime dramas and I know police procedure. I did not contaminate the scene.'

'Okay, okay,' accepted Addison. 'Did you see anyone else anywhere near the body? Anything unusual at all?'

Gibson shook his head dolefully.

'No. If there was anyone else in, and there are usually a few ... resident undesirables who are terribly rude to Lulu and me, then they were asleep or unconscious. We went back down the hill as quickly as we could and went back into the flat where I called nine, nine, nine immediately. Well, I had a large brandy then I called. I hope that was okay?'

Addison sighed again.

'Yes, Mr Gibson. I don't think the delay was crucial. So you saw or heard nothing all the time you were in there?'

'Well, yes. There was the noise.'

'The noise?'

'Yes. I nearly died. Oh ... I mean, I shouldn't have said died. I'm sorry. Sorry.'

'What noise?' Addison growled irritably.

'Well ... Lulu and I were halfway down the hill when she suddenly stopped, and so I did too. I listened and there was nothing, but then there was this scuffling sound in the bushes and a noise like someone hurrying away. I nearly had a heart attack on the spot.'

'And did you hear anything after that?'

'No, no. But I wasn't for hanging around to find out. I was back in the flat as quick as my feet could take me,' Gibson answered breathlessly.

'Well done,' replied Addison with the fakest smile that Winter had ever seen him muster. 'Mr Gibson, I'll need you to show the constable the spot where you say you heard this noise. If you could go with him now, please. You've been very helpful. We will be in touch.'

'Oh, it's no problem. We're glad to help. Aren't we, Lulu? If there's anything else at all that we can do to help, then please let us know.'

Addison turned his back on the man with a cursory nod and walked closer to the constable who had been taking Gibson's statement.

'Have you been inside this guy's flat yet?' he muttered softly.

'No, sir,' the uniform replied equally quietly. 'Not yet.'

'Well, do it. Mark off the area where he heard his noise, then take him inside on the pretence of getting his statement down in full and check his place out. I never trust a man who likes cats.'

'Yes, sir.'

Addison turned to leave but saw Winter chatting to Gibson.

'That's a beautiful cat you have there, Mr Gibson,' the photographer was saying.

The man beamed and looked down at his pride and joy sitting patiently at the end of its pale-pink lead.

'Would you mind if I took a photograph of the two of you?' Winter asked.

Gibson brightened considerably, puffing himself up.

'Well, if it helps. It's the least we can do. Will it help?'

'It might,' Winter assured him. 'You can never tell what might make the difference in a case like this.'

Gibson nodded enthusiastically and stood up straight, pulling at Lulu's lead to get her the same.

Winter rattled off a succession of frames of the strange man in the blue pyjamas and the striped dressing gown with his preening ginger tabby. He wasn't sure if he wanted them just for the novelty value or as some bizarre photographic counterpoint to what was on top of the hill, but it didn't matter. The picture was his for ever.

'Fruit loop,' was Addison's assessment as the two men climbed back up the path to the scene.

'Because he has a cat or because he might be gay, you big-oted sod?'

'*Might* be gay?' Addison retorted. 'He owns a cat.'

'That's it? You rest your case? Did the entire second half of the twentieth century pass you by?'

'Fuck *that* case,' Addison snarled. 'It's the one up there that I'm bothered about.'

'What do you think the noise was he heard in the bushes?'

'Who knows? Rabbits, deer, some other "cat walker" looking for companionship. Anybody's guess for now. We'll get Baxter and his people down there to see what tracks they can find.'

'Deer?'

'There's loads of deer in here. Cute-as-fuck Bambi types, if you like that sort of thing. Some bastards even hunt them with dogs. Eric Paterson, the super over at London Road, is really hot on it. He makes it a personal mission to chase down the sods responsible.'

'The same way you're going to deal with whoever did that on top of the hill?'

'The very same. Come on. Let's see what they've got.'

They climbed the hill again and, as they did so, the sun came up and the glowering figure of John Knox could be seen towering over the sepulchres, mausoleums, monuments, obelisks, statues and cherubim. The frown worn by the man who led the Protestant Reformation was perhaps caused by the multidenominational *memento mori* below him in Gothic, Celtic, Moorish and Jewish.

'Think he saw who did it?' Winter asked with a nod to the twelve-foot-tall figure of Knox perched on a sixty-foot-high Doric column.

'Probably too dark,' Addison replied. 'But, even if he did, chances are he'd blame it on a Catholic.'

When they got back to the scene, they saw Narey and Baxter standing off to the side, discussing the scraps of evidence they had accumulated. Fitzpatrick was still working her way fastidiously over the body, the poor girl's naked form not yet afforded the dignity of being covered.

'Okay,' Addison said as he breezed into the scene, not waiting for anyone else to finish their conversation. 'Listen up.'

Narey, Baxter and Fitzpatrick dutifully stopped and paid attention, their annoyance at having to do so barely concealed.

'Our only known witness is worse than useless,' Addison went on. 'All we have to go on for now sits on top of this hill. Here's what we need. Her name. And we need that as soon as possible. Shoes. I want to know where her fucking shoes are. Lipstick. I want to know the make and colour that wording was written in. Her movements. I want to know where she was last night and who she was with. Most of all, though, I want to know who had a reason to write "SIN" on this girl's stomach. Someone who knows her would be the best guess. A boyfriend maybe. Or ex-boyfriend. Find him and find the person most likely to have done this. Okay?'

Narey and Baxter looked at each other ruefully, but it was Fitzpatrick who replied.

'I might be able to give you a partial answer to the last of those, Inspector. And Tony? You might want to get your camera out again.'

Winter's itch twitched as he and Addison converged on the pathologist as she raised the girl's purple-tinged body onto its side so that they could see her back. Narey and Baxter had obviously already been let in on the discovery and Addison looked pissed off at being the last to know; but, far more than that, he was eager to know what it was.

'I'm no expert on tattoos,' Fitzpatrick continued. 'But I would say this was done fairly recently.'

Under the glare of the temporary spotlights and the fleeting brilliance of Winter's flashgun, they saw it. Arched across the curve of the girl's lower back was the depiction of a writhing snake, working its way round bold letters separated by beating hearts. Despite the skin's discoloration where the lividity had settled after death, the name could clearly be made out.

Addison stared at the tattoo as Winter fired off a series of shots. Finally, the DI spoke low and steady, little more than an angry rumble that they had to strain to hear against the rising wind.

'Well, what are you waiting for? Find out who the hell Razor is and bring him in.'

Chapter 3

Glasgow, July 1972

He checked himself out in the mirror, tilting his head left and right, trying different expressions on for size. He'd do. He'd more than do.

The cut of his suit was pretty special; two weeks' wages that had cost him but it had been worth it. Three-piece, royal blue with a thick gold stripe running through it. The guy in Slaters who had sold him it said that it had come from Carnaby Street and was the only one in Glasgow. The trousers had four buttons on the waist and the waistcoat was cut high enough to show them off. Nice flared bottoms on them, too, above a pair of righteous three-inch platform shoes. Dead gallus, if he said so himself.

The tie was as wide as the Clyde and he'd thought twice about wearing it. What the hell, though. It looked good; *he* looked good. You couldn't be going to the dancing wearing just anything: you had to look the part. That was true even if you were just going there to try to get off with a lassie. Which he wasn't. Not quite.

It still mattered, though, making the effort. Same with his hair. He pushed his hands through it, making it appear even bigger, his sideburns thick and dark. Some guys still wore Brylcreem like it was fashionable. Could you believe that? The idiots wouldn't know style if they fell over it. Like he'd listen to what they had to say about anything.

It was going to be a big night, he could feel it, the nerves just bubbling under the surface. His blood was pumping with what-ifs and he already felt the need of a drink to slow them down. He couldn't have more than a couple, though. Big night. He needed to keep a clear head. Anything else was far too risky.

He blew a stream of air towards the mirror and flapped his lips, making the noise come out in a jumpy rat-a-tat-tat, shaking his shoulders at the same time. He wanted, needed, the worry out of his system. He couldn't afford to be nervous, not tonight.

He played with the knot in his tie, fingering at it, easing it towards his throat and away again until he was comfortable with the look. It wasn't like he was really into it; the clothes and that. But he could pull it off. Better than that, he'd look like he wasn't even trying to pull it off.

He pulled his hand up towards his mouth and breathed hard into the palm, trying to catch the smell of his breath. He did it again, just to be sure, but it seemed okay.

Moving closer to the mirror again, he made his eyes crease at the side the way that Steve McQueen did. Took him ages to get that right. He'd gone to see *The Thomas Crown Affair* at the Cinerama on Eglinton Street. Loved that film. Totally cool, like McQueen himself.

Smile. Then look mean. Grin. The McQueen eyes. Mean and moody. 'Are ye dancing?' he asked out loud. Too loud.

'Did you say something in there?' came her voice from the other side of the bathroom door.

He froze. Guilty way before the event. Stand still, say nothing, pretend he hadn't heard her.

'Ah said, did you say something in there?'

'Eh . . . no, no. I was just thinking out loud, love. Wondering where the hairbrush was.'

He stared at himself in the mirror, not seeing McQueen. Not seeing cool. Seeing embarrassed. Seeing guilty. He shook himself again, blowing away the shamefaced cobwebs. It was going to be a big night and he didn't need his head full of shite. Get a grip.

She was standing there when he came out of the bathroom, looking at him oddly, seeing the suit for the first time. He could see that she liked it and yet she didn't.

'You're looking kinda smart, are you not? Where did you say you were off to?'

'Ah didn't. I'm working, though. Look, I'll try not to be too late back, but don't you bother waiting up for me. Sorry, I'm running late as it is. Better rush.'

The front door closed behind him and he could hear the theme tune from *The Thomas Crown Affair* echoing in his head. Echoing like windmills in his mind.

The bus into town was busy, full of people chattering away as if it were just a night like any other. He knew it wasn't, and they should have, too.

Behind him, two girls were singing 'Get it On' by T.Rex and

in between verses they were giggling about how the band were coming to Glasgow and they'd die if they didn't get to see them. They were both in love with Marc Bolan and each said they loved him more than the other one. All he could think of was how unlikely it was that not seeing a band would be the death of them.

Someone else started a singsong at the back, three young blokes who quickly drowned out T.Rex with a raucous version of 'Chirpy Chirpy Cheep Cheep'. The two girls glared at them at first but soon gave in and within minutes the entire bus, conductor and driver included, were singing the song on the way into town. Everyone but him.

It was a warm night and the windows of the bus were open, letting the singing escape into the night air, treating Maryhill and then St George's Cross to chorus after chorus. They weren't fooling him, though: it was whistling in the dark, showing that Glasgow wasn't afraid of the bogeyman that nobody mentioned. Was that why he wasn't singing, because he knew that they should have been afraid?

When the bus hit the city centre, he got off at Buchanan Street and walked the rest of the way. Klass was on the third floor of a building at the top of West Nile Street and, as it was a Friday night, it was easily recognisable by the queue of people that snaked all the way down onto the pavement.

The queue wound up the narrow stairs and left only enough room for those not allowed admittance to make their way back down the steps and onto the street. When he got nearer to the entrance, he could see people doing their first dance of the night, a nervy quickstep as they moved from one foot to the other, waiting to find out if they'd be knocked back. It was the best disco in town and tough to get into. 'Not tonight, boys' was the usual line from the bouncers, and he saw shoulders sag as they had to deal with the embarrassment of not getting in. He'd get in, though; there was no doubt about that.

He scanned the queue, looking for likely candidates. Glasgow in all shapes and sizes but not one that immediately jumped out as being what he was looking for. There would be plenty more inside, though, and more still as the night went on.

The bouncers gave him the once-over and then the nod.

The place was teeming with people, sticky with summernight body heat. It smelled of beer and cigarettes, perfume and hormones. It was light enough to see everyone and dark enough to hide a few imperfections.

Ages ranged from distinctly underage up to early thirties. On another night he'd be interested in the underagers, but not tonight. Everybody was glammed up but the styles were all over the place. The Brylcreem boys were still there, refusing to give up their slick. The hippies and the rockers were there, too, mimicking London and New York fashions but doing it their own way with whatever clothes they could lay their hands on. A few of the guys had classy suits but he reckoned his more than held its own. The gold stripes were getting a few looks.

You'd have thought that maybe people would seem nervous, but it didn't look that way. Maybe it was all front. Like him. All show. But, inside, hearts going nineteen to the dozen. It would have to be playing on your mind, surely. Especially the girls. You wouldn't know it, though. If you'd landed from

Mars you'd never have thought they had anything more to worry about than when the band would be on and whether they'd pull by the end of the night. Life was in that room and nothing else mattered.

That night's band was at number three in the charts and had played at Green's Playhouse the month before. They'd gone down a storm then but this place would have been full anyway. It was where it was happening, in more ways than one. They came on and played and half the crowd danced and the other half stood and watched or sat at the tables at the side and clapped. He watched too. He watched other people's eyes and where they were looking. He watched for signs of something wrong, something that didn't quite fit. And he watched for the person he was looking for, even though he had little idea of what he might see.

As the hours slipped by, the room got hotter and louder, the walls closing in as the bodies multiplied, hazy mirages under the glitter ball's shimmer, all wrapped in a fug of cigarette smoke. He got himself a lager to slake his thirst and to make sure he looked right, his back against the wall and everything before him. He checked out the room for the umpteenth time, careful not to catch the eye of anybody who looked likely. The last thing he wanted to do was let them know he was hunting them. It wouldn't do to scare them off.

He was aware he was breathing heavier than he should and that his senses were heightened like a wolf ready to attack. He had to calm down. Could people tell that he was like that just by looking at him? Could they sense that he wasn't the same as everyone else there? It would ruin everything if they could.

There was a couple standing by the far wall, the bloke a bit too close for the girl's liking. The fellow was leaning in on her, his face leering just inches from hers. She wanted to retreat but couldn't, her back against the wall and nowhere else to go. She was uncomfortable. He could see that, even from the other side of the room, and it made his pulse quicken. He saw another bloke circle the room, clearly checking out the talent but making no effort to ask anyone to dance or to chat them up. He was a watcher, too.

The band had finished their set and the DJ had taken over again: a tall, blond-haired guy wearing an outrageous black leather suit with a red waistcoat and towering platforms. He soon had the dance floor full and the temperatures raised another notch. The dancing was good; it always had been in Glasgow but people were learning new moves now that the old dance-hall steps had had their day.

He sensed a different movement out the corner of his eye and heard the sound of several pairs of feet moving quickly. The adrenalin pumped through him and his hands balled into fists, his feet ready to run. Just as quickly, however, his eyes took in what was actually happening and he breathed again, hoping that no one had noticed his reaction.

The flurry of movements was the waitresses, all four of them, hustling round the tables at once. He glanced at his watch and realised the reason for their sudden scurry. It was quarter to eleven and they had to get food on all the tables before eleven o'clock. If you wanted a drink anywhere in Glasgow after eleven - and everybody did - then you had to have a meal. In Klass, the meal was laid on for you and you had to eat it. Every table got paper plates laden with spam and chips. The rule was that everyone had to eat at least one chip.

That meant you stayed within the law, that the disco could officially be classed as a function and the booze could flow for another hour.

The hour flew, the quickest of the night, like a river rushing downhill towards a waterfall. It was nearly closing time and the whiff of desperation was rising above the smell of sweat. The DJ put another record on the deck and, as soon as the first strains were heard, there was no doubt that it was the Last Chance Saloon, the undoubted moment of truth. 'When a Man Loves a Woman', the perennial Klass closing number, a guaranteed smoocher.

He saw anxious eyes looking around the room in the hope of finding someone who would agree to dance the last slow number. If they failed now, it would be the chippy and the last bus home. Eyes met eyes, lonely desperation met the same. He saw grudging shrugs of acceptance, wide-eyed nods of excitement and drunken indifference to anything other than a pulse as bodies paired off and moved together.

Female eyes sought out his. He blanked them, watching but dodging calls for attention. They weren't what he was looking for, not quite.

As the last few bars of Percy Sledge trailed off into silence, newly formed couples were fixed in fervent embraces, lips locked as if they were the one and only. The lights came on and bouncers called for movement, some smoochers oblivious to the lack of song or the harsher light until they were tapped on the shoulders and told to move along. He watched them leave in their new pairs and as dispirited singles.

There was nothing doing, not tonight, anyway. He'd be back, though, and he'd get what he wanted. He needed to.

Chapter 4

Saturday, mid-morning

Two hours after leaving the Necropolis, DS Rachel Narey parked up outside the multi-storey in Bridgeton, observing that the tower block's cream-and-terracotta make-over spectacularly failed to hide the fact that it remained another ugly high-rise.

The multi – there were three of them in all, each made up of two fifteen-storey, L-shaped towers clutching onto each other for dear life – stood precariously on the corner of Ruby Street and Baltic Street. It looked down on Dalmarnock Primary School and a warren of new-build housing that formed part of the East End regeneration. The high-rises were still there, untidy neighbours that had escaped the ASBO; slumlords of all they surveyed. The multis were supposed to have been communities on stilts but instead they'd made strangers out of people living on top of one another.

This area seemed to change every time she visited, slowly pulling itself up by its bootstraps on the back of the Commonwealth Games cash that had been invested. There was plenty still to be done but at least more people were getting to live within touching distance of the ground.

Narey had the new DC, Fraser Toshney, with her and it was the nearest of the tower blocks that interested them. The eighth floor was said to be home to one Robert Wylde, a.k.a. Razor, and their prime suspect as the boyfriend of the murdered girl. He was known to the police and a DS at London Road had offered Wylde up a warning: Wylde was quick on his feet and had been given the Razor moniker for a reason.

'Because he likes to shave regularly?' Toshney asked with a snigger as they sat in Narey's car awaiting the arrival of the blue-and-yellows that held their uniform back-up.

Narey just looked at him, expressionless, until Toshney was forced to swallow and turn his attention to the rain that was beginning to fall softly onto the windscreen. Toshney had been with them for only two months, but it had proved plenty of time for Narey to come to the conclusion that he was a pain in the arse. He was getting assigned to her far more than she liked, and she made a mental note, yet again, to have a word with Addison about it.

Other officers were also out searching for a clue to the murdered girl's identity. Teams were knocking up tattoo-parlour owners and asking them to check their records for jobs that matched the one on the girl's back. Others were working their way through missing persons or going door to door in the area around the cathedral. Something burned in her stomach, praying that her info on the nickname, slim as it was, was the one that would hit the target first. She wanted this. So much of the rest of her life seemed out of control or simply so messed up that work had become even more important. She was losing more of her dad to Alzheimer's with every passing day and the pain and the guilt and the practicalities of that had led her to turn Tony away. She'd tried to deal with one hurt and just caused another. Worse still, she knew she was keeping him dangling, unfairly offering him hope of a distant maybe. Her job mattered because it was the one thing she had control over.

The squad car arrived, pulling up so it was nose to nose with Narey's Megane, immediately drawing curious, guilt-ridden glances from those on the street. It would take seconds rather than minutes before everyone within the shadow of the tower block would know the cop car was there and so it was time to move.

Narey slipped out of the driver's door, leaving Toshney to follow in her wake and knowing that the uniforms would be right behind them. She pushed her way through the red-framed glass door and into the bowels of the Ruby Street multi, seeking out the lifts. She pressed eight and said a silent prayer of thanks when the elevator lurched noisily into life.

Toshney stood against the opposite wall, occasionally glancing up as if he were ready to say something but thinking better of it. The constables, Boyle and Murray, were looking at each other as if playing out some silent conversation of their own that involved sly smiles and secret nods. Narey vowed that, if Toshney wasn't the target of their joke, she'd rip their balls off. She glared at them and they, too, suddenly became interested in the shine on their shoes.

The lift groaned to a halt on the eighth floor and Narey put a finger to her lips before leading the three men out onto the landing. She and Toshney advanced to Wylde's door and she positioned Boyle and Murray at either end of the corridor, mindful of the warning from London Road to be careful.

Narey rapped on the door twice, warrant card in hand, listening intently for signs of movement inside. She heard the sound of feet padding around and knocked again, louder. 'Robert Wylde. Police. Open up.'

A shadow passed across the door's peephole and the door was slowly edged back. The short, fair-haired man in his early twenties who opened it looked half asleep, pulling on a T-shirt above tracksuit trousers and still barefoot. Wylde took a half-step back to allow Narey and Toshney into the flat, then rocked forward again, bursting between the two of them and into the corridor, a pair of trainers swinging from his left hand. Narey managed to get an arm up in time to make a grab at his shoulder but he slipped from her grasp. Toshney hadn't even moved.

Wylde looked at both ends of the corridor, seeing the constables closing on him and desperately sizing up his options. Murray, slightly the smaller of the two cops, was at the same end of the landing as Narey and Toshney, so Wylde spun and hared towards the bulkier figure of Boyle. The PC spread himself, arms wide, blocking Wylde's path as the other cops closed in on him from behind.

Wylde made a hopeless lunge towards his right, trying to squeeze himself through the tiny gap left by Boyle. The officer moved over to close what little space there was and, as he did so, Wylde spun on his left foot and pirouetted in the opposite direction, leaving Boyle floundering as he flew past him and towards the top of the stairs. As Wylde's fair hair disappeared from view, Narey screamed at the men who were standing and looking at each other.

'What are you waiting for? Toshney, get down the stairs after him. You two get in the lift. And remember he's dangerous. Christ Almighty! You're bloody useless.'

Toshney bolted for the stairs, knowing full well that his chances of catching Wylde were minimal unless the runaway tripped or fell. Boyle and Murray tumbled into the lift, grateful for the easier task and confident that it would beat Wylde down the eight floors to the street.

Shaking her head at their departure, Narey knocked on the door of the nearest flat that faced out onto Baltic Street, simultaneously reaching for her Airwave radio. The door was opened by a small, dark-haired woman in her early fifties who recognised Narey for a cop before she'd managed to raise her warrant card to eye level.

'Aye, what is it?' the woman asked warily, looking beyond Narey's shoulder.

'I need to use your flat, please. You're not in any trouble. I just need to look from your window onto the street.'

'Of course I'm no' in any trouble. What would I be in trouble for? Bloody cheek. Ah suppose you can come in but I'm no' happy about it. Do you want a cuppa tea?'

Narey smiled to herself at the woman's instinctive hospitality despite being put out at the intrusion. She quickly turned down the offer before speaking into the Airwave as she marched across the room, easing open a window and looking down towards the street. 'I need back-up. The nearest car you've got to Baltic Street in Bridgeton. And hurry. A suspect is fleeing on foot.'

A man's voice crackled back, asking her to wait while they contacted cars. 'Sergeant, there's a car on Swanston Street. It will be there within two minutes.'

As Narey listened, she looked down to see a figure burst out of the front door to the tower block and race across the street. From her high vantage point she could see the direction Wylde was running in.

'Okay, good, get me another one. Get it to ... the end of the street that runs away from the flats on Baltic down past the primary school. I think it's Albany Street. There's some old disused red-brick at the end. The street's a dead end for traffic, so get me a car at the other side.'

The street door flew open again and Narey watched Toshney run across the road in futile pursuit of Wylde. She knew she could have saved him a bit of sweat and worry by letting him know the cavalry was on its way, but she was rather enjoying watching him huff and puff in Wylde's wake. Moments later Boyle and Murray appeared and they, too, took off after the runaway, both quickly gaining ground on Toshney but not the suspect.

'Get the Swanston Street car onto Albany Street. Suspect on foot. Tell the drivers to avoid hitting officers in pursuit. Well, the uniformed ones anyway. They can hit the detective constable if they want.'

She heard the patrol car before she saw it. The blaring siren cut through the morning air and drifted up eight floors a good bit before the car arced round the corner at speed, instantly overtaking Toshney and then Boyle and Murray. Wylde heard it coming and was looking left and right, desperate to seek a way off the road, but there was the red-brick to the left and new-build houses to the right. He zigzagged one way, then the other, trying to buy himself enough time to get to the end of the street, where the concrete bollards would knacker the patrol car.

Just as it looked as if he would make it, the second cop car roared into view, screeching to an immediate halt at the other side of the bollards. The two cops inside were on the street in seconds and, with the Albany Street car squeezing Wylde towards the wall, there was nowhere for him to go.

Wylde braced himself with the railings and overgrown weeds of the old red-brick school at his back, bending at the waist and sucking up lungfuls of air. The patrol-car cops approached, Boyle then Murray not far behind. Wylde seemed to have given up the flight, bent double.

'Just watch him,' Narey murmured from the window.

As the two uniforms reached out to grab him, Wylde straightened and made a swift crisscrossing action with his arms in front of him. Both cops staggered back, one of them clutching at his cheek, the other grabbing at an injured shoulder. Wylde was named Razor for a reason.

Narey, cursing loudly, instinctively knew that both men had been cut with blades, double-sided razors that were probably hidden in his trainers. She saw that neither of them was fit to tackle Wylde, who was about to leg it past their car and onto Dunn Street and away. Boyle was only a yard behind and Narey wanted to scream out a warning.

Boyle had seen the other cops fall, however, and had sussed the reason. He could see the bright flash of red that was already scarring one officer's cheeks and had been round long enough to know the cause. In his final stride, he'd withdrawn his baton and lashed out as soon as he was within arm's length of Wylde, sending it crashing into the man's right wrist.

Wylde shrieked and turned towards Boyle, his left arm arcing through the air armed with a razor blade. Boyle swung again, missing and sending nothing but air past the razor's edge. He brought the baton back up as quickly and as hard as he could, hearing the satisfying crunch of metal on bone and Wylde screaming.

Murray and Toshney were there now and they bundled on top of Wylde, pinning his arms and making sure he'd dropped his blades. Narey watched them haul Wylde to his feet, seeing him dance furiously like some demented puppet on a string.

Narey got back onto control and ordered an ambulance for the two injured cops and someone to take their patrol car back to base, before speaking to Toshney.

'Get Murray and Boyle to take him on to Stewart Street. And get yourself a gym membership. You sound knackered. And ask those other two muppets how Wylde got to the bottom before the lift.'

'Yes, Sarge,' Toshney panted into his Airwave. 'And I already asked them. They said the fly bugger pressed the lift call button on the sixth floor and the third. Meant the lift stopped on both floors when they were going down.'

'Yeah, well, those other two cops paid the price. Don't mention the murdered girl whatever you do. For now, we charge him with resisting arrest and two counts of serious assault on a police officer. Once we get him into Stewart Street, we'll see what else he knows.'

Chapter 5

Saturday afternoon

'So why did you run?'

Robert Wylde's eyes were scrunched angrily into little balls of defiance, the scowl on his face a statement of intent. Whatever it was, he didn't do it. Except of course that he did. They'd all seen him cut those cops, the blood still staining Albany Street.

'No comment.'

'Something to hide?' Narey was doing the questioning. Addison had joined her but taken up a watching brief, standing against the far wall alongside Constable Sandy Murray. The duty solicitor, Mr Malcolmson, a grumpy middle-aged man with bad breath, was riding shotgun.

'No comment.'

'Innocent people don't do a runner when the polis knock on their door, Mr Wylde. Why did you run?'

'No comment.'

'Change the record, Robert. You're not a celebrity being

interviewed by the papers. You know why we're here and you know you're going to tell us all about it, so why not save everyone's time by talking now?'

'No comment.'

'Where were you last night, Robert? Or should I say, Razor? Where were you in the early hours of this morning?'

For the first time, Wylde's eyes flashed towards Narey, hints of confusion and worry evident. He pulled his stare back to the wall but she had his attention now.

'Were you near Glasgow Cathedral this morning, Robert? Near the Necropolis?'

'No. No comment.'

'Which is it? No or no comment?'

'Please, don't badger my client, Detective Sergeant Narey.' Malcolmson's interruption was no more than for show.

'Which is it, Robert, no or no comment? Were you near the Necropolis?'

Everyone in the room could see Wylde doing mental calculations, desperately trying to work out what answer would work better for him, the truth or a lie.

'No.'

'I see. Okay, at least we're getting somewhere. So you weren't near the Necropolis but you decided you had to run. Something you didn't want us to know. Or to find. You got a girlfriend, Robert?'

Wylde lost his spot on the wall again, his eyes betraying him as he looked at Narey properly for the first time. He looked away again quickly but she'd seen his fear.

'I asked if you had a girlfriend.'

'No comment.'

'Right. Can't really see there being a queue of girls daft enough. You're hardly God's gift, Robert. What do you think, DC Toshney? Hard to believe there's some girl out there with this eejit's name tattooed on her back.'

Wylde's head flew round, his eyebrows knotted and mouth open, fighting the urge to ask or answer but with a fever clearly building inside. His solicitor saw the look and was uncomfortably aware that there was something he knew nothing about.

'What information is it that you seek, DS Narey? I may need time to speak to my client alone.'

Narey bent down so that her face was just an inch from Wylde's. 'What's her name?'

'No comm—'

'I said what's her name?'

Wylde screwed his eyes up as if to shut Narey out. 'What's this about?'

'What's her name?'

'DS Narey. I insist you do not continue to repeat questions in my client's face.'

Wylde exhaled heavily. 'You probably mean Kirsty.'

'Probably? How many girls have got your name tattooed on their backs?'

'Just the one that I know of. Kirsty McAndrew.'

Narey stood up and backed away from Wylde, giving him a moment of breathing space. She swapped glances with Addison, who continued to stand there silently.

'Would you describe Kirsty for me, please, Robert.'

Wylde looked at the duty solicitor, who in turn stared at Narey, doubtless trying to second-guess her motives. He nodded at Wylde. Answer.

'She's twenty-two. Blonde hair. Um, blue eyes. Pretty. About five feet four.'

Both Narey and Addison felt the need to turn towards each other and share something, but resisted. It wasn't yet time.

'Okay, Robert. Good. When did you last see her?'

'Two weeks ago. We split up. What's this about?'

Wylde turned to his lawyer but Malcolmson was way ahead of him and was probably already counting future earnings. He gave Wylde the briefest of nods and said nothing. Narey continued.

'Who dumped who?'

'She … We … Well, it was just time to call it a day.'

'So she dumped you, Robert. Couldn't have been nice. Mad at her, were you?'

Wylde was still trying to do his best to keep his face impassive but Narey could see the uncertainty and alarm that was eating away at him from behind the mask. She just needed to give him a final kick over the edge.

'How angry were you at her, Robert? Angry enough to have killed her?'

Wylde's jaw dropped open and he made useless attempts to form words, his lips closing and retracting but never meeting. He finally managed one word. 'What?'

'Kirsty McAndrew was found murdered this morning.'

'No. No. That can't be … No. And you think that I …? No. No way!'

Wylde stood, kicking his chair back and swinging his handcuffed wrists in front of him. Addison and Murray calmly walked round the desk, one fronting him up while the other grabbed him by the collar and forced him down into the chair, which was positioned underneath him again. Wylde slumped back down, his mouth again jabbering the same silent song as before.

His eyes were on the floor now. Narey let him be for a moment, then, taking advantage of Wylde's preoccupation with the floor, looked to Addison for an opinion. She got a shrug and a frown that said maybe. And maybe not. She continued.

'Mr Wylde, when did you last see Kirsty McAndrew?'

'Two ... two weeks ago. I told you. Two weeks ago.'

'Where were you last night?'

'At my flat. And out for a bit. Had things to do. I didn't ... I didn't do that to her. No way did I do that.' He paused, brain whirring. 'Is she really dead?'

'Yes, Mr Wylde. She is.'

'Wisnae me.'

'Can you prove that, Robert? Who can vouch for where you were?'

Wylde's face crumpled. 'No one. I can't give you a name. No one.'

'Okay. Where does Kirsty McAndrew live?'

'With her mum and dad. In Elcho Street, no' far off the Gallowgate.'

'What's her mum and dad's name?'

'Um. Donald and, er, Geraldine. Donny and Geraldine. Oh, fuck, they'll be ... It wisnae me. Honestly. It wisnae.'

'Hmm. Mr Wylde, you assaulted two police officers today. Will you confirm that for the tape?'

The duty solicitor coughed and tried to interrupt, but Wylde spoke over him.

'Yes. I cut them. I'm sorry. I thought . . . I . . . I cut them with razor blades. But I didn't touch Kirsty. I swear it.'

Chapter 6

Saturday night

Her back was pressed against the cold, grey granite of the Victoria Bridge, at the beginning of Gorbals Street. Her front was pressed against his chest, his mouth seeking hers. Somewhere on the fringes of the kiss, she heard a car horn blare and the hiss of air brakes as a bus slowed on the vast junction with Clyde Street on the southern fringes of the city centre. It was way after midnight but the crossing was still busy with traffic.

'Come on, I'll walk you home.'

'No, you won't. There's no need. You know it's only going to take me twenty minutes to walk it. Look, I can see my flat from here.'

He followed her gaze to where the twin towers of Caledonia Road were in sight, albeit nearly a mile away. Giant twinkling shadows on the other side of the river.

'Aye, Hannah, twenty minutes at this time of night.'

'You wouldn't be coming in, anyway. I'm working in the morning and my mother wouldn't like it.'

He looked away but couldn't hide a smile. 'That's not why I'm offering.'

'Course it isn't.'

'I'm just not happy about you walking home on your own. You know that.'

'Gary, I'll be fine. Anyway, how am I going to manage that half-marathon next week if I can't walk home? It's only a mile.'

'Yeah but—'

'But nothing.' She leaned in and kissed him again, knowing he would give in, just as he usually did.

Moments later she pulled herself away, her hands flat against his ribcage, teasingly holding him off. 'See you tomorrow night?'

'Yeah. Pick you up?'

'No, I'll get you in town. I'm going to meet Emma first for a couple of drinks. I'll text you.'

'A couple of drinks? I know what you and your sister are like when you get started. Try and be sober when I get there, eh?'

At that, she slipped away from him and backed off, grinning at him as she reversed. 'You'll just have to wait and see. Can't promise anything. Like you said, you know what I'm like when I get started.'

'Tease.'

'You love it. Byeeee.'

She waved and turned with only the slightest hint of unsteadiness, caused as much by her heels as the unknown number of vodka-and-cranberries. She was still waving as she began the march across the bridge, the Clyde inky black below its five broad stone arches. She didn't look but she knew he would be running across the junction in search of his bus or possibly a last drink.

How many times had she walked across this bridge? Thousands, probably. Sometimes she'd take the Albert Bridge from the Saltmarket and get onto Laurieston Road that way. It was six and half a dozen in terms of distance. She liked the walk, even if Gary wasn't keen on her taking it. She'd done it thousands of times before she'd met him and with probably a couple of thousand more to come.

There was a point, midway across just as she reached the central arch, where she always made a little hop. She'd done it since she was a kid, walking either to or from town with her mum and dad. It marked, in her head at least, the halfway point in the river, the moment she crossed south of the Clyde, as she was doing now, or north, as she'd done earlier. As she got older, the hop got a little smaller. At least it did if other people were around. Now it was heading for one in the morning and she was half cut. She gave a proper, six-year-old's hop.

As the bridge turned into road, she gave another hop as she landed on dry land, accompanying it with a stifled giggle. On the other side of the road were the gardens belonging to the Central Mosque, its red-brick wall and railings soon giving way to the mosque itself with its glass-domed roof and minaret. It was one of her favourite landmarks on the walk home. On she walked, singing quietly to herself and happy in her place in things. On past the multis on one side of the road and the Citizens Theatre on the other.

When she got to the junction where Gorbals Street forced

Cleland Street to become Bedford Lane, she made a point of crossing to the other side of the road. The building on the side of the street that she'd been walking on had always freaked her out. People called it the old Linen Bank building and said it was the last of the old Gorbals tenements. She'd never known it anything other than disused, standing lost and alone like a survivor of a nuclear holocaust. The bricked-up door and boarded windows, the red ashlar walls, gothic scrolls and weird head carvings all gave her the heebie-jeebies. She hurried past it and tried not to look.

Her next landmark was the Brazen Head, another few hundred yards up the street and more than halfway home. Its famous – or infamous – green and white walls marked where Gorbals Street became Cathcart Road, not long before she'd take a left onto Caledonia Road. It was a route she knew like the back of her hand. She could see the pub up ahead, peeping at her under the railway bridge, its lights still blazing. As she passed, she heard raised voices and the threateningly cheery chink of glasses.

Immediately after the pub there was the strange, low, bricked archway to her left that led onto Laurieston Road. She always found herself taking a few steps to her right, away from its dark recess, an instinctive reaction to the possibility of someone stepping out from the gloom. A few strides more and she was under the next railway bridge, its rusting blue hulk throwing the pavement into near darkness. On cue, a train rattled overhead, deafening her with its roar through the bridge supports.

As the train faded, she wouldn't have been able to say when she heard the footsteps behind her, or when she realised that they had been in time with her own but now were gaining. All she knew was that it dawned on her with a cold, creeping certainty.

The Brazen Head shrank into the distance and the giant twin multis on Caledonia Road seemed much further away than they had a few moments before. Her pulse was racing and something that must have been her heart was crashing into her ribcage.

Up ahead on the left, a hundred yards or so away, were the remains of the old Caledonia Road church, sitting marooned in the triangle created as Cathcart and Laurieston Roads came together. She couldn't see its tall, obelisk tower for the eaves of the railway bridge but knew it was there all the same.

She looked over her shoulder and saw the shape, dark and hunched, gaining on her with every step. If she walked, he would probably catch her. If she ran, he would run after her. She ran.

Shit. Running was harder when you were a bit pished. And much harder when you were wearing heels. Run. Her thoughts were tangled, tripping over each other. Scared. Very scared.

She needed somewhere to go into that would be safe, but the church had lain empty for nearly fifty years, since local neds burned the insides out. All that was left to offer her any kind of sanctuary was the gaunt, foreboding shell. And yet, maybe if she could get to the far end where the acropolis pillars stood high on the wall, she'd be in the open and someone would see her. And see him.

Run faster. Reach the church. She'd never make it: the sounds on the pavement behind were getting closer with every breath. As soon as the bridge support vanished on her left, she pushed off into the scrubland where a beaten path ducked in behind the church walls. She told herself it was a shortcut. Her only hope.

Get your heels off, she thought. Can't run in heels. She slowed just enough so that she could push her right instep down against her left heel. Now the other . . .

Something hit hard against her back, low on the right side just above her hip. Breath rushed out of her, choking out in a single painful gasp of surprise. Worse, it threw her off her stride, pitching her forward awkwardly. His footsteps were so close and the church walls just a yard away.

Turn. Fight. She could hear Gary saying it. Turn and fight. She spun clumsily on her single shoe, bracing her legs so that she could swing, claw, punch at whoever, whatever, was there. Too late. As she turned, a gloved hand was in her face, blinding her, pushing her back and down, into the shadow of the old church.

She could feel the dampness of the woollen glove, its fibres tickling her skin, scratching it. Her heart screamed and she slowly, quickly began to drown in fear and adrenalin.

Darkness came.

Chapter 7

Early Sunday morning

For the second morning running, Winter had been woken by the sound of the phone ringing. For a few seconds, just long enough to depress him when he realised the reality, he'd thought he was in Rachel's bed rather than his own.

He fumbled for his mobile, anxiety making his fingers buttery. Early-morning calls were rarely good news.

'Yeah. Um, yeah. What? Fuck. Yes, got it. Okay. I'm leaving now.'

He pressed the button to end the call and blew a stream of air from his lips before letting the phone tumble onto the bed. It had been Denny Kelbie, a DCI at New Gorbals. The news was the sort of wake-up call that had you doubting you'd ever been asleep in the first place.

A dead girl. Seminaked and found draped round a monument in a cemetery.

The facts assaulted him, stirred him. But for the fact that she'd been found not in the Necropolis but in the Southern

Necropolis across the river, Winter might have thought it was some macabre form of déjà vu.

After a quick drive through the ghost of a Sunday-morning city, he parked his Honda Civic on Caledonia Road in the shadows of the tower blocks and directly across from the Gothic gatehouse that formed the entrance to the Southern Necropolis. The imposing sandstone edifice, looking for all the world like the gateway to a medieval castle that was no longer there, was guarded by two of Scotland's finest and a line of police tape.

The gatehouse was dwarfed by its modern neighbours on the other side of the street, yet managed to retain its own sense of size and an odd, almost surreal, grandeur. The twenty-foot-high archway and the avenue of trees beyond it were the entry point to another world, one where the residents, two hundred and fifty thousand of them, were all dead.

After taking his camera bag from the boot of the car, he crossed the road and flashed his ID at the cops. They nodded him on without a word and he crossed through the archway into the city that always sleeps.

The cobbled roadway that ducked under the bowed arches of ancient yew trees was bordered by verdigris headstones, most nearly two hundred years old, each of them winking at Winter as he marched deeper into the bowels of the cemetery in search of the urgent voices he could hear within. It was another damp morning, and a rising mist clung mournfully to the crypts, lending the Southern Necropolis an eerie air that it didn't need.

The cemetery was huge – space enough to hold an endless

array of football pitches, studded with teeth of headstone granite. Pathways were guarded by twisted arboreal sentries, their gnarled arms reaching down to touch gravestones choked with ivy or crumbling under years of neglect. It was death on a grand scale.

Winter followed the distant voices and the scent of death that tickled his nose, winding his way down grey paths amid the green until he came upon a gaggle of crime-scene officers and cops wrapped up in bunny-suit white. They faced him as he advanced down the cobbled track, one or two with hands on hips, including a diminutive figure at their heart who rocked from side to side with impatience.

Denny Kelbie stood little more than five foot five and probably weighed no more than ten stone when soaking wet. Yet he was a carnaptious wee sod who was continually growling at people around him like a Jack Russell with distemper. Sure enough, he barked at Winter as soon he arrived.

'And where the hell have you been? It's been twenty minutes since I called you, get her photographed and get the fuck out of my way.'

Kelbie was bristling, as if looking for a fight. His eyes were daring Winter to respond, the corners of his mouth already curling back to deliver his next putdown. To his annoyance, Winter took no offence and offered no rebuttal. Instead, he walked straight past the DCI and stepped into the breach as the crowd parted to reveal the reason that they were all there.

She was clinging onto the base of the monument, her head resting against the cool of the stone as if sleeping off the effects of a hard night before. If that was the case, then it was the hangover from hell.

His camera came up to eye level instinctively and he popped off shot after shot, his fingers curling, adjusting, moulding, capturing.

Her hair was dark and short, bobbed, framing her pretty young face. Early, maybe mid-twenties. She was tall and long, her bare legs stretched away from her, one knee tucked crookedly under the other, her single black high heel scraped with dirt and grass. Her mouth hung open, flycatcher wide, lipstick smudged. Her skin was ivory white, bloodless and cold, kissed by the early-morning chill. Her hands were clasped together in front of her, in prayer or contemplation. At first look, her eyes seemed captivated by the grassy verge at the statue's feet, but a closer examination showed she was glassily uninterested.

The right side of her head was broken and bloodied. Vivid stains of firebrick red, occasionally speckled with pale fragments of flesh, streaked down the statue's base, showing where the two had come into violent and fatal contact with each other. His camera picked out passive blood drops on the foliage and a spray of impact spatter on the granite. It seemed her head had been battered again and again against the stone.

The young woman's Saturday-night clothes looked cheap and incongruous draped over her Sunday-morning deathbed. Her black cotton top plunged in a cowl towards her cleavage and left her shoulders uncovered and dappled in dew. Her short black skirt was round her waist.

Winter made his lens retreat so that it took in the statue that the girl hung onto, saying a silent apology for revelling in the vivid counterpoint it offered. The weathered figure of a woman, her head veiled and bowed, looked down sadly, curiously, at the girl who lay dead at her feet. The statue's hands were missing, the victims of time or vandals, and an evergreen climbing plant had made her right side its own. She made a poor excuse for a guardian angel.

'The White Lady,' a familiar voice shouted out from behind him, breaking his dark reverie. 'Careful she doesn't look at you or you'll turn to stone.'

'What the fuck are you doing here, Addison?' DCI Denny Kelbie sounded as if the vein on his forehead was going to burst. 'You get lost looking for Stewart Street?'

Addison feigned puzzlement. Narey was at his shoulder, the merest hint of a smile directed at Winter. Both of them were already suited up in uniform white.

'No, sir, I didn't,' Addison told Kelbie pleasantly. 'Do you know the story about the White Lady? It's your patch, I'm sure you must.'

Kelbie glared back incredulously, eyes bulging. He began to answer but Addison continued, seemingly oblivious to the DCI's indignant fury but, in fact, simply talking over it.

'Two women from Langside Avenue, a carpet manufacturer's wife and her housekeeper. They were coming back from church in the pouring rain. Chucking it down it was, so they had their umbrella up and crossed the road straight into the path of a tram. The wife, Magdalene, died before she got to hospital and the housekeeper, Mrs McNaughton, followed two weeks later. A terrible thing. Local legend has it that, when you walk past the White Lady, her head turns and follows you. But if you look her in the eye then you'll turn to stone.'

'Look, Addison . . .' Kelbie's fury was rising.

'But you can guard against that by running round her three times, shouting "White Lady, White Lady". Think you should maybe give it a go to be on the safe side, sir?'

Kelbie, his cheeks flushing, marched right up to Addison until his head was, almost comically, level with the DI's chin. Winter knew there was no love between the two men and had heard there had been a falling-out a few years before, when they were both detective sergeants. Addison had never talked to him about it but the word was that punches had been thrown – although, as they now faced each other, it struck Winter that Kelbie would have had to stand on a box to land one on Addison's chin.

'Are you forgetting who you're talking to?' Kelbie demanded.

Addison made a poor attempt at innocence. 'No, sir, not at all. What makes you think that? How is your wife, anyway?'

'I asked you a question already, dickhead. What the fuck are you doing here?'

'Deid body, sir. It's my job.'

'Not in New Gorbals, it isn't. And how did you know about it?' With that, Kelbie turned his head to fire a look at Winter, knowing full well that he and Addison were mates.

'Not guilty,' Winter protested. 'I jumped in the car and headed straight here without calling anyone.'

'Aye, and about that,' Addison replied, without taking his eyes off Kelbie. 'Why the hell didn't you call me? You must have seen the connection to the other girl right away.'

'Christ, I can't win,' Winter groaned. 'Look, why don't you two argue about it while I take some photographs.'

'What connection?' Kelbie interrupted, sneering. 'You've been watching too much television, Addison. You have a murder vic and I have a murder vic. That's it. Stewart Street isn't hijacking this case.'

Addison lowered his head and his voice. 'You sure about that? *Sir.*'

The DI was looking down at his superior officer, nearly a foot below him and smiling, fully knowing the risk and reward of doing so. The reward was immediate. Kelbie's lips curled back behind his incisors and he snarled again as both of them moved even closer until each could feel the other man's breath on his face.

'I'm going to do what I should have done years ago,' Kelbie growled. Addison smiled again.

'What are you two muppets frigging playing at?' barked a voice from farther down the path. The wide, muscular frame of Detective Superintendent Alex Shirley was bearing down on them, his close-cropped, steel-grey hair worn like a halo in the early-morning mist. 'Do I need to remind you there's a dead girl at the foot of that statue?'

Kelbie groaned at the sight of the Stewart Street Detective Super, known to all and sundry as the Temple. He glared again at Addison's taunting face before turning to Shirley.

'Sir?'

'This is our case now, Denny. I know you're not going to like it but I've already spoken to your guvnor and it's been sorted. Phone Billy Devlin and he'll fill you in.'

'*What?*' The exclamation came not from Kelbie but his DS, a moaning, nasally, ginger named Ferry. 'That's not on.'

'Too fucking right it isn't,' Kelbie howled. 'It's bang out of order.'

It was now Shirley's turn to go face to face with Kelbie, Addison grinning infuriatingly as he stepped away and wandered towards the girl's body.

'The decision has been made, Chief Inspector.' Shirley's voice hardened, expecting no further argument. He got one, anyway.

'I'm not having this. I'm not having *him* take my fucking case.'

'Sorry, Kelbie, but this is ours. And watch your language. I don't know how much you know about the Necropolis killing but it's too pat for it not to be linked. If it's unrelated you can have it back.'

'Sloppy Stewart Street seconds? Cheers. And it's way too early to say this girl was killed by whoever did yours. Other part of the city, no necklace used to strangle her. No forensics in yet. Sir, I have to insist that we wait until—'

'DCI Kelbie,' Addison interrupted, his voice heavily spiced with something that Winter couldn't identify, 'you were saying?'

Addison was crouched by the side of the girl's body, his gloved hand holding the bottom of her black cotton top with its distinctive cowl. He was signalling Kelbie and the others closer, beckoning them with a single cocked finger. When they were within a few feet, Addison paused. Stony-faced, he eased the top up to expose the girl's pale midriff.

To his credit, if he took any satisfaction from seeing Kelbie's jaw drop, Addison never showed it. Instead he carefully smoothed the girl's top back into place and stood up to move aside to let Winter and his camera in instead.

If there had been any merit to Kelbie's argument that her murder was not related to the body found in another cemetery just two miles away, just twenty-four hours earlier, then that argument had been lost. The scrawled lipstick lettering on her torso made certain of it.

Chapter 8

SIN

The same heavy, bludgeoned lettering in violent, waxy red. The wording identical.

The only sounds in the cemetery were now coming from Winter's camera. The clicks, whirrs and fizzes of buttons, motors and flashes punctuated a morbid silence that consumed the handful of people who stood behind him. He had a front-row view on the three letters that they were all staring at, so close that the word filled his vision and not just his viewfinder.

So close that he saw the contours of the lipstick as it smeared her soft, pallid skin, tainting it in daubs of pigments, waxes and oils. So close that he could see the fury that it had been written in. So close that he could see the jagged edges where it met her flesh. So close that he could smell it.

The girl had been branded by her killer. With just three letters, he had labelled her, disparaged her and declared her as one of his. With one word he had laid claim over her. She was his second victim and no one could doubt it.

The picture he had taken barely a day before, the image on the girl's stomach high on the hill above Glasgow Cathedral, filled Winter's mind. Addison's words at seeing the first one came back to him too, about how it was 'psycho stuff'. Winter knew that this didn't just make it doubly bad: this was much more than the sum of two parts.

He stood up and away from the body, his movement the signal for the remaining cast to stir and sound to erupt. Alex Shirley swore under his breath before barking orders at the Stewart Street squad who had arrived in the cemetery: the crime-scene manager, Brem Dawson, steering his own team more quietly but no less feverishly; uniforms, detectives and forensics going where they were told and doing what they knew best.

Narey stood to the side of the stage, her expression set and her eyes fixed on the girl. Winter tried to catch her eye but she was lost. In a rookie cop or someone more faint-hearted than Rachel, he might have taken it for weakness or sentimentality but he knew her better than that. She was angry.

The Temple summoned Kelbie and his DS, Jim Ferry, plus Addison, Narey, Winter and Brem Dawson to him with energetic sweeps of his arm. They formed an impromptu huddle yards from the White Lady and the girl she'd so poorly guarded.

'I want an information lockdown on what we've got here. Bare minimum goes out to the press. Girl's body found, suspicious circumstances, family to be informed et cetera. Nothing, and I mean *nothing*, about that word. It does not leave this cemetery. I do not want one single person knowing that doesn't have to. You all understand? DCI Kelbie, your officers that were here fall into the category of not having to know.'

Kelbie chewed agitatedly on his lip before nodding thoughtfully.

'It looks to me as if I'm back on this case, then, sir. I'd say that necessity dictates it.'

'What?'

'You're right, sir. We obviously can't take the chance on this wording getting into the press. We don't want to give the killer the oxygen of publicity and we don't want to run the risk of copycats. The best way to ensure that nothing leaks out is to keep us on the inside.'

Shirley's eyes widened and flashed in anger.

'Are you saying that I can't trust you to obey frigging orders and follow protocol if you aren't on the case?'

'Not at all, sir. Of course not. But it will be much easier for me to keep a lid on whatever rumours float through New Gorbals if the team there aren't pissed off at having nothing to do with a case on our turf. Put me and Ferry on your team and everyone wins. I'm sure Superintendent Devlin will okay it.'

'Rubbish!' Addison broke in, his jaw jutting towards Kelbie. 'You just tell your people to keep their mouths shut. Simple as that.'

'He's right, Derek,' Shirley sighed, cutting off Kelbie's reply. 'DCI Kelbie and DS Ferry are now part of the investigation team. It's the only practical decision.'

'And, as DCI,' Kelbie sneered in Addison's direction, 'I assume I will be senior investigating officer.'

Shirley shook his head wearily. 'You assume wrong, Kelbie.

I'll be SIO. I'm taking charge of this myself, I'm not risking you two idiots behaving like children. You will keep me fully informed of every development. Understood?'

'Sir.' Kelbie managed to puff and preen at the same time.

'Good. Strategy meeting in Pitt Street at three this afternoon. Now get to work.'

Kelbie allowed himself a final triumphant glance at Addison before taking his DS by the arm and turning away from the group. Addison opened his mouth to speak but Shirley pre-empted him.

'Save your breath. I'd rather have Kelbie on the inside pissing out than on the outside pissing in. At least this way we can keep him under control. And for chrissake, Derek, remember that he is your superior officer, whether you like it or not.'

'That will be not, sir.'

'I don't give a toss. What we have here is even bigger than your ego. Now go catch the bastard that did this. All of you.'

Brem Dawson was the first to leave, corralling his forensic troops and ordering them to begin the painstaking task of examining the site for evidence and removing the girl's body to the morgue. A clear path had already been made to allow access to the scene, but now every other inch had to be checked and rechecked.

Winter fell into an uncomfortable threesome on the secured path to the crime scene, Narey and Addison at either side. It was uncomfortable for him at least: Narey refused to catch his eye and Addison was consumed with his fury at Denny Kelbie.

'It's my own fault,' the DI cursed. 'I could have kept the

lettering back until we'd got that nasty wee shite and his plods off the premises.'

'So why didn't you?' Narey demanded.

'Because I wanted to rub his snotty nose in it, obviously.'

The three of them stood and watched the forensics work, perversely fascinated by the sight of the bunny suits picking their way assiduously over the cemetery's green and cobbled skin. Winter had his camera at his waist now but his trigger finger kept popping off discreet shots, knowing that a fair few would hit their unsuspecting targets.

'How do you know so much about this place?' Narey asked Addison. 'All that White Lady stuff.'

'My dad used to bring me here when I was a nipper. He was brought up just a couple of streets away. The place has always given me the creeps. You'll be loving it, though, wee man. Right up your street.'

Winter ignored the jibe.

'You ever heard of the Gorbals Vampire?' Addison continued.

Winter shrugged but his curiosity was obvious.

'It was long before our time. Nineteen fifty-four. The story went round among the local kids that there was a vampire on the loose and that he'd already kidnapped and eaten two boys. I know it sounds stupid but the whole city was gripped with the idea. The vampire was supposed to be seven feet tall and had iron teeth. You'd maybe think that would be enough to scare kids, but not if they came from the Gorbals.

'Instead, they put the word out. They weren't going to wait for the vampire to take another of them: they were going after him. As soon as school was out they were to head for the cemetery wall and wait for it to get dark. And the wee buggers were armed to the teeth. The wall is what? Seven feet high? They all got on top of it and, as soon as they got the shout, they piled in.

'Half the kids in Hutchensontown were in the cemetery, prowling between the crypts armed with penknives, stakes, stones, whatever they could get their hands on. The local bobbies were eventually called and they reckoned there were four hundred kids in here, aged from four to fourteen. My dad was one of them.

'He couldn't get hold of a knife, so he got the biggest stick he could find and whittled the end to a sharp point with a knife he borrowed from his mate, Bertie. He told me he was scared shitless and my old man didn't scare easily. I suppose it's different when you're only six. The cops cleared the lot of them out of the cemetery but they came back the next night and the night after that. My papa gave my dad a whack round the ear and kicked his arse. That was the end of his vampire-hunting days. But the old bugger still brought me in here when I was a kid and told me the story, knowing full well it would scare the crap out of me.'

'Explains a lot,' Winter said, and smiled at him. 'No wonder you're such a miserable sod.'

'That's rich coming from you. See that gatehouse you passed through on the way in here?'

Winter nodded.

'The guy who designed it is buried just over there. Ashes to ashes, dust to dust and all that. What comes around goes around.'

'Christ, you're quite the philosopher.'

'I know. It's a gift, wee man. Okay, Rachel, what's your take on this?'

Narey deliberated.

'One killer. Psychopath. Hates women. Has moral issues judging by the word he wrote. Or else the girls are linked but that seems less likely on the face of it.'

Addison nodded. 'Agreed. Anything else?'

'I don't think Kirsty McAndrew's ex-boyfriend fits this. I'd say he was genuinely shocked when we told him what had happened to her. And he's still in custody. But there are obvious similarities in profile between the victims. Age, gender, build, both good-looking, both dressed for a night out.' She paused. 'Both vulnerable.'

Addison looked at her for a moment before replying. 'Okay, so those are the similarities. What about the differences? The first girl had no shoes, this one does. One strangled with a chain round her neck, this one's head battered in. The first one had a bag, emptied. This one doesn't. How many girls do you know that go out without a bag?'

'None. He's taken it. Trying to cover his tracks probably.'

'Looks that way.' Addison sighed heavily. 'Okay, let's get on with this. First we need to find out who she is and see if there's any connection with the McAndrew girl. Whatever we learn, we keep it to ourselves for now. I'm not sharing any information with that wee shit Kelbie, whatever Shirley has to say. As far as I'm— Oh, for fuck's sake!'

Narey and Winter followed Addison's gaze and saw four or five young heads popping up above the cemetery wall, all adorned with baseball caps. They were either standing on something or on the shoulders of their mates. One young tracksuited gymnast was even sitting on the wall, his legs dangling over the edge.

'Jesus! Rachel, get uniforms to patrol the cemetery perimeter and get those silly sods down. The last thing we need is them looking in here. I'm not having a repeat of the hunt for the Gorbals Vampire.'

'We're not going to be able to stop them all from looking.' Narey raised her eyes and the two men followed her gaze, seeing the pair of blue and cream giants that towered over them. The Caledonia Road flats filled the skyline and offered hundreds of uninterrupted views onto the crime scene.

Addison stuck a two-fingered salute up at the tower blocks. 'Stare at that.'

Chapter 9

Sunday afternoon

The hurriedly arranged strategy meeting in Pitt Street wasn't held in the largest available room but rather in one where the smallest number of people were likely to be walking past. It had been done with as little fuss as he could; Alex Shirley was determined to keep as much of a lid as he could on news of the matching words on the stomachs of the two murdered women.

Every murder was a very big deal, even in a city like Glasgow, where it wasn't exactly unusual. But this was different. It was what it was but it was also what it could become. There was both a brutality and a potential randomness about these killings that had even hardened detectives concerned. Shirley was shitting himself at the prospect of this being only the start of something.

Winter took a seat at the back as usual, all the better to see without being seen. He knew that it was only that he'd been there from the first victim being found on the Necropolis that saved him from being outside the scope of Shirley's need-to-know policy. Two of his photographs were on the wall facing the rows of chairs that were swiftly being filled by the backsides of the force's CID. They were his passport to the case and he revelled in the fact that they drew the attention of every cop in the room.

They were both close-ups of the faces of the girls, blown up, full and glossy but losing nothing from the increase in size. They were pixel-perfect in their grotesque beauty. Kirsty McAndrew, her blonde hair wet-dark and licking at her pretty features. Girl number two, as yet unknown but staring helplessly into the abyss, her mouth wide as if dumbfounded by what she saw.

Winter looked at the back of Rachel's head as she sat in the front row, seeing her sitting so close and yet so far away. Just someone he used to know in a room full of people. There were ten bodies sitting in front of Winter by the time the door opened to allow Alex Shirley to march in and advance directly to the table that faced the rows of cops. The superintendent took his place under Winter's photographs, flanked on either side by Addison and Kelbie. Among the ranks facing them were Jim Ferry from New Gorbals, DS Andy Teven, DS Rico Giannandrea, a handful of detective constables including Fraser Toshney and Rebecca Maxwell, plus Superintendent Jason Williams representing uniform. They collectively shut up as soon as Shirley got to the top table.

He stood facing them, examining papers in front of him with pursed lips even though he'd already read every word they contained. When he lifted his head again, he was ready.

'Ladies and gentlemen, thank you for being here. I know some of you have had to change shifts to accommodate this and I'm grateful for that. For those of you who don't know him, may I introduce DCI Denny Kelbie from New Gorbals. He will be assisting on this enquiry along with DS Jim Ferry.'

Kelbie gave the briefest of nods, his face moulded into a picture of earnestness. Addison stared ahead as if Kelbie's name had never been mentioned.

'The young woman with the blonde hair behind me is Kirsty McAndrew. She was twenty-two years old from Elcho Street in Bridgeton. She was a shop assistant and lived with her parents. She was murdered sometime in the early hours of Saturday morning and her body was found in the Necropolis. The young lady with the dark hair is Hannah Healey.'

The name landed heavily. To Winter, she had been decaying flesh and broken bone but now she had a name. Now she was real.

'She was twenty-three years old, a hairdresser and lived with her mother in a flat in one of the high-rises on Caledonia Road. The flat overlooked the Southern Necropolis, where she was found this morning. Her neighbours later made a positive identification from the crime-scene photographs.'

Shirley paused, seemingly finding something else of interest in his notes but, in truth, giving everyone in the room time to catch their breath along with their thoughts.

'We have no doubt that the two deaths are linked and that the killer was almost certainly the same person. That is not information we shall be sharing outwith the confines of this room. If asked, you refer them to media services or to the agreed statement, which you will be provided with on leaving this briefing. But be in no doubt that we are dealing with a potential serial killer.'

The phrase jagged its way across the room, screeching like nails down a blackboard. Shirley let the thought settle on his audience as he bent to click the mouse at his fingertips, causing the photographs behind to be replaced by two more that Winter had taken: the matching stomachs of the two girls and the identical lettering. Enlarged as they were, the similarities in the handwriting were obvious. Small involuntary gasps slipped from the mouths of some of those who hadn't seen them before.

'The images before you were written on the victims in lipstick. That information remains sacrosanct. If it goes into the force at large or, God forbid, into the public arena, then I will be holding people in this room responsible and I will not be pleased.'

The Temple glared round the room, seeking any wavering eyes, determined that his message hammered into the skulls of his detectives. There was no dissention.

'Ladies and gentlemen, forgive me for stating the frigging obvious, but we are dealing with an extremely disturbed and dangerous individual. Both girls were raped. Both were strangled. Hannah Healey also suffered severe and violent head injuries. What I want you to do is to apprehend him before this' – he gestured behind him – 'happens again. Whatever else you are working on takes second place. No, it takes third place. This investigation takes first *and* second place. I will not have another victim, not under my watch. Do I make myself clear?'

'DI Addison,' Shirley started again, his tone as fierce as before, 'bring everyone up to speed, please.'

Addison got to his feet, the briefest of unrequited glances over at Kelbie as he did so.

'Kirsty McAndrew had been on a night out with friends. They were in Citation in the Merchant City and also Bacchus. We have … this image from Citation's CCTV.' A grainy still shot showed five attractive young women dressed up for a night out. 'Kirsty walked home alone and we believe she was attacked en route. CCTV has some images of her walking on the Trongate at twelve-thirty. Time of death is estimated at around two a.m. She was strangled, partly by use of the necklace that she was wearing.

'Her bag was present at the scene, its contents found dumped some distance away. Her shoes were not present and remain missing. She was wearing them in the CCTV, so she may have lost them in a struggle or the killer may have taken them.

'We've only known of Hannah Healey's identity for a couple of hours so we don't have as much information on her as we'd like. Your job will be to put that right as soon as possible. We are currently aware of no confirmed link between the two of them. If there is one, you will need to find it and fast. If there isn't, our job will be a hell of a lot harder, and whoever killed them is a bona fide serial nutjob.'

Shirley's eyebrows shot up at Addison's language, provoking a matching sneer from Denny Kelbie. Addison wasn't particularly fussed by either but he had to stop when Shirley placed an arm out in front of him and scraped his chair back as he stood up again.

'Let me interrupt at this point to make something quite clear. I have no doubt that a link does exist between these two young women. They may have frequented the same pub or club, used the same gym, had the same ex-boyfriend. I don't know. Check their entire histories: school, work, family, personal lives, everything. There *is* a link. Find it.'

Addison allowed Shirley to retake his seat, watching his boss vigorously smooth his suit jacket back into place. He cleared his throat theatrically and continued.

'Kirsty McAndrew had this' – he clicked the mouse, and a new photograph appeared on the whiteboard – 'tattoo on her back. DS Narey has established that it refers to her former boyfriend Robert Wylde. Narey and I have interviewed Wylde and believe it is unlikely that he was involved in her murder. He's got a busy charge sheet and some history of violence but I don't think he's our man.'

Addison caught the maliciously raised eyebrow offered }up by Kelbie for public consumption and managed to swallow down the retort that yearned to burst free from within him, refusing to give the DCI the satisfaction. 'We are of course not ruling Wylde out and will explore every avenue open to us. With that in mind, Rico, I want you to take over coordinating a look into the tattoo parlours in town. We think this was done relatively recently and might give us something to work with. There's already been groundwork done and Jason will fill you in on where his people have been.'

DS Giannandrea nodded, taking the printed copy of the tattoo that was passed down to him. Winter, looking over his shoulder, followed the contours of the angry snake that inked its way round the small of Kirsty McAndrew's back.

'Andy, go over every inch of the CCTV from Citation and whatever Bacchus has,' Addison continued. 'Also get everything you can between there and Elcho Street. Talk to her friends and the staff, see if anyone was hanging around, paying Kirsty special attention, that sort of thing.'

'Narey, coordinate further door-to-door round Caledonia Road and surrounding areas. Trawl her route home. We need details on her movements last night, boyfriends, friends, family. Take Toshney with you.'

Winter couldn't see the look on Rachel's face but he could picture it, and allowed himself a smile. He knew just how much she enjoyed having Toshney as a sidekick. But he also knew Addy. The fact that Rachel didn't want Toshney would have been reason enough for her to get him.

'DS Ferry you – and your DCI – talk to her parents, her friends and whatever other close family she had. Talk to Wylde again and see if there was another boyfriend or someone she'd maybe knocked back. See if we can set up a reconstruction as well. Someone must have seen her walking alone even if the cameras haven't.'

A low rumble escaped from Kelbie's throat and the skin around his eyes reddened.

'Thanks for the advice, DI Addison. If you're also going to teach us how to suck eggs then can you wait till this investigation is over? In the meantime, maybe we can discuss the most significant piece of information that we have to hand. The one you haven't mentioned yet.'

Addison stared and Winter could tell he wasn't sure whether Kelbie was bluffing or not. The self-satisfied look on Kelbie's snarling face made Winter fairly sure that he wasn't.

'What information is that?' Addison couldn't help himself.

'The fact that Kirsty McAndrew's bloodstream contained heavy levels of benzodiazepines.'

'Where the fuck were you keeping that little nugget of information?'

Addison paused, seeing the reproach on Shirley's face. 'Sorry. Where the fuck were you keeping that little nugget of information, *sir*?'

Kelbie smiled smugly, enjoying Addison's fury. 'I took the liberty of having a wee chat with your lab people. Very accommodating they were, too. The toxicology tests aren't complete yet, as some of the samples have yet to be returned, but the blood samples suggest Kirsty McAndrew was heavily sedated. Some derivative of Rohypnol, most likely.'

Shirley leaned forward, deliberately cutting off the space between Addison and Kelbie. 'Thank you, DCI Kelbie, good work. Derek, contact the lab and ask them to match the results against the samples taken from Hannah Healey.'

'No need.' Kelbie grinned like a pit bull licking raw meat. 'I've already asked them to check. They'll get the results back to me by the morning.'

Chapter 10

Late Sunday afternoon

Addison and Winter followed Cat Fitzpatrick as she led them through a set of swing doors and down the pale, narrow corridor on the first floor of the Scottish Police Services Authority building. Winter saw that Addison's gaze was focused admiringly on the pathologist's rear and gave him a frown of disapproval that the DI cheerfully shrugged off.

'I don't mind acting as tour guide,' Fitzpatrick was saying, albeit in a tone that suggested she did mind. 'But I'm not sure Sam will have results for you by now.'

'If they're not ready, they're not,' Addison replied, his stare never wavering. 'I'm just keen to find out the conclusions. Before anyone else does.'

Winter knew full well what the last comment meant, and so too, by her reply, did Cat.

'Such admirable dedication. And I'm sure that it has nothing to do with a visit this morning by DCI Kelbie. And why have you got Tony with you, anyway? I can't see any need to photograph lipstick samples.'

'Do you two mind not talking about me as if I'm either not here or stupid?'

They both ignored him and Addison coughed unconvincingly before answering. 'I feel it will help to record the process. For evidentiary purposes. And because we have to attend another location immediately after we leave here.'

'The Station Bar by any chance? I hear that place is full of highly suspicious characters.'

'I have no idea what you're talking about, Miss Fitzpatrick.'

'Course you don't. Okay, here we are.'

Fitzpatrick opened the door into the lab and led them inside. Winter was struck, as he always was, by the suffocatingly clinical nature of the room. Diffused lighting, sterile workspaces and numerous trays of blue plastic test tube holders. There were phials and bell jars and endless computer monitors. Above all, there was a pervading sense of seriousness.

Cat Fitzpatrick looked around the lab, obviously not seeing the person she was looking for. 'Sam?'

'Two seconds.'

An impossibly tall and slender young woman in a white lab coat emerged from behind a screen, her hands resplendent in bright-purple nitrile gloves and a pair of protective glasses pushing long dark hair back onto her head. She unashamedly looked Winter and Addison up and down, seeming to take a particular interest in the DI's lanky six-foot-four frame. Rather than address either of them, however, she spoke to Fitzpatrick, betraying the hint of an accent that might have been Aberdonian beneath its educated overtones.

'Hi, Cat. I take it these are the long legs of the law.'

Fitzpatrick tried to hide the smile that fought its way onto her face at seeing Addison on the receiving end of a sexist remark for a change.

'It is indeed. Detective Inspector Derek Addison and photographer Tony Winter. DI Addison, this is Sam Guthrie, one of our chemists. She's been taking care of the lipstick for your collar.'

Winter watched the sideshow, seeing an uncustomary awkwardness in Addison as he realised the joke, and that the innuendo was at his expense.

'Aye, very good. Thanks for seeing us, Miss, er, Ms . . .'

The chemist smiled and her eyes showed amusement at the DI's unease.

'Sam. It's short for Samantha.'

'Sam. Thanks.'

Fitzpatrick and Winter swapped glances, both enjoying Addison's discomfort and happy for him to know it. The DI glared at them.

'Right, I'll leave you to it. I've got things to do. Play nice.' Fitzpatrick hesitated and glanced at Guthrie. 'Both of you.'

Guthrie smiled at Addison, her right arm out playfully as if guiding the way. 'This way, gentlemen, and I'll bring you up to speed on where we are with your sample. Do you know anything about forensic discrimination of lipsticks?'

Both men shook their heads, causing the chemist to tut in mock disapproval.

'It's an interesting science. There was an excellent paper done on it by the Forensic Science Society of Malaysia in 2011. Bit of a field leader. The key is to apply a little TLC. Do you know what TLC is, Detective Inspector Addison?'

The DI seemed to swallow before answering. 'Um, tender loving care?'

'Thin-layer chromatography. Lipstick samples that are indistinguishable during visual analysis can be discriminated from each other by a combination of TLC and GC-MS.'

'Okay, I'll bite. GC–MS?'

'Gas chromatography–mass spectrometry.'

'Right, obviously.'

'We analyse the colouring agents with TLC and the organic components with GC–MS. Okay, see these two lipsticks?' Guthrie held up two seemingly identically coloured tubes of red within an inch or two of her own lips. 'What colour would you say they were?'

Addison shrugged uncomfortably. 'Like I'd know. Well, they're kind of blood red. Actually, this is one for you, Tony. Miss ... um, Sam, you may not know but Tony here has his own patented colour chart for blood. He's just the man to answer that question.'

Guthrie looked at Winter curiously. 'Hmm, I think I may have heard about this. Canteen chat. You differentiate blood by colour according to the degree of oxygenation, right?'

Nice attempt at deflection, Addy, Winter thought. But, fair enough, he'd play along.

'Yeah, that's pretty much it. I can make a fair stab at time of death, or at least the time of bleeding, by visual analysis. When it spills from the body, the haemoglobin is fully oxygenated and the blood is bright red like candy apple. Later it loses oxygen and becomes dull and listless like sangria or burgundy. It's not an exact science but I've had plenty of practice.'

Guthrie turned to look at Addison and raised her eyebrows in bemusement.

'Is he a bit ... sick in the head?'

'No, he's just a bit ... special.'

'Hmm. Interesting. Okay, Tony, so what colour would you say these lipsticks are? According to your ... chart.'

'I'd say they represent something like three-hour-old blood. Maybe firebrick red or carmine.'

Guthrie examined Winter for a while as if he were something at the bottom of a Petri dish, before shaking her head at him and turning back to Addison.

'Not exactly what I would call suitably sexy names for a lipstick, are they? I'd suggest something like "passion", "heat" or "sensual". What do you think, Detective Inspector?'

Addison looked from Winter to Guthrie and back again as if he'd stumbled into a madhouse.

'Do they seem the same colour to you, Detective Inspector?'

Addison nodded resignedly. If it was a game, he was losing.

'They do look very similar,' Guthrie conceded. 'But I've analysed them with TLC and here's an overlay of the chromatograms showing the analysis of both lipsticks. One in red and the other in green. See the different peaks?'

Addison looked at the chart offered to him and saw rising, simultaneous, coloured peaks but in each case the red and green crests were at varying heights, sometimes wildly different.

'Different lipsticks?'

'Completely. Even lipsticks that are the same colour can be made up of a different combination of colouring agents and have different chemical structures. The TLC can screen them quickly and separate one from the other. That's what we've done. I might need GC–MS to confirm things further down the line but the TLC has been enough to reach one basic conclusion.'

'Which is?'

'That it's none of these.' Guthrie stepped back and swept her arm wide to show a huge range of lipsticks of similar hues that were lined up on a desktop to her right.

Addison blew hard. 'How many have you got there?'

'Seventy-four.'

'Jesus, Accounts are going to love you.'

Guthrie smiled. 'A girl can't have too many lipsticks. As proven by the fact that I'm going to have to get some more. There's no match in this lot and they are the most popular on the high street. I'll need to widen the search.'

'Fuck's sake! How many shades are there?'

Guthrie rolled her eyes theatrically. 'Okay, let's see. I like Bobbi Brown. It has—'

'Was he not married to Whitney Houston?'

'No. It's a she. And, no, Bobbi Brown has fifty-two different shades of lipstick.'

'What?'

'Max Factor currently do about fifty. Rimmel do more.'

'How many manufacturers are there?'

'Revlon, Elizabeth Arden, L'Oréal, Esprit, Color Riche, May-belline, Clinique, Beautify …' She paused for breath and thought. 'Mac, Calvin Klein, Dior, Cover Girl, Lancôme—'

'Aye, okay. I get the point.'

'I went into Debenhams' online site and they stock eighty-eight different lipsticks. That's *before* you add in shades. The good news is that far fewer of them are red these days. It's a bit old-hat. Pinks are much more popular. Plus browns, purples, you name it. What colour of lipstick do you like on a woman, Detective Inspector?'

Addison's obvious reticence in answering allowed Winter to steal into the breach. 'He's not too fussed about colours really, Sam. He's happy as long as they're breathing.'

If Guthrie took any pleasure in Winter's dig at the DI, then she failed to show it. Instead, she furrowed her brow and again regarded Winter as if he were just a bit odd.

'Unlike you, then, Tony. The word is that you're much happier photographing them if they're dead. I'd say the detective inspector's preference for women to be breathing is far healthier.'

Jesus, Winter thought. If this is how she acts after Cat Fitzpatrick told her to play nice, how is she when she wants to get nasty? By the look on Addison's face, he was deliberating as to whether he wanted to find out.

'So, going back to the lipstick. We're no closer to knowing what the hell it is?'

Guthrie sighed and shook her head at Addison, as if he were a schoolboy who had asked a particularly stupid question.

'On the contrary, Detective Inspector. We're a *lot* further forward. We know what it isn't. And that is the good news. If it were one of the popular lipsticks that I've tested then it could have been bought by any one of tens of thousands of women in hundreds of different retail outlets or online. As it's not one of these, then the odds of identifying a purchaser and a place of purchase will have improved significantly. I would say that's good news, wouldn't you?'

'Um, yes. Of course. Well, you'll let us know when you've performed a bit more TLC and have a definitive result.'

Guthrie looked at Addison as if he'd just questioned whether the sun would come up in the morning.

'Of course I will. It's my job. Now run along, boys. I've got work to do.'

As the door closed behind them and they began a chastened walk away from the chemist's lab, a broad grin spread across Winter's face. Addison caught the look and scowled.

'Aye, and you can fucking shut it as well, wee man.'

Winter's grin grew even wider.

Chapter 11

July 1972

It was getting to him how the world, or at least the part of it through which the Clyde swam darkly, was continuing as if nothing had happened. On Sauchiehall Street or Partick Cross, on buses into town or the subway out west, life went on just as it had before. Men and women drawing on cigarettes or munching fish and chips, talking twenty to the dozen and saying nothing.

He wanted to scream at them, grab them and shake them. Rattle them around in their clothes until they got the message. Life wasn't the same. Couldn't be the same. Life was different because lives had been lost. Lives had been taken.

It should matter.

In his head, there was little else. Every waking moment and most of the sleeping ones, too. He could think of nothing else, yet they seemed to have forgotten already. In and out of shops, punching in for work, listening to music, pushing babies around in prams. They just went on and on.

Oh, they talked about it, of course they did. How could

they not? It was the talk of the steamie, gossiped about in every pub and every parish. Everyone knew somebody that fitted the description. Everyone had a suspect in mind. It was him. Or him. They had as many theories as they had fillings in their teeth.

But they talked just as much about this new Common Market thing that was going to happen next year and how we'd all end up speaking German or French. They were still trying to get their heads round the new decimal currency and asking how much things cost in real money. They shouldn't change it until all the old folk are deid, that's what his gran had said.

Everything was changing. The shipyards on the Clyde had been saved after the work-in and now they were changing their names and thousands of men were keeping their jobs. People were bothered about the cost of milk and Ted Heath's Tory government. They worried about their jobs and whether they'd get a ticket to see David Bowie at the Apollo. They made sure they had enough cash to get a skinful at the week-end and any other night they could afford it. They wondered whether they'd get into Klass on Friday night. And then, maybe, they'd talk again about what happened there.

He wanted it in every paper, every day. In front of their eyes as they sat down at breakfast or supped a pint in their local. He wanted the headlines to be bigger, louder, bolder. He didn't want them to be reading about Bloody Sunday or the upcoming Munich Olympics or Rangers fans still making their way home after winning the Cup Winners' Cup in Barcelona. It should all be about what happened.

It should matter.

It was the first thing he thought about when he woke and the last thing on his mind before he fell asleep. What happened. And what was going to happen next.

He hated their ability to get on with things, shove it all aside and function normally. Even people who were closer to it than they knew just did what they'd always done. Her at home, she was more worried about how many Kensitas Club coupons she'd need for that new table lamp she had her eye on in the catalogue. As soon as she'd smoked her way to enough coupons, he'd be dispatched to the gift centre on Cambridge Street. In their house, items were commonly referred to as the Kensitas toaster or the Kensitas food mixer. Everyday stuff. Everyday matters.

They all busied themselves with things to stop thinking about it. Buying things, selling things, smoking things, drinking things. All designed to stop themselves from getting scared. It wasn't like that for him of course. It *was* his thing. And he was the one who had nothing to be scared of.

Two young women. Dead. And it wasn't finished. He was sure of that.

Chapter 12

Sunday evening

'That wee shite Kelbie knows full well that the reason we hadn't asked the lab for the toxicology report is that they weren't finished,' said Addison. 'He may be a halfwit – in fact he's *definitely* a halfwit – but he knows that to get back samples of blood, urine and tissue takes bloody time. He deliberately jumped the gun to look like a smartarse.'

'I'd say it worked,' Winter offered.

'Don't wind me up, I'm fizzing as it is.' Addison took an angry gulp of Guinness, choked it past his throat in one draining and resumed his rant.

'Playing Sherlock fucking Holmes with his Rohypnol shit. He asked a question that he wasn't yet entitled to ask and got an answer that any clown walking in off the street could have got. The little rat is a glory-hunting wee—'

'Another pint, Addy?'

'Aye, obviously. Standard Scottish round-buying convention. I'm nearly finished, you're not, but it's your round, *ergo* you should be getting off your arse and up to the bar before I get near to the bottom of this glass.'

'Most people would just have said, "Yes, thanks."'

Sunday night in the Station Bar was quiz night and so was normally avoided by Winter and Addison on the basis that they had enough unanswered questions without listening to any more. This time, though, Addison had said that they would just ignore the anoraks and get a drink inside them. Between Kelbie and Sam Guthrie, the DI's cage had been well and truly rattled.

Winter returned with two perfectly poured pints of the black stuff, a midnight sky topped with orbits of ivory cream. He sat them down on the table and a large, contemplative mouthful disappeared from Addison's tumbler long before Winter was able to park himself in his seat. Addison's gaze was on the stout but his mind was elsewhere. In case it was still on Denny Kelbie, Winter tried to move the conversation away.

'So do you think there's a link between the two girls like Shirley says?'

Addison stared deeper into his pint in the vain hope that the answer might be found at the bottom of it. The frown that formed suggested he didn't find it.

'Nope.'

'That's it? Just nope.'

'Look, the Temple is desperate for there to be a link. He'll have us jumping through hoops to find one. The reason for that? He wants there to be one. If there is a link then there's some sort of pattern, some sort of reason. The alternative is that we have a complete psycho on our hands and that these girls were killed at random. My gut says it's a random, whether Shirley likes it or not. The two girls were young, pretty and on a night out. That's it. That and dead. You'll be happy, though: plenty of sick pictures for you to take.'

The truth, as is often the case, causes the most offence. 'Piss off. Seriously. That's bang out of order.'

'Yeah? Boo hoo.'

Winter slammed his pint down on the table and glared hard into Addison's face.

'Fuck off, you prick. I know you're pissed off about Kelbie, and that chemist was winding you right up, but that doesn't give you an excuse to take it out on me. Being my friend doesn't give you that right.'

Addison glowered back, nostrils flaring and eyes wide until he made a soft noise like the air coming out of a balloon. He rubbed wearily at his eyes. 'Aye, fair enough. Whisky?'

'Is that code for sorry?'

'No, it's code for whisky. Don't be such a girl. You want a half with that or not?'

'Aye, why not? I'll need another one if I'm going to listen to you.'

'Wise words, wee man. Wise words.'

Addison spent longer than necessary getting the two whiskies on account of being distracted by Nadia the barmaid. Or, rather, of trying to distract her from her job. She wasn't for playing, but it didn't stop the DI from trying.

When the drinks finally arrived, Winter did something he knew he shouldn't, but he still stung from Addison's jibe about sick pictures.

'So what is it with you and Kelbie? What's the bad blood all about?'

Addison grinned sourly. 'Apart from the fact that he shouldn't be a DCI because he's got no more time on the job than me and only got fake-promoted because of the restructuring when we went to a single force? And that he's an irritating, useless little arse? Forget it, Tony. There's not enough Guinness in the tap there for you to hear it all.'

Winter raised his eyebrows, running his finger round the rim of his pint glass and making it sing softly. 'That bad, huh? Must have been a girl.'

He saw Addison's teeth clench for just long enough to know that he had hit a nerve. As a good friend, he had no option but to hit it again until it rang.

'So who was she?'

'You're talking rubbish. As usual. You going to the game on Wednesday night?'

'Deviation and deflection. Must be bad. Not like you to get so uptight about a woman. What was it? Were you in love with her or was it your mother?'

For a split second, Winter was sure Addison was going to punch him. And, for a split second, he was. Addison burned with a fury that Winter had seen often but rarely turned in his direction. When he spoke, it was low and cold.

'Earlier, when I said you'd be happy that you'd have plenty of sick pictures to take?'

'Aye.'

'Well, I apologise. You're right. It was bang out of order.'

Winter read between the lines. 'And I'm bang out of order too?'

Addison nodded. 'Aye, you are. It wasn't my mother, you cheeky little prick. It was my sister. That little shite Kelbie shagged my sister.'

The malt, which Winter quickly realised was actually a double, had already disappeared down Addison's throat and he was clearly contemplating a replacement for the Guinness. He was absently moving the glass from hand to hand, his anger barely under the surface.

'As if that wasn't bad enough ...' Addison sank another fierce gulp of his stout before urgently fingering the froth away from his lips, the vein on his temple throbbing in time to the memories that made him halt. He nibbled at the inside of his cheek but when he was ready to speak, he had to choke his words back for a different reason. The table next to them began shouting at the quizmaster to repeat the question, drowning out Addison's words. 'Kelbie was married to someone else but—'

The quiz team erupted into another outpouring of trivia fury. Three guys in their late forties were waving their arms about in protest at something or other and clearly pissing off Addison in the process.

'So, *anyway* ... the wee shite finally fessed up to Marie and she told him where to go. Me, I wanted to—'

When Addison was interrupted once more by a noisy debate about Henry VIII and his wives, he'd had enough. He turned to study the three guys, each alternately shouting and whispering as they huddled across their pints of lager, all of them dressed as if they were some ill-advised throwback to the seventies. Addison reached back in his chair and thrust an arm into the middle of their table, plucking a mobile phone from the hands of one of the three.

'Bobby?' he called to the bar manager who, in the middle of pulling a pint, turned at the sound of his name. Addison tossed the mobile across the bar, where it was deftly caught. 'You maybe want to keep that till the quiz is finished.'

The owner of the phone turned with a distinct 'what the . . .?' look on his face, anger and bewilderment all in one.

'The answer's Catherine of Aragon, ya cheating halfwit,' Addison informed him.

'Hey, now wait a minute.' The guy got halfway out of his chair.

'Leave it, Les,' one of his pals warned him. 'It's no' worth it.'

'But he took my phone, Paul. My phone. You saw him, Neil. He took my phone.'

'Oh, dry your eyes,' Addison told him. 'You're lucky I didn't shove it up your arse. Now keep the noise down. We're talking.'

Les's mouth opened and closed like a fish's, as he saw the danger of continuing to argue. He and his teammates sensibly dropped their heads and turned back to their own table.

'As I was saying,' Addison resumed with a final glare at the quizzers and lowering his voice to an angry buzz, 'Kelbie was married to someone else at the time but neglected to tell my sister that.' He continued through gritted teeth, 'He told her a pack of lies just to get into bed with her.'

A phrase involving pots and kettles leapt into Winter's mind but he sensibly didn't voice it.

'Marie thought he was single and I don't know what the hell she possibly saw in him, but she fell for the prick. That baldy wee nyaff? I know women are strange but that takes the fucking biscuit.'

'So what happened?'

'Marie took a phone call from some woman threatening to claw her eyes out. Marie obviously makes a polite request asking what the fuck the mental cow is talking about and makes a few choice threats of her own. The woman says she's Kelbie's wife. Says she's going to kill Marie for stealing her man.'

'Nice.'

'Aye.'

The bitterness was swallowed down with a double mouthful of Guinness that emptied the glass.

'Kelbie had convinced his wife that Marie had made all the running and that he was oh-so-fucking sorry for allowing himself to be trapped or conned or whatever he told her. The little ratbag got away with it.'

'From you, too?' The surprise in Winter's voice was obvious. It wasn't the kind of thing that his mate would let lie.

'Yeah. From me, too. Marie was embarrassed even though none of it was her fault. She made me promise to let it go rather than make things worse by cutting Kelbie's dick off and shoving it down his throat. So I did what she wanted. And every time I see the little shit I hate myself almost as much as I hate him.'

Addison was squeezing the life out of the empty pint glass and Winter thought it might actually smash in his grip. He reached out and put his own hand over his pal's. 'You want another one of those?'

Addison looked down at Winter's hand, then slowly back up to face him, disbelief spreading across his features.

'Aye. Of course I do. But it's my round. And don't go getting all sister act on me. Touch me again and you go on the same list as Kelbie.'

Winter sighed and was about to reply when Addison turned halfway out of his seat, the two empty glasses like ready weapons in his hands, the hubbub of the pub quiz clamouring behind him.

'I'll tell you something, wee man. This case is huge. I'll be fucking damned if I'm going to let that wee shite get to the bottom of it before I do. This is personal.'

Chapter 13

Sunday evening

Emma Healey's flat was a traditional red-stone tenement in Hill Street, not far from the Glasgow School of Art. Incongruously, to its left and up the hill, sat the modernist Junior School building belonging to St Aloysius College, with its glass-sided balconies and broad, floor-to-ceiling external blinds. Across the street was the time-and-grime-blackened elegance of the Chandlery Building, the original home of the college in its Italianate palazzo style with its pillared portico, a hundred and fifty years of Glasgow weather and pollution seemingly proving impervious to the powers of sandblasting.

Architecturally, there was no doubt that the tenement where Emma lived was the poor relation of the neighbourhood, but it was Glasgow working-class and bloody proud of it. Narey remembered reading that four recent Turner Prize winners had lived in Hill Street and wondered if Hannah's little sister was an arty type.

Narey pressed the buzzer to the second-floor flat and moments later a hesitant voice and the rasping sound of the intercom indicated that she and Andy Teven could enter. They climbed the tenement stairs in silence and found the door to the flat open.

Mother and daughter sat huddled together on the sofa in the white-walled living room, the decor drawing what little colour was left from their faces. Emma Healey's eyes burned red from tears, contrasting raw against her bloodless cheeks. She looked up hopefully when Narey and Teven came in, searching their faces for signs that a terrible mistake had been made. Finding none, she slumped back in her seat. Her mother Mary, equally pale, sat open-mouthed, barely looking up as the officers entered the room, her fingers intertwined, working round each other feverishly.

Narey and Teven had already decided that they'd get better results if she led the interviews. A woman's touch he'd said, more than a little sarcastically. Whatever he thought, they both knew she'd manage more of a connection with the Healeys.

'Mrs Healey? Emma? I'm Detective Sergeant Rachel Narey. This is Detective Sergeant Andy Teven. Thanks for agreeing to speak to us. I won't say I know how difficult this must be for you because I don't. But I do feel for your loss.'

Both women nodded but Mary Healey did so without being able to look up at them. Her bottom lip quivered.

'Sit down, Sergeant, please. Both of you.' Emma Healey, a year or two younger than her sister but with the same pretty features and short, dark, bobbed hair, waved an arm in the direction of the two chairs in the room, and the two detectives settled into them. 'My mum's going to stay with me for a night or two. Can I get you something? Tea, coffee?'

'No, thank you. We'll try not to keep you too long. You've had a long day and it must be a lot to take in. But I do need to ask you some questions about Hannah if that's okay.'

It was as if the mention of her daughter's name woke Mary Healey from her near-trance. She looked up at them for the first time.

'She's a good girl, Sergeant. Never any bother like some you see going around. Neither of them ever been any bother.' Mrs Healey reached out an unsteady hand and stroked her younger daughter's face. A tear began to trickle down Emma's cheek, dampening her mother's fingers.

'She's never done drugs. Never got into trouble with the police. Never stayed out all night. Never any bother. She's my baby girl. My baby.'

Narey hesitated, the mother's words falling awkwardly between them. The silent gap seemed to stretch as she deliberated how to respond, but Mrs Healey ended it for her.

'I know she's dead, Sergeant. I can feel that she's gone. I just don't like talking about her as if she's not here. You understand?'

Narey breathed out. 'Yes. I think I do.'

'What do you want to ask us?'

'We need to build up a picture of the people in Hannah's life. Who she was in contact with. Anyone who may have had anything against her. Who may have harmed her.'

Emma shook her head vigorously. 'No one. Hannah didn't have an enemy in the world. She wasn't some goody-goody. We both . . .' She cast a sideways glance at her mother. 'Neither of us was angels but everyone loved Hannah. Honestly, Sergeant Narey. I can't think of anyone who'd have wanted to hurt her.'

'Well,' Narey said, trying to soften her voice as much as she could, 'someone did. And we'll do everything possible to find out who it was. We know her boyfriend was Gary McGregor. How—'

'It wasn't Gary,' Emma interrupted. 'No way. He'd never have—'

'It's okay. We know Mr McGregor was in town when Hannah was attacked. We've seen him on CCTV and our interviews with him have confirmed that. We're not considering him a suspect. But how long had he and Hannah been going out? Were there previous boyfriends?'

Emma's hand went to her eyes, rubbing at them. 'They'd been seeing each other for about eighteen months. I used to wind them up that they were love's young dream. Besotted with each other, they were. I think they would have got married in a year or two . . .' Her voice trailed off.

'So there's no way she'd have been seeing anyone else? Sorry but I have to ask.'

'No way.' The answer was clipped and resentful.

'And previous boyfriends?'

Emma shrugged. 'They seem so long ago. A boy named Keir Colvin lived in the next block of flats. But that was years ago and I think he moved to East Kilbride. There was another boy – what was his name, Mum? Lewis. Lewis . . . Jackson. I still see him around now and again and I think he and Hannah still talk to each other. Just friends like.'

Narey nodded, seeing Teven take a note of both names.

'And has she ever mentioned anyone showing a particular interest in her? Chatting her up or pestering her, maybe?'

Emma shrugged again. Then a look crossed her face.

'There's Mr Grey. But, well, it's probably nothing and I'd just be getting someone into trouble.'

'Let me judge whether it's nothing or not. Who's Mr Grey?'

'Just this guy who goes into the hairdresser's where Hannah works. Worked. And his name's not really Mr Grey. That's just what Hannah called him. He was called Ronnie something or other.'

Narey leaned forward in her seat. 'Tell me about him.'

Emma Healey wavered, cast another long look at her mother before speaking. 'He was a perv, that's what Hannah said. He gave her the creeps. He always went in there and asked for her even though he had to pay three times what he would in a barber's. He spent the whole time looking at her in the mirror and she reckoned he was ... well, playing with himself under the apron. She called him Mr Grey because of the colour of his hair and after the guy in *Fifty Shades*. A right perv, she said.'

The girl's mother looked at her, puzzled by the sudden insight into Hannah's life. 'What are you saying, Emma? Who is this man?'

Emma's face looked apologetic. 'I maybe shouldn't have said anything. He probably just fancied Hannah. It doesn't make him a—'

She choked on the word but Andy Teven picked it up, speaking for the first time.

'A killer? It might. You not think, DS Narey?'

Narey looked at the drained faces of the two women in front of her and nodded slightly. 'Yeah. It might. Emma, tell me everything you know about him.'

Chapter 14

Monday morning

CINDERELLA KILLER: SHOELESS GIRLS FOUND DEAD

The newspaper headline screamed at them from the billboard outside the corner shop next door to the Hyndland Café on Clarence Drive. Winter had got the subway to Partick and walked over while Narey had, unusually for her, shaken off the cobwebs by strolling there to meet him from her flat at the foot of Highburgh Road.

Their meeting had been billed, unofficially, as a catch-up. Winter wasn't even sure what that meant but was fairly certain it meant something different to him from what it did to Rachel, just as he'd interpreted things differently when she'd said they'd have to take things slowly for a while, as she needed to concentrate on looking after her dad. He'd interpreted that as his being dumped and little had happened since to convince him otherwise.

She'd wanted to move her dad out of the care home and back into his own house or even in with her, but his condition just hadn't allowed it. The Alzheimer's had deteriorated such that Alan Narey simply couldn't be left on his own. Rachel had decided that whatever spare time she had had to be dedicated to him rather than to Tony. He understood, sort of. But he didn't like it.

They'd both cried, perhaps for the same thing, perhaps for something different. He'd gone back to his flat and she to hers, a mile and a half of loneliness between them. It occurred to him that although Rachel spent a lot of her time with her dad, she was even lonelier than he was.

This morning, she'd got to the café just before him and was standing staring at the board in all its shouting block-capitals glory. He could see her right foot tapping furiously and knew instinctively that she was angry. So much for the catch-up.

'Jesus. Addy is going to go absolutely mental.'

'Oh, he sure is. At least I might get that useless tosser Toshney out of my hair.'

'You think it was him that spoke to the press? He's not that stupid surely?'

'Well, someone is. Thing is, even if it wasn't Toshney, Addison is going to blame him anyway. I wouldn't want to be in his ... shoes.'

'No mention of what was written on their stomachs?'

'You can see what I can see, can't you?'

He sighed softly. 'You want me to get the paper or just read the free ones in the café?'

'Go and buy any paper that has this in it. I don't want to have to wrestle it out of someone's hands. And I would.'

'Oh, I know you would. Get me a bacon roll and an orange juice, will you?'

It was only the *Sun* that had the story. Plastered over three pages including the front. They'd managed to get hold of photographs of both Kirsty McAndrew and Hannah Healey, the girls smiling incongruously out of the page. The headline conveniently ignored that Hannah had one shoe on. Or else it disregarded the fact that Kirsty had one fewer than Cinderella.

A quick scan showed no mention of the lipstick scrawl, so that was at least something. There was a lot of play about the two cemeteries with words such as *ghoulish*, *macabre* and *grisly* featuring throughout the piece. It was manna from heaven for the tabloids but Winter doubted that Addison or Shirley would see it that way. Or Rachel, come to that.

His eyes tried to follow the report, but they kept drifting back to the eyes that gazed at him from the paper. He couldn't help but compare the images to the ones he had taken in the Necropolis and on Caledonia Road. Couldn't stop himself from comparing the faces in front of him to the sleeping bloodied forms he'd photographed. Eternity stared back at him from the ink.

He closed the newspaper over, shutting the girls away, and handed over his cash to the shopkeeper. When the bell rang to betray his entrance into the café, he saw that Rachel was sitting in the rear wooden booth and already had a copy of the *Sun* in front of her. The way her mouth was knotted suggested that she was far from impressed.

'If it's Toshney, then I'm going to kill him myself,' she hissed, her hands tightening their grip on the paper.

'You get brown sauce on that roll?'

'Just bloody eat it once it comes. I think this shoe stuff is bollocks. Why no shoes, then one? It doesn't make any sense. I'm not buying it. Addison's going to go ape shit though. This Cinderella stuff will have him diving off the top board. Christ, at least there's nothing about the writing on their stomachs. Although it does mention the first girl's hands being placed palm up and the other's clasped in prayer.'

'You sure it came from inside?'

She looked up at him, as if realising that she'd been talking out loud and had said more than she'd meant to. Even when they'd been together, she'd always tried to keep their personal and professional lives completely separate, putting up a barrier and on a need-to-know basis that annoyed the hell out of him. Even voicing her opinion of the missing shoes was more than he'd normally get.

'Yeah. Probably. Maybe.'

He heard the all-too-familiar sound of the cell door slamming shut in his face.

'You do remember that I took photographs of those girls? And that I was there in the Necropolis? And that I know about the shoes? And that we were more than colleagues?'

She smiled back at him sarcastically and perhaps slightly sadly. 'Yes, I do remember. Doesn't mean I should be talking to you about them. Or talking about who might have leaked this to the bloody paper.'

'You mean Toshney?'

She glared at him and glanced around the café before

opening her mouth to retort. The words never came though because she was interrupted by the waitress setting down an orange juice and a coffee. By the time the girl had left, Rachel's tone had softened.

'Sorry. Didn't mean to shout at you. It's just been ... difficult lately.'

Winter nodded. 'How's your dad?'

Her face fell. 'Not good. He's gone through a bit of a bad spell.'

'And how are you?'

She shrugged but he could see the pain behind her eyes. He wanted to hug her yet knew he couldn't. Shouldn't. 'If there's anything I can do to help ...'

His hand edged cautiously towards her across the table. Rachel stared at it, seemingly considering the offer. 'Tony ... I want to ...'

Her mobile phone rang and vibrated on the desk, slicing through whatever was passing between them. Rachel looked at the screen and mouthed an apology. She hit the answer button on the phone but didn't have the chance to say as much as hello before the voice on the other end began blaring through. Even from the other side of the table, Winter could tell it was Addison. His own conversation was over.

Narey put the mobile to her ear but just as quickly had to take it away again and hold it a foot away as Addison ranted down the other end. 'Yes, I've seen it,' she eventually managed to say. 'I've got a copy of it in front of me now. No, I don't know. Of course it bloody wasn't me! Yes, I know you think it was him. Yes, maybe but—'

Addison continued his tirade, an angry buzzing bouncing off the wooden panels of the booth. Narey grimaced at the noise and made several stuttering attempts to butt her way into the onslaught before finally managing to bring the DI to a halt.

'Look, *sir*, I'm not exactly Toshney's biggest fan, as you know. No ... no ... Let me finish. Everyone at the scene heard you hammer Toshney for that. As soon as you did that ... Hang on ... As soon as you did it gave everyone else a free hurl at blabbing it to their friendly local journo, knowing full well that Toshney would get the blame. Or even just mentioning it to someone else who then told the paper. No ... no, I'm in the Hyndland Café. No, I'm on my own. Right, okay, see you soon.'

Winter raised his eyebrows questioningly at Narey as she hung up, but she shrugged unapologetically.

'The more Addy ranted that it was Toshney, the more I felt inclined to defend the twat. Anyway, I'm right. Everyone at the scene at the Necropolis heard Toshney make that stupid Cinderella joke. It could have been any of them. It could have been you.'

Winter just looked back at her, his face impassive. 'I thought we were going to have a chat.'

She sipped on her coffee, eyes closed. 'Sorry. We can't. I've got to go. Now. Addy wants a brainstorming situation. Which is ironic, given that he's already doing my brain in.'

'Bit of a bad mood?'

'He could probably run his car on the steam that's coming out of his ears.'

'Yeah? I've had better starts to the day myself.'

'Sorry.'

In moments she was gone, swept through the front door in a bustle of coat, leaving him sitting alone in the booth. Winter pushed aside the bacon roll, appetite disappeared, and stared at the space where she'd sat.

Five minutes later, he left the café, trying his best not to look as crestfallen as he felt and headed back to Partick station to get the subway into town. He still had a while before he was due to start work but he decided to head into Pitt Street early. God knows, there was enough for him to do.

He cut through a housing estate on his way to Crow Road, his head full of questions about relationships and shoes and tattoos and young women lost in the night. The camera in the bag on his back still held images taken in the two cemeteries, and a bit of him itched to take it out and go through them. A more rational part resisted and he left the camera where it was, weighing down on his shoulder like a nagging conscience.

At the foot of Crow Road he turned left onto Dumbarton Road and hoofed it the rest of the way to the station. The Glasgow underground was the third oldest in the world after London and Budapest. It had just two routes, the inner and outer circle, meaning that there wasn't necessarily going to be a station near where you wanted to go.

The trains rattled round in circles all day long. Until recently, they were liveried in a colour that was officially something other than orange, even though orange was exactly what it was. Only in Glasgow would it have to be formally described as 'Strathclyde PTE Red' to appease sectarian sensitivities. It made even more of a joke of the subway's supposed nick-name – the Clockwork Orange. A joke because no one in Glasgow ever used the phrase.

Winter descended to the platform, walking despite the escalator. As he got down to track level, his eyes were imme-diately drawn to the LCD screen that showed the local television headlines. A report about NHS funding lingered briefly before being replaced by a bulletin that mimicked the morning paper. MURDER HUNT FOR 'CINDERELLA' KILLER. Below the heading was a photograph of uniformed cops stationed outside the Southern Necropolis and below that was the sub-heading SHOELESS GIRLS KILLED AT CITY CEMETERIES.

There weren't many people waiting for the next train, but Winter saw a young couple nudge each other and nod in the direction of the screen. The girl, a neo-punk with platinum-spiked hair, cuddled into her boyfriend for protection. They turned away but Winter stood and stared. He watched the screen change to the next story and waited patiently for it to come round again, willing in vain for it to have new informa-tion by the time it next appeared. But each time it rolled around there were two girls dead and nobody seemed to be any the wiser.

On the train, he took up a seat opposite a large woman in her early fifties who was evidently viewing the screens on the platform wall behind him.

'Oh my. You see that?'

Winter hoped she was talking to someone else but, on lift-ing his eyes, he saw she was looking for an answer from him, shock and incredulity writ large on her doughy features.

'What's that?' he asked, despite knowing the answer.

'Two lassies killed. Oh, my Goad. Killed in cemeteries, it says.'

'Aye. Ah read that in the paper this morning,' another chipped in, a twenty-something girl who looked like a student. 'Two of them murdered. Took their shoes aff them and everything. Left their bodies in the graveyard.'

'Oh wheest,' the older woman breathed. 'That no' terrible? In a graveyard, that's dead creepy, that is.'

'Ah know,' replied the student. 'According to the paper, one was the same age as me. Just oot for a night oot, too. Terrible.'

'It is. You better watch yoursel', hen. Dinnae be going oot by yourself. An make sure your mammy knows where you are.'

The girl gave a shiver. 'Well, my mammy's deid but, aye, ah know what you mean. Makes you think, eh?'

'Ah saw this programme last night about a murder,' butted in a man with a beard and a woollen hat pulled down low on his forehead. 'This guy killed three women.'

The student and the older woman looked at each other and both shivered. 'In Glasgow like?' the student asked.

'Naw, New York. It was pretty good.'

'Pretty good?' the older woman shrieked.

'Aye, him that used to be in the West Wing was in it. You know, the one with the hair. It wisnae real if that's what you were thinking.'

The two women breathed again. 'Aw, that's awrite then. Him with the hair? The good-looking one that was in that thing with Meg Ryan?'

Winter closed his eyes and tuned out. He'd been on the London Underground dozens of times and had never once heard strangers have a conversation. Sometimes – quite often, in fact – he wished that Glaswegians had the same view of people they didn't know. In Glasgow, a stranger was just a friend you hadn't had an argument with yet.

He got off at Cowcaddens and instinctively looked at his watch. It wasn't that he wanted a drink but he was only a few hundred yards from the Station Bar and checking if it was opening time was a reflex action. It was just after 10.30, so the answer was an emphatic no in any case.

He wandered over to Cambridge Street and from there on to Sauchiehall Street, where he walked against the rising tide of humanity who were going up the hill towards the city centre. Late workers and early shoppers, some sticking their faces in windows to see what they couldn't afford, others interested in nothing more than the cracks in the pavement. At Antipasti, he turned left into Pitt Street, soon seeing the corner of the crumbling, red-brick monolith of the force's HQ up ahead.

As he got closer, he saw a man pacing agitatedly outside the main entrance. It was hardly unusual given the nature of the place: there was always likely to be somebody worried about someone or something inside. It was only when Winter got nearer that he recognised the broad figure for who it was.

'Uncle Danny. What the hell are you doing here?'

Danny Neilson was Winter's mother's brother. A former police sergeant himself, he had virtually brought Tony up after the death of his parents. The two were close, although it was a strange kind of closeness. They could go months without seeing or talking to each other but slip back into a certainty of understanding within minutes.

Danny was Danny. A big, bluff, understanding man who had been there, seen it and told it to sit on its arse. He was the smartest man Winter had ever known, even though a first glance might make you think he was the oldest nightclub bouncer in town. The one thing you rarely saw with Danny, however, was him in any kind of fluster. And that's exactly how he was now.

'Danny, what's up?'

'About time, Anthony. What kind of time do you call this to start work? Half the day's gone already.'

'It's called shift work, Uncle Danny. Come on, spill. Were you working late last night? You look like shit. What's wrong?'

Danny was a taxi-rank supervisor, working all hours and in all weathers, even though he'd retired from the police twelve years before. Winter had told him often enough that he didn't need the hassle of refereeing drunks, but Danny always said it was his job and he'd keep doing it. Now, he ran his hand through his full head of grey hair, blowing hard and angry. Winter had never seen him like this.

'I worked till two but that doesn't matter. It's those eejits in there. Where do they get them from these days? I spent half an hour trying to get past the muppet on the desk and, when I finally got to speak to someone in CID, I was back on the street in fifteen minutes with my arse barely touching the street on the way out.'

'Yes but what—'

'Then I said I wanted to speak to you but they gave me some shit and said I couldn't. I had to give it the old "Do you know who I am?" bollocks again and that's when they said you hadn't started yet. So I waited. Either for you or for anyone else that I knew by sight who I could speak to.'

'But why, Danny? What's this all about?'

'Those murders that were in the paper this morning. The two girls found in the cemeteries?'

'Yeah?'

'Well, I know who did it.'

Chapter 15

The King's Café on Elmbank Street is, despite its name, a chippy. However, there are tables and chairs enough that it doesn't contravene the Trade Descriptions Act, and Winter and Danny sat down and ordered two cups of tea. Winter's mind turned briefly to Addison's lyrical waxing over the best chips-and-cheese in town, but the consideration lasted all of two seconds before his stomach lurched in protest.

They had the place to themselves and the sole member of staff paid them no attention after handing over the steaming cups of tea. That seemed to suit Danny fine. He continued to be agitated and had told Winter that he wouldn't explain anything until they were sitting down away from the eyes and ears of others.

'So?' Winter asked.

'So what do you know about these killings? Were you working the case? I know you'll know more than was in the paper.'

'Danny, I thought you were going to tell me something rather than ask questions. What's got you into this state?'

'Son, did you photograph these girls?'

'Yes. Yes, I did. But you know I can't just go blabbing to you about what was there.'

Danny's gaze hardened and Winter saw what a lot of men had seen over the years: a look that would make them think twice about arguing with the man in front of them. Danny had never given Winter any reason to be afraid of him, just as he wasn't now, but he saw the look and what it meant.

'Okay, son. Here's what we'll do. I'm going to tell you what I think. What I'm fairly sure of. Then I'll expect you to tell me what you know. Okay?'

'Maybe. Why don't you tell me, then we'll see?'

'When the fuck did you become the play-it-by-the-book guy, Anthony? Never mind. When you hear what I've got to say, you'll tell me.'

Danny blew on his tea, buying himself a few seconds. He sipped on it, the three-sugar sweetness failing to remove the sour taste that had so obviously taken up residence in his mouth.

'There was a case, years before you were born, but you'll know it. The Klass killings.'

Winter's brow slowly furrowed in scepticism. 'Right. The Klass. You think these two murders are connected to that? You think this is *him*? Come on, Danny.'

Danny gave him the look again, even fiercer this time. Shut up. Listen. His next statement came out low and slow, like a growl.

'Son, I worked the Klass killings for two years solid. I lived and breathed it. I know as much as anyone alive about that case except for the bastard that did it. And I *know* there's a connection to those two girls. I *feel* it.'

The two men stared at each other for an age. Winter tried to make sense of Danny's words, seemingly so unlikely, yet had to weigh them up against the look of hard certainty that was chiselled onto his face. Danny stared back, intent on convincing Tony of every word he said.

Of course Tony knew about the Klass killings. Everyone in Glasgow knew about them. They were as much a part of a kid's education as never answering the question about what team you supported or never eating yellow snow.

Four young women had been murdered across two separate weekends in the city, two months apart. All four had been to Klass, the disco on West Nile Street, easily the most popular in the town. All four had been raped and strangled.

It was the early seventies and the city descended into genuine panic. Girls weren't allowed out and young men who remotely resembled the suspect were stopped for questioning. For months, maybe years, a shadow haunted every night out in Glasgow. All the cops ever had was two names – one imagined, one real. They never made one fit the other.

The name of the legend was Red Silk, so called because witnesses spoke of a man with a red silk handkerchief in his jacket pocket who had been seen talking to two of the victims. It was a name that caught on. It fitted newspaper headlines and fired imaginations. *Red Silk's gonnae get you. Careful that Red Silk disnae catch you on the way home.*

For forty years, the name had been a fixture in books, newspaper articles, documentaries, even a movie. Red Silk grew bigger even than the horrendous acts he'd committed – simply because he'd never been caught. There were theories – dozens, maybe hundreds of them. Academics, journalists, ex-cops, psychics and psychologists – everyone had an idea of who Red Silk might be. And everyone had an idea of why the killings stopped as suddenly as they started. It was a cottage industry based on the ferocious murders of innocents.

The real name, the one that the theories finally agreed upon, came years later. A man convicted of other vicious crimes against young women. A killer whose murderous brutality certainly matched the handiwork of Red Silk and who had lived and worked in the city at the time before moving south.

His name was Archibald Atto. A former English teacher who was serving consecutive life sentences for the sadistic murders of four women but was suspected of many more. He'd been in prison for eleven years and across that time had twice directed police to the unmarked graves of victims in return for prison privileges. No one was in any doubt that he knew the precise locations of other bodies but that he kept the information to himself as a future bargaining tool when he required it.

No fewer than nine other families were desperate for Atto to give them some measure of peace by disclosing the locations of their daughters, sisters, nieces and granddaughters. They'd ask if he would even just confirm that they were dead and that he'd killed them. Atto chose to give them nothing except silence. The search for the missing girls and the families' continued suffering kept the case in the headlines and his name in lights. It seemed that Atto enjoyed both.

Not everyone thought Atto had committed the Klass killings and it was something he'd never confirmed or denied. There was even a school of thought, endorsed by a former chief constable, that there was no single Klass killer, no Red Silk. His view was that the killings were unconnected, merely tragic coincidences. It wasn't a view shared by many.

But Atto had been inside for over a decade. How could Danny possibly think that he was connected to the killings in the cemeteries?

'Like I said, I know the Klass killings inside out. I know every other case that Atto has either been convicted of or suspected of. I know how he works and this stinks of him. The report in the paper said that the first victim had her palms turned up, the second had hers clasped together. That's not natural. It's how Atto would place his victims.'

'But Danny—'

'Yeah, he's inside. I know that. I'm not senile yet, son. And it doesn't change anything. I know what I know. Killings on successive nights over the weekend, girls on a night out, strangulation, rape. Girls disappearing into thin air and emerging dead somewhere else. The hands. The locations where they were found too – classic Atto. I've never believed in coincidences, Tony, and I'm too old to start now.'

Winter exhaled hard and rubbed at his eyes. 'So what happened when you went into Pitt Street?'

'They basically told me I was nuts and that I should bugger off. Some DS, Teven his name was, took my details and pretended to write down what I said. He didn't even make an effort to hide the fact that he saw me as a stupid old sod, stuck in the past and with some harebrained idea to get himself noticed again. He thought I was a crackpot and the report's probably already in the bin.'

Danny was angry and agitated. Being dismissed on account of his age and sell-by date was never likely to be something that would sit well with him. But heaped on top of his age issues was frustration. Winter knew all of that but couldn't help himself from pointing out the obvious.

'You can't really blame them, Danny. You've been behind that desk and seen the nutters crawl out of the woodwork whenever something like this happens. I know you're not a nutter, but Teven doesn't know you from Adam. Look at it from his point of view.'

Danny growled. 'I'm looking at it from a cop's point of view. He should do the same.'

A silence fell between them. Sips and gulps were taken of unwanted tea.

'Okay,' Danny started again, looking out of the café window but seeing nothing. 'So I need to give DS Teven a bit more to work with, something to convince him that there *is* a link. You've got the photographs you took, right?'

'No way, Danny. You know I can't do that. I *cannot* do that. I'll get fired if I'm lucky and arrested if I'm not. Dan, you know I'd do anything for you, but that's asking too much.'

'Anything? And yet not something that anyone else will ever know about?'

'They won't know about it because it's not going to happen. This is crazy.'

'Son, that's the second time today that someone has suggested I'm off my head. I didn't expect it from you.' He threw a couple of pound coins on the table. 'That's for the tea. If I had thirty pieces of silver, you'd be welcome to them.'

'Danny . . .' Winter's plea was in vain as his uncle turned his back and walked out of the café, the door slamming shut behind him.

Chapter 16

July 1972

The queue outside Klass ran a good thirty yards down West Nile Street as well as up the three flights to the disco itself. It was another warm night without even the rumour of a breeze, and he knew it was going to get hot inside.

He'd ditched the three-piece suit on account of the heat. He'd been loath to give up on the gold stripe but it had to be done. The last thing he could afford was to look out of place, so he'd gone for a pair of new hip huggers with particularly wide bell bottoms teamed with blue platforms. His light-blue floral shirt was half covered by the width of his navy paisley-patterned tie. It was a fair leap from the suit, but he liked it.

The queue shuffled its way slowly inside the building and edged up the stairs an argument at a time. The bouncers must have been in an even tougher mood than usual because a succession of dejected young guys came back down, muttering about the bastards on the door, the volume of their protests getting louder the further they got away from the doormen. The crowd on the stairs were still chirpy though. It had been a full week since the last incident and that was a lifetime ago.

The reminders were still there though. At the top of the first landing was a big poster: HAVE YOU SEEN THIS MAN? Under the words were an artist's impression of the only description that the police had. Not that it was worth much. It could have been anybody. It could have been him.

At the top of the second landing, there was another copy of the same poster plus three that had been made by the *Daily Record*. Each one had a sketch of one of the three women with the words DID YOU SEE HER? in large lettering. Under the drawings were the words 'RED SILK' MURDERS and two telephone numbers to call. Red Silk, he thought, what a stupid name. Half the crowd didn't even bother looking at the posters but some of those who did, particularly the girls, shivered and turned away as quickly as they could. Better not to think about it.

He looked at the posters, though. He stared at them. He stared and tried not to be seen to be staring.

The queue snaked its way higher, the stairs becoming hotter and stickier as it neared the entrance. Those let in by the bouncers tried to look cool as if they fully expected it, but he knew that inside they were swimming in relief. Others weren't faring so well, but some of them had a few tricks up their sleeves. Two girls, whom he could see only from the back – but one was a tall brunette and the other shorter with long, bright-red hair – were on the top step before the door and the bouncers were shaking their head at them. One of the girls, the redhead, told them that they were friends of the DJ. The guy on the door didn't look convinced but he went inside and, two minutes later, the blond-haired DJ appeared at the door, dressed in a yellow suit with blue stripes and enormous red platform shoes. He looked the two girls up and down and winked at them before telling the bouncer that, sure, they were with him. In they went. A couple of other girls cottoned on quickly and shouted up the stairs. 'Hey, us too. You do remember us, don't you?' They also must have been good-looking enough, because the DJ grinned and said yeah, and they were allowed in the door.

It didn't go down too well with the blokes in the queue. There was a lot of grumbling, but they couldn't afford to do it too loudly or else there was no way they were getting past the bouncers. He'd be fine, though. Top of the stairs and, sure enough, the bouncer just looked him in the eye and signalled him inside with a backward movement of his head.

It was already pretty busy, murder clearly not being bad for business. Klass had been in every newspaper in the country for three weeks and it did look like there was no such thing as bad publicity. The thought both bothered him and encouraged him.

The DJ was back behind his decks, no sign of the supposed friends he'd invited in, and he had the dance floor almost full already. Foreheads glistened as people moved to the beat, record immediately following record as the DJ made them work. The guy was full of himself, jumping up and down, pointing to girls in the crowd and acting the big man, but he could make them dance.

After a bit, he slid the volume down on Elton John's 'Rocket Man' and spoke over it. 'Awrite there, people. Welcome back. I'm Jumping Jimmy Steele and this is Klass, the best disco this side of New York City. I'll have you groovin' and movin' again in two seconds flat but first a few announcements. Next Friday night is Red Silk Lookalike night. You've all seen the posters and there will be a very special prize for the guy – or gal – who looks most like Mr Red Silk. An', as if that wisnae enough for youse, on the following Saturday we are having Glasgow's very first Be Red Silk for a Night night. Guys, youse are no' getting in unless you've got yoursel' a red-silk hankie in your top pocket. Youse have been warned. And, as if that wasn't enough, next week's band is currently in the top twenty and will be here live on stage. It's the Sweet! We're Klass and it's all happening here. I'm Jumping Jimmy Steele and this . . . is the Sweet themselves with "Poppa Joe".'

He felt a rage building as the crowd cheered the DJ's nonsense. It was Glasgow all over, gallus as anything, but it wasn't excuse enough. It wasn't right, nowhere near it. If only they knew.

He pushed his way through the punters near the bar and ordered himself a pint of lager. It poured fast and fizzy, turning golden before him. He handed over a fifty-pence coin and had a large mouthful of the lager down his throat before the barman came back with his change. The liquid was gassy, tepid and already a bit stale, but it washed away a nastier taste that had gathered in his throat.

Feeling slightly better for it, he turned away from the bar, pint glass in hand, and, as he did so, his elbow clattered into that of a girl standing behind him. Half of her glass splashed onto the floor at her feet. She just looked at him in mild astonishment, but her friend, a tall brunette, didn't hold back.

'That wis a Martini and lemonade. Now it's jist *half* a Martini and lemonade. The bar's ower there.'

He didn't say anything. There was nothing to say. He spun on his heels and queued at the bar again, returning minutes later and proffering the glass towards the redhead, who was draining the last of the glass he'd spilled. He'd seen her only from behind as he'd queued to get in, but it had to be the girl who had said she was friends with the DJ. Hair as red as that wasn't very common, even in Scotland. She wore black, fake-leather hot pants, brown, knee-length suede boots and dark nylons. Her top was the same colour as her boots and seemed to hug a good figure. Her eyes were a vivid, lively green.

'Sorry,' was all he managed to say. Hardly the sharpest of patter but, then, he wasn't there to talk. He would have come armed with snappy chat-up lines if that had been his purpose, but he had something more serious in mind.

'Not much of a talker, are you?'

'Sorry.' He said it again, regretting it immediately. He wasn't there to chat her up but he didn't want to sound like an idiot, either. The snigger from her pal, the brunette, suggested he'd failed.

'Aye, so you said.' The redhead laughed as she pushed her hair back out of her eyes. 'Do you just go around elbowing women and saying sorry?'

'Not at all. Sometimes I don't say sorry.'

'That's not very nice, is it? Did your mammy not teach you any manners?'

'She taught me to be wary of girls with red hair.'

'Ah. A wise woman. Did she teach you how to dance as well?'

'No. My big sister taught me that. She wasn't very good, though.'

She looked at him as if waiting. Her eyebrows rose in part exasperation and part amusement until she finally sighed in frustration.

'So . . . are you dancing?'

This wasn't quite in the plan. He didn't want to draw attention to himself. That would be far too risky. But was it more risky to dance or to refuse? There was no doubting that she was very easy on the eye, the flames of her hair shimmering under the glitter ball and her green eyes sparkling with the capacity for mischief. To hell with it, he'd dance. Just the one, though.

'Aye. I'm dancing.'

They placed their drinks on the nearest table and took to the floor. He knew the song, Jo Jo Gunne with 'Run, Run, Run'. Could he dance to that? He'd just have to. He was a big guy but he was light enough on his feet and had done enough 'proper dancing' in his day, and this couldn't be that different. He just had to move, whether it was to follow her or do his own thing.

She was into it; he could see that right away. The bright-green eyes closed over and a smile spread wide across her face as her hips swayed and her feet danced. Her arms were above her head and then by her side, the leather-look hot pants shimmying and her slim legs always on the move. She looked good and she danced well.

He looked beyond her as well, though, taking the chance of being on the dance floor to look and to watch. The dancers round him were into their moves and their partners and so not paying any attention to where his eyes were going. It was too good an opportunity to miss. He saw where they were looking and read what he could into their clothes, expressions and mannerisms. And then he looked back at her.

When the song faded, segueing into America's 'Horse With No Name', she smiled coyly at him, looking him straight in the eyes. Before they had started, he'd decided it would just be the one dance but, when she said thanks and turned away, something still stung. She took a couple of steps, then looked back over her shoulder.

'What's your name?'

He hesitated, wondering whether to make something up or give her his real name. What harm could it do? Anyway, something inside him wanted her to know.

'I'm Danny. Danny Neilson.'

Chapter 17

Monday. Noon.

The lurid pink shop sign on Alexandra Parade read SCISSOR SISTERS in a large florid font. Just in case the pun wasn't crushingly obvious enough, there was a huge pair of silver scissors underneath the lettering and a pair of identical blonde manes, one at either end.

Narey had for once managed to ditch the insufferable presence of Toshney and instead had the much more relaxed presence of DC Rebecca Maxwell, who had not long moved over from uniform but could be relied upon not to stick her feet in her mouth. Almost as one, they turned to look at each other on seeing the sign and raised their eyebrows in disapproval. This was going to be good.

The sisters in question were Melanie and Maria McAllister – M&M's, as Maria had blurted out before Melanie had glared at her to remind her why Narey was there to visit them.

'Sorry, sorry. Oh, ma Goad. Ah'm sorry. We pure loved Hannah, so we did. She was a great wee worker and never any bother. Brilliant wi' highlights, so she wis. Ah've been greetin' my eyes oot since we were telt. We both huv. Ah didnae mean—'

'Oh, zip it, Maria, for God's sake!' her sister ordered her. 'Stop babbling oan. The sergeant's no here to listen to you talking rubbish.'

The Scissor Sisters were in danger of giving hairdressers a bad name. Matching big blonde cuts that were a dare away from platinum, fake bakes that might have been browned in a Greggs oven and teeth so white you needed shades. With matching green eyes and dolly smiles, they could have been twins, but Melanie was clearly the elder of the two, even if only by a matter of minutes. She was the one in charge and wee sister Maria knew her place.

'Sorry, Mel. It's just that ah get nervous, you know that. An wi' wee Hannah getting … Oh, ma Goad, ah cannae say it. I cannae even say it.'

Melanie's eyes closed over briefly and she shook her head at her sister for what Narey guessed to be the millionth time in her life. 'Oh, shut up, Mar. Seriously. You're showing us up. Again. Sorry, Sergeant. What can we dae for you?'

Narey smiled gratefully while sighing inside. She needed an easy one, just a simple 'here's what you need to know' all wrapped up in a pretty piece of ribbon. Mel and Mar didn't seem to represent a great chance of her getting that.

'Thanks for seeing me. I know it's a difficult time.'

The Scissor Sisters nodded in unison.

'How long did Hannah Healey work here?' Bog-standard technique. Start with questions you already know the answer to and work your way towards those that you don't.

'About a year and a half?' Melanie looked towards her sister, who nodded. 'Yeah, about a year and a half.'

'And how would you describe her?'

'Brand-new.' 'Great.' 'All the clients loved her.' 'She was a star.'

The replies spun one over the other and Narey wasn't entirely sure who said what, but she got the idea. Hannah was well liked. More than that, she had her 'in' for the question she really wanted to ask.

'So she was popular with the customers?'

'Oh, aye, definitely.'

'So I suppose some of them would be regular clients? Booking their appointments with Hannah?'

The sisters with the scissors nodded enthusiastically. 'Oh, yeah. She had her regulars. We all do,' Melanie agreed.

'Just women, or men too?' Narey steered them where she wanted to go.

'Men anaw,' Maria answered proudly. 'We're unisexual.'

Narey did her best not to catch DC Maxwell's eyes, instead forcing herself to remember why they were there. Melanie McAllister tutted at her sister. 'Hannah had male clients as well. We dinnae get as many men as women, but there's a few. Guys who like to look good, like.'

'Anyone in particular ask for Hannah?'

Melanie and Maria looked at each other.

'Well ... aye,' one of them started. 'There's—'

'Ronnie,' the other one answered.

Bingo. Narey made sure she didn't respond too quickly.

'Who's Ronnie?'

Maria did an exaggerated shudder. 'Ronnie Dance. He

ayeways asked for Hannah and if she wisnae available he'd just go away and come back another time.'

'Was ayeways glad he did,' Melanie agreed. 'Wouldnae have wanted him to get me to do him.' The sisters looked at each other and shuddered again.

'Oh, Goad, me anaw,' blurted out Maria. 'Pure weird, so he is. Ah wouldn't trust him alone in a room with a rubber doll.'

'Mar!' Melanie tutted again. 'But she's right, though. Pure weird.'

'In what way?'

'Just kinda ... sleazy. Pervy sleazy. When Hannah did his hair he wis always just, like, staring at her in the mirror. Ugh.'

'So what does this Ronnie look like? What can you tell me about him?'

Mel and Mar looked at each other, confused and a bit scared.

'Ronnie? You think . . .?'

Narey turned her mouth down at both sides, making a show of looking doubtful that there was likely to be anything at all in the route she was taking.

'We're just checking everything out. We have to consider all possibilities in a situation like this.'

'Oh ... okay.' Melanie took charge. 'He's quite a big guy. About six foot. Maybe early forties. Grey hair. No' really the kind that would come in here normally. More of a barber's kind of man. He's got these dark eyebrows, bushy things. Would be awrite-looking if he wisnae so creepy. He said he was a painter. No' a decorator, like. A proper artist painter.'

'I didnae believe him,' butted in Maria.

'Me neither. Full of shit if ye ask me. I've got an address for him if you want.'

'Really?'

'Yeah. We keep a list so we can send out Christmas cards at the end of the year. Somewhere in Dennistoun, I think. I can get it for you.'

'Hang on, sis. Is that no' breaking that client privy … privy … um, thingy.'

'Naw, Mar. We're no' bloody doctors. Hang on, Sergeant, I'll get it.'

A couple of minutes later, Melanie McAllister returned, a vivid pink leather book in her hands, thumbing through its pages.

'Here it is. Ronnie Dance, 103 Roslea Drive, Dennistoun. Flat 3/1.'

Narey and Maxwell were there in less than ten minutes. They'd have been there even sooner but they had to go through the process of asking the Scissor Sisters some more questions that they were barely interested in the answer to. They were interested in Ronnie. Mr Grey.

A hundred and three Roslea Drive was a blond sandstone tenement behind a robust hedge, the street-level windows protected from view, one by vertical blinds and the other by net curtains. Up on the third floor, Flats 1 and 2 had their windows topped with dark stone lintels, curtains open and a light shining on each side.

'You think this guy might be our man, Sarge?' Maxwell sounded hopeful and anxious all in one go.

'One way to find out. But he's a definite maybe, I'd say.'

She pushed the button for 3/1 and waited. A few moments later a gruff male voice answered.

'Aye?'

'Mr Dance?'

'Who? Naw.'

They heard the intercom close and Narey buzzed again. The voice was more irritable now.

'Whit is it?'

'I'm looking for Mr Dance.'

'Piss off. There's no Mr Dance here. Gie's peace.'

The intercom died again. Narey buzzed long and hard.

'Whit the fu—'

'This is the police. Open the door. Now.'

Silence. Then a heavy sigh. 'Prove it.'

'Jeezus. Look out the bloody window.'

Narey backed away from the door looking up at the window and holding her warrant card up by her head. She saw a figure by the window, flashes of a grey hoody coming close to the glass, then disappearing. The intercom crackled and the latch dropped.

When they got to the third floor, the hoody was waiting for them by the door. Inside it was a young guy, early twenties maybe, with a thick head of dark hair, looking half worried, half angry.

'DS Narey. DC Maxwell.' Narey introduced them and offered a closer inspection of her ID.

'What is it?'

'We're looking for a man named Ronnie Dance. We are led to believe he lives here.'

'Well he disnae. Never heard of the guy.'

'What's your name, sir?'

'Aaron Pearson. And I've lived here for nearly a year. The guy before me was called Davis or Davidson, something like that. You can check with my landlord.'

'We will, thank you. The person we are looking for is about six feet tall, with grey hair and dark eyebrows. Early forties. Ring any bells?'

'Naw. Whit's this all about?'

'I'm afraid I can't discuss that, Mr Pearson. Now, can you give me a contact number for your landlord?'

Pearson sighed and nodded.

Narey and Maxwell knocked on every door in the block, getting answers from three out of the other five, but no one knew of anyone ever living there who fitted the description of Ronnie Dance. Mr Grey, whoever he was, had given the sisters a false address.

Narey made a call into Stewart Street and minutes later got word back that a check on the voters' roll failed to find a single Ronnie Dance in all of Glasgow, far less one that fitted Mr Grey's age.

False address, false name. Mr Grey was very interesting but very hard to find.

Chapter 18

Monday afternoon

DS Rico Giannandrea pushed through the door of the Ink Sync tattoo parlour on Stockwell Street, DC Sandy Galbraith in his wake. The bell on the door alerted the guy behind the counter but he didn't look up as they entered, just shouted out to them. 'Be with you in two minutes. Just finishing something off.'

The skin-coloured walls of Ink Sync were lined with enlarged examples of tattoo designs and photographs of the shop's handiwork. Tigers and scorpions fought for wall space with Celtic crosses and flaming skulls. A bandana-wearing Jimi Hendrix was squeezed between a distraught angel and a gun-toting, basque-wearing warrior maiden. Babies' footprints complete with names and dates of birth were next to a dripping-maw zombie.

Giannandrea had never fancied the idea of having a tattoo, and his mother would have killed him if he ever did. Still, he couldn't help but stare at the dedication to their art by customers whose inked bodies were on display. An exposed left arm showed a blue-skinned tiger advancing south towards the wrist through jungle foliage, every piece of skin covered and the beast looking ready to spring from the painted biceps. A girl's back, blonde hair just showing at the nape of her neck, was covered in a beautiful depiction of a female samurai in front of a blooming cherry tree.

Rico was fourth-generation Scottish and second-generation policeman, his great-grandparents having emigrated to Troon during the wars from Barga in Italy, then working their way up the west coast to Glasgow. Great-Granddad Geraldo had opened a chip shop on the Ayrshire coast, then a bigger one in Kelvinbridge. Rico's dad, Gerry, had walked the beat in the city centre and told his son to stay the hell out of it. Rico went to university in Manchester, got a degree in criminology and then came back to Glasgow to do the very thing that his old man didn't want him to do in the first place. Except he was going to do it his way.

That was Rico all over. All the things he loved about Scotland and the things he hated were pretty much identical. He couldn't tell you the difference even if he wanted to. Tattoos were a good case in point: love them, hate them, don't understand them, fascinated by them.

'What happened to hearts with arrows through them or "Scotland Forever"?'

The man behind the counter looked up and grinned. 'They went out with mullets and Spangles. Strictly homemade stuff if anyone has those nowadays.'

The accent was English, Midlands somewhere, Giann-andrea reckoned. Skinny and dark-haired, he was in his early twenties, wearing a Nirvana T-shirt that exposed both arms, showing the left one covered in an intricate spider's web with what looked like angels caught up in it, while the right arm was bare.

'Do that yourself?' Giannandrea asked.

The guy looked at his arm as if seeing it for the first time. 'No. You don't get many artists that ink themselves. You don't get the same quality of work. What are you thinking of having done?'

'Nah. Not my thing. I'm here to ask you a few questions.'

The man looked at him suspiciously. 'Health and safety?'

'Police. I'm DS Giannandrea. This is DC Galbraith. Mr . . .?'

'Stark. Ritchie Stark. Listen, if it's kids getting body art then they must have used false ID because we make certain they have proof of age if they look under eighteen.'

'No, it's not that.' Giannandrea pulled a photograph from the brown envelope in his hand. 'Do you recognise this tattoo?'

Stark took the A4-sized photograph of Kirsty McAndrew's lower back showing the snake writhing its way round the lettering of her ex-boyfriend's nickname. He studied it for no more than a few seconds before handing it back to Giannandrea.

'It's one of Stevo's.'

'Stevo?'

'Stevo Barclay. He's the other inker that works here. He owns the shop. This has his signature all over it. It's definitely one of his.'

'This her?' Giannandrea showed him a photograph they'd got from the family. Stark studied the picture but offered only a shrug. 'Don't know. Haven't seen her before.'

'Her name was Kirsty McAndrew. Ring any bells?'

'No.'

'But you're sure this was done by your mate Stevo?'

'Positive. Most tattoo artists in town could probably tell you it's his.'

'They did. That's why I'm here.'

Stark scrunched up his face. 'So why didn't you just say that?'

'I like to be awkward. Where is Barclay now?'

'He'll probably be at— Wait a minute. Was? You said the girl's name *was* Kirsty McAndrew.'

'You obviously didn't read the paper this morning, Mr Stark. She's dead. Murdered.'

Stark's jaw dropped and quickly lifted again. 'Shit. That's . . . Christ.'

'Hmm. You were about to tell me where Mr Barclay is.'

'At home probably. He's not working till this afternoon.'

'I think Stevo will need to start early today. Phone him and ask him to come in.'

'Why, what's this all about? This tattoo . . . the girl . . .?'

'Just ask him to come in, please, Mr Stark. Now.'

Stark looked as if he wanted to argue but instead picked up the phone behind the counter and punched in a number from memory.

'Stevo. Ritchie. You need to get your arse in here, man. The police are in the shop and they want a word . . . No, nothing like that . . . Nope, it's non-negotiable. Okay, okay. See you.' He put the phone down. 'He'll be here in twenty minutes.'

*

135

When the bell dinged behind him, Rico turned to see a stocky, shaven-headed man in his early thirties with a thick goatee beard push his way inside. His eyes searched the room, obviously not used to seeing suited types like Giannandrea and Galbraith inside.

'You Stevo?'

The guy nodded, clearly anxious and unhappy. 'Yeah. What's this about?'

'Something to worry about, Mr Barclay?'

Stevo screwed his face up as if Giannandrea had said something stupid. 'I'm dragged in here early because the police want to speak to me? Aye, I'm worried. Doesn't mean I've anything to hide, though.'

'Fair enough, Stevo. Why don't you and me and DC Galbraith here go through to the back office and have a chat?'

Barclay stood his ground, as if wondering if he had any choice, before offering a shrug and a questioning look towards Stark. Before they could move, the door opened again and a heavily tattooed and pierced figure slipped inside, a tall guy wearing a studded, black leather jacket, with scarlet hair shaved at the sides and the rest crested into a Mohawk. Giannandrea smiled at him.

'You looking for the nineteen eighties, pal? I think they're further down the street. You'll find them if you're lucky. Do ya feel lucky, punk?'

'Eh?'

'On your way, son, this place is closed.'

'Hey,' shrieked Stark. 'You can't do that. You're losing us custom.'

'You know what? This is a murder investigation and you're

shut until I say so.' Giannandrea watched Stevo's eyes widen at the word 'murder', then turned back to the bewildered punk. 'Sorry, Swampy, but no piercings for you today. Why don't you go home for a bath, then maybe try one of your maw's earrings on?'

'Eh? What you mean? What you trying to say?'

'I'm saying goodbye. Arrivederci. Ciao, baby, ciao.'

Giannandrea nodded at Galbraith, who promptly ushered the punk out of the door and closed it behind him, switching the sign to CLOSED.

'Right, Mr Stevo. Let's you and me have a wee natter.'

Barclay reluctantly led Giannandrea and Galbraith through a red door into a cramped office, where piles of drawings were stacked on a desk next to multicoloured boxes of inks and assorted machine parts. A television was on the wall above the desk and a telephone could just about be seen amid the mess. Barclay lifted four or five boxes, which Giannandrea could see were labelled as needles, off a chair and offered it as a seat. He cleared another chair in the corner for himself, placing more boxes onto the floor. Galbraith was left to stand, notebook in hand.

'This your work?' Giannandrea asked, shoving the photograph of Kirsty McAndrew's tattoo in front of him. Barclay's gaze went to the photograph and immediately back to Giannandrea, his eyebrows knotting darkly. 'Yeah. Why?'

'What can you remember about the young lady that had it done?'

'I don't know. It was—'

Giannandrea thrust a photograph of Kirsty into Barclay's face, watching for a reaction but didn't get one.

'Yeah. I remember her. That's her. She was in here ... I'd need to check my records but ... maybe a couple of months back. She had to strip to the waist to get it on her back. It can be ... well ... intimate kinda work. So, yes, I remember her.'

Giannandrea leaned in close, smiling, man to man. 'Fancy her, did you?'

'No! Well, aye, I suppose she was ... What's this all about?'

Rico stared at him for a bit, making an obvious show of weighing Barclay up. He leaned forward further, his chin resting on his hand, staring some more.

'This girl? She's dead. Murdered.'

The news seemed to take time to percolate through Barclay's brain but, when it did, he opened and shut his mouth a couple of times, his face reddening as he got to his feet, pointing at Giannandrea.

'And you think I've got something to do with it? No fucking way! No ... how ...'

'Sit down, Mr Barclay. Sit down!'

Barclay had taken a half-step towards Giannandrea, causing Galbraith to move off the wall ready to intercept before the DS waved him back into place. Barclay put the brakes on himself and stood fuming for a moment before slumping back into his chair.

'Hell of a temper you've got on you there, Mr Stevo. Lose it often, do you?'

'Piss off. So the girl got a tattoo done here? So what? We do thousands of people a year.'

'Aye, and how many of them end up dead? It's a bit worrying. You not think so?'

Barclay braced himself against the armrests of the chair as

if about to get to his feet again before thinking better of it. Instead, he spat back at Giannandrea, 'I've got nothing to do with this. Ask me anything you want.'

'Oh, thanks very much. Okay, where were you last Friday night?'

'What time?'

'Any time. You tell me.'

'I was out. Drinking in Blackfriars on Albion Street. And across the road in O'Neills.'

'Who was with you?'

'No one.'

Giannandrea smiled pleasantly. 'That's convenient.'

'Disnae fucking look like it, does it?'

'What time did you get home?'

'I don't know. I was blotto.'

'Dear, dear. A terrible lifestyle, Stevo. I hope you weren't the same on Saturday night.'

Stevo's head sank into his hands until something slowly dawned on him and his head came up again. He wasn't angry any longer. He was scared.

'Friday and Saturday night? Those two girls that they were talking about on the radio? No, no, no. No. No way, man. You've got to believe me. That wisnae me. Jesus Christ, I'd never do anything like that.'

'No?'

'No!'

Giannandrea looked back at him for a while, making a show of deliberating, but in reality just making the man sweat. 'Maybe I believe you, Stevo. But I think we might have to take a wee trip down the station to continue this chat. You seen this girl – her name's Kirsty by the way, seeing as you ask – since she came in here to get her skin desecrated?'

'No. I only ever saw her on the day she got it done and the day she made the appointment. That's it. Not before or since.'

'Hmm. Who owns this place?'

'My old man does, but he doesn't have anything to do with it these days. He probably hasn't been through the door in four or five months. He just lets me and Ritchie get on with it.'

'Okay. And how long have you known Ritchie?'

'Just under a year. He'd moved up from down south and was looking for work. His timing was good because I'd just lost the guy before him.'

'You gave him a job just like that?'

'Well, obviously I got out some practice skin and gave him a trial to show me what he could do. The guy was good, so I took him on. Ritchie's sound. Wouldn't do anyone any harm, if that's what you're thinking.'

'Even I don't know what I'm thinking, Stevo, so don't waste your time trying to guess. Okay, you sit here for now and nice DC Galbraith will keep you company. I've got to make a phone call.'

Giannandrea closed the office door behind him, leaving a furious Barclay to sit and fret under Galbraith's stare. Ritchie Stark was pacing the middle of the shop floor waiting for him to emerge.

'So, Ritchie. You haven't lived in Glasgow for too long?'

'Nearly a year now.'

'Where did you move from?'

'Near Nottingham.'

'So why did you move?'

Stark stared back at Giannandrea, seemingly unsure whether to answer. 'Am I being interviewed here? I didn't tattoo that girl. I didn't even meet her. I told you.'

Giannandrea held both hands wide, his face a picture of well-groomed innocence and charm under his dark, thick locks. 'Interviewed? We're just chatting, dude. My mother brought me up to be polite and be interested in people. She wasn't wrong, was she?'

Stark blinked. 'Um, no. Just chatting. Okay.'

Rico smiled genially. 'So why did you leave Nottingham?'

'It was just . . . personal stuff.'

'Tell me.'

'I broke up with a girlfriend and just felt like I needed a fresh start. I'd been to Glasgow a few times and liked the place so it seemed as good a place to go as any.'

'Yeah, well, it's a good place, right enough.' Giannandrea just smiled and held Stark's gaze long enough to make him uncomfortable.

'You like it here?'

By the look on his face, Stark was obviously trying to work out if he was being tricked in some way. 'Um, yeah. It's great. Great place.'

Giannandrea smiled broadly. 'That's good to hear. Makes me proud to be Glaswegian.' He left another pause long enough for Stark to squirm in.

'Where were you on Friday night, Ritchie?'

'I thought this was just a chat?'

'Oh, it is. And now we're chatting about what you did on Friday night.'

'Um, I was with my girlfriend.'

'Ah, nice. No better way to spend a Friday. And she'll obviously confirm this if we ask her.'

'Yes. Of course.'

'What's her name and where is she?'

'Faith. Faith Foster. And she'll be at work.'

'Where?'

'She's an assistant in a vet's surgery. Drummonds on Duke Street.'

'Do you live together?'

'Yes, she moved into my flat a couple of months ago. It's on Tobago Street in Bridgeton. I can tell her that you want to speak to her when she gets home.'

Giannandrea smiled. 'That's all right, Ritchie. No need for you to go to that bother. We'll speak to her ourselves. Now, if you'll excuse me, I've got to make a phone call.'

'Oh right. I'll just, um ... I'll be over there out of the way.'

Giannandrea took his phone out and hit a number from his contact directory. Addison answered on the second ring.

'Sir, it's Rico. I'm at Ink Sync, the tattoo shop on Stockwell Street. I've been having a chat with the owner. He's the guy who tattooed Kirsty McAndrew. He's flapping and has a right temper on him.'

There were a few moments before Addison replied, sounding distinctly edgy and distracted.

'Yeah? Haul his ass in here, then, Rico. Let's have a word with him. Oh, what the fu— I don't fucking believe this. Rico, you got a telly where you are? If so get it switched on. BBC1.'

Giannandrea waved his arm in the direction of Ritchie Stark, beckoning him over. The tattooist immediately started towards him.

'Ritchie, does that television in your office work?'

'Yeah.'

'Put it on for me, please. BBC1.'

Stark swiftly changed direction towards the office door, a wary look plastered across his face, and hauled it open. Inside, Barclay and Galbraith looked up expectantly.

'Stay on the line, Rico,' Addison instructed. 'And watch his face when he sees what's on. Although I can hardly believe my own bleeding eyes.'

Giannandrea nodded at Stark as if wondering what he was waiting on and the tattooist reached under the drawings on the desk and emerged with a remote control. He pointed it at the television and it flickered into life. Stark switched the channel and the screen changed to show DCI Denny Kelbie standing in front of a microphone. The ticker running along the foot of the page said it was an emergency press conference in the 'Cinderella Killer' investigation.

'Seriously?' Giannandrea asked out loud.

'. . . and that is the reason that we have decided to make an announcement at this stage. There has been sensationalist and unhelpful speculation in the media today which, if left unhindered, may cause unnecessary panic among the general public. We have firm leads in this investigation and are actively pursuing these as I speak. There is no reason to believe that there is a killer at large, randomly attacking young women. It is our belief that these murders are linked.'

Kelbie was the picture of sincerity as he looked directly into the camera – calm, reassuring, authoritative and concerned. He even looked taller on TV, mainly because no one was standing next to him.

'It is important that while the public, particularly young women, continue to take normal precautions for their safety, there is no need for panic. I can assure you that every possible step is being taken to identify links between the two victims and to apprehend their killer. I will take some questions.'

'I've got a question, you daft little fucker,' Addison raged at the TV screen, right into Giannandrea's ear. 'What the fuck do you think you're doing?'

'DCI Kelbie, can you confirm that both victims had their shoes removed by the killer?'

'Yes, I can.'

'No, you bloody can't!' Addison ranted, causing Giannandrea to hold the phone a foot away from his ear.

'The reference to a "Cinderella Killer" in this morning's press was lurid but essentially accurate. Kirsty McAndrew's shoes had been removed and, similarly, so was one of Hannah Healey's. It may be that the killer was disturbed before he had the opportunity to remove her other shoe, but that is merely speculation on our part, and the last thing I would want to do at this stage is to speculate.'

'No, of course you fucking wouldn't. Rico, can you believe this prat?'

'Without asking you to speculate, DCI Kelbie, do you think there may be some sort of sexual element to the removal of the women's shoes?'

Kelbie screwed his face up, smiling to make it clear that there was something he wanted to say but couldn't. 'I can't really comment on that at this juncture. Let's just say it is an avenue that we are not ruling out. Next question.'

'Not ruling out? Jesus suffering.' Addison's rising anger and incredulity threatened to burst Giannandrea's eardrum. 'You might as well tell him that you're convinced it's some shoe fetishist.'

'DCI Kelbie, are you investigating the possibility that there's a foot or shoe fetish involved in these murders?'

'No comment. Next question.'

'What are the links that you think exist between the two victims?'

'I can't comment on those for operational reasons, but you can be sure that they are being investigated and will be confirmed. Okay, that's all for today. Thank you for your attendance.'

The press conference ended with Kelbie posing for a couple of shots from the photographers, giving one final look of studied sincerity before turning away. The screen cut to an announcer in a studio and the programme moved on to something else. Addison roared a final obscenity into the phone.

'Jesus H. Christ! So what did your tattooist make of that, Rico?'

Barclay had barely taken his eyes off the screen except for a few nervous glances at Giannandrea and some confusion at the stream of incoherent but very obviously swearing coming from his mobile. Stark's reaction was almost identical.

'Well, there's two of them, sir. And they're very interested. Very interested indeed.'

'Two of them? Right, bring both the buggers in. I'm in the mood for some ritual torture.'

Chapter 19

Monday afternoon

Narey had been landed with what Addison referred to as basic policing but what she less charitably thought of as work for Sergeant Dogsbody. She had three detective constables and a fleet of uniforms out to follow the route that they presumed Hannah Healey had taken after she left her boyfriend on Victoria Bridge.

While it was possible that she had been attacked anywhere in the mile between the bridge and her home, they had been able to rule out the first quarter-mile after seeing Hannah on CCTV images near the Citizens Theatre. So they began from there, Narey directing them to pick over every bit of pavement in the hope of finding the spot that she'd been taken. There was no useful evidence on the body so their only hope was discovering the point of abduction, which was also quite possibly the spot where she'd been killed.

It was a thankless, laborious task, as much suited to a street cleaner as a detective. Taggart, eat your heart out, she thought

146

miserably. She'd sighed as she watched Toshney blunder from one bit of the road to the next, making stupid and no doubt inappropriate jokes to other cops as he went. There must be a way to get rid of that muppet, she thought. And the sooner the better.

She hadn't been in the best of moods to start with. The visit earlier to Scissor Sisters and Roslea Drive had proved a frustration, just providing more questions than answers. Now she was stuck on Gorbals Street with Toshney for company. It was hardly what you would call a secure crime scene and any number of people would have walked along it in the twenty-four-plus hours since Hannah Healey had been killed. That didn't mean that it wasn't worthwhile looking, just that it was a pain in the bum. Anything that was useful could have been moved, removed, run over or kicked away. She dispatched officers left and right off the main drag when they passed likely places, beginning with the car park immediately after the Citizens and then the rose garden on the opposite side of the street. At the traffic lights, she had them investigate the grounds of the creepy, desolate, Gothic building that stood on the corner of Bedford Lane. If she were going to murder anyone, she would have done it there. Either that or she'd just watched too many episodes of *Scooby Doo*.

They painstakingly made their way up the road, scouring the grass verge on the right after the lights and the rubble on the left, where some demolition work had recently taken place. Up ahead under the railway bridge looked another likely spot but yielded nothing, despite their spending half an hour on it. Narey looked further down the road and saw the green and white frontage of the Brazen Head and her heart sank, as she cursed Addison for what was sure to follow.

A few punters were already standing outside the pub smoking, but, as she watched, the throng grew, no doubt being called by their mates to see the police sideshow that was approaching. She sent Toshney to the right with a handful of uniformed cops, ostensibly to search the area around the boarded-up windows of the newsagent and the abandoned former takeaway premises, but in reality to keep him away from the Brazen Head.

'Afternoon, officers,' came the first shout from outside the pub, a dozen or more ruddy-faced regulars now standing there. Something involving the word 'pigs' swiftly followed from someone hidden at the back of the group. Here we go, she thought.

Narey crossed the road and confronted the group, preferring to meet them head on than have them think she was intimidated. Catcalls, wolf whistles and laughs broke out as she approached, making her hackles rise even further. She'd think of a reason to arrest the lot of them if she could but the last thing she needed was this lot kicking off.

'Afternoon, gentlemen. We are carrying out an operation in the area this afternoon and I would appreciate some cooperation from you.' This was the point where she hoped they wouldn't just laugh.

'This to do with the wee lassie that was killed along the road? The one that was in the paper this morning?'

'Yes, it is. Have any of you seen or heard anything that might be useful to us?'

Surprisingly enough, she got nothing more than blank

faces and shrugged shoulders. Even if they knew something, it was unlikely they were going to offer information to cops in front of their mates. Even though a young woman had been murdered, there was a thin line between cooperating with the police and grassing.

A grinning, leering guy with an Elvis quiff broke the silence. 'Do you want tae take doon ma particulars, darling?'

'Not at the moment, thanks. Maybe later.'

'Oh, well, ah'll keep ma fingers crossed, then, eh?'

'You do that. But it might have been better if your mother had kept her legs crossed.'

The smart guy turned out not to be that smart and got her dig long after his mates did, their laughter alerting him to the fact that she'd taken the piss out of him. His face flushed with anger at them for taking her side against him, but he didn't say anything else.

'Were any of you gentlemen in the pub on Saturday night?' More blank faces. She would get nowhere with them and knew that she'd be as well getting them out of the way.

'Okay, in that case I'm going to have to ask you to get off the pavement as my officers need to continue their search of the area.'

A brawny shaven-headed guy with a bull neck and a face even redder than his cohorts' nearly burst a blood vessel at being asked to shift. 'Away to fuck, what we got to move fur? We're allowed to smoke out here.'

'Well, for a start, I can charge you with obstructing the public highway.'

'Aye, right.'

'Yeah, right. You want to test me?' Six burly cops had

instinctively appeared at Narey's shoulders, fully ready to enforce her request, but she was equally determined not to rely on them.

The loudmouth stuck out his jaw, not wanting to take a step back in front of the others, and, as if to physically prove it, he advanced to the low railing that separated the drinkers from the police. Narey knew he'd probably rather get nicked than back down. She'd happily arrest him but it could be the first in a set of dominoes falling. 'What's your name?' she asked him.

He hesitated. 'Lex. That's all you need to know.'

I'll decide what I need to know, she thought, cursing him for being so stubborn as to make it more difficult for her to give him a way out. 'Okay, Lex. Here's the thing. A young woman got murdered just along the road there. She could have been your wee sister or someone else's daughter.'

Lex said nothing but he was listening. 'We want to catch the person that did it. None of you is suspects but we need help to catch her killer. My guess is that the rest of these guys listen to you, so what I'm asking is that you go and talk to them, see if anyone does actually have any information, and you can come and talk to me. Not grassing, nothing like that. It's called catching a murderer. What do you say?'

Lex glanced around at the other pub customers and Narey knew that if anyone of them had looked at him accusingly the deal would have been off. Instead the others looked at their feet or shrugged as if to say, 'Why not?'

'Aye, okay,' Lex muttered. 'I know the lassie's mother. We'll talk and I'll get back to you. You got a number?'

The question provoked some more infantile giggling and

the beginning of a beery cheer that was silenced not by Narey but by Lex's glare. He looked around, defying them to take the piss, and the punters settled for a few muffled laughs. 'Right, we're goin' in,' he told them.

'Fuck's sake!' a few of them muttered. 'Ah take it I can keep smoking in the pub, then, darling?' another of them moaned. 'Seein' as how you're making us go back inside.'

'No, you can extinguish your cigarette and then go in. Or go away. I don't care which. And put your fags out in the bin provided. If you drop them on the ground then I'll do you for it.'

The wolf whistles and 'whoaars' had been replaced with muttering and grouching, which was exactly as she'd hoped. The pub's punters stubbed out their cigarettes and shuffled back into the boozer, a few brave mumbles about pigs and fascists their last attempts at saving face.

Narey exhaled and turned back to the street to instruct the constables where to search next. Behind her, one anonymous voice made a final shot at bravado.

'Nice arse, darling.'

She shook her head despairingly and tried not to laugh. Tossers, she thought. Toshney had caught up, his expression making it clear he'd found nothing.

'Okay, there's next to no chance of it being right in front of the pub but go over the ground anyway. And pay attention to that arched underpass after the pub. It's got abduction point written all over it. The rest of you move on to the bit under the next bridge. Toshney, take half a dozen of them and go beyond the bridge. We need to move this thing along.'

It quickly became obvious that the shadows under the

railway bridge had no secrets to offer up and Narey walked on underneath it, seeing the area of grassy scrubland to her right before the ruins of the old church. Her senses heightened immediately: she knew that, if she were walking alone, that would be exactly the kind of area that might have her cross the road to avoid. Prime suspect, she thought.

She saw Toshney near the sandstone side wall of the church, a bricked-up doorway immediately behind him. She somehow knew he was going to signal to her even before he did it. Expectancy and reality blurred as her instincts infused her and she saw Toshney waving both his arms excitedly above his head. Her stride lengthened and broke into a near run despite herself.

There was something at his feet and he was reaching for it. 'Toshney! Don't touch it, whatever it is.'

He froze mid-reach and didn't seem to know whether to twist or stick, instead wobbling uncertainly. She got closer and could see what had got him so agitated. A shoe, black and high-heeled. It was immediately familiar.

'Get your arse out of there, Fraser, will you? And watch where you're stepping. Try not to trample on any more ground than you have to and avoid standing on any footprints unless you can be sure they're your own.'

'You think this is it, then, Sarge? Where she was attacked?'

'If that's her shoe, then yes. Now get out.'

Toshney turned awkwardly, his eyes at his feet as if he were walking through a minefield in clown shoes. He took an ungainly step to his right, then jumped towards an untouched patch of ground, then made another leap back onto the tarmacked area, seemingly pleased with himself as he landed. He was more pleased with himself than Narey was, despite his find.

She pulled out her phone, at the same time waving her arms at the uniforms to come off the waste ground. 'Tape up the area and get it cordoned off ... Hello ... DS Narey. I need forensics at the old Caledonia Road church in the Gorbals. No ... now. And contact DI Addison as well, please, and tell him I need him down here.'

With Toshney safely back out of harm's way, Narey carefully advanced towards the shoe. It was fairly new, the heel barely worn, hardly the thing that someone would throw away. Someone lose it while drunk? Always a possibility, but someone losing it while running or being attacked seemed much more likely. More than that, though, it just *was* the same shoe.

Compared with the rest of the scrub, the ground near the shoe was roughed up as if there had been people moving around on it. Her gut as well as her rationale had no doubt. This was the place.

Campbell Baxter, the heavyweight senior scene examiner, heaved himself out of the cruelly tight confines of his car just twenty minutes after Narey had made the call requesting his attendance. Baxter - or Two Soups, as he was universally known behind his back - wasn't exactly the most popular of the SPSA staff as far as the police were concerned but he was nothing if not thorough. If there was anything at the scene that could be used, Baxter would make sure that his staff found it.

He calmly huffed his way towards Narey, pulling on his coveralls as he did so, finishing the performance by squeaking on two pairs of nitrile gloves with the uncharacteristic flourish of a final noisy smack of latex against his hand.

'What do we have, Sergeant?'

'A shoe. From here it's a similar make, size and colour to the shoe missing from the Southern Necropolis murder victim. This road is on the route she was known to have taken after she was last seen. There has to be a strong possibility that this is where she was attacked.'

Baxter nodded grimly. 'Okay. I assume no one has contaminated the scene by going over to the shoe.'

Narey looked towards Toshney, who reddened slightly and screwed his face into an apology.

Baxter harrumphed loudly, expelling air and disgruntlement. 'Wonderful. Just wonderful. Take your shoes off, young man. Off, I said. Will someone competent please take prints of this idiot's shoes for comparison purposes. Heaven help us. Can't you keep them under control, Detective Sergeant Narey? I thought you knew better.'

'Look, I'm as annoyed about this as you are. I can't be everywhere at once, though. Don't worry, Toshney and I will be having words later. Except he won't be doing the talking.'

By now, a small army of white-suited troops had assembled at the scene under Baxter's command, the uniformed constables pushed back to the periphery of the battle. Two Soups continued to grumble under his breath as he patrolled the perimeter, eyeing potential access routes.

'Mr Burke,' he called to one of this team. 'Find yourself a clearway. I'd suggest in here.' Baxter gestured with a wave of his arm. 'Get us a few shots of the positioning of that shoe, then please remove it for examination. I'm going to get the case notes from the previous scene. Don't let anyone trample over anything in my absence.'

Baxter returned to his car, quickly re-emerging with a computer tablet in his left hand. Using the built-in 3G technology, he tapped into the R2S, the Return to Scene software, as he walked. Once he'd bypassed the system's security he was able to access all the case notes and photographs from Brem Dawson's team at the cemetery where the second girl's body was found. In seconds, he had clear, close-up photographs of the single shoe that Hannah Healey was wearing.

Paul Burke photographed the shoe from various angles, dropping a scale next to it to indicate size, and making sure its precise location and angle were recorded. That done, he slipped a pen under the heel and carefully lifted it into the air before depositing it safely into an evidence bag. Retracing his steps through the scene, he handed the bag over to Baxter.

Two Soups held the evidence bag up to the light in his left hand, his eyes squinting and his right hand rummaging thoughtfully through his woolly, grey beard. He looked at the markings on the sole: the maker's logo and the size clear to be seen. Baxter's mouth tightened, pushing his fat lips up towards his nose in a display of deliberation.

'Clearly, I cannot offer a definitive opinion until we do the relevant tests, DS Narey. However, I will be surprised if those tests do not tell us that this is the partner to the shoe that the victim was wearing. Now, if you will excuse me, we need to get to work. This is, ostensibly at least, a crime scene and we have evidence to find. We will start with the footprints in the area around where the shoe was. Including those of DC Toshney!'

Narey had barely begun to sigh when she became aware of a commotion at her back. She turned to see Denny Kelbie and Addison both emerging from their cars at the roadside, Kelbie with DS Ferry trotting at his heels. By the look on the DCI's face, he wasn't surprised that they were both there, but Addison certainly was. He fired an angry look first at Kelbie and then at her. Great, she thought, it will somehow be my fault.

Kelbie and Addison both began striding towards the scene as if in a race where neither of them was allowed to run. The diminutive DCI and the lanky DI didn't look at each other, but Addison was clearly aware of the smug grin on Kelbie's face.

'You called me here, DS Narey,' Addison said pointedly when the pair of them reached her.

'And the control office called me,' Kelbie added without being asked.

'Under whose instruction?' Addison asked sarcastically.

Narey looked back defiantly at both men. 'I'm not getting in the middle of this. With all due respect, sirs, if you want to get into a pissing contest then leave me out of it. We've found what looks like Hannah Healey's missing shoe and most probably the place she was attacked. Mr Baxter's staff are about to collect evidence from the scene. Other than that, it looks like we might be a bit overstaffed here, don't you think?'

Addison and Kelbie glared at each other, their mutual loathing obvious and neither wishing to back down. Narey stepped into the breach again.

'We're not going to have much success with potential witnesses. Nobody could see anything from that direction.' She pointed at the bleak solidity of the brick wall across the road under the railway bridge. 'And the church blocks out the view from the road ahead. It only leaves the houses over there – and they must be two hundred yards away – or the multis back there behind Cumberland Street. And it was pitch dark.'

Kelbie ignored her. 'Where's the shoe?'

Addison brightened. 'Oh, aye, the shoe. I'm with DCI Kelbie on that one. I'd love to see the shoe.'

Narey and Kelbie looked at Addison, hearing the sarcasm that was dripping from his voice and seeing the beginning of a smirk appearing on his face.

'I saw you on the telly earlier, sir,' Addison continued, his grin growing. 'Interesting theory. About how the shoes were key to this. How the killer had a fetish for shoes. Very psychological, that. You might be on to something there, sir. It turned out to be quite convenient that the papers got that "Cinderella" line, didn't it?'

'What are you suggesting? You better watch your step, Addison.'

'Oh, I'm watching it, sir. I'm watching where I'm putting my feet. Are you? Because, if you're not careful, you'll be putting yours right in it. Which is a wee bit ironic, don't you think?'

Kelbie squared right up to Addison, stretching his neck to make any kind of vertical parity that he could, his voice dropping so that he couldn't be heard by anyone else. 'You keep taking the piss, Addison, and I'll have your guts. You're a loudmouth smartarse and I'm sure there are plenty of senior officers who would be glad to see the back of you. I can make that happen.'

Addison dropped his head down nearer to Kelbie's until they were almost forehead to forehead, his voice also softening so that only Kelbie would hear. 'You can't make that happen because you are a useless little shite who's only been a DCI for five minutes and only then because of some clerical cockup. If you were going to have a quiet word in a superintendent's ear, then you'd need to stand on a chair. And even then you'd need to take your tongue out of his arse to do it. Sir.'

Kelbie's lips drew back into one of his canine snarls but Addison beamed broadly at him and moved before the DCI could reply, calling on Baxter to ask where the shoe was. He strode off towards where he was directed, leaving Kelbie seething.

'It's Hannah Healey's all right,' he announced loudly, holding the evidence bag up before him, ostensibly to the light but actually so everyone in earshot could see what he was referring to. Given that Addison was talking at full volume, 'in earshot' meant every cop and forensic at the scene.

'It is hers, DCI Kelbie. Wouldn't you say, sir?'

Kelbie took the bag from him, examined it fiercely and grudgingly nodded. 'It certainly appears to be a match.'

'Bit of a pity, sir. In fact I'd go so far to say it's a great disappointment.'

'Why's that, DI Addison?' Kelbie forced the question out through gritted teeth. Addison smiled as if he'd never been so pleased to be asked a question.

'Because I thought we were really onto something with your theory about the shoe fetish. The one that you announced all over national television. That could have been the breakthrough that we needed, but it looks like ... unless ... Mr Baxter, you're an expert on all things anatomical and physiological. In your experience, how many feet do human beings tend to have?'

Two Soups began to answer the question before realising the nature of it. 'Two of course. I don't ... Really, DI Addison! I've got work to do.'

Addison made a face of exaggerated disappointment. 'That's it, then. Our only chance was that Hannah would have worn three shoes, but, seeing as she didn't, then your theory is a bit, well, fucked.'

Kelbie's face was flushed with anger, his ears glowing and the vein on his forehead ready to pop. 'This disproves nothing yet.'

Addison laughed. 'No offence, but I think it probably does. If I follow your theory right, what must have happened is that our killer with a shoe fetish has taken one of her shoes – not two, mind, just one – and brings it here to dump it rather than getting himself away safely and taking it with him? He really is a twisted genius, this guy, isn't he?'

Kelbie tried to get close so he could again speak to Addison without anyone else hearing but the DI backed away on the pretence of walking nearer to the place the shoe had been found, forcing Kelbie to raise his growl. 'So what's your bright idea, then?'

Addison shrugged genially. 'Well, what we actually have is one victim with shoes and one without. Hardly much of a pattern, is it, sir? I think, sadly, we have to file that theory under "pile of shite". Should we call the television to tell them?'

Kelbie advanced halfway to where Addison stood before

halting, acutely aware of every eye on them, his finger twitching to point at Addison but somehow stopping himself. 'I want a full report on every bit of evidence found at this site on my desk by the morning. I want every house over there doorknocked for witnesses and the same with the flats back there. And *you*' – he jabbed his forefinger at Addison – 'and I are going to have words.'

Kelbie spun on his heel, DS Ferry falling into line behind him, and marched back towards his car. As he stormed away, Addison made a mock salute. 'Yes, sir. Looking forward to it. We can work on some more theories.'

Narey walked to Addison's side and they both watched Kelbie's car drive off.

'Sir?' she asked quietly. 'You do know that he's a DCI, right? And you're not.'

'Is he? I hadn't noticed. But I did notice that he's a wee shite and I'm not.'

'Well . . . you're not wee, sir. I have to give you that.'

'Insulting language to a senior officer, Rachel? I can't be having that. C'mon, let's see what Baxter's boys have found. The key to this case is here. I can smell it.'

'Aye, okay, but you do know that if you keep poking the fire like that you'll eventually get your fingers burned?'

'Ach, dinnae worry. I've got asbestos fingers, Rachel. Asbestos bloody fingers.'

Chapter 20

Monday evening

At rush hour, it was a ten-minute walk or a twenty-minute drive from his office in Pitt Street to his flat in Berkeley Street, but sometimes Winter still took the car. It depended on how much gear he had with him – camera equipment was heavy and cumbersome – or simply whether it was raining. It rained a lot.

That evening he walked. It was just after eight, he had his rucksack over his shoulder and everything that he was likely to need was inside. He was walking down Bath Street, dodging his way through other late workers with their noses glued to the screens of their mobile phones. One or two were caught accidentally on purpose by the corner of his bag, justice for not looking where they were going.

After his morning fall-out with Danny, the day hadn't got much better, being long on routine and short on excitement. The investigation into the two murders whirled around him but, today at least, he couldn't reach out and touch it. He'd already photographed all that there was to see in relation to the killings and had processed it all by mid-afternoon. The remainder of the day was spent catching up on more mundane filing: a stabbing from Bilsland Drive and a hit-and-run at Anniesland Cross.

A few times, when the monotony of the electronic paper-work got the better of him, he'd brought up photographs from the two cemeteries onto his screen, fighting off a fit of guilt as he did so. There was no sense of titillation or rubbernecking. Instead, it further tested his admittedly skewed theory that there was a beauty in death. Two young women, having done nothing more than go for a night out, brutally murdered. How could there possibly be any beauty in that?

Winter's unknowing mentor was the Mexican tabloid pho-tographer Enrique Metinides, the man who had spent fifty years taking extraordinary pictures on the violent streets of his capital city. Metinides chased police cars, ambulances and fire engines to capture the results of shootings, road accidents, suicides and stabbings. Despite the inevitable horrors that he had to photograph, Metinides contrived to show a grace and dignity in the bleak. His work was unsettling, intimate, and had an exquisite, irresistible attraction. Death isn't beautiful but it can be made to look that way.

Metinides once said that he 'got to witness the hate and evil in men'. That was what Winter was seeing when he viewed his own photographs of Kirsty McAndrew and Hannah Healey. Not beauty but hate.

He shook the images from his head as he headed down Bath Street to walk the bridge across the M8 towards Berkeley

Street, the domed splendour of the Mitchell Library on the other side and nose-to-tail traffic on the motorway thirty yards below. He glanced at his watch and made an instant decision to have a quick one in the Black Sparrow before going up to his flat. The pub was only yards from him but he didn't drink in it too often. It was a cracking little boozer but, if anything, it was just *too* close to home.

Tonight, however, it did the job just fine. A pint of heavy was in front of him within seconds and he savoured the sight of it for as long as he could bear before washing the dust of the day down his throat. Winter looked around, happy not to see anyone he recognised in the bar, but observing that one or two others had already assumed the position of solo drinker. He joined them in their splendid isolation.

Of course, the beer wasn't capable of washing away thoughts of the Necropolis or its southern neighbour and, if anything, standing drinking alone simply gave him more time to contemplate it. Addison had hit a nerve when he had accused Winter of relishing the prospect of having plenty of sick pictures to take. Winter wanted to think that his mate was wrong but he couldn't easily convince himself that that was the case. If there were more killings, God forbid, then he knew he'd want to be at the front of the queue to photograph them. It was the way he was made.

This wasn't doing him any good. He forced the remainder of the pint down his neck and made for the door. He was bad enough with one drink inside him and more was only going to make matters worse.

It was a murky night and the gloom was already beginning to settle as he pushed his way back onto North Street, ignoring the spicy temptations of the Koh-i-Noor, and ambled the last few yards towards his flat. At the corner, he was struck, not for the first time, by the sandstone splendour of the Mitchell Library and the contrast with his own modern apartment block directly opposite. The Mitchell was lit up in its evening finery, making the Berkeley Street building seem even more clinical in comparison.

Winter let himself in and took the stairs up to his flat, the weight of his camera reassuringly heavy on his shoulder and every whack against his side an urgent reminder to download what was inside. As he reached his landing, he threw the camera bag onto his other shoulder and reached for the lock with his key, only to stop dead in his tracks. The door was closed over but already open.

He froze, his heart clattering into his ribcage as he came to a sudden halt. He pushed gently at the door with his fingertips, feeling it float away from him. He was as sure as he possibly could be that he'd locked it that morning before going to meet Rachel in Hyndland. His mind raced up and down the stairs, wondering about the noise he'd made climbing them, wondering whether there was someone inside who may have been alerted by the clang of his feet.

The only thing that he had that resembled a weapon was the bag on his back. He'd often carry a tripod that would have delivered much more of a blow, but that lay in his office back in Pitt Street. If he needed to, he'd have to rely on the bag plus the staple Glasgow stand-by of fist, feet and head. He feathered the door open and stepped inside, cursing the squeaky laminate flooring as he did so.

One more step and he was on the silent safety of the

hallway rug, the strap of the bag gripped tight and ready to be turned as shield or blunted sword. His breathing was loud in his ears, drowning out even the pounding in his chest. Conscious of leaving his back unguarded, he pushed open the door to the living room and stepped inside, seeing no one and nothing out of place. Wait. There was a coffee cup sitting on the table in the middle of the room. He knew it wasn't his, because he never drank the stuff and kept the cups only for the very occasional guest.

He turned so as to avoid backing out of the room and stood in the hallway again, listening and looking. The door to the bathroom was open and that, as best as he could remember, was the way he'd left it. The kitchen door was closed and that, too, was how it should have been, even though the rogue cup gave the lie to the suggestion that it hadn't been entered. The spare bedroom, the room whose walls were lined with his photographs, was also ajar and there was a light on inside. He never left the door open in case he returned with an unexpected visitor. The wall was his own business and not something he wanted to share. The light he couldn't remember leaving on or not.

There was a pool of shadow visible on the floor inside, something he'd never remembered seeing before. Shit. Whatever he was going to do, this was the time to do it. He slowly took the bag from his shoulder and placed it in front of his chest. His plan, such as it was, was simple. He was going to barge the door and, if there was someone standing inside, hopefully it would take them clean off their feet. He braced and breathed deep, taking a step back, ready to put everything he had into the door frame. As he did so, a familiar deep and gruff voice came at him from the other side of the bedroom door.

'You really are one sick puppy, Tony. How the hell can you sleep at night with this stuff on your wall?'

The air leaked from Winter like a punctured tyre, relief and nerves escaping through his lips.

'Uncle Danny, what the fuck are you doing in here? And how the bloody hell did you get in?'

Winter pulled back the door and saw Danny standing with his back to him, his gaze fixed on the wall of framed photographs.

'Are you supposed to have these in here? Silly question: of course you're not. The book might have closed on most of them but they will still be the property of the Fiscal. Or whatever police authority you worked for when you took them. Not yours, though, son, not yours. What's with this picture of a decapitated head? Not very nice, is it?'

'How did you get in, Dan? And why?'

'Getting in was the easy bit. You know me: picked up a few tricks in thirty years on the force. As for the why, well, I wanted to see these.' Danny turned and Winter saw that he was holding a collection of A4 prints in his hand. Winter knew what they were even before Danny fanned them out like a pack of playing cards.

The Necropolis. Kirsty McAndrew. Caledonia Road. Hannah Healey. Strangulation. A battered head. Witnessing the hate and evil in men.

Danny held them out for Winter to see as if they were somehow making his point, justifying his actions.

'You've no right doing this, Danny. No right at all. Breaking into my flat, for God's sake.'

Neilson waved a hand airily in front of him, dismissing the accusation as irrelevant.

'Good photographs, these, Tony. Bad, bad stuff but good pictures. There's no—'

'Danny, are you just going to carry on as if you've done nothing wrong here?'

'—no doubt in my mind now, son. None at all. This is him. This is *definitely* him.'

Winter just looked at Danny, sensing that any more questions about right and wrong were a waste of time. The eyes looking back at him were angry and resolute, not for being argued with. Winter hesitated, getting the unmistakable sense of being about to open a door that couldn't be closed again.

'Okay, why are you so sure? How can you be?'

A light switched on inside Danny and he flashed a grim smile. 'Come and sit down. This might take some time. I've already had a coffee while I waited on you but I wouldn't say no to a beer. You've got some Peroni in the fridge.'

Winter shook his head ruefully as he went to the kitchen, pulled back the fridge door and pulled out two bottles of beer, swiftly ripping the heads off them with a bottle opener. When he got back to his living room, Danny was sitting on one side of the table with six of Winter's photographs laid out in front of him. The coffee cup that had looked so out of place before had been relocated onto the floor.

'I know you well enough, son,' Danny began as Winter took his seat opposite him. 'You'll have looked at these pictures more than once. Studied them closely, I'll bet. But there's always things you won't see if you don't know what you're looking for.'

Winter said nothing but couldn't hide a feeling that was creeping over him, a familiar sense of anticipation that was as much eagerness as dread.

'See the way the first girl is laid out on the flat gravestone? How her hands are positioned before her? Read this.' Danny dug a sheaf of papers from his inside pocket and leafed through them before shoving a clipping into Winter's hands.

In each of the so-called 'Red Silk' murders, the perpetrator left the victim arranged in a manner that was almost ritualistic. These included, in the case of Brenda MacFarlane, her arms being outstretched as if in supplication on the cross. Criminal psychologists believe that the killer was displaying overt power over his victims by asserting his ability to make them at his mercy.

'And this.'

Danny handed over another piece of paper, this time a faded sheet torn from a notebook. Winter recognised the handwriting immediately.

The killer has some kind of God complex. Lays them out as if they are praying to him. Or as if to prove he can do what he wants with them. He arranged Brenda M as if she was praying to him. It's more than just the killing for him. He enjoys the power.

Winter looked up from the paper, seeing Danny eager for a reaction. The dawning of some acceptance in Winter's eyes seemed to be enough.

'That was Brenda. Now read this about Mary Gillespie.'

Another time-soiled sheet was handed over, Danny's hand-writing again. He pointed at a section halfway down the page.

> Mary G had her head resting on a low wall. It was like she was resting on it or laying her head at his feet. He wants us to find them like that. He's playing with us.

'We managed to keep this stuff out of the papers even though the press were all over this story for months on end. Nobody else knew.'

Winter pushed himself back from the table and exhaled hard, still saying nothing.

'I know the guy, Tony. I chased him for two years. I know what he did to these girls. I know what he did to women else-where. This has got his prints all over it. These pictures prove it. You see that, don't you?'

'Maybe. Tell me more. I know the story but only what I've read in the papers. I wasn't born then, remember.'

Danny sighed. 'Oh, I remember, son. Brenda MacFarlane had been dancing at Klass on a Friday night in June 1972 with her sister Frances. Brenda was nineteen and Frances was a year younger. Their parents thought they were both at a friend's house but they'd hidden away their going-out clothes and got changed in a pub toilet, then hid their gear, aiming to pick them up and change back after the disco.

'Disco was the new thing. The dance halls were still going but, for the younger crowd, it was disco. They could still dance but there were live bands as well. This was the music that was in the charts and the bands that played it. You wouldn't believe how many of them came up to Glasgow to play at a disco like Klass. Slade, Bowie, Status Quo, Elton John. They were all there around this time. So all the old "are ye dancing?" stuff still held good: you could go out and still get a slow dance at the end of the night.

'At some point on that night, Frances MacFarlane got dancing with a boy. She ended up snogging him but says she came up for air long enough to see her sister dancing with some guy wearing a black velvet suit with what looked like a red silk handkerchief in the top pocket. She looked again and the two were chatting away. When Frances eventually surfaced after the lumber number – the last slow dance – Brenda was nowhere to be seen. She figured her sister had got off with the guy in the velvet suit and didn't think too much about it. But when she was outside, and Brenda didn't turn up to get their other clothes and catch the last bus to Partick Cross, she began to worry.

'Brenda was found the next morning. Raped, strangled. Her clothes around her waist and her arms stretched out wide. Her sister screamed, then cried for a month. She became an alcoholic and looked fifty by the time she was twenty-five.

'The next night, the Saturday, police were all over Klass. Interviewing everyone there and asking what they'd seen the night before. The place was still open, though – best way to make sure potential witnesses were in the one place. Slade were playing and they were massive in Scotland at the time so they weren't easy to cancel. One of the customers was a girl called Isobel Jardine. She went home on the last bus to Govanhill with her pal. They parted at Allison Street and Isobel walked the rest of the way home herself. She was found the next morning in Govanhill Park. Raped and strangled, half dressed, crouching on her knees and leaning against the building that was the old bandstand.

'All hell let loose then. When it was realised that she had been at Klass the night before, then all bets were off. Isobel's pal, Meg Johnstone, didn't remember any guy in a black velvet suit but said the bus back from town was pretty full and there were too many people to remember who was on it.

'We had officers at Klass every night after that. Interviewing everyone that went in, showing them the sketch that was done from the description that Frances MacFarlane gave. The sketch could have been anyone, though, and we didn't even know if Brenda had left with the guy in the suit. We didn't know if the Klass connection was a coincidence. All week, nothing happened, nothing turned up of any use. Then it was two weeks later, the Saturday night. Or, more to the point, the Sunday morning.

'Mary Gillespie was found murdered in an alley behind tenements off London Road, not far from Glasgow Green. She was found lying on the ground but with her head resting on the wall. She'd been partially strangled but finished off with her head being smashed against the wall. She'd been raped. Mary was married and her husband said she'd been visiting her sister on the Saturday night. The sister said this was true and all efforts were concentrated on the area between the sister's house in Bridgeton and Glasgow Green. But the way she'd been attacked was too similar to the Klass killings and so detectives went back to the sister and kept on at her. Two weeks later, they broke her down and she admitted Mary hadn't been with her at all. She'd agreed to cover for her if her husband ever asked. Mary had been at the dancing in town.

'We went back to Klass and people said they'd seen someone matching Mary's description on that Saturday night. Only problem was that we also asked in Clouds and Joanna's as well and people there said they'd seen her or someone looking like her. But in Klass one girl said she thought she'd seen Mary talking for ages to a guy who was wearing a black-and-white-checked jacket – with a red silk handkerchief in the pocket.

'That was all that people needed to know. It was Klass and it was the guy with the red silk handkerchief. The description went out and of course the press latched onto the handkerchief and called him Red Silk. It didn't help us much, though. We knew that if the guy had any sense – and from what he'd done we knew he was smart enough to have got away with it so far – then he'd never wear that red silk hankie again. Maybe he'd never worn it before.

'But the town went into meltdown. People were terrified. Didn't stop them going out, though, and it didn't stop them going to Klass. In fact, the place was busier than ever. Klass even ran Red Silk Lookalike contests. One night they had Be Red Silk for a Night night, when the guys only got in if they had a red hankie in their top pocket. Only in Glasgow, eh?

'Of course, none of this made the chief constable very happy. He wanted this guy caught and fast. Any man in his twenties who looked remotely like the Frances MacFarlane description was stopped in the street or pulled into the station and asked to account for their movements on the night of the killings. Door-to-door enquiries took place all over Glasgow. We were sure someone must know something.

'Everything pointed to Klass, though, and somebody in high office came up with the bright idea of getting young detectives inside the place posing as punters. They needed men and women who didn't stick out like sore thumbs, who weren't obviously cops. I was the youngest detective sergeant in the city, so I was a natural for it. Got my glad rags on and went dancing, size-eleven feet and all. For weeks and weeks we were in Klass every minute it was open.'

Winter shook his head at the thought of Uncle Danny shaking his stuff in a seventies disco. 'That must have been some weird job. Did it work?'

Danny glowered, genuine anger in his voice. 'Stupid question, son. He killed again, didn't he?'

Neilson tipped the bottle of Peroni back and half of it disappeared down his throat before he abruptly snapped it away from his mouth again.

'Three weeks later. Christine Cormack. Twenty-one years old. She worked in the Tunnock's factory in Uddingston and was in Glasgow for a night out with two friends. She was in Klass, so were six coppers, including me, and so was the man that killed her. She was found in the alley behind the club, her mouth gagged with one of her stockings, strangled, beaten and raped. A red silk handkerchief was found near the scene. He did it there, right under our noses. Shoving our noses right in it.'

Danny stared into the beer bottle in his hand for a few seconds before thrusting it to his mouth again and draining it. He held the empty bottle out to Winter. 'Get me another one, son.'

Winter retreated to the kitchen, secretly relieved to temporarily escape from the intensity of Danny's reminiscences. Even his own taste for the dark was being smothered by the depth of his uncle's anger. This stuff hadn't happened forty years ago as far as Danny was concerned: it was as raw as the day before. When he returned, another two beers in his hands, Danny was studying the crime-scene photographs in front of him.

'One thing I don't get, Tony: what the hell's with the word written on their stomachs? That doesn't fit with anything.'

'I don't know, Dan. All I know is that you're not supposed to know.'

Danny screwed his face up. 'Seriously, Danny. Alex Shirley's drawn a three-line whip under this. He's paranoid about *that* getting out. He finds out that anyone has blabbed about that word outside the case team, then their arse won't touch the steps on the way out.'

'It won't get out, Tony. What the hell do you take me for? The only person I'll talk to about this is you.'

'Why doesn't that make me feel any better?'

Danny shrugged. 'Because you're a natural-born worrier? Everything else about these killings screams Klass to me but this ... this doesn't fit. What does the case team make of it?'

'Jesus, Danny. I told you. Shirley's going mental about the word and making sure no one discusses it with anyone.'

Danny sighed heavily. 'Have you not got it yet, son? When I mentioned Archibald Atto to CID, they told me they think I'm a silly old fool and to go away and not bother them any more. Fine, I can do that. But what I can't do is let this go. So I'm going to have to do it myself. With a little ... no, a *lot* of help from you. I want to know what you know. You're best pals with Derek Addison. He'll know everything that's going on. And Rachel, too, she'll know.'

Winter jumped to his feet, his arms spreading wide. 'No way, Danny, I can't do it. You'll get me sacked. You're right: Addy *is* my pal. But you don't go around spying on your pals so that you can give information to someone else. You don't put their careers at risk. And as for Rachel, well, we're ... not seeing a lot of each other at the moment.'

Danny looked back at Winter, snorting a heave of frustration through his nose and his features twisting. He leaned forward and grabbed at the photographs, scooping them up in his hands at the second attempt and brandishing them before Winter. 'Are you really going to make me spell this out, son?'

Winter's eyes furrowed, trying to make out what Danny was alluding to, the penny finally dropping, slow and ugly. 'You're fucking joking me. You wouldn't.'

'Yes I fucking would!' Danny threw the photographs at Winter, their sharp edges cutting at his chest.

Winter just let the photos tumble to the floor without reacting. As Danny's head sank into his hands, Winter slowly bent down and picked up the prints.

'I'm sorry. But don't force me to do it, son.'

'It means that much to you?'

'Yes.'

'Jesus.' Winter paced back and forth across the room, shaking his head in disbelief at what he knew he was going to say. 'I can't believe this but, okay, Danny, okay. I'll do it. But just to be clear: I'm not doing this in case you tell someone about these photographs. I'm doing it because you would have to be desperate to even threaten to do something like that to me.'

Danny's eyes closed over and he nodded. 'Aye. Sorry, son.'

'Why does this mean so much to you, Danny?'

Neilson hesitated, the answer that was on his lips changing into a sudden snarl.

'He's a killer. Other young women are being killed. That no' enough for you, Tony?'

'That's enough.'

Danny's voice softened. 'Good. And thanks. Atto is in Blackridge Prison, the new one between Glasgow and Edinburgh.'

Winter's heart sank. 'And why do I need to know that?'

'Because we're going to visit him.'

'Christ.'

'Listen, we need to do this. These killings? They're not finished. If I'm right – and I'm as sure as I can be that I am – then this isn't over. If Atto has anything to do with it, or if someone is copying his killings, then there's more to come. I'd guarantee it.'

Chapter 21

July 1972

It had been the hottest July in years and there hadn't been a drop of rain in two weeks. Everyone in Glasgow was dry – dry and thirsty. The crappy beer in Klass was flowing fast and often. No matter how tepid it was and how quickly it got stale, it was rushing down throats as if the punters had walked the Sahara. Some of the girls were on sweet stout but most sipped on martini or Cinzano, glasses chinking with ice that fought a losing battle with the summer swelter and the packed body heat. A disco that had been popular was now the only place to be. The killings hadn't killed trade: it had multiplied demand.

Danny laughed inside to see that some of the blokes were still strutting their stuff in mohair suits despite the rising temperatures inside Klass. They were too proud of their gear to ditch it just because it was so damn hot. They must have itched and sweated like pigs in a Swedish sauna in those suits. A tall chap with fair hair stood next to him at the bar, wrapped up in a navy mohair that might as well have been a straitjacket with a built-in electric blanket. His white kipper tie was loosened at the neck but he still twisted at it to let a comfort of damp air steal inside. His forehead was clammy, sleek rivulets of sweat dripping down his neck.

Looking good was important but Danny wasn't sure it was worth frying to death for. Sure, he felt a pang of regret at the temporary demise of his three-piece with its stylish stripe but he'd have regretted the heat more. Instead he'd got himself togged out in a new yellow Hardy Amies shirt that went with the brown floral tie that she had bought for his birthday. His brown high-waisters had a cool, wide flare and his white shoes gave them a summer look that said Saint-Tropez or Majorca. But he was still too hot.

The real bonus of the high temperature was the clothes that the girls were wearing. Of course, it wasn't why he was there, but it didn't do any harm to look. This was the seventh time he'd been on Klass duty and it was beginning to wear thin. Long sweaty nights with little sleep and no results was making everyone tired and irritable. Relations at home were being stretched to the limit and there wasn't even a hint of the man they were calling Red Silk. So the girls were a welcome bonus. Tiny miniskirts and bare legs tanned by the unusually good weather, skimpy hot pants and singlet tops that slipped off exposed shoulders. Peach hot pants with bib and braces, white silk shirts with mutton sleeves, and pink suede platform boots. Even those with long dresses wore them thin and they clung to curves in the heat. Maybe the swelter made the dancers think they were on holiday, or else their blood was getting hotter, too, because he had seen them pair off as if driven by their basest instincts. Every degree that the thermometer rose, so too did their primeval passions. Drink was drunk and dances were danced. Faster, hotter, sweatier. The whole room was steaming.

He'd given up on his own self-imposed ban on drinking much while on duty there. It wasn't just the heat-induced thirst: he'd also convinced himself he was standing out by not doing what everyone else was doing. So he took his share of the draught lager and when that ran out he turned to the McEwan's Export and swallowed that. There were three of them in Klass that night: he, Billy Moffat and Geordie Taylor. They made a point of never talking to each other, but couldn't help but swap quiet nods and knowing glances, maybe pointing one another in the direction of someone they thought might be worth checking out. Billy and Geordie were knocking back pints, too, wiping clean their lips with the backs of their hands and eyeing up the customers.

They'd been christened the Disco Dancing Division by the other lads, or Triple D Squad for short. Six of them took their turns, four male officers and two female. The women, Alice McCutcheon and Liz Grant, went on about how they weren't particularly happy with the duty and moaned about being set up as potential targets for a murderer. He knew they didn't mean it. Liz in particular would have loved it if Red Silk actually made a move against her. She carried a little clutch bag with half a brick inside and wouldn't think twice about battering someone around the head with it. She could look after herself, and so could Alice.

It was Alice who had said to him that every man in a disco like Klass was a predator, on the prowl for what he could get. She said they were having to find a hunter among a room full of hunters. He didn't much like hearing that but found it hard to argue with. The evidence was all around them.

He watched two blokes, one in a light, beige safari suit and the other broiling in a navy velvet jacket, standing either side of a slim girl in a green miniskirt and halter-neck top. They were crowding in on her, stealing her space and the little fresh air that there was. It was obvious that she didn't know them, or at least hadn't done until a few minutes before. The girl was laughing, but something in it seemed nervous, anxious not to annoy them. The two lads weren't together, either – that much was obvious from the way they reacted to each other. Consciously or not, they'd teamed up to hunt as a pair, but they were also competing against each other, forcing her to choose one or the other. They'd need an eye kept on them.

He was abruptly distracted, though, by movement near the door. Three girls had added more than their share of body heat to the human pool already inside. It was her. The redhead. She and two friends, one of whom he recognised as the mouthy brunette she'd been with on her previous visit, were making their way through the crush towards the bar, alternately asking and pushing and nudging until they cleared a path for themselves.

She saw him and he knew immediately that she'd remembered. Her eyes smiled without the rest of her face betraying a flicker, and he liked that. She was still looking his way as they forced the last body to move aside and allow them into the tiny oasis of space before the bar. She had on hot pants again – very hot pants in this weather, he couldn't help but think – and a white calico blouse that emphasised the lustrous red hair that tumbled onto her shoulders. Her slim legs were bare and ended in strappy platforms that added three or four inches to her height.

He heard the voice almost before he'd realised it was his.

'Martini and lemonade, isn't it?'

She smiled and her friends laughed. 'Well remembered, Danny Neilson. But there's three of us.'

'Oh, aye, sure. What do your pals want?'

The friends laughed again and ordered up a Babycham and a rum and blackcurrant with ice. He wedged himself into a damp space between two other blokes at the bar and waved a pound note in the direction of the short bald-headed barman. He got a curt nod in return that signalled he'd been noted. Minutes later, three glasses were in front of him. He briefly wondered what the hell he was doing but another voice in his head told him to shut up and just do it.

He passed over the drinks to the two friends first and finally gave the martini and lemonade to her, standing square on as he did so, forcing her to face him and hopefully talk.

'Thanks, Danny. Just what I need.'

He instinctively moved his pint glass towards her smaller one, and she gave a little laugh as they clinked together, making her ice cubes giggle and a flurry of bubbles rise in his beer. Over her shoulder, he saw Geordie Taylor looking at them, eyebrows furrowed in curiosity. Stuff him, nothing to do with him. He was fitting in, that was all. Just fitting in.

'I'm Jenny.'

'Danny.'

'I know.'

'Yeah, sorry. Forgot.'

She laughed at him, her eyes lighting up. 'That's a bad memory you've got there. You also forget that your mammy warned you to stay away from red-headed women?'

'Nah, I'm just living dangerously.'

'We're all living dangerously these days, Danny.'

'You mean the killings?'

The words were out of his mouth before he could stop them, a step down a slippery path that he knew would be better avoided.

'Yeah. Of course. It's not you, is it?'

'What?'

'The man that murdered those poor women. It wasn't you, was it? Are you Red Silk?'

He faltered, tongue-tied. He knew she was joking. She *had* to be joking. He'd hesitated for far too long. She was probably taking that as some sign of guilt and was going to run out screaming. Then she laughed, her eyes shining and creasing at the sides.

'Your face! I'm just kidding you on. You're not, are you?'

'No, of course I'm not.'

'Yes, but you would say that, wouldn't you? That's what that Christine Keeler said. You wouldn't exactly admit it if you were Red Silk.'

'I'm not.'

'I know. I wouldn't be standing here if I thought you were him.'

'Don't suppose you would. You not worried about being in here after what's happened?'

'Well, yes, but it's not going to happen again, is it? Not here. Surely he wouldn't come back here. Anyway, I've got my pals with me. As long as we stick together, nothing's going to happen to us.'

'I hope not.'

She laughed again. 'Thanks. You're sweet.'

Sweet. That's what she called him. His wife.

'And also' – she leaned in close and whispered into the hot air between them – 'I've heard that there's police in here. Plain-clothes. Trying to catch the Red Silk guy.'

'Where d'you hear that?'

'My pal Carol. She said she was talking to a polisman and he told her. Said that they were in here dancing. Poliswomen too.' She looked him over. 'I don't think you're a cop, though. Not in that shirt. Hardly plain-clothes, that, is it?'

He glanced down at the yellow shirt with its flowery swirls and felt a bit hurt. He really liked that shirt.

'Your face,' she giggled. 'Do you take everything to heart?'

'No. Well, sometimes maybe. Anyway, I like this shirt.'

'So do I. I was kidding. Again. Where did you buy it?'

'Arthur Black's.'

'The place on St Enoch Square? It'll be handmade, then. And cost a week's wages. Nice. Not so sure about the tie, though.'

'It was a present.'

'From your mum?'

'Um, yes.'

'Really?' she laughed again. 'That *is* sweet. Terrible tie, though.'

Maybe it was the guilt that made him look past her again and see Geordie Taylor staring at him and then throwing a look towards his left. He followed the copper's gaze and saw

Billy Moffat looking at him too. Sods. It wasn't good, though. If they were looking at each other and him, then someone else would twig the three of them were linked. He put his pint down and took her drink from her hand, putting it on the table next to his.

'Let's dance.' He took her hand as he asked, leaving her little choice but to move with him.

'Okay, Red Silk,' she giggled. 'If I refuse you might kill me.'

They writhed through the bodies at the edge of the dance floor and emerged onto the heaving, broiling space, he leading the way and she quickly following. He'd barely thought to listen to the music but could now hear that it was 'Son of My Father' by Chicory Tip. Not that it would have mattered.

Even in the crowded room and above the beat of the record, he could hear her platforms clicking on the wooden floor as her feet marked out the rhythm, immediately falling into time with the sounds thudding from the DJ's turntable. The white calico blouse floated as she moved, offering fleeting glimpses of the soft, glistening flesh beneath. He tried not to look but his eyes won out over his mind. They did the same with the hot pants that gyrated, swung, swayed and teased.

Bodies moved all around them, steam virtually rising to the roof, but he couldn't see anything but her. Her hair flowing, her eyes alive, her hips twisting, her legs swaying, skipping, captivating. He knew it was wrong. He knew it spelled trouble.

When the DJ segued into Free's 'A Little Bit of Love', they shared a look and stayed on the floor, simply changing their steps as the music dictated. Part of him wanted to look to see if Taylor and Moffat were watching, but a larger part wanted to remain and look at her. Part of him wanted to scan the room and see if there was anyone there who might have been the man he'd come to look for, but a larger part of him wanted to dance with her.

So they danced. And then they danced again.

Chapter 22

Early Tuesday afternoon

'Thanks for meeting me.'

The girl looked up at him, pushing her fringe out of her eyes and smiling as if he'd said the strangest thing.

'You're my granddad. Why on earth wouldn't I meet you?'

It was a perfectly reasonable question, or at least it would be if you didn't know any better. And she didn't. Danny Neilson knew, though. He knew everything, and that was why he was as nervous as he ever remembered being in his adult life. Thirty years as a cop and never as bad as this. It was also why he didn't answer the question, at least not directly.

'How's your mum?'

Chloe rolled her eyes theatrically. 'Doing my head in. As always.' A guilty look then crossed her face and she seemed to have thought better of it. 'She's all right really. I'm nineteen and she isn't. I guess it's always going to be a bit of a war.'

'Well, I don't want to make things worse,' he offered. 'The last thing you need is her getting mad at you because you're meeting me.'

Chloe nodded quietly. The same thought had obviously occurred to her already. 'That's why I'm not going to tell her.'

Oh, great, he sighed inside, he'd got the girl lying to her mother. That was almost guaranteed to improve the situation.

'Are you ready to order?'

She shook her head and ducked it back down into the menu, giving him the chance to look at her up close without her noticing. Her green eyes were hauntingly similar to her mother's, and there were also hints of Barbara in the high cheekbones. The fiery red hair and pale skin came from her father, though, the arsehole Mark, who had fled from the scene when she was just a toddler. She was a pretty girl and that wasn't just him being biased. Actually she wasn't a girl any more and that was scary. She'd become a young woman and he'd missed so much of it.

Still, he was finally doing what he'd promised himself to do for so many years. He wasn't proud that it had taken the ghosts of his past to force him into action but at least he had done it. Archibald Atto and the Klass copycat killings had dug up secrets that he knew had to be confronted.

They were in Velvet Elvis on Dumbarton Road – Chloe's suggestion. It was a trendy bar and grill, not really his kind of place but he did like it, even though it was decidedly strange. It was a converted butcher shop and still had meat hooks hanging from the ceiling and a huge wall of Edwardian tiling that had been there since James Burrows and Sons had been pushing out sausages and black puddings. The tall red patio doors to the street opened up in the summer making it into a pavement café and attracting the local arty-farty types.

'I'll have the Velvet Elvis burger with hand-cut chips,' she announced. 'And could I have cheese and bacon on it?'

'Sure. You're not one of those girls that just eats lettuce leaves, then?'

Chloe rolled her eyes again, this time at him rather than her mother. 'As if. Lettuce is for rabbits. I like my burgers. I guess I'm lucky: I just don't get fat when I eat them.'

'Well, I do get fat but I'm having the beer-battered fish and chips, anyway.'

'You're not fat, Pap …' She paused, looking perplexed. 'What should I call you? I'm not five any more and Papa Danny doesn't seem right now, somehow.'

He shrugged, just glad that she was talking to him at all and not caring what she called him. 'Up to you. Papa? Granddad? Grandpa? Old git?'

She grinned shyly. 'Hmm. Yeah maybe old git. I'll think about it and get back to you.'

'Okay, you do that. Do you want something to drink?'

'Just a Coke, please.'

'You can have … I mean, you don't have to have juice just because …'

She laughed a bit. 'I know. Coke's fine. I'm going out tonight, anyway, so I'll have enough then.'

Danny bit his lip, determined to not actually be an old git and go on about the amount that some girls drank. He'd seen them often enough when he supervised the taxi rank into the early hours. He knew it probably made him sexist but it scared the shit out of him when he saw them barely able to walk. It wasn't that he thought they shouldn't get drunk if they felt like it: it was their ability to look after themselves in that state that bothered him. Short skirts, high heels and bloodstreams overflowing with alcohol made them targets for the boozed-up bampots who were also on the streets.

A tall blonde waitress came and took their order, leaving them with nothing to say. Chloe mustered a smile towards him, albeit a bit awkwardly, and let her eye wander round the bar, settling on the old black jukebox that sat against the wall, a sign above it inviting customers to PLAY THE JOOKIE. 4 PLAYS £1.00. The machine, a Galaxy 200, had actual records in it, vinyl 45s, and Danny wondered if she'd seen such things before.

'Do you want to put some music on?' he suggested.

She wrinkled her nose to say no. 'I probably haven't heard of any of them. Wouldn't know what to pick. But thanks.'

They were both relieved when their drinks arrived, giving them something to do with their mouths rather than talk. Chloe reached quickly for her Coke and took a long sip, keeping the tall glass close to her lips. He took an equally grateful gulp of beer and examined the top of the pint tumbler for inspiration.

'So how is . . .?' 'Are you still . . .?' They both started at once and both immediately retreated to let the other one speak. 'No, no. You go. Please.'

'How is college going?'

'University,' she corrected gently. 'Yeah it's great. I'm really enjoying it.'

'And what is it that you're actually studying? I know I should know but . . .'

'English along with journalism and creative writing. It's a

pretty cool course. Hopefully I'll finish up with a BA joint honours.'

Danny felt a surge of pride that was in danger of breaking into a stupid grin and he covered it with a mouthful of his beer.

'That's brilliant,' he gushed, the beer diversion not quenching his pride in the slightest. 'I knew there would have to be some brains in the family eventually. What do you want to do after you graduate?'

She reddened briefly. '*If* I graduate. I don't know. Maybe journalism or something in films would be great. I'll see.'

'What does your mother want you to do?'

A heavy sigh. 'Join a nunnery or become a teacher. Sometimes I'm not sure what she wants. Sorry ... I shouldn't ...'

He shrugged, tempted by the prospect that their shared issues with Barbara might be the thing to bind them, but knowing it was the wrong road to go down.

'She just wants what's best for you, that's all. It's not been easy for her having to bring up a daughter on her own.'

Danny got a sudden flash of fire from her eyes that nearly burned him in his seat. All she actually said was, 'Hmm.' But the look in her eyes spoke volumes. Basically, it said, Back off. You don't know what you're talking about because you weren't there.

She was a fiery one and that red hair didn't come without an extra kick.

Their food arrived and they both tucked in, letting the unspoken spat subside and making only polite noises to enquire about each other's meal. Two strangers passing the salt and the time of day.

He considered telling her how much he had actually seen of her in the years since they had last met. The times he'd sat in his car at the end of their road waiting for a glimpse of her on the way to the park or back from swimming. How he'd watched her win the hundred-metres at a school sports day when she was nine, knowing that her mum was working and wouldn't be there. Or how he'd kept every photograph that had appeared in the local paper. Or how he'd sent a Christmas present every year until she was twelve, finally giving up after each and every one was returned unopened.

'Are you still working nights at the taxi rank?' she asked eventually. 'Mum never really says but that was the last I knew.'

'Yes, still there. It keeps me in beer money.'

'Do you not get a bit fed up with all the madness out there at night?'

'Am I not too old for that, you mean?'

'No. Well, yes. Maybe I meant that a bit too. But the town is just full of nutters, especially at taxi o'clock.'

'You okay when you go out? Safe, I mean.'

He got another little burn of flame from her eyes – not as much as before, though, just a mild singeing. 'I'm fine. Built-in self-preservation sense. If I get too out of it, the homing signal kicks in and I head back to Mum's.'

'That's good. It's a very handy skill to have. Listen, Chloe, I'm sorry I wasn't there when you were growing up.'

He half expected her eyes to flash angry again but they didn't.

'It's okay. You don't need to apologise.'

'I'm not. I'm saying that I'm sorry I wasn't there. I wish I had been.'

She nodded. 'Okay. I know it wasn't your choice. You going to tell me why Mum's so mad at you?'

'No. Not today. It's too long a story. Let's just say she had her reasons and I'm not blaming her for being like that.'

Chloe looked at him for a while, maybe working out if it would be worth trying to get him to talk about it.

'Okay, not today. Does that mean we'll meet again?'

'Yes. If you want to.'

'Yeah. Okay.'

'Good.'

Back out on a damp, springlike Dumbarton Road, they prepared to go their separate ways, a palpable awkwardness between them at how to say goodbye being finally settled by a clumsy hug.

'Thanks for coming,' he said.

'I told you, you don't need to thank me. Anyway, I enjoyed it.'

'Did you?'

'Yes.'

'Good. Me too. Listen … there's something else I wanted to say. You know these murders that happened in the city centre? Well … I know I don't have much right to lecture you after all these years but … it's dangerous out there. Just be careful, will you?'

She wrinkled her nose at him, obviously amused, then leaned in and kissed him on the cheek. 'Okay, Papa. I will.'

Chapter 23

Tuesday afternoon

Walking down the SPSA corridor to the chemist lab, DI Derek Addison was aware of a feeling that he was almost completely unfamiliar with. Dredging his memory banks, he realised that it was probably something that other people called nervousness. Given the length of time since he'd last experienced this phenomenon, he wasn't entirely sure how to deal with it.

What he did know was that the source of his nerves was waiting at the end of the corridor. Sam Guthrie had left a message saying that she had completed the lipstick analysis and asking him to drop into the lab for the results. She'd also added that she could contact DCI Kelbie if he preferred ...

He was bothered less by the suggestion that she might call Kelbie than by the fact that she so clearly knew that she could wind him up by saying it. He'd never quite understood the attraction other guys had for confident, intelligent women. Give him vulnerable and vacuous any day of the week. Guthrie was annoyingly sharp, self-assured and intellectual, but he could have just about coped with all of that if she hadn't been so bloody good-looking as well.

He'd asked around about her, purely for professional reasons. She was originally from farming stock near Stonehaven and had gone to university in Edinburgh, gaining two degrees and seemingly being a stellar student. She was twenty-six and had been in the SPSA in Glasgow for two years. She was single.

Addison paused just as he was about to push open the door into the lab, seeing her through the glass panel, head down over a piece of equipment. That weird sensation flushed through him again and he knew he didn't like it. It was time to adopt the Addison persona. It never failed.

He shoved the door back wider than was necessary and strode through without the courtesy of a knock or the politeness of a hello, his hands thrust into his pockets and an uninterested look fastened to his face. Guthrie didn't look up but instead made a show of sniffing at the air.

'Sounds like testosterone. Smells like testosterone. It must be DI Addison. Take a seat. I'll be with you in a moment.'

He stopped mid-stride and mid-attitude. 'Look, I don't have time to—'

'Yes, you do. Sit down and try not to break anything.'

Addison's mouth opened and closed before turning into a disgruntled frown. There was a chair in front of the desk near Guthrie and he dropped himself into it, crossing his lanky legs in a show of pique.

'And don't pout,' she called to him, still not having taken

her eyes off the machinery in front of her. 'It's not very macho, is it?'

He fretted for a bit before having another stab at asserting himself. 'You said you had the results of the lipstick analysis.'

'Yes, I did.'

'And that you would let me have it.'

She looked up for the first time, eyebrows raised enquiringly. 'Yes, I did.'

'I meant the results,' he gabbled, aware that he was losing.

'Of course you meant the results. What on earth else could you have meant?'

'I ... never mind. Do you have the results and will you kindly tell me what they entail?'

Guthrie sighed. 'I do and I will. Hadn't we established that? Okay, Detective Inspector, walk this way.'

The scientist rose elegantly from her chair, her long legs taking her to the rear of the lab in just a few strides, leading him to the shelf where the array of lipsticks had been on his previous visit. In their place were just three tubes of the stuff and three printed charts. Guthrie turned so her back was against the edge of the worktop, her ankles crossing neatly in front of her and her arms folding across her chest, looking at him the way she might look at something unusual at the bottom of one of her test tubes.

'You look tired, Detective Inspector. Tough case? Not sleeping much?'

'Um ... busy time.'

'I can see that it must be. You look as if you're in need of some TLC.'

He hesitated. 'Thin-layer chromatography?'

Guthrie tilted her head to the side in curiosity, but her eyes were laughing. 'Why on earth would you need thin-layer chromatography to help with a lack of sleep? Tender loving care, Detective Inspector, that's what you need.'

His nerves had been justified. The woman was a nightmare.

'The scientific TLC does have its uses, however.' She pushed herself gently from the worktop and picked up the charts behind her. 'I have a positive identification on your lipstick. Do you remember the chromatograms I showed you on your previous visit?' She didn't get an answer. 'The little red lines and the little green lines?'

'Yes, of course. I just didn't know that it was called . . . Jesus, will you just tell me what you've found?'

'Tut-tut. Impatient *and* intemperate. Hardly desirable qualities in a profession such as yours, Detective Inspector. Okay, you see the overlay in this chart?' The red and green peaks rose together but the heights varied very slightly. 'That shows that they are almost certainly made by the same manufacturer. Whereas *this* chart' – in the second, the coloured peaks were completely in alignment – 'indicates that we have a winner.'

'Okay, I can see that. Definitely the same lipstick? Do you not need to check with the . . . er, GCSE?'

Guthrie sighed. 'It is, as I suspect you well know, GC–MS. And, yes, surprisingly enough, you are correct. As well as having analysed the colouring agents with the TLC, I also studied the organic components with GC–MS. And, as you can see from the final chart' – she held it in front of him – 'it confirms it. It is, scientifically and unequivocally, the same lip-stick.'

'Which is?'

'Hollywood by Ava Duvall. It's a real old lady's lippy. It used to be very popular in the seventies and eighties much in the same way as something like Old Spice aftershave was for men. But tastes change and it just went out of fashion. Duvall doesn't even make lipstick any more. They just make fragrances these days.'

'So when would this have been bought then?'

'Well, I checked that out with them and they say they stopped production in 1995, but there was probably still some stock being sold into the late nineties. It means, obviously enough, that there is no chance of tracking down a stockist or time and place of purchase. However, it's not all bad news. I'd suggest that you could reasonably postulate that—'

'That someone who has access to a fifteen-year-old lipstick is less worried about fashion and more about some senti-mental attachment to it. It perhaps belongs to a mother or grandmother. Then again, maybe it was just found in an old box of make-up. Either way, it looks highly unlikely that it belonged to Kirsty McAndrew.'

Guthrie nodded thoughtfully. 'And you interrupted me because I'd moved from a scientific analysis to an investigative one. My apologies for treading on your toes, Detective Inspector.'

'No, that's, um ... Sorry for, um ... interrupting. Is there anything else you can tell me about this?'

The chemist smiled and Addison ducked internally, won-dering what she was going to throw at him next. 'Not about the lipstick, no. However, I've also been involved in processing the trace evidence found on the ground adjacent to the Caledonia Road church and can tell you that we believe we have successfully extracted DNA from it. It's not the quality we'd wish for but it's there.'

Addison blinked at her, his nerves and awkwardness disappearing like snow off a dyke. 'What the bloody hell didn't you tell me that for? What have you got? Jesus H. Christ, woman, you're blabbering on about an out-of-date lipstick and don't bother to mention that you've got fucking DNA that probably comes from a double murderer?'

Guthrie didn't bat an eye but she did let her eyebrows rise far enough to show amused disapproval. 'I wouldn't go as far as probable, Detective Inspector. Such premature decision-making doesn't bode well at all. Perhaps I'd be better contacting Detective Chief Inspector Kelbie if and when we get a match to the DNA.'

'What? You really don't want to do that. Premature? Kelbie shoots his bolt quicker than an ADHD kid with a crossbow. Look, Ms ... Sam. I'd very much appreciate it if you made a point of conta—'

'Ask me out for dinner.'

'What?'

'Ask me out for dinner and I'll make sure you are the first point of contact once the results of the DNA tests are delivered.'

'I ... uh ... now look ... um ... Okay. Would you like to go out for dinner with me sometime?'

'No, thank you.'

'What? You said—'

'I said I wanted you to ask. I didn't say I'd accept. That's the bargain upheld, though, and I'll let you know as soon as we get something positive.'

'Yeah but ... okay ... when do you think you'll get something?'

'Soon. And you'll be the first to know.'

Addison needed a drink after his second round with the Guthrie woman. Truth was, he would have gone for a pint or two anyway but he certainly felt as if he deserved it after her dicking him around like that. Not dicking around – bad choice of words. Any expressions relating to the male sexual organs had to be avoided when he was thinking about her. Avoided like the bloody plague.

He'd walked over to the Station Bar, twice texting Winter en route but not getting an answer. A pity, but it would hardly be the first time that he'd drunk alone, nor the last. Maybe his own company would be better, anyway. The last thing he wanted was Winter blabbering on about either Sam Guthrie or Kelbie.

He was passing the Piping Centre opposite the top of Hope Street, just a couple of hundred yards from the pub, when his mobile rang. Winter.

'Awrite, wee man? What's happening?'

'Hi, Addy. Don't think I'm going to make it for a pint. Got a man to see about a dog.'

'Aye, very good. You go chasing dogs and just leave me to drink on my own. It's good to know who your friends are. What you been up to, anyway?'

'Och, just this and that. Getting some routine stuff

processed. Did I hear you were back down in the chemist lab today?'

'Who told you that?'

Neither of them could miss the defensiveness in his answer.

'Keep your hair on, Addy. Paul Burke saw you going down there. Did the lovely Ms Guthrie have anything interesting for you?'

'Piss off and don't start on me.'

'Oh, sore point, is it?'

'I said piss off.'

'Calm down, man. And anyway that wasn't what I meant. I meant did Sam have anything interesting about the case? Did she have the results of the lipstick analysis?'

Addison hesitated, still unsure whether Winter was taking the piss. 'Yeah, she did. Turns out it's some old-fashioned lippy that you can't buy any more. The company stopped making it years ago.'

'What was it called?'

'Eh? Hollywood by Ava Duvall. What difference does it make?'

'Just wondered. What else are they working on down there? They got results back from the Cathcart Road site?'

'What is this? You're giving me more hassle than Shirley. Glad you're no' my boss. Naw, she's not got anything on it yet. Next couple of days with a bit of luck. Think I've persuaded her to come to me with the info as well rather than that wee shite Kelbie.'

'Aye? How did you manage that, then? The old Addison charm?'

'I told you not to start on me about that. If you're not

coming out for a drink, then you've lost the right to wind me up.'

'Calm down, big stuff. I was only pulling your— Hello? Hello? Addy?'

Addison's phone was back in his pocket and he began the march on the Station Bar in earnest. Drinking alone had become a lot more preferable to drinking with someone who wanted to ask questions.

Chapter 24

Tuesday evening

Outside Hillhead underground station, Winter tucked away his mobile and the conversation with Addison that had disappeared in a huff of smoke. The stress in the DI's voice was obvious and Winter suffered a wrench of guilt for having wound him up, but it faded fast. He had his own problems to deal with.

Across the other side of Byres Road, he saw the corner of Highburgh Road, knowing Rachel's flat was just yards beyond it. It had been only a month since he'd last been there but so much had happened in between that it seemed an age ago. Hell, so much had happened since they'd tried to meet for breakfast the day before. The rescheduled 'catch-up' was on her home turf.

A group of four young women passed in the other direction as Winter made his way down Ashton Lane's cobbled access. One of them, a tall, attractive blonde, made eyes at him as they went by. Winter blanked her, as much out of confusion as to what he was supposed to do as anything else.

He climbed the stairs into the Grosvenor Cafe, picking out a booth in the corner and ordering a couple of drinks: a bottle of beer for himself and a glass of white wine for Rachel, putting them together on the table in front of him. He hadn't seen her all day and had only her text from that lunchtime suggesting the meeting. He'd heard whispers through the forensic grapevine that something had been found on the route near the Southern Necropolis killing, but no one seemed to know if it had amounted to much. Ten minutes later, almost on time for her, she arrived, looking tired and grouchy.

'Bad day?'

'Long day,' she sighed, rubbing at her eyes.

'I took a chance and got you a glass of wine.'

She looked at it doubtfully – just what she needed and the last thing she should have. 'Thanks.'

They fell into the kind of awkward silence that can happen only between people with lots to say to each other but are not sure where to start. She pushed at her glass without drinking it and he sipped at his beer for something to do.

'Are you ...'

'What happened with ...'

'Sorry, you go first.'

'No it's okay. You.'

They both hesitated, words stuck, and reached for their drinks instead, their hands brushing against the other's. His hand recoiled slowly, hers as if it had been electrocuted.

'You go first.' It was more of an order than an invitation.

He took a mouthful of his beer, buying time and drinking her in over the rim of the glass. Tired or not, she still looked good. He fought the need to tell her.

'So how's your dad today?'

Rachel sat forward and her hands flew to her head. 'Oh, shit, no. With everything that was going on, I forgot to call the home.' She looked at her watch, but one glance told her that it was far too late to phone him. 'Shit.'

The symptoms of her dad's Alzheimer's had begun to emerge the year before and had, inevitably, got worse as the months had passed. Rachel's guilt at his being in the nursing home never left her but she did phone or visit every day. Or at least she tried to. With her mum having died six years earlier, it was down to Rachel to be there for him, but her job didn't exactly make that easy.

'Don't worry about it,' he said, trying to sympathise. 'It's not as if . . .' – he faltered – 'he wouldn't understand the pressures of your job.' Her dad had been a cop too but Winter knew it wasn't a good enough save to stop her from working out the pause.

'It's not as if he would remember that I called, anyway? Is that what you were going to say? It's not the bloody point and you know it. And he had a really good day yesterday, if you must know. He knew who I was as soon as he answered the phone. Do you know how good that makes me feel? If he'd been the same today . . .'

She wavered, her hands covering her face, then pushing back through her hair, fatigue and remorse making her look older. She pulled the wineglass to her lips but pushed it away again and rested it back on the table.

'I don't really want wine. Can you get me a Diet Coke, please? And see what they've got for eating behind the bar. Not something off the menu, just a snack. I should eat something.'

Winter, happy of the excuse to get away from talking about her dad and knowing that he'd put his foot right in it, shoved himself up from the seat and headed to the vast central bar, bottle of beer in his hand. He wove through people, not really seeing them, just aware of them in his way. A barmaid asked him what he wanted and he got the Diet Coke plus a packet of salt-and-vinegar crisps, salted peanuts and a chocolate bar.

'Andy Teven said he was speaking to some old copper at Pitt Street yesterday.' She stretched as he returned. 'He didn't give a name but the description sounded like Danny.'

Winter held out the choice of the crisps, nuts and chocolate, and she took all three. He'd never understood why someone who loved food as much as Rachel did never got remotely fat.

'Every old copper looks like Danny. Did I hear word about something being found on your sweep of the route that Hannah Healey took?'

'I don't know. Did you?'

'Yes, I did.'

'There you go, then. Mystery solved,' she mumbled through a mouthful of crisps.

When they'd been together yet secret, touching wasn't allowed in public. Her rules. He didn't like it but he could live with it as he could always touch her later. Now, not being allowed to touch her because they weren't whatever it was they had been . . . that was much more difficult. It hurt.

Her bag abruptly beeped and she delved into it in search of her phone. He recognised the tone: she had a text. Pulling the mobile out, she seemed to make sure the screen was turned away from him as she studied it, her eyes flickering to his to see if he was watching.

'Answer that if you want.' The words were dry in his mouth.

'No. It's okay. I'll get it later.' She didn't look at him. 'So it wasn't Danny at Pitt Street, then?'

He took a large gulp at the bottle in his hand, his mind racing.

'You'd have to ask him. So, did you find something belonging to Hannah Healey?'

'No idea. You know how long it takes the lab to get back with answers to anything. If only it was like on those *CSI* shows on the telly and we got immediate results. How is Danny these days, anyway?'

'Oh, you know Danny. Never changes. He was asking for you, though. In fact he was asking how you were getting on with the case.'

'Interested in the case, is he?'

'Isn't everybody? Two murders in two days. Bound to be the talk of the town. Only natural that people want to know if you're any closer to catching the guy.'

'I suppose it is. And Danny being a former cop ... Guess that instinct never leaves you. You think he still wishes he was on the job?'

'You know what they say. Old policemen never die: they just cop out.'

'And old photographers never die: they just stop developing. Was that answer a cop-out?'

'I don't know. Was it?'

'I don't know. You know what, though?'

'What?'

'I'm tired. I think maybe we should call this a night before one of us actually has to give a straight answer to a straight question.'

'You know what?'

'What?'

'I think you're right.'

Chapter 25

West Lothian, Wednesday

It was officially named HMP Central Scotland, but was known universally as Blackridge for the small town in West Lothian that it was nearest to. It was generally pronounced as *Blackrigg*, the same way the locals said it. The town picked up a bit of business from the prison but, for all that, they'd just as rather it weren't there. The supposed £100 million that it cost to build 'the big hoose' outside the town would have gone a long way in Blackridge, a tiny place still recovering from the closing of the colliery fifty years before.

The jail sat almost plumb between Glasgow and Edinburgh, as near midway as the planners could make it, so as to avoid offending the sensibilities of either end of the M8 corridor. Prisons were as political as anything else when it came to disputes between the capital and the biggest city.

The stark, grey structure, its anonymous walls fifteen feet high topped with coils of barbed wire, seemed to have been dropped into the lush, rain-sodden countryside from outer space. All care had been given to its security and none at all to its being sympathetic to its surroundings. It stood alone but for a large car park that might have been pinched from outside a major supermarket. Only a red-brick building that resembled the gable end of a nondescript modern family home broke the monotony of the grey wall. It was the gatehouse, Union and Saltire flags billowing in the fresh spring wind before it. Winter and Neilson made their way towards it in silence.

In the car, as they drove along the M8, Danny at the wheel, he'd talked at length about Atto and his crimes – the ones they knew about and the ones that they didn't. The latter list was longer than the former.

'Atto was an English teacher, specialised in offering extra tuition for kids that needed to up their grades to get into university, or to get into a better university. He made good money but never stayed in one place too long. He had excellent references and always came highly recommended. Never worked in schools, though – kept under the radar in that sense. Seems he was popular with the pupils, particularly the girls. Paid them a lot of attention.

'In 1999, he was convicted of killing two sixteen-year-olds, Beverley Collins in Dumfries and Emma Rutherford in Leicester. By the time Beverley's body was found, ten years after she was killed, it was impossible to tell if she'd been sexually assaulted. Her corpse was still bound at her ankles and wrists and she'd been gagged. Emma was found by chance in a shallow grave just three days after she'd gone missing. A springer spaniel partially dug her up and the dog's owner called the cops. Emma's throat had been cut and she'd been both raped and anally assaulted. Atto's DNA was found on her clothing.

'At this point, he had made headlines, quite a few of them. But maybe it hadn't been enough for him. He let a name drop in a police interview, nothing accidental, mind. I've seen and heard the tapes and he hesitates for an age before he says it, making sure everyone there is hanging on his every word. He lets them know that he used to live in a street named Huntington Road in Coventry. It doesn't mean anything to any of the cops or lawyers present but they go check it out. It turns out Huntington Road is two hundred yards away from where a nineteen-year-old named Melanie Holt went missing in 1991. Sure enough, they find out that Atto lived very close to her.

'They go back to Atto and say, "Did you kill Melanie Holt?" Atto smiles and says yes. They say, "Where's her body?" and he smiles but says nothing for ages. Then he says, "Greening Place in Ipswich." Obviously, they say, "Is that where Melanie's body is?" He gives this sly grin and says no, that he lived there.

'They check out the address and, sure enough, a girl had gone missing from there too. Louise Shillington had been twenty-one when she was last seen in 1993. Atto had lived on the same street. So they ask him, "Did you kill her?" Yes. "Where is her body?" Nothing. For months they questioned him and for months he stonewalled them. Melanie and Louise's parents both wrote to him but he wouldn't budge.

'Then the case team, now three times the size that it had been, create a timeline of Atto's movements: jobs, houses, medical records, the lot. They come up with a list of nineteen possible victims: eleven murders of young women and eight violent rapes. They confront Atto with the list and he looks at it curiously, making a big show of remembering things, some of them obviously very pleasurable to him. Then he looks at them and coldly asks, "Is that all you could come up with? You underestimate me."

'So they ask if he's admitting he killed and raped those girls. He says no. He says he's admitting nothing, wasn't in those places, didn't ever meet those girls. Sure enough, none of them was girls he taught. Then, a year later, when the media interest in Atto is dying down, he asks to talk with the case team again. Says he made a mistake. He did meet Heather Ryan, he remembers now. "Did you kill her?" "Maybe. I don't really remember."

'The bastard has been dicking the case team and the families around ever since. So he's serving four consecutive life sentences when it should perhaps be seventeen or more. Some people say it doesn't matter because he'll only ever leave prison in a box. But that's not the point. These families, they need to know. They need to have a funeral and they can't because he won't tell them where the bodies are. So, yeah, I'm glad he'll die in prison, but part of me wants that to be right now and another wants him to rot in there until he tells everything he knows.

'Archibald Atto is a psychopath, a nasty, vicious, brutal, murdering piece of shit. But he's more than that. He's clever. Devious. He has a dangerous combination of high intelligence and low cunning. He tortures people's emotions because he can, because he believes he's smarter than them.'

'So is he Red Silk?' Winter asked. 'Did he carry out the Klass killings?'

'He's never admitted to it. Never even acknowledged that it might have been him. He did live in Glasgow at the time and moved away not long after the final murder. But so much of it is similar to what happened later. Beverley Collins's skeleton was bound in a way that it was believed she'd been forced into a kneeling, praying position. Her hands were bound *in front* of her rather than behind. Emma Rutherford was buried on her back, her arms spread wide. Not the thing you'd do if you wanted the grave to be as small as possible and reduce the chance of it being found.

'After Atto was convicted the police went back to witnesses from 1972 and showed them his photo. Of course, they'd all seen him on the news by this time and impressions had formed in their minds. Plus, they were a lot older and memories were playing tricks. The person with the best look at Red Silk, Frances MacFarlane, was dead. But plenty of those asked said aye, that's the man. That was the guy that was in Klass when those girls were murdered.'

To get a visit to a convicted prisoner in Blackridge, the visit has to be booked by the inmate. You couldn't just turn up at the door and ask to visit the infamous serial killer Archibald Atto. They didn't encourage that kind of thing. Atto had no family, his elderly mother having died a year after he was convicted, and, not surprisingly had no known friends. Or at least no one who would admit to it. His visitor schedule rarely got near to fulfilling even the statutory minimum of two hours in any period of twenty-eight consecutive days.

Danny, inevitably, knew a man who knew a man who worked in Blackridge. The warder got a message to Atto saying that an Anthony Winter and a Daniel Neilson wished to visit him, with news of Christine Cormack. He also let it be known that the news was something that was likely to interest the media. Danny knew that Atto hadn't had his face on the front pages for a while.

They were sitting in the prison car park, a couple of hundred yards from the main building, the only sound the intermittent squeak of windscreen wipers tackling the softly falling rain. Danny was staring ahead, psyching himself up for what was to come.

Winter could almost see the play that was going on behind Danny's eyes, seeing them tighten as hard thought followed bad memory. 'Stop me if I do something stupid, son.'

'You likely to?'

'I don't know. I know I want to. I know I'm going to want to punch his lights out.' Danny's voice got louder. 'I'm going to want to want to rip his head off.'

Danny lashed out, banging his fist into the steering wheel, causing the horn to blast and making a couple of people walking across the car park look and wonder what the hell was going on. Winter waited till he was finished.

'The anger's not doing you any good, Danny.'

An ironic little laugh escaped from Neilson. 'You think not? Look at my hand, Tony.'

Danny held out the back of his hand in front of Winter. 'What do you see?'

Winter looked at the large, beefy hand dotted with liver spots, a road map of thick veins showing the way from wrist to fingers. The skin was loose and sat in dishevelled folds, the fingers broad and strong. He shrugged. 'It's a hand.'

'It's an old man's hand, son. Look at the loose skin. But watch this.'

Danny slowly clenched his hand into a fist and the skin tightened until the loose folds disappeared, leaving the back of his hand as taut as the day he was twenty-one.

'That's why the anger's doing me good. It takes years off me. You'll always have a reason to live if you have something to make you angry enough.'

'So that's your only reason for living?'

Danny sighed. A noise that came from deep within him. 'No. Not the only one. I met Chloe yesterday.'

Winter swung round to look at him. 'Seriously? How long's it been since you've seen her?'

'Too long, son.'

'And does Barbara know about this?'

A bitter laugh was followed by a long silence. Then, 'What do you think?'

They walked from the car park to the gatehouse, a shimmer of smirry rain dusting them as they made their way across the tarmac. Winter saw Danny's jaw clench tighter with every step they took towards the prison.

'You okay now, Dan?'

'I'm fine, son. I've waited a long time for this, that's all. Forty bloody years.'

From the gatehouse, they were directed to the visitor centre, a dark-grey building just thirty yards away. Apart from staff, there were a handful of people inside, all mooching about in various states of embarrassment and shamelessness. Winter noticed that a couple of likely lads in tracksuits clocked

Danny and immediately saw cop, instinctively turning away so he didn't see their faces.

A broad, shaven-headed officer had a Labrador on a lead and was wandering in and out of the waiting crowd, the dog clearly sniffing for drugs and causing anxious looks on a few faces. The man on the other end of the lead looked a lot meaner than the dog, his dark-blue tie knotted uncomfortably round a thick, fatty neck as he stared aggressively at everyone in turn. Danny, being Danny, stared back, giving as good as he got. The officer clocked it and walked over, keen to check out the unfamiliar faces.

He pulled his dog over to where Winter and Neilson stood, forcing the dog to go through the routine of sniffing them even though it didn't seem remotely interested. Danny made a show of looking at the guy's name badge, CRIGHTON, and lingered on it just enough to annoy him. It worked.

'Visitor forms,' he demanded, standing confrontationally close to Danny and thrusting his hand out to receive the request form they'd been issued. Danny didn't take his eyes from the officer's as he fished in his pocket and brought out both forms and handed them over.

The man scanned through the forms, checking their names and the date and making his authority clear. He seemed about to hand the forms back when something he read made him stop and his face creased in consternation. He looked up at Danny and Winter, obviously unhappy, and gave the forms back without saying anything.

'Nature's always full of surprises, isn't it, Mr Crighton?' Danny asked him, causing the officer's face to show further confusion.

'What do you mean?'

'Well, it's no' every day you see a bulldog taking a Labrador for a walk, is it?'

Crighton took a step towards Danny, eyes furious, but halted himself. 'Your first time here, is it?'

'Yeah.'

'Aye, and maybe your last. See that desk over there? Get yourselves there now. The officer there will take your photographs.'

Danny grinned at the officer before he and Winter strolled casually over to the spot Crighton had indicated. Another member of staff clicked a remote button and a desktop camera took individual photographs of them. Winter, in particular, was irked at the process, never being comfortable on the other side of the lens. They then had to offer up photographic ID of their own, and supporting proof of their names and addresses. 'You'll be in the system now and we'll be able to confirm your identity if you return,' they were told.

Both men were given keys for lockers where they had to leave everything they had on them, before having to remove their jackets and shoes and being frisked. The officer had already told them they could take up to ten pounds in cash into the visit room but they'd both declined, figuring that there wasn't a whole lot they would want to spend it on. The niceties over with, they were passed on to another officer at the end of the holding area, being told that he would lead them into the visit room.

The officer, tall and thin, eyed them suspiciously when they approached. 'First visit?' he asked stony-faced. Both men nodded.

'Rules. The visit will last for forty-five minutes. You will enter the visit room and take a seat at a table. I will give you a number and you will sit at the table I tell you and not at any other. You and the prisoner will not share food or drinks of any description from the same container. You will keep your hands in sight at all times. Chairs will remain in a face-on position at all times. When time is called at the end of the session, the prisoner will exit the room. You will remain seated at the end of the session until you are invited to leave. You will not approach or converse with any other prisoner throughout the duration of your visit. Do you understand?'

'Yes.'

'Okay. Names?'

'Neilson and Winter.'

The officer consulted the sheet of paper on the clipboard in his hands. He looked up at them again and then back at the sheet, just to make sure, his eyebrows slowly rising as he did so.

'Well, well. It's not every day, that's for sure. Relatives? Friends?'

'Naw.' Danny growled.

The officer glowered at Danny's bluntness. 'Okay. This way, gentlemen. Mr Atto awaits you. You're in for a treat.'

Chapter 26

Wednesday mid-morning

They were driving to Bridgeton again, Narey at the wheel, wondering about the whereabouts of the mysterious Mr Grey, and Toshney whistling something exasperating that was managing to burrow its way into her head. Although they were investigating a double murder, she was seriously considering whether a third body would make things that much worse. Perhaps she could convince him that there was something on the road in front of the car and then, just accidentally, step on the accelerator. Who would doubt her? Which jury in the land would convict her? In the end, she decided against murder on the basis that it wouldn't look good on her record. Instead, she settled for regular sighs, tuts and glares in his direction. When that failed she told him to shut up.

They parked on Tobago Street, a rundown spot even by East End standards that lay in the old badlands between the Gallowgate and London Road. Much of the surrounding area was being regenerated as part of the Commonwealth Games project but this strip of scrub and boarded-up buildings was more in need of a revival than most. Ritchie Stark's sandstone tenement sat atop a small row of shops at the corner with Stevenson Street, although it was difficult to tell whether the shops were closed or abandoned. Certainly forsaken was a boarded shack with a hand-painted sign that read JOHN'S BAR. It propped up the flats above, but John, whoever he was, had long gone.

The area across the street had once held a row of houses but they too had disappeared years before and the foundations were grassed over, home now only to two mongrels who were sniffing and snapping at each other in an age-old mating dance.

'Why the hell would you come here if you moved up from Nottingham?' Toshney asked aloud.

'You've obviously never been to Nottingham,' Narey told him. 'Although you do think he'd have been able to get something a bit more salubrious than this.'

'Do you think he could have got somewhere *less* salubrious? He must be a real charmer to persuade his bird to come here.'

Stark's girlfriend, Faith Foster, had confirmed they had been at the flat on both the Friday and Saturday nights of the murders and that Stevo Barclay, Stark's boss at the tattoo parlour, had been drinking with them on the Saturday.

Addison and Narey had both wanted to know more though and, on the part-pretence of confirming the alibi, she was going to take the opportunity to ask Faith about Barclay. Addison was suspicious of Barclay's lack of credible proof as to where he was those nights. Rico Giannandrea had originally asked Barclay about his whereabouts only on the night that Kirsty McAndrew was murdered and the explanation that he'd been at the flat on the Saturday had been something of an afterthought.

'You think the car's going to be safe if you leave it here?' Toshney asked her, looking round warily.

'Probably not, but the alternative would be to leave you here to look after it, and I'm not sure you'd be any safer. Let's go up and see what they've got to say.'

In the doorway, Narey pressed the wobbly plastic shield that covered a handwritten piece of paper with 'Stark' written on it, and moments later the intercom crunched and an English accent crackled through. 'Yeah? Who is it?'

'Police. DS Narey and DC Toshney. Can we come up, Mr Stark?'

There was a silence at the other end of the intercom before the man replied. 'Um, yeah. I thought we'd sorted this.'

'We'd still like to ask you a few questions, Mr Stark. It won't take long.'

'Um ... okay. Come on up.'

The door catch was released and Narey and Toshney made their way into the tenement and up the stairs towards Stark's flat. The concrete internal staircase was gloomy and didn't exactly smell wonderful, causing Toshney to complain by blowing out a sharp blast of breath. 'It's reeking in here.'

Stark was waiting at the door to the flat, dressed in skinny jeans and a sleeveless Foo Fighters T-shirt that showed off the bizarre spider's-web-and-angels tattoo that covered his left arm. His dark hair was swept back on his head and he looked as if he hadn't shaved for a couple of days. 'Come in.'

They went past him into a narrow hallway with two closed doors off it and headed towards the sound of a television set at the end of the hall, where a third door opened into a large living room. The room was sparsely decorated, just a couple of framed rock-gig posters on a jet-black wall at the door and another on one of the three white walls. In front of the window, with its picturesque views onto the derelict land on Tobago Street, sat a black leather sofa and on that sat a girl clad in black, a shy chameleon seeking camouflage. Faith Foster was probably only about five feet tall but five-inch platform shoes considerably added to that. She wore a long, black, crushed-velvet skirt, a plain black T-shirt and mesh gloves that ran to her elbows. The whole goth look was topped off by the pale make-up on her small round face, her short dark hair and the black lipstick on her thin lips.

Stark reached down and switched off the television set. 'This is Faith.'

The girl looked at them nervously, a half-hearted attempt at a smile on her lips. 'Hi.'

'Hello, Faith. I'm DS Narey and this is DC Toshney. I believe you spoke to one of my colleagues on the phone, DS Giannandrea.'

'Um, yes. I told them where we were on Friday and Saturday. We were here.'

'Yes, I know, but I'd just like to ask you a bit more about it.'

'Why?'

The girl's voice was soft yet demanding and Narey wondered whether she was emboldened by the disguise that she wore.

'Faith, two young women, more or less the same age as you, have been murdered. Anything that we learn might just be the breakthrough we need to find out who did it.'

'Okay. I don't see how we can help, but okay.'

Stark sat beside his girlfriend, the two of them making an odd pair. He was a few years older than she was, wearing a similar uniform of unconformity and yet somehow wearing his more naturally. Faith gave more of an impression of being at a fancy-dress party that had never stopped.

'So, if you don't mind, could you tell me what you told DS Giannandrea. It will help if I can hear it fresh.'

Faith gave an uncertain look towards her boyfriend, who gave the tiniest nod of approval.

'We were in here. It's as simple as that. On the Friday, I got in about seven-ish. We ordered in a pizza from Dominoes. Had a bottle of wine and watched telly. And we ... we did stuff.'

'Stuff?'

'Sex. You want me to tell you how many times or positions?'

'No, thank you. And what did you watch before you had sex? And did you both stay here all night?'

'Just the usual Friday-night rubbish. A couple of soaps, then some Channel 4 comedy stuff. Then sex. For a while. And, yes, we both stayed here all night.'

'How did you pay for your pizza?'

'What?'

'Cash or card?'

'Oh, for God's sake. Cash. But we phoned up so the shop will probably have a note of the delivery. You can check.'

'We will, thanks. And on the Saturday?'

The girl sighed sulkily, her eyebrows theatrically reaching for the ceiling. 'Much the same, except we had a Chinese rather than pizza. And Stevo Barclay was here. We watched telly and had quite a bit to drink. Only difference is we didn't have sex. Not until after Stevo left, anyway.'

'And what time was that?'

Foster shrugged expansively. 'Don't know. After one o'clock, anyway. Probably nearer two. I couldn't give you an exact time when we had sex. Sorry.'

Narey wanted to give the girl a slap. 'Look, this isn't anything personal, Miss Foster. It's just routine. We need to check everything. Everything and everyone that we can rule out brings us one step closer to finding who did it.'

Faith made a face but nodded reluctantly. 'I know. Sorry. I get it.'

'Do you ever go to the tattoo parlour?'

The girl seemed to relax slightly, the tension and the confrontation easing out of her. 'Yes, sometimes. I pop over for lunch now and again and if Ritchie isn't busy then we can go out or just hang out in the shop.'

'Did you ever meet Kirsty McAndrew? The girl who was murdered.'

'No. At least I don't think I ever did. I saw her picture in the paper. Her and the other girl. But I don't think I recognised either of them. There's been so many people in and out of the shop. Jesus, I can't bear to ... It's horrible.'

'Do you have tattoos yourself?'

Faith hesitated, looking at Stark and then at Toshney. 'Well, yeah. Ritchie does them for me. But I'm not showing you them. Not here. Not in front of him. They're ... in a couple of personal places.'

Narey saw Toshney try to hide a sudden burst of interest in the conversation and she made a mental note to chin him about it when they were finished.

'It's okay, you don't have to show us. I just wanted to get an idea of how much you were around Ink Sync. Do you know Stevo Barclay well?'

Faith screwed her face up a bit, then shared another look with her boyfriend. 'He's Ritchie's boss. I'm ... not exactly a fan, though. I don't like him very much.'

'And yet he was over here eating Chinese and drinking on Saturday night?'

'Yes, he was. We said so,' Stark butted in. 'Stevo's all right. He's a good guy and he gave me that job. I know he's a bit ... hot-headed, but he's okay. He's just got a bit of a temper on him sometimes. He had nothing else to do so he came over and we had a few beers.'

Narey looked straight at the girl. 'And do you ever feel threatened by him, Faith?'

Instead of answering, Foster looked at Stark, but Narey wasn't having that. 'No, Faith, look at me, not Ritchie. It's me that's asking you the question. Do you ever feel threatened by Stevo?'

'Um, well ... yes. Sometimes. He's just a bit ... angry, I suppose. Nothing definite. Just kinda angry.'

'Is he ever violent? Again, don't look at Ritchie. Just tell me what you think.'

'No. Not that I've seen. Well, when he's had a drink he sometimes tries to start fights but I've never seen him actually have one.'

'Me neither,' added Stark, even though he hadn't been asked. 'And, like we said, he was here on Saturday till late.'

'Okay. Okay. Do you think Barclay ever saw Kirsty McAndrew again after he tattooed her?'

Stark shrugged, looking doubtful. 'If he did he never mentioned it. Look, I'm sorry but I don't know what else I can tell you. I can't believe that girl was murdered and she'd been inked in our shop. But it's just a coincidence. It's got to be.'

'Maybe, Mr Stark. Let's hope so. But you understand that we will have to continue with our enquiries and we may need to speak to some of your other customers.'

'Really? Well, okay. Whatever you need, I suppose.'

'Well, that's exactly it, Mr Stark. Whatever we need.'

Back on the cracked pavements of Tobago Street, Narey was relieved to see that her car had indeed survived intact. One of the mongrels from the wasteland opposite was sniffing around the rear tyres and thinking about marking its territory but retreated when Narey strode towards it. She glanced up at Stark's flat and saw a shadow step away from the window as she did so.

'What did you make of them?' she asked Toshney.

'Stark and his girlfriend?'

'No, Brad Pitt and Angelina Jolie. Of course Stark and his girlfriend.'

'Oh, right. Em, she seemed a bit nervous. Always looking to him to see what she should answer.'

'Yes, good spot.'

'And those clothes she was wearing. Weird, man. Never understood goths.'

'Right, stop while you're ahead, Toshney. Let's get back to the station. And, before we get in the car, no bloody whistling. This case is doing my head in as it is.'

Chapter 27

Wednesday mid-morning

Winter and Danny were led through a narrow corridor, other visitors before and behind them, until they entered a large open room that resembled a school dinner hall – although, if it had been used to serve up lunch to pupils, then it appeared they'd spread dessert on the walls, as all four were the shade of pink blancmange. The room was studded with tables painted in a neutral yellow with matching yellow chairs parked in front of them.

The handful of visitors shuffled left and right, seeking their allocated tables and quickly taking their seats. Winter and Neilson slid into the chairs behind Table 14, Danny looking tense and ready for a fight. Winter tried to catch his eye but the older man was having none of it. He stared at the door on the far wall and was seemingly willing it to open. He wasn't alone: almost every pair of eyes was on the door that linked to the prison halls. Each of them was waiting for someone from the segregation unit – prisoners separated from the herd, either for their safety or someone else's.

An officer advanced to a glass panel by the door and seemingly got the nod from someone on the other side, because he pressed buttons on the wall and the door slid open. Seconds later, the first of five identically dressed men walked warily through the door, his eyes lighting up as he saw the person there to visit him. Some looked more pleased than others at the sight of their visitors but all seemed at least grateful to be somewhere different. Last of all was the man they'd come to see. He emerged slowly, his eyes scanning the room until they alighted on them. He stood there looking at them curiously, impassively, seemingly enjoying the power of making them wait. Visitors on other tables were looking at him, ignoring their own loved ones and staring at the infamous serial killer.

The prison officer tried to take him by the elbow but the gesture was casually shrugged off as if by someone unused to physical interaction. Instead, he stood for a moment longer, then strolled to the table, gliding across the polished floor, making no more sound than a breeze whispering across a dark street. Without looking at them, he eased back the chair that faced them and slid his frame into it, barely brushing the floor as he settled it in front of the table again.

He kept his eyes down as he rearranged his clothing to suit him, pulling at the crease in his trousers and the folds of his jumper until he was satisfied that all was as he wanted it to be. Then he patted them down again, pulling here and tugging there. At length, he slowly lifted his head and took in the men opposite, knowing full well that he had every ounce of their attention.

The most immediately striking thing about Archibald Atto was how ordinary he looked. A nondescript face under a neat, sensible haircut in mildly greying brown, with regular features devoid of distinguishing marks. He was a man who wouldn't get a second glance or be remembered two minutes after being seen. You'd maybe take him for a retired accountant or librarian if you bothered to look at him at all.

He wore the same navy-blue jumper and light-brown trousers as every other prisoner who had come through the door, but he would have been anonymous even without the prison-issue clothing. Of medium build and average height, middle-aged, he was cloaked in the invisibility of his ordinariness. The only things you might have noticed as being uncommon about Atto were sleepy dark eyes that could have been stolen from a corpse, so little did they reveal about what was inside.

Yet the inside was the one place where Atto was markedly different. Winter often wondered whether the world would be a better place if people were turned inside out and everyone could be seen for what they were. If, instead of false smiles or hidden personalities, they wore words like 'Liar' or 'Thief' or 'Murderer', the lettering running through them like sticks of Blackpool rock. Most people are content to suffer their own failings as long as they're not on public display. Atto's were locked behind his Mr Average façade.

He looked slowly from Neilson to Winter, then back again, weighing them up but showing little interest in what he saw. He looked back at them blankly, clearly waiting for them to make the first move, armed with the patience of someone who had been locked up for fourteen years.

Danny looked back, but his face was far from as expressionless as Atto's: his had resentment and anger smeared all over it. He pushed himself back in his chair and crossed his arms, ready to play the pointless game and not give Atto the satisfaction of talking first. His resistance lasted as long as it took him to lean forward again.

'Mr Atto, I am—'

'Daniel Neilson. Detective Sergeant Daniel Neilson.' The response came within a heartbeat of Danny's beginning to speak, the voice level and calm. 'Did you think I wouldn't recognise the name? You were mentioned in dispatches, Sergeant Neilson. Or "Mr Neilson", as it must be by now. It was such a long time ago, but I still remember vividly reading about the so-called Red Silk case in the newspapers. You never did catch your man, did you, Mr Neilson?'

'Not yet.'

Atto laughed at Danny's growled response, a high-pitched chuckle that seemed out of place and came without an accompanying smile.

'Well done, Mr Neilson. Never give up, that's the spirit.'

'You better believe it.'

'Oh, I do.' The tone was now patronising. 'And Mr Winter here ...' The sound of his own name snapped Tony from a strange reverie and he realised he'd been looking at Atto's hands as they rested on the table, imagining the things that they'd done. 'Mr Winter here must be your ... nephew. You look a bit alike but you don't share a surname. Given the age difference, nephew would seem the most likely thing. Am I right?'

Neither Winter nor Danny said a word and Atto took that as his answer. 'I am, aren't I? So, tell me, Mr Winter, what is it that you do? I'd say that you haven't followed your uncle into the police. I don't get that feeling from you. Not quite.'

'I work for the SPSA. I'm—'

'Ah, the Scottish Police Services Association. I hear lots of good things about them, although not from many people locked up in here. Don't mind telling you that there's some of us grateful that the kind of fancy techniques you have now were not available forty years ago. But I rudely interrupted you and for that I apologise. Please continue.'

Winter hesitated, unsure of how much of himself he actually wanted to reveal to Atto. However, they did want him onside. 'I'm a police photographer.'

Atto's head tilted to the side in a show of mild confusion. 'I thought that kind of thing was undertaken by scenes-of-crime officers these days.'

'They generally are, but I'm a specialist.'

'Well, well. How impressive. A specialist. And so you fill your days photographing victims? Bodies? Is that your speciality, Anthony?'

The sound of his first name stung and Winter snapped back. 'I photograph lots of things.'

Atto nodded, his sleepy eyes beaming as if something had achieved the rare feat of making him happy. 'I see.'

'Are you aware of the two murders in Glasgow last weekend, Mr Atto?' Danny had tired of the conversation and wanted to talk business. Atto's eyes never left Winter, but he was clearly listening.

'I am aware of them, yes. We're only locked away, not living in a cave. Murder is something of a popular topic in here.'

'Something of a specialist subject of yours, too.'

'That's really funny, Mr Neilson. Maybe you would have been better suited to being a stand-up comedian than detective. At least you could have caught a few laughs.'

'If you are aware of the killings, then perhaps you'll be aware of the nature of them. Was there anything in them that seemed at all familiar to you?'

A hint of a smile played on Atto's lips. 'In what way "familiar", Mr Neilson?'

Danny leaned forward and lowered his voice, dropping both volume and pitch. 'In the sense that they were carried out by a sick psycho freak that gets his kicks from humiliating and torturing innocent women before murdering them in an attempt to prove that he's some kind of big man.'

Winter saw it, however briefly. The fleeting shadow that passed across Atto's eyes. It was like the eruption of a solar flare, except happening somewhere on the dark side of the moon. All three of them blinked and it was gone, replaced by the calm scorn that had preceded it.

'That's not really much in the way of detail for me to go on, Mr Neilson. Sadly, I can see why your police career didn't reap much in the way of success.'

Danny took a breath. 'You got real successful in your ventures, didn't you? That's why you've been locked up in here for fourteen years.'

'Ah, but the fun I had in the meantime. And all the fun I had that the likes of you never found out about.'

'Like I said, not yet. There are similarities between the two recent murders and your own ... pathetic little attempts at making a name for yourself. They were carried out by someone with a similar need to make up for his inadequacies by proving himself more powerful than a woman half his size.'

Atto's dark solar flares surged again and Danny knew he'd found a tender spot. 'But the person that did this didn't prove himself more powerful than anyone, did he? He just showed that he was weaker. A pathetic little prick with a tiny little prick. Someone craving attention to shore up their own lack of self-esteem.'

This time Atto's mouth tightened into a petulant snarl as his eyes burned into Danny's. His upper body rocked back and forth, his eyes slowly closing over, the grimace as tight as a heart attack. The prison officer hovering near them strode across, clearly agitated at the sight of Atto. Danny and Winter instinctively knew it was a sign of imminent rage that the guard would be familiar with. As he stood a foot away, seemingly unsure what to do, the rocking slowly came to a stop and Atto re-opened his eyes.

He shot a look at the officer, who hesitated before walking backwards to resume the spot and stance that he'd had. Atto re-tuned his gaze to Danny, the fires gradually subsiding.

'I can be an angry man, Mr Neilson. Very angry indeed. As to why that is, I'm not entirely sure. And it's certainly something I've considered over the years. I had a good childhood, brought up by loving parents. Loved neither too much nor too little by my mother, before you ask. I was neither beaten, sexually abused nor humiliated by my school peers and I've never perpetrated physical harm on a pet.'

'I want to talk to you about the two recent murders in Glas—'

Atto scowled at the interruption. 'Patience, Mr Neilson. If

you wish to talk about that, then you will indulge me in conversation. As I was about to say, I've experienced none of those clichés and yet I fit every accepted definition of a psychopath. I've come to the conclusion that there is something wrong with the executive functions of my brain. I think that I'm not quite right in the head.'

Atto smiled at his own joke, a sneer of a smile that tugged at only one side of his mouth. His eyes didn't join in.

'Not crazy, though. I've done a lot of reading about it. What they call my cognitive processes are well above average, as is my ability for perception and reasoning. But I don't do so well when it comes to empathy, and I have sometimes lacked in what other people regard as self-control. Are you aware of the paralimbic system? Mine is a bit ... wonky.'

Neither Neilson nor Winter spoke but merely looked back at Atto blankly, one seething with rage and the other with disquieted fascination. Atto took the silence of both as evidence of stupidity.

'The paralimbic system,' he intoned, 'is a behaviour circuit of the brain. It includes the amygdala and prefrontal cortex. Have you heard of a man named Brian Dugan? An American, convicted of the murder of three girls. Two of them were seven-year-olds and that's not right.

'After being scanned, Mr Dugan was found to have extremely low levels of density in his paralimbic system, something the neuroscientists said was responsible for his lack of empathy, guilt or remorse. It's led to a legal debate about whether the judicial system should accommodate the belief that behaviour such as his or mine is what they call "hot-wired".'

'Bollocks.'

'So succinctly put, Mr Neilson. Never mind that my argument was articulate, pertinent and derived from a position of understanding that few people could manage. Still, you sweep it away with a single word.'

Danny's grip on the table in front of him tightened, deliberately chaining himself to it in case he got up and went to the other side, aware that the nearby prison officer was eyeing up his whitened knuckles. 'It's bollocks because you're a murdering bastard who is dreaming up reasons you shouldn't rot in hell.'

Atto delivered another of his lopsided smiles.

'You know what, Mr Neilson? You bore me. You're the latest in a tedious line of little policemen demanding answers. Your nephew here on the other hand . . . he interests me. You don't need a scanner to see inside me, do you, Anthony? You see it.'

The statement threw Winter completely. He knew he must have been staring at Atto throughout the self-serving explanation about brain activity. He was morbidly fascinated by the monster who sat before him so blithely warbling on about the reasons that led him to rape and butcher. But he hadn't meant that interest to be so transparently obvious. He said nothing, determined not to give Atto something to work with.

'You know what it's like to see death, don't you, Anthony? You must have seen even more of it than I have.'

The tension between the three men crawled like ants over damp skin. Danny tried to take control of the conversation back from Atto.

'You know more about these recent killings than you are telling us, don't you?'

'Tell me, Anthony, what do you feel when you photograph a body?'

'What do you know, Atto? Who is doing this and why?'

'Do you ever tire of it? Ever lose that thrill that you had when you photographed your first corpse?'

'Atto, these murders have your signature all over them. You know it and I know it. What's your involvement with this? Or is it just another pathetic bit of playing with yourself because you can't actually do what you want to do?'

'I don't think I'd ever get over that first rush of excitement, Anthony. Every time would be like the first. Is it like that with you?'

Winter's gut churned and he wanted to smash his fist through Atto's face but refused to give him anything in the way of a reaction. The trouble was that Atto didn't seem to need him to react.

'You must have seen the look on the faces of the dead, the ones that were terrified. The ones that had just crossed over when they least expected it. It's quite something, isn't it?'

Winter stared back at Atto, desperately trying to keep him out of his head. Danny tried again.

'Do you know something about the killings in Glasgow? I'm asking you.'

Atto's head snapped to Danny. 'Yes, I do. I know rather a lot about them. Now shut up. I'm trying to have a rather more interesting conversation with your nephew.'

Danny's eyes widened briefly before darkening, his face scowling fiercely and his voice gruff and low. 'What do you know, and how? Atto, if you want another fifteen minutes of fame then you will need to talk to us.'

'I don't *need* to do anything. The *need* is yours. The power is mine. And I choose to speak to Anthony here. Tell me, why do you think men kill, Anthony?'

Winter still hadn't spoken but felt exhausted by the conversation that he was and wasn't part of. He just stared back at Atto, trying to keep his face blank but fearing he was failing. Atto didn't need an answer: he came back at him as if he'd received one anyway.

'Come on, now, indulge me. You and PC Plod here are keen to pick bare the bones of my knowledge and yet you're not prepared to offer me even a conversation in return? That seems a bit rude, don't you think?'

Winter and Danny looked at each other, swapping resigned shrugs. A pact with the Devil was something that Winter was very reluctant to sign up to, but the look on Danny's face told him he had little choice.

'Okay . . .' he began slowly and hesitantly. 'I guess men kill for lots of reasons. For money, for survival, for revenge.'

'No,' Atto sighed, a look of disappointment on his face. 'That's why men *have* to kill. I'm talking about why men *want* to kill. Like me.'

Winter looked back at him for an age, disturbed that he was to have a seemingly logical conversation with a man like Atto. A beast who revelled in killing innocent women. His own messed-up fascination with death did not extend to an interest in the motivations of a murderer. Or did it?

'Men who want to kill . . .' – Winter saw Atto hanging on his reply – 'they clearly have something wrong with them. It is unnatural to want to take someone else's life for no reason.'

'It might not be natural for you, Anthony, but it is extremely natural for me.'

Danny's face contorted but he took another grip on the table and stayed on his side of it, making no effort to disguise his contempt.

'It is unnatural,' Winter continued, 'for the vast majority of people. It's something they couldn't even contemplate. So I suppose the question is whether people like you are born with something wrong that makes them act in that way or whether something happens that fashions them into a killer.'

'Okay – nature or nurture. That, as you say, is the key debate. In fact it's much more relevant than you might think. But that's just going for the obvious. I'd hoped for better from you, Anthony. I could have received that sort of superficial response from anyone.'

Winter's desire to punch Atto in the face burned again, as he imagined the satisfying smack of flesh and bone on the patronising, sneering, smug features opposite him. Maybe the prison officer would be so pleased to see him do it that he'd conveniently look the other way. Then again, maybe he wouldn't. Somewhere deep inside himself, he sighed.

'Well, if we assume for a moment that it is something you are born with, then the question would be whether that's genetic, like an inherited trait or characteristic. Or whether it's like you were talking about, a deformity in your brain. Something . . . biochemical. That you're wired up wrong. I can see how that would explain it.'

Atto nodded thoughtfully, saying nothing. Winter went on.

'But, then again, perhaps more people than we know of are born with this – what did you call it? – low-density brain area in the para-whatever. But maybe these people don't ever kill anyone. Maybe it takes something else to trigger it, to turn people into—'

'Cowardly murdering bastards.' Danny finished the sentence for him.

'Yeah, that. Maybe it's nature *and* nurture,' Winter continued. 'Maybe you always had it in you and something happened to bring it out. What was it?'

Atto gave another of his ill-fitting, high-pitched chuckles. 'Good try, Anthony. But we aren't talking about me: we are talking about people *like* me. So … if such people are born the way they are, with some brain deformity, as you put it, how should that reflect the way that they are sentenced and treated?'

Danny could restrain himself no longer and leaned forward, his jaw jutting right at the prisoner.

'How would it affect sentencing? Atto, I would chop your balls off with a pair of rusty knitting needles and then stuff them down your throat.'

Atto smiled disdainfully. 'It's amazing, Mr Neilson. Civilisation has advanced through five thousand years and yet the caveman still walks among us. Darwin would look at you and shake his head in disappointment. Evolution's passed you by.'

'Civilised? You think there's something civilised about the things you've done? Because you are badly mistaken if you do. You are the lowest of the low, the scum of the earth, and, if there *is* a Hell, then you'll surely burn in it. Something wrong with your brain? No shit.'

The prison officer near them was getting agitated again,

glancing at his watch and obviously hoping that visiting time was nearly over. 'Quieten it down there. I won't tell you twice.'

Atto looked at Danny for a while, condescension writ large, then switched his gaze back to Winter.

'So, Anthony, what would be your approach to sentencing and rehabilitation of such killers if it's proved that something like an irregularity of the paralimbic system is the root of psychopathic behaviour? If someone like me was a natural-born killer?'

Winter weighed it up for a while, staring into Atto's dull, soulless eyes and wondering what they'd seen. Scenes far worse than anything he had photographed, he was sure of that.

'If someone was born with that kind of defect . . . you'd have to take it into account. Rehabilitation wouldn't be an option, though, not if you were born that way. And as for sentencing . . .' He paused and looked deeper into the black pools of Atto's eyes. 'I think I'd go for Danny's suggestion: rusty knitting needles.'

Atto's face tightened and Winter saw the fury flame in his pupils before his eyes slowly closed over and he began to rock back and forth again, gradually increasing in speed and intensity. He was still rocking when a bell abruptly shrieked through the room, signalling the end of the visiting session.

Prisoners at the other tables got to their feet, saying their goodbyes, but Atto remained rocking until the officer walked over and put his hand on his shoulder. Atto shrugged it off and sat for a few moments before he deigned to stand up, his newly opened eyes never leaving Winter. He eventually stood and was pushing the chair neatly back into the place that it had been in when he arrived, when Winter broke the silence.

'Mr Atto, one last question. Why is the debate about nature or nurture more relevant than I might think?'

Atto stared back before giving a final lopsided smile and turned away.

Winter and Neilson were at the back of the small crowd of visitors making their way down the narrow corridor that linked the visiting room with the holding room. They all trudged slowly behind the officer at the front leading them back towards fresh air and open space.

Danny was staring at his feet while shaking his head, obviously still fuelled by anger. Winter saw his hands balled into fists and knew that the prospect of punching a hole in the corridor wall appealed to him.

'Good call, though, son,' he finally said as they emerged into the next room.

'What was?'

'Going for the rusty knitting needles. Good call, Anthony.'

'Danny?'

'What?'

'Do me a favour and never call me Anthony again.'

Chapter 28

Wednesday afternoon

Narey's attempts to get some kind of line on the mysterious perv known as Mr Grey were proving less than successful. All they had to go on was a ropey description of an early forties male with grey hair and dark eyebrows. Needless to say, he hadn't been back to Scissor Sisters since the murder of Hannah Healey.

Almost the only productive part of the investigation, although not in a good way, was Toshney's seemingly endless series of awful puns. Each was delivered with the adolescent hope that it might be the one greeted with laughter rather than scorn. It never was.

New *strands* of the investigation. Mr Grey being on the *fringe* of the case. Mr Grey being *hair* today and gone tomorrow. Wondering what *lengths* they might go to to find him. The *cutting* edge of policing. On and bloody on. If Addison didn't get Toshney out of her hair soon ... Oh, bloody hell.

She spoke to her contact in London Road but no one there had heard of Grey. It was the same in divisions all over the city.

Maybe not surprising if he'd never actually committed, or been caught for, anything. Leering and the possibility of a bit of undercover fiddling were offences that didn't generally get as far as the police.

Along with Rebecca Maxwell, she visited the city-centre salon where Kirsty McAndrew had her hair cut, but none of the staff there had any tales of dodgy customers, never mind anyone who fitted the description of the man who called himself Ronnie Dance.

She pulled records on sexual harassment, indecent exposure, voyeurism, indecent communication, whatever she could think of. Nothing. Was she wasting her time? There wasn't that much reason to like the guy for the killing, given what he was said to have done in the salon, but the fact that he'd lied about his identity changed things big time. Addison was keen for her to push it, his nose twitching as much as hers at the fact that the perv felt the need to create a false name and address.

In the end she had no option but to fall back on the tried and tested. Talk to people. She got as many officers as she could into hairdressing salons, taking Scissor Sisters as a starting point and working out in a circle from there. Although she hated herself for it, almost to the point of hearing Addison's chauvinistic chuckling as she did so, she got female cops to visit the shops wherever possible. She needed gossip, she needed girl-talk. Jesus, she needed whatever she could get.

If Addison said it was woman's work he'd run the risk of a kick in the balls.

The word back from her hairdresser scouting patrols came in slowly, but then, as Toshney was quick to remind her, there were no shortcuts in this kind of case. Just about the only kind of business that Glasgow had more of than hairdressers was pubs.

She let it do its thing in the background, confident there was nothing else she could do to rush it. And it wasn't as if she didn't have enough to be getting on with.

The first tickle came after Rebecca Maxwell visited a salon on the Gallowgate, no more than a quarter-mile from where Kirsty McAndrew lived. She came into the operations room, dropping her coat and bag into a chair and making her way towards Narey.

'I might have something on your Mr Grey, Sarge.'

Narey looked up, noticing something different about Maxwell's own fiery red tresses. 'Yeah, you might have had a haircut on his account by the look of it.'

Maxwell grinned and ran her hand through her hair. 'Seemed the best way to get the conversation started. Anyway, it was only thirty quid and I reckon expenses can stand that.'

'If you've got something out of it, then maybe.'

'Well, it's something. I'm just not sure how far it will take us. The girl who did my hair said that another member of staff, a Lorraine Victors, had been complaining about some guy who kept eyeing her up. Seems she's a pretty girl and it's not that unusual with male customers but this guy just struck her as creepy. Thought he might be touching himself under the robe but could never be sure.'

'And?'

'And the description given was about six foot, early forties, dark eyebrows, grey hair.'

'That sounds like a full house if we were playing Mr Grey bingo. Did he give a name?'

'Yes. Scott Duke.'

'Scott Duke? Sounds bollocks. You checked it out?'

'Just about to.'

'Go do it. Good work. And nice haircut, by the way.'

Later, one of the WPCs, Imelda Couper, got a similar response from a girl named Tracey in a salon on Union Street. She said that one of her regular customers, a guy calling himself Mike Majors, was a bit of a weirdo. Always asking for her, always staring and some uncomfortable fidgeting going on down below while he got his haircut. The description was bang on.

Before long, they also had a Jason Prince visiting a hairdresser's on Howard Street and a Ryan Race, who was a regular at a salon on Hope Street. In each case he got his hair cut by arguably the prettiest girl in the place, never let anyone else do it, and was considered a sleazeball by all and sundry. In each case, the hairdresser was alive and accounted for.

'What the hell have we got here?' exclaimed Narey. 'A serial killer or a—'

'A serial curler?' offered Toshney.

'Oh, shut up, Fraser.' Narey rubbed at her eyes and pulled a hand through her long brown hair, idly trying to remember when she last had it cut. 'I want this guy in Stewart Street by this time tomorrow. Whoever he is, whatever his game is. Just find him and drag him in here.'

'Bring me the head of Mr Grey,' sniggered Toshney, grabbing the top of his own hair and holding it up as if he were carrying it. Narey slapped Toshney's hand away, causing him to yelp.

'Ow. That's—'

She raised her eyebrows, inviting him to finish. He changed his mind.

'Um, no. It isn't.'

Narey's exasperation was close to breaking point. 'Good. Now that's settled, go bring him in here.'

Chapter 29

Wednesday evening

'I swear if that prison officer hadn't been there, I'd have happily wrung his neck with my bare hands.'

'Not sure that would have done us much good in getting him to talk about the two new killings, Danny.'

'No, I don't suppose it would, son, but it would have done me a hell of a lot of good. That smug look on his face ... I just wanted to smash it, wipe it off his gub with a single punch. Just sitting there, thinking about what he did to all those girls. Thinking about the parents who don't know what happened to their daughters, don't know where they're buried. I wanted to kill him. God forgive me but I actually wanted to kill him.'

Winter looked at his uncle, the man he'd always respected more than anyone else in his life, his own parents having both died when he was too young to have properly known them, and saw something he'd never seen before. Danny had always been big and strong, rough and wise, but Winter had always thought of him as basically a gentle soul. Sure, he'd seen him put people in their place and on their backside but this was different. Danny meant what he said. Given the chance, he would have ended Archibald Atto's life.

They were back in Winter's flat in Berkeley Street, a beer each already drunk and another in front of them. Both men knew it was going to take more than one to wash away the taste of Blackridge Prison and the man they'd gone to see.

'He revels in it. That's what gets to me as much as what he's done. He loves pulling our chains and making us dance through bloody hoops to get anything out of him. He enjoyed what he did and enjoys rubbing our noses in it. All that bollocks about low brain density and paralimbic whatever it was. He's a cold-blooded killer and I don't care whether it's his brain, his mother, his primary-school teacher or whether he was bitten by a rabid dog. He did it and he pays the price. The reason doesn't make any difference to me.'

'I get that, Dan, but what if it makes a difference to why the two girls were murdered? What if it can help us work out the connection, if there *is* a connection, between Atto and what happened last weekend?'

'Oh, there is a connection. He said so. And I know he might have been saying it to keep our attention or just to wind us up, but I don't think so. He said he knows a lot about these new killings. A lot.'

Winter saw Danny's fist close over again, the lines on the back of his hand disappearing as his anger emerged anew. 'Okay, what about the nature-or-nurture stuff he was talking about. He said that was "more relevant" than I might think. What do you reckon that was all about?'

Danny slugged on his beer, a serious swig that accounted for nearly half the bottle. 'I don't know, son. Like I said, I don't care about the psychobabble of why he's the crazy murdering bastard that he is. That might have been just one of his games. Or maybe he was hinting at something. But I don't see how his parents or his upbringing could be relevant to what's going on now. We need to go back and see him again, though. We can't leave it at that.'

Winter mulled over the beer and the thought. Something nagging away at him like a bad tooth.

'He was playing with us. No doubt about that. But I also think he was giving us something.'

Danny laughed grimly, wiping at his mouth. 'Giving *you* something more like. He wouldn't have pissed on me if I was on fire, but he liked you. Not that I would think that was a good thing if I was you.'

'No, I don't think it's a good thing. All that shit about me seeing death and being able to understand him. Made me want to puke. I tell you, Dan, it made me feel like I need a shower after talking to that guy.'

'Yeah? Well you might just have to get used to it because I need to know what it is that he knows, and, if him having some kind of freaky connection with you is what makes it happen, then so be it.'

'Jesus Christ, Danny. The guy is a monster. A proper fucking monster. I don't know. Even today, he was trying to mess with my head and I don't know if I want to let him in there.'

'Scared of what he might find?'

'Piss off.'

Danny's eyes closed over and his hands covered his face. 'Sorry, son. Honestly, Tony, I didn't mean ... Jesus. Look, I was just ...'

'Forget it. The guy's messing with your head, too, Uncle Dan. Look, if it means that much to you – and I know it does – then I'll talk to him again. But I reserve the right to tell him where to go. Okay?'

'Okay.'

'Okay. Now, like I was saying, I think he was giving us something when he started on that nature-and-nurture stuff. It was like some kind of test. The clue was there if we were smart enough to work it out. But I don't think it has to be what you were saying about his parents or—'

Before Winter could finish, he was interrupted by a sudden and violent banging on the front door. Four or five loud thumps resonated through to the living room where they sat. The two men looked at each other.

He got to his feet, noticing that Danny had instinctively done the same, readying himself for any possible confrontation. Winter waved him back into his seat but Danny shook his head and stood his ground.

The banging continued as Winter got to the front door. 'Who is it?'

'Police! Open up.'

The voice ... Winter thought and moved in one action, his hand turning the snib and releasing the door catch. As soon as it was unlocked, the door began to swing towards him, the speed of it forcing him to take a step back. Derek Addison strode through the gap, fury on his face and the flat of his hand pushing straight at Winter's chest and driving him backwards. Behind him was Narey, face set hard and as angry as Addison.

She threw the door closed behind her as Addison continued to push Winter back, nearly forcing him off his feet as he shoved him back into the living room. Danny had emerged from the room and looked ready to step in and go for Addison, but a near scream from Narey stopped him in his tracks as he wound back an arm.

'Don't even think about it, Danny. Things are bad enough as they are.'

Addison disagreed, though, his features curling into a confrontational snarl at Danny as he pushed Winter back and back until he finally made him tumble into a leather armchair. 'No, go on, do it. After the shitty day I've had it would be the perfect ending if you take a swing and I get to belt you one and then arrest you.'

Danny's arm did swing back but he didn't get the chance to throw a punch as Narey strode between the two men, shoving a hand against the chest of each and forcing her way through till she stood over Winter, who sat in the chair with a look of bewilderment on his face.

He looked up and saw her face tighten, her mouth draw up and in as she sucked on her teeth, a sure sign of anger. Her eyes burned furiously at him, a look he was used to – but this was a new level of intensity. She looked at him until her lips curled back and she shook her head in an obvious fit of disgust, reaching into her coat pocket and producing a set of handcuffs.

'Anthony Winter, I'm arresting you on suspicion of perverting the course of justice and interfering with a police investigation. You don't have to say anything but anything you do say will be noted and may be used as evidence. Do you understand?'

Chapter 30

Wednesday night

She'd cuffed him. She'd actually cuffed him. It had all happened in such a whirl that Winter wasn't sure just what the hell was going on, but he'd looked down at his wrists bound in two circles of steel and black moulded plastic. There was something that looked like tears of frustration forming in the corners of her eyes, and that was never a good sign. From behind her, a raging Addison shouted, 'What the fuck have you two muppets been up to?'

Danny's voice had roared back. 'This is ridiculous. Look, I don't know what you think's happened but you can't just—'

'Don't you start, Danny,' Narey had spun and bawled at him. 'Don't you dare start. He's just an idiot but you should know better!'

She'd snapped her head back at Winter, daring him to argue, daring him to say anything that would give away their former relationship to Addison. He'd never seen her look at him the way she was doing right now.

'What's this all about?'

'Good question, wee man.' Addison's head had appeared over Narey's shoulder, his expression no less livid than hers. 'A very good question. And it's just what I was about to ask you.'

He'd bent down so that he was eyeball to eyeball with Winter, his face aggressively up against his friend's. 'And you better be clear that, when I ask you that question, I want an honest answer or – pal or no pal – I'm going to rip your head off and stick it up your arse. You've been taking me for a mug, Tony. All those questions about the case? I'm not very happy with you. You understand me, wee man?'

Winter hadn't exactly been in a position to argue, so had simply nodded. Addison had nodded back, slowly.

'So what have you two idiots got to say for yourselves?'

Winter and Danny had looked at each other, unspoken messages flying from one to the other. The silent consensus had been to say little or nothing. It had left Addison no choice – they could see that now – but it had seemed like a good idea at the time.

It didn't seem quite so clever now. Winter and Danny were in separate interview rooms in Stewart Street and had already been thrown into separate cells, staring at four walls and wondering what the hell was going on.

Rachel had sat in the front seat of the patrol car that had driven Winter to Cowcaddens, he slung in the back, she staring silently straight ahead, not once catching his eye in the rear-view mirror.

The look on the booking sergeant's face had been priceless. Winter got the distinct feeling that all the photographs he'd snatched of cops on duty over the years was fuel to the fire of the sergeant's pen. He was booked in with some enthusiasm and left to stew.

Winter's sullen silence when he was dragged into the interview room was driven by not knowing what Danny was saying when he was sitting before Narey and Addison. His loyalty to his uncle and his determination not to let him down was taking precedence over his ties to the two cops who were interrogating him.

Maybe that was why, after unsuccessful attempts at interviewing them separately, Winter and Danny found themselves sitting at the same side of a wooden table, Addison and Narey on the other, two uniforms standing by the door.

'I think you must have got your wires crossed, son,' Danny told Addison sternly. 'In my day we called this unlawful arrest.'

Addison laughed bitterly. 'In your day? In your day cops were allowed to give kids a cuff round the ear and smoke in their panda cars. Must have been great. But times have moved on. And the only thing I've got crossed is my fingers that you two aren't as big a pair of fuck-ups as you seem to be.'

'Piss off.'

Addison's face went within an inch of Danny's. 'Wrong answer, old man. I want to know what you two have been up to, and I'm not taking any of your shit in the meantime.'

'Don't know what you're talking about.'

'Do it the hard way, right? Okay, fair enough. You're old and probably a wee bit muddled, so you might think that's a good idea, but young Tony here knows making me even more pissed off than I currently am isn't the best plan I've ever heard. Don't you, Tony?'

Winter looked from his pal to his uncle to his ex-girlfriend and knew he couldn't win. He opted to do what he usually did when he was in a hole: he kept digging. 'I don't know what you're talking about.'

'Let's just charge them,' Narey scowled.

'A good idea, DS Narey, but I'm nothing if not famously fair. Right, time for a very quick story. Then I want answers.'

Danny and Winter sighed, the inevitability of what was coming next settling on them.

'First of all, I have a conversation with DS Andy Teven. He tells me that he had some ex-copper come into the station wanting to talk about the cemetery killings. Says the old boy was up to high doh and said the murders were linked to the Red Silk killings of the seventies. That we should be looking at Archibald Atto. Andy reckoned the old boy had been at the cooking sherry a wee bit early in the day. Sounded like a crank to me, too, but I asked for the ex-cop's name. Danny Neilson, he says. Well, well, says me. Not only a well-respected former polisman but the uncle of one Anthony Winter of this parish. Interesting, I thought. Particularly interesting that said Anthony Winter, despite being an acquaintance of mine, never thought to mention it. With me so far?'

The two men said nothing but took a close interest in their shoes.

'So I spoke to DS Narey here. She also thought it a bit odd that Tony hadn't said anything. She and Tony are, I believe, on good speaking terms and yet he hadn't mentioned it to her either. So, unlikely as it seemed, what with Archibald Atto having been locked up in prison for the past fourteen years, we thought we'd check it out. Sure enough, he was safely tucked up in his cell. But we also asked if he had had any visitors recently. Funnily enough, he had two just today. Want to guess who?'

Winter and Danny swapped weary glances but didn't speak.

'I asked if you wanted to guess,' Addison roared. 'And you better make sure it's a good guess because you only get three lives each.'

'And you're about to use at least one of them up,' Narey seethed beside him.

'Jesus, what do you want us to say, Addy? You obviously know we were there.'

'What do I want you to say? Let me think. Maybe what will win the three-thirty at Haydock or why women talk so much without actually saying anything. Or hang on, I know: maybe you could fucking tell me why you were visiting a serial killer who you seem to think is involved with an active murder case?'

'Because he's involved in your bloody murder case!'

Danny's blurted reply brought a smile to Addison's face and caused Narey's grimace to deepen.

'Okay, so now we're getting somewhere. Not anywhere sane but at least it's a start. Right, Danny, so tell me why you think he's involved. And how the bloody hell he can be.'

Danny sighed and rubbed at his eyes, a rueful frown stealing its way onto his face. He shook his head and sank into his chair.

'I've already been through this with your DS Teven. I told him chapter and verse and he wasn't prepared to listen.'

'Obviously he did listen and obviously he told me. And I'm listening now. But it better be good.'

'No, it isn't good, son. If I'm right, it's all bad. These killings stink of the Klass case. Stink to high heaven of it. Jesus Christ, do your computers not tell you that? The way the victims were laid out, the positions they were in? Pure Atto.'

Addison turned to look at Winter. 'Aye? And how exactly do you know the positions they were laid out in? If it involves crime-scene photographs, then someone is in deep shit.'

'Never mind that,' Danny came back at him. 'The point is they are so similar. The positions of subservience, begging, praying. The killer making out he is all-powerful and taking the piss out of the victim and the cops. The age of the victims. The time-frame between killings, the city-centre locations. It's either Atto or someone copying him. It's too pat to be a coincidence.'

Addison stared at Danny, thoughtfully though, rather than with the angry bemusement of earlier. He turned to Narey and the pair shrugged at each other, too smart to dismiss what the old cop said but too smart to think it could be true.

'Okay, copycat I can just about buy,' he said finally. 'That's worth looking at. But Atto being involved? That's just nuts.'

Danny's eyebrows rose furiously. 'Son, I've already had your DS Teven dismiss me as crazy. I'm not keen on it happening twice.'

'Right, haud your horses. It was a turn of phrase. I know you're not nuts. But this whole situation is. How the ...? How can Atto be involved with this?'

'Because he's devious. Because he is highly intelligent and twisted beyond belief. Because he's always had a way of manipulating people to do things that he wants. DI Addison, I don't know how he's involved. But I'm sure he is.'

'Jesus, I can't believe this.' Narey's patience had snapped. 'Danny, the guy's been locked up for fourteen years. Seriously?'

'Rach, I know how hard it is to believe but trust me: this guy is capable of just about anything. You can rule nothing out where he's concerned.'

Addison's brows furrowed slightly and Winter recognised a familiar mischievous look in his eyes, a look that usually spelled trouble for someone.

'*Rach*? So how well do you two know each other?'

Narey didn't blink. 'We've met.'

'Hmm. Cosy. Okay, here's how it is, Danny – and dickhead. We will look into Atto and any link to this case. But you two idiots have way overstepped the mark. I have to decide whether you'll face charges. In the meantime, you're going back in those cells. But if I do decide you will be let out then you will not go anywhere near Atto again. Understood?'

Winter looked to Danny but his uncle looked straight back at Addison, deadpan and determined. 'I can't promise that, DI Addison. I'm sorry but I can't. This means too much to me.'

Addison returned the look. 'In that case I can't promise I won't arrest you again and put you away.'

'Fair enough.'

'No, it bloody isn't,' Narey said, standing, exasperated. 'This is stupid. Two women have been murdered and we've not got time either to go on wild-goose chases or to run after these two idiots. We need to get this nipped in the bud here and now. Just charge them.'

'Rachel, Atto is involved in this, believe me.' Danny had both hands flat on the table, ready to push himself to his feet. 'He told us as much when we spoke to him. Don't dismiss this because it seems unlikely. You're better than that.'

'What did he say, Danny? What do you mean he told you as much?'

'He said he knew a lot about what had happened. I asked him what he knew about the cemetery killings and he said he knew a lot. And it wasn't just what he said: it was the way he said it.'

Addison dropped his head into his hands while Narey wheeled away, shaking hers, unable to stand in one place and take in what she was hearing. Addison looked up, a pained expression writ large. 'The way he said it? Jesus, Danny. How do you know he wasn't just winding you up? The guy's famous for pissing people about with his stories.'

'I heard him, son. He knows about these killings. He knows way more than he's telling.'

'Tony?'

Winter nodded. 'I agree. I didn't want to be any part of this and I didn't want it to be true. But Danny's right. The way Atto said what he did? I'd say he meant it. I know how crazy it sounds and I'm not telling you I've got the first idea of how he's involved, but I'd say he is.'

'Enough,' Addison shouted, waving his arms at the two uniformed cops. 'I've had enough. Take them back to the cells. If only you two eejits had the brains to make life easier for yourselves.'

Winter and Danny trooped out, the interview room door closing behind them. Addison pinched the top of his nose, his eyes screwed shut. 'Christ, if this is even half ... This is all I need. Rachel, do you have any idea where the circus is these days, because I'm going to run off and join one. These two clowns should probably do the same. Archibald Atto? My arse. It just can't be.'

The tirade that was just building up a head of steam was abruptly curtailed by Addison's phone ringing in his pocket. He pulled it out irritably and stared at the screen, clearly not knowing who was calling.

'Yeah?'

Whoever was on the other end of the phone, their voice made Addison's face change. 'Oh, hi ... Miss, um ... Sam. Hi.'

Narey could hear the soft lilt of a female voice escaping from Addison's mobile and watched his face, as he was obviously self-conscious about speaking in front of her.

'I'm very well, thank you. And you? Good, um ... You do? Well that's ... What do you mean? I don't see how it can't ... What? You're fucking joking me. You seriously have to be fucking joking me. No ... sorry ... I know you're not ... and there's no doubt ... Fuck me gently. No ... I mean ... I'll call into the lab. Yes, yes, bye.'

Addison thrust his phone back into his pocket, his face perplexed and clearly none too happy. His mouth was tight and skewed to one side. He looked at Narey looking at him and shook his head despairingly.

'That was Sam Guthrie at the lab. The DNA results from the trace evidence that Baxter's people picked up at the side of the church have come back in. She wanted to give me a heads-up on this before it got to Kelbie and Shirley. They've got a match.'

Narey's features crossed into some bewilderment of her own. 'Great ... Isn't it?'

Addison's head tilted to one side and his mouth turned upside down. 'Maybe not so great. The DNA they found was a match to Archibald Atto.'

Chapter 31

1972

It sounds awful, but when you go into the station on a Sunday morning, probably nursing a head from the night before, the last thing you need to be told is that some wee lassie has been murdered. Actually, the last thing you need is to be told that you're the one that's been landed with investigating it.

Look, it's human nature. Maybe not exactly at its best but it's the way it is. You've already got enough on your plate, maybe juggling fifty cases, and there's a good chance there's already a murder or two among them. It's Glasgow, those are the odds. Then the CID clerk welcomes you through the door and hands you another one.

You might huff, probably sigh, complain about the lazy sods on the night shift or moan about why some other bugger couldn't do it. Anything, everything, except thinking what you should think. A wee lassie's been murdered.

You become hardened to bad news in the morning so that even such a terrible thing becomes another number, a form 3:24:1 to be filled in and handed over. A crime that will become a 3:24:2 if it's cleared. One piece of paper that gets turned into another.

The CID clerk tells you that the wee lassie has been raped and strangled. God help you but the first thing you think isn't that it's the end of the world. Of course, inside, you know that it's the end of someone's world and those who knew her. But, outside, those pieces of paper have to keep getting filled in.

You tell yourself that wee lassies get killed in big cities and you can't save the world by treating each one as if she's your daughter or sister. That can only lead to the nuthouse or the bottom of a bottle. You give them your best. Everything else you keep for the people at home. Those are the rules for survival.

And sometimes you break them.

Sometimes they sneak past your defences, coming to whisper to you in the night. Not ghosts as such but just as capable of haunting you. They get under your skin, smiling up at you from collect photographs, calling out to you in the voice of their mother or sister, demanding justice. Demanding that you deliver it.

That's how it was with him and Brenda MacFarlane. Eventually.

Looking back, of course, there was guilt at the indifference he felt when George Scott, the CID clerk, first handed her over to him. The old boy stood at the uniform bar and called him over with a conspiratorial wave, as if he were doing him a favour. And he probably thought he was. In the morning, the clerk was armed with every crime that's happened on the night shift – maybe thirty or forty in a city-centre station like Cranstonhill – and, if he liked you, he might just give you the good stuff to work on. If he didn't like you or you'd pissed him off, you'd get the crappy jobs that no one wanted. This was George giving him a good one but for him it was just yet another case and another job to do.

It changed. Not only did Brenda become a real person with a sister and parents and friends whom he had to talk to, but before long she wasn't alone. She was joined by Isobel Jardine, then Mary Gillespie. He'd been picked up by a tornado and placed at its eye, Brenda, Isobel, Mary and half of City of Glasgow police revolving around him till his head spun.

No one on the force ever called it the Red Silk murders. It would be the Springburn murder for victim one or the Govanhill Park murder for victim two. Not until the third killing, the London Road murder, when the Klass connection had been made and the major-incident room set up, might they collectively be known as the Klass murders. Even then, that was informal. The Red Silk tag was a figment of the press's imagination and for their use only.

It wasn't just another case – or just another three – but in many ways it had to be tackled as if it were. Same procedures, solid police work, lots of boot leather worn out, lots of doors knocked on, lots of familiar faces spoken to. Notebooks filled with barely legible scribbles that had to be transcribed quickly or their sense was lost for ever. Pieces of paper for everything.

They would work for all they got and hope to force that little something extra. A guilty conscience, an informer or a set of fingerprints. Fingerprints were the holy grail of detection. Stick-on certainties for conviction and brilliant, except for the bloody mess you had to make to get the things done. If he had a pound for every time he covered his hands in black bloody ink he'd have been able to afford a fortnight in Spain.

He was regularly banging on to his inspector about how they should get some training in how to do this properly, but he'd have been as well shouting at the moon. Jock Binnie was old-school and training was something you did round football parks in the dead of winter. When he'd suggested to Binnie that they get specialists to do that sort of thing for them he was told that soft modern coppers didn't know they were born.

So it was, quite literally, a case of getting your hands dirty and hoping for the best. Flicking through endless A4 sheets of prints, giant blow-ups of offending loops, whorls and arches, seeking a match. And, if you were lucky, you might even have forms that had been filled in properly.

Each page of prints had a descriptive form filled in by the arresting officers, but sometimes the guys got bored on long night shifts and filling in forms got old pretty quickly. So, after a while, instead of being asked 'eyes' and putting blue, brown or whatever, they'd put 'two'. He'd even seen forms where, when asked if suspects had any distinguishing peculiarities, some jokers had written 'Roman Catholic'.

God knows, they'd all either done that sort of thing or been tempted to, but it wasn't what you wanted to read when you actually needed proper information and some other idiot had done it.

Still, the fact that he had an absence of usable fingerprints made it someone else's problem for now. He had the streets, the tenements, the nights in Klass and an array of contacts to speak to. All the open doors and the closed ones. All the avenues that might be lubricated with the help of a little alcohol.

It was a fact that the best way to crack a case was often to crack open a bottle. Pub owners were usually glad to see a familiar face from CID at closing time, as it would be guaranteed to get any lingering bampots on their way without too much fuss. Once the doors were closed, a bottle would be opened and all sorts of secrets and interesting gossip would tumble out. Few people heard more about what was really going on than the boss man behind the bar.

The same trick worked for contacts, informants, call them what you will. Whisky was much more likely to get them talking than a set of thumbscrews. He remembered Jock Binnie telling him that the heat of the sun would take the coat off a man's back more quickly than the strongest wind. So pour them a large dram, sit back and listen. Although, wouldn't you know it, all that was changing too.

A year earlier, they'd got a new chief constable, David McNee, and he'd come down on them like a ton of bricks. Nae bevvying. It was as if he'd told them they had to stop arresting crooks, the fuss that was made.

McNee had come up through the ranks from being a beat bobby, so he knew just how much booze the guys were shifting before, during and after their shifts. Legendary amounts, so it was, and everyone could tell you a tale about their mate being pissed on duty. Listen, they were good guys doing hard jobs in a city where people liked a drink, so it was hardly surprising that they did the same; but McNee knew it had to stop.

He put the word round, backed it up with action, and within no time everyone knew the score and everyone knew the rhyme. Only drink tea or you're in front of McNee.

It didn't stop them all. For some, it was so ingrained that they'd take their chances. But it was the beginning of the end. The irony for him, of course, was that he was boozing officially, supping lagers and whisky in Klass on Davie McNee's tab.

Irony wasn't exactly in short supply, though, so he didn't fuss too much. The rules said that treating the victim as if she were one of your own would lead to the bottom of the bottle, but that was probably okay, since the boss had knocked drinking on the head yet was actively encouraging you to do it on duty. There was no point in trying to work out the sense of that one.

He'd learned a different truth. Wee lassies might always get killed in big cities, but only if people like him didn't stop it from happening in the first place. Catching the bastards who did it was all very well, but stopping it from happening – that was the thing. It was too late for Brenda, Isobel and Mary, but not for the next one. And if he got his fingers burned by caring too much then so be it.

Chapter 32

Thursday morning

The swivel chair behind the desk in Alex Shirley's office was empty, almost ominously so, but in front of it three seats were already filled. Addison, Kelbie and Winter sat silently in mutual resentment. None of them and all of them wanted to be there.

All three seemed to find a disproportionate fascination with the bare walls of the office, it being preferable to looking at each other. Only Addison, being Addison, allowed his gaze to drift occasionally to the family photograph that sat on the superintendent's desk. It wasn't the first time he'd admired the portrait of Shirley's wife and 20-something-old daughter, and probably wouldn't be the last.

When the door behind him flew open and just as quickly slammed shut again, he wrenched his eyes from the photo and joined the other two in studying the paintwork. He sensed rather than saw Shirley storm past them and drop forcefully into the chair opposite. Only then did all three pairs of eyes switch dutifully to the man behind the desk. It took one look to see that Shirley was raging.

He stared fiercely, taking them in in one all-encompassing glare that managed to be an accusation and a string of questions. Each of them sat and wished that one of the others would say something so that Shirley would stop bloody staring. Finally, he spoke.

'What the frigging hell is going on?'

None of them spoke. Winter was sure it wasn't his place to do so, knowing that, if anything, he was there to get bollocked. Or worse. However, neither Addison nor Kelbie seemed keen to put his neck on the line first. Shirley had to make the choice for them.

'When I ask a frigging question, I expect a frigging answer. DI Addison, I understand that you were the one who spoke to the lab, although I would like to know why that was the case, so you're it. What is going on?'

Addison took a deep breath and began to open his mouth, but, before he said a word, Kelbie cut across him.

'I'd also like to know why the lab gave the DNA results to you, Addison. If you were trying to subvert procedures, then I for one won't be happy.'

'Shut up, Kelbie,' boomed Shirley. 'If there's points-scoring to be done, then I'll be the one doing it. Addison, speak.'

Addison allowed himself a sideways glare at Kelbie before answering, taking satisfaction in the smacked look on the DCI's face.

'Well, you know the basics, sir, and the basics are still pretty much all we have. DS Narey's sweep team found the shoe at the ground adjacent to Caledonia Road church. We have since confirmed that the shoe belonged to Hannah Healey and that it matched the one that she was wearing when her body was found. Mr Baxter's team collected trace evidence from the scene, strands of hair caught in the wall of the church, and proceeded to extract DNA. The results came back and were passed on to me. The reason for that being that I was trying to solve this case and catch a murderer.'

Kelbie sighed but got only a glower from Shirley in return.

'The DNA was put through the system and they came up with a positive match. It was only a partial match but a match nonetheless. To Archibald Atto. Obviously this presents more questions than answers, but the computer doesn't take this into account. The computer says Atto.'

'Please tell me how this can be,' Shirley asked wearily. 'Because I'm only a simple old polisman and I can't get my head round this.'

'I'm not sure any of us can, sir. Atto hasn't left the prison. Sounds obvious, but it was the first thing we had to ask. No home visit, no transfer to court or hospital. He hasn't been outside the walls of Blackridge since he had a minor op six years ago.'

Shirley's eyes were closed over and his face scrunched, his breathing deep. 'The match is definite?'

Addison nodded. 'Partial but definite.'

'Christ almighty! So could he have somehow got out of Blackridge and then back in again? The perfect alibi?'

'We're looking into it, sir. Doesn't seem likely, but it's possible. Obviously, Blackridge swear it couldn't happen, but they would say that, wouldn't they? The DNA is his.'

The Temple seemed to be ageing by the minute. 'Check

everything. If he's got out ... if he's done this ... Holy shit. Somebody will get crucified and I'm damn sure it's not going to be me. Give me an alternative – how else could this have happened?'

Addison spread his arms wide, groping for possibilities. 'The alternative is transference. Somebody was in physical contact with Atto, that person was then at the scene and, accidentally or intentionally, left the hair behind.'

'Okay, so who do we know that has been in contact with Atto?' Shirley finished his question and let his gaze swing slowly round to Winter. Addison had anticipated the query and was ready with an answer.

'Tony has met with Atto but it was after the murder of Hannah Healey and after the evidence was recovered from the church. We've checked the visiting records and he hasn't visited before. Atto doesn't get many visitors at all. Hardly surprising really. The odd, probably very odd, psychologist, social worker and appointed prison visitor. That's it. We are checking all of them out. Apart from that he only comes into contact with other cons and the prison staff.'

'Are we checking them out too?'

'Yes, sir,' Kelbie interrupted again. 'I've taken charge of that, sir. It's obviously a long process but we're looking at every prisoner in the segregation unit that has been released in the past six months. If that draws a blank, then we'll look at everyone that's come out in the past year. And we're pulling files on all the staff.'

Shirley shook his head slowly, despairingly. 'Okay, okay. That brings us to you, Mr Winter. Tell me why I shouldn't have you sacked right here, right now.'

'Sir, I think that Tony—' Addison's intended defence didn't get started.

'DI Addison, may I suggest that you shut up and let Mr Winter speak for himself. Unless you want to run the risk of following him into unemployment.'

'Yes, sir.'

Winter felt the need to stand up and make his speech but wasn't entirely sure why. It wasn't just his neck on the line but Danny's and possibly Addison's as well.

'Detective Superintendent Shirley, I know how bad this looks. But I was only trying to help my uncle, Danny Neilson, because he was convinced that there was some connection between the cemetery killings and the case he was working on in the seventies. We weren't trying to interfere with the current investigation. We were trying to ... help it.'

Shirley looked back nonplussed. 'I need more than that, Mr Winter. Much more. I knew of your uncle back in the day. A good policeman with an excellent record. He's the reason you haven't been sacked already.'

'My uncle worked the original case. It means a lot to him. It's ... unfinished business. He approached a member of the case team but didn't think he'd been taken seriously. He felt the need to take things on himself and persuaded me to help him. He ... we thought that if we could talk to Atto then we could come back with something that could convince others that Atto was somehow connected to these killings.'

'Hmm. Regardless of the fact that Mr Neilson felt he wasn't taken seriously, and that is something we will address' – Shirley fired a look at Addison – 'your behaviour has been unacceptable. You are under suspension, Winter. If you or your uncle go near Archibald Atto again, you will be arrested. If you or your uncle approach officers actively involved in this case, you will be arrested. And I still reserve the right to charge you over what has already happened. Do you understand?'

'Yes, sir.'

'And you will make sure your uncle understands?'

'Yes, sir. Although he's ... single-minded about some things.'

Shirley sighed. 'Did you not hear me properly? He will be charged. I'm not having bloody vigilantes getting under my feet on this. Get to your office, take what you need and then piss off out of my sight.'

Winter avoided Addison's gaze as he got to his feet, shoving the chair back into position and leaving the room. Being suspended he could handle – it was the chance he'd taken as soon as he'd agreed to help Danny – but being off the case meant not being there if this killer struck again. Missing out on that hit home hard. It wasn't his only problem, though: telling Danny he ran the risk of getting arrested was likely to be of as much use as shouting at a rainstorm and telling it not to hit the ground.

Back in Alex Shirley's office, a new silence fell on the three officers. The detective superintendent was looking at Addison and Kelbie as if he'd never seen them before and was wondering how the hell they'd ever got a job. The two of them resumed their hope that each other would speak first and dig an almighty hole for himself. In the end, they never got the chance.

'You,' Shirley began, levelling Addison with a hard stare.

'You are friends with that idiot that just left. In the past, you have persuaded me to let him take priority position on some high-profile cases. That leaves me questioning your judgement. It also leads me to wonder whether you knew what he was up to.'

Addison knew that he shouldn't but, as ever, he couldn't help himself. 'No way. I had no idea whatsoever that he was going to visit Atto or that he even had any interest in him. Okay, if you want to question my sense in being his mate, then fair enough – I'm wondering that myself right now. But I will not accept the allegation that I knew what he was doing.'

Alex Shirley's face darkened and reddened. 'Not accept? Not frigging accept? Addison, do you not know when your head is on the bloody block and it is better to shut up?'

'No, sir. Apparently not. I'll take any criticism coming my way but what you suggested was way beyond that, and I'm not having it. Whatever the consequences.'

Shirley got redder. 'Enough! Don't push it, because you don't want to find out the consequences, and I don't have the time or the manpower to execute them while all this is going on. But don't force me to make decisions when this is done.'

This time Addison said nothing and Shirley moved on to his next victim.

'Kelbie, you can take that sleekit grin off your face. Just because Addison has stuffed up doesn't mean that you are off the hook. This investigation is a frigging shambles and you're the senior officer. What the hell was all that nonsense about the shoes in the TV interview?'

Kelbie squirmed uncomfortably in his chair, his tie tight. 'There seems to be some ... er, misunderstanding about the shoes, sir. I was certainly not suggesting any firm link or motivation on the part of the perpetrator, although I admit that does seem to be how it was construed by some sections of the media.'

'You don't say,' Shirley barked sarcastically.

'Yes, well, it is perhaps unfortunate that they took that line but, operationally, it works to our advantage.'

'And how do you figure that out?'

'The misplaced concentration on the shoes diverts public attention from the real point of our investigation and temporarily at least takes the heat off the situation. Now we have the Atto lead and we can get on with that without interruption.' He took a sneering sideways look at Addison. 'As long as we can trust everyone to keep that under wraps.'

Addison bit. 'If there is an insinuation in that, then you better back it up with something more explicit. But there's a tiny chance you can back it up because there's a very small chance that there could be any truth to it. And, while we're at it, there's little wonder the media jumped on your slight blunder with the shoes. Jumped right in there with both size fives, didn't you?'

Kelbie glared at Addison briefly before swivelling his head to Shirley as if to ask that the DI be reprimanded for the height jokes, but Shirley blanked him. At least he did until Addison started again.

'Although maybe you were on to something after all, because Atto wears shoes. I'm sure he does, I read it in the papers. Maybe he has an accomplice on the outside. Probably someone who wears shoes. Maybe you should look into that.'

'And maybe you should shut up and show a modicum of respect, DI Addison,' Shirley cautioned.

'A modicum? That's just a small amount isn't it, sir? A smidgen, a wee bit, a tiny, insignificant little amount.'

'Addison!'

'Sir.'

Addison couldn't help but notice that both Shirley and Kelbie were very red around the eyes. Good. That made a bugger of a day slightly more bearable. There was, however, always a price to pay.

'We need to speak to Atto.' Shirley made sure they knew what he meant. 'Properly. He's the only person likely to be able to give us an explanation as to how his DNA was at the scene. If Winter was right and Atto claims to know about these killings, then we need to get it out of him, and fast. We cannot let him mess us about. If we need to offer him some extra prison privileges to get him to cooperate, then do it. DCI Kelbie, I want you to speak to him.'

'What? But sir, I—'

'You heard me, Addison. Just think yourself lucky you're still on the case. If DCI Kelbie wants your assistance on this then he can ask you. It's up to him.'

Kelbie turned in his chair to look at Addison, unable and unwilling to keep the smug grin off his face.

'Thank you, sir. I'll contact Blackridge immediately and make the arrangements. And, as you say, if I need DI Addison then I won't hesitate to call on him. Although I have to say that there's little chance of that being necessary. A very small chance indeed.'

Chapter 33

Thursday noon

Rebecca Maxwell and Imelda Couper had gone back round the hairdressers Mr Grey had been known to frequent and urged the staff to alert them when he showed up again. The salons hadn't needed much encouragement, not given the customer's sleaze rating. Each had taken numbers and promised they'd be straight on the phone the minute he showed up.

In the end it had taken less than a day. The manageress at Shear Genius on Hope Street called Maxwell to say that their Ryan Race had just walked in the door and asked for Libby, his usual stylist. Libby was with another customer but 'Ryan' had said he'd wait. The salon was halfway down Hope Street, near the corner of West George Street, and so no more than a ten-minute walk. Maxwell put a shout out for Couper, and, finding her in the building, set off with her down Hope Street at a canter.

'Think he's dangerous?' Couper asked as they hustled past the newly and slightly oddly renamed Royal Conservatoire of

Scotland, which would always remain the Royal Scottish Academy of Music and Drama to passing Glaswegians.

'Well, if he's the guy that killed those two girls, then yes.'

'And we're going to go in there and nick him ourselves?'

'I don't see anyone else here, do you?'

Couper grinned. 'No, and I must admit it's worrying me a bit. Should we not have back-up? You have told Narey about this, right?'

Maxwell shrugged and screwed up her face. 'I left a note saying where we were going.'

'Jesus, Becca. We mess this up and we'll both get our arses chewed.'

Maxwell smiled broadly, her eyes never leaving the road as they crossed over Sauchiehall Street. 'Yeah, but get it right and we reap the rewards. You do want into CID, don't you?'

Couper exhaled noisily. 'Aye, okay. Come on, let's get this over with.'

The hill was steeper now, running away from them down towards the river. The gold and black signage of Shear Genius was visible just a couple of hundred yards away on the other side of the road. They crossed and walked the last bit of the way in silence.

Maxwell entered the salon first, catching sight of the grey hair in the hairdresser's chair as she pushed her way through the door. She looked into the mirror and saw the face looking back at her: early maybe mid-forties, dark, bushy eyebrows, an expression of curiosity. She watched and saw the expression change as Couper followed her through the door. The man's eyes opened wide at the sight of her uniform.

In an instant he was out of the chair, the stylist Libby being pushed as he got to his feet, staggering backwards till she collided with Maxwell. Still wrapped in an apron, the six-foot-tall client rushed towards the door, barging his way past a startled Couper. The place was in uproar. At least one customer and one member of staff were screaming and a pile of magazines were sent flying as the man fled across the room.

Mr Grey had the door to Hope Street open before anyone could move and was halfway through it. Couper threw herself at the door, using her weight to slam it closed, trapping his trailing arm inside the salon. The man screamed in pain and frustration but Couper kept the door hard against the arm, knowing that if he freed it he'd be gone.

'Get my cuffs, Becca,' Couper hissed through the exertion of pressing the door against the man's desperate efforts to free himself. Maxwell took the handcuffs from the belt around Couper's waist and locked one round the customer's flailing wrist and one round her own.

'Okay, got him.'

Couper released the pressure on the door and the man immediately began to pull his arm through and run. Maxwell was ready for him, though, and braced herself, halting his movement and then swiftly pulling back to yank him clean off his feet. Couper grabbed a handful of the man's shirt and together they hauled him back inside the salon.

As Couper twisted the man's arm behind his back, she looked at Maxwell with a rueful grin on her face. 'Okay, now can we call for back-up?'

'Yeah, why not? We may as well get a lift back up the hill.'

The man lay on the floor below them, breathing hard and looking up at them, wild-eyed.

'I didn't do it,' he screamed. 'I didn't touch her.'

'Touch who?' Maxwell asked him.

'Hannah Healey. I didn't kill her. I know that's what you think but I didn't. I didn't.'

Chapter 34

Thursday afternoon

DCI Kelbie and DS Jim Ferry were standing next to their car, wearing matching dark raincoats and grim expressions, viewing the clinical exterior of Blackridge Prison and taking a moment before crossing the car park and going inside. They'd worked together for four years and there was no need to say anything or to explain their hesitation. Ferry knew how much it meant to Kelbie and it was a big deal for him too. Promotion for one probably meant an overdue step up for the other. They both wanted it badly. Atto was a stepping stone to a better future for them.

'C'mon,' Kelbie muttered as casually as he could. 'Let's get in before the flaming rain starts again.'

The men hurried across the car park, dodging puddles and casting anxious glances at the low clouds glowering blackly at them from above. The heavens looked about fit to burst and, if they did, it was likely they'd return to find their car sitting abandoned in a tarmac swimming pool.

Kelbie delved into his pocket as they hustled past the

sodden flags dripping from the flagpoles in front of the gate-house. He brought out his ID and clenched it in his right hand, ready to show it as soon as they were inside. He had no intention of waiting in any unnecessary queues or being given any less than the attention and respect that they deserved. The staff inside wore uniforms but they weren't cops; they had to be shown who was in charge right from the off.

There were a few people in the queue waiting to be seen at the gatehouse but Kelbie wasn't having any of that. He walked behind them and flashed his warrant card at the man behind the desk. 'Police. DCI Kelbie. This is DS Ferry. We're expected and in a hurry. Where's the visitors' centre?'

The man didn't look best pleased and neither did those in the queue, but nothing was said. Instead, the officer just pointed, leaving Kelbie to charge on, satisfied he'd scored his first point. He and Ferry pushed their way inside the holding hall and Kelbie looked around for assistance. He knew there were all sorts of procedures for getting into the visit but they didn't apply to him. A stocky officer with a bullet bald-head was a few yards away, scouring the room with a drugs dog, and Kelbie shouted to him.

'Hey, you. Police. I need some help over here, now.'

The officer's thick, shiny head turned as did plenty of others at the use of the word 'police'. He didn't exactly seem enamoured with Kelbie's manner but did wander over towards him, albeit with a demeanour that suggested he was as likely to chin the cop as help him.

'What's your name?' Kelbie demanded as soon as the man was within a few feet.'

'Officer Crighton. And yours?'

Kelbie flashed his ID again. 'I'm DCI Kelbie. This is DS Ferry. Okay, Crighton, you're my man. We've got an appointment to interview a prisoner in the segregation unit and I want you to get us in and out of there without any of the usual hassle. I'm not standing in line with these scumbags. Park your dog somewhere if you need to but let's get on with it.'

The man grimaced at the suggestion. 'There's procedures that need to be—'

'Listen, I've not got time for that shite. That's why I'm talking to you. Make one quick phone call to your governor and then get us in there. You people should have known we were coming. C'mon, shift.'

'Who is it you're here to visit?'

Kelbie leaned in close and dropped the volume of his bark. 'Archibald Atto.'

The officer's eyes widened. 'Atto? That's his second visit within a couple of days.'

'Aye. You got a problem with that?'

'No. Not at all. Just . . . surprised. I'll make the phone call.'

Kelbie sneered with self-satisfaction as the man turned his back and walked a few yards to an internal phone. He returned just moments later, looking much less happy than the dog that trotted obediently at his heels. 'I'll take you through.'

'Right, let's go.'

The officer led Kelbie and Ferry to a room off the visiting hall, a sparse pink-walled space with just a single table, one chair behind it and two in front. The two cops took up the chairs and waited. The officer, Crighton, left them there and closed the door behind him, assuring Kelbie that he would remain outside and escort them back outside once they were finished.

Ferry sat to his boss's right, his chair slightly withdrawn so that he was further back from the table. As well as taking up an obvious position of deference, it allowed him to watch Kelbie without being seen. The DCI was edgy, anxious to get started rather than nervy, but drumming his fingers on the table and shifting in his seat. He kept glancing at the door opposite as if that would make Atto appear, his trademark snarl creasing the side of his mouth at every minute that passed without the door sliding back.

The rap of Kelbie's fingers on the wooden table echoed round the room, marking the beat for their shared tension and impatience. 'C'mon to fuck,' he finally muttered, his digits digging harder into the tabletop. They must have been the magic words because the door slid at last and Atto walked through it, a prison officer at his back.

Atto looked at Kelbie and Ferry, obvious disappointment on his face and seemingly undecided whether to take a seat at the table. He stood there, slowly studying the men in front of them before eventually, reluctantly, easing his way into the chair with barely a sound. He let his eyes drop and fiddled with his navy jumper, rearranging the position of it and pulling at his trousers until he was fully comfortable.

'Atto, I'm DCI Kelbie and I'm here to talk to you' – Atto's gaze swung towards Ferry, completely ignoring the man who was talking to him – 'about the murders of Kirsty McAndrew and Hannah Healey. I believe you have already indicated that you …'

Atto was staring unblinkingly at Ferry, locking into his eyes and shutting Kelbie out of his view. Ferry turned his head to look at the DCI talking and saw the annoyance on Kelbie's face as he spoke without any response from Atto.

'That you were aware of the deaths of these two women and that you had some knowledge of what happened to them. I want you to . . .'

Ferry thought he could feel Atto still staring at him but was convinced that it was just paranoia on his part. He'd been looking at Kelbie for long enough and surely Atto must have had enough of whatever game he was playing by now. He didn't turn his head but let his eyes swivel quickly to his right towards Atto and saw immediately that the man was looking straight into his eyes. He dragged his own gaze back to Kelbie.

'. . . tell me everything that you— Will you look at me when I'm talking to you!' Kelbie's hair-trigger temper had shot its bolt but it did nothing to make Atto shift his eyes.

'Atto! Mr Atto, I want you to tell me everything that you know about the murder of Kirsty McAndrew and Hannah Healey. We have reason to believe that you are directly connected to this investigation. Are you fucking listening to me?'

Atto didn't move his head from the direction it was facing but let it slowly bob up and down, showing agreement. Ferry could see by the look on Kelbie's face that Atto had reacted and turned to see the prisoner's eyes still boring into his own.

'Okay, good,' Kelbie growled, his jaw tightening in frustration at the lack of control he had over proceedings. 'Now tell me what you know. We know you like your name all over the papers, so why don't you buy yourself a few front pages and tell me what you've got to do with this?'

Again Atto continued to look straight towards Ferry, but this time his head swung slowly from side to side, in the laziest, most casual shakes of dissension, saying nothing.

'Stop fucking looking at him and look at me! And talk to me! We have a DNA match to you that was found at the scene where one of those girls was attacked. How do you explain that?'

For the first time, Atto blinked. He turned to look at Kelbie, his nondescript features showing mild interest in the DCI for the first time, cogs clearly turning behind his sleepy, dark eyes. It didn't last long, though, and after just moments he let his head and his stare swing back to Ferry.

'Yeah, you heard right. DNA found at the scene where the girl was assaulted before she was murdered. *Your* DNA. Don't turn away from me. The evidence is quite clear. Don't you want to claim another victim? Another notch for your belt?'

Atto didn't look, didn't answer, didn't shake his head. Instead, he looked at Ferry, the DS twitching under his relentless staring, his eyes betraying him and regularly flickering back to his tormentor.

Kelbie was fit to burst, his irritation ready to let loose like the storm clouds that were gathering over the prison's roof. His fingers thumped onto the table in front of him, banging out a tune that Atto refused to dance to or even pay any attention to. Frustration boiled over into desperation.

'If you don't talk to me I will have no alternative but to arrest you in connection with these two murders. Are you listening to me? We have your DNA from the scene. Fuck you. Archibald Atto, I am arresting you in connection with—'

A high-pitched chuckle escaped from the side of Atto's

mouth, a barely suppressed but lopsided smile appearing on his lips. His eyes never left Ferry but he let the irregular smirk spread across his face until it was a full sneering smile.

'Do you think this is some kind of joke, Atto? Because let me—'

Atto's grin disappeared and his head rolled round to face Kelbie. He stared at him contemptuously for a few moments, before finally speaking for the first time in a low voice that demanded to be heard.

'He's not finished.'

'What? Who's not—'

'Your killer. He's not finished yet. Get me Anthony Winter.'

'What?'

'I will speak to Anthony Winter. And no one else.'

Chapter 35

Thursday afternoon

Mr Grey turned out to be Mr Brown. Brian Brown, a car mechanic by trade and currently shit scared by nature. He trembled as he sat in front of Narey, hands shaking and eyes darting nervously left and right.

'I didn't do it,' he said for the fifth time since she'd sat down in front of him. 'I promise you I didn't.'

'Promises aren't good enough, Mr Brown. I need you to prove that you didn't. Tell me all about you and Hannah Healey.'

Brown looked to his solicitor, a fresh-faced kid who looked about fourteen, and received a nod in return.

'Hannah Healey was my hairdresser.'

Narey sighed. This part of the investigation was already looking much less fruitful thanks to the revelations about Atto, and she didn't have time to waste being pissed about.

'Mr Brown. We know Hannah was your hairdresser. We need you to tell us more than that.'

The man was still shaking but he let his eyes linger on Narey as he thought about his reply. Her skin crawled.

'I liked her. So I went there for a haircut. Nothing wrong with a man fancying a girl. All it was.'

'Is that right? And yet, when the officers entered the salon on Hope Street, you ran. Why was that?'

The man squirmed. 'I read about what had happened to Hannah. Terrible. I couldn't believe it. And I knew people might think I had something to do with it.'

'Why would they think that?'

Brown glared. 'Because people are suspicious. And because ...' He glanced at his solicitor. 'Because maybe I fancied Hannah a bit too much. But I wasn't even in Glasgow the night she was killed.'

Narey already knew. She'd felt it. Brown was a certifiable sleazebag but nothing more. The development with Atto made it seem certain she'd been chasing the wrong lead with this one and the vibes coming off Brown confirmed it.

'So where were you?'

'Edinburgh.'

'You can prove that?'

Brown looked to his brief.

'Detective Sergeant Narey, my client visits a hotel in Edinburgh on occasion. He pays in cash and there will be no paper or electronic confirmation of his visit. The owner ought to be able to identify him and corroborate the time of his stay there.'

Narey laughed. 'Your client's alibi is a stay in some back-street knocking shop where rooms are rented by the hour from someone who is going to be far from keen to speak to the police? Try again, Mr Martin.'

Even as she argued, she wanted out of there. She knew this

lowlife wasn't the man they were after. She'd make sure he was done for something but it wouldn't be what they wanted.

'Mr Brown, your alibi is next to worthless. Your motives are clear. Your character is repellent. We have a string of people who will testify to your habits while having your hair cut. Is there anything you want to tell me?'

Brown and Martin put their heads together. The conversation was brief and had clearly already been had.

'Detective Sergeant Narey,' the solicitor piped up again. 'My client is willing to make a statement confirming that he behaved inappropriately on occasions while within the confines of the Scissor Sisters establishment. We stress that this behaviour fell short of public indecency but we would be prepared to accept that it may have constituted a breach of the peace.'

As the solicitor spoke, Brown stared at Narey, seemingly fascinated by the configuration of her buttons.

'Mr Martin, I believe your client just made another breach of the peace. Mr Brown, you look down my blouse again and I'll make you wish you'd been born without sight. You understand me?'

Brown's eyes immediately fell to the table and he nodded furiously.

'How many places do you regularly get your hair cut?'

'Well . . .'

'How many?'

'Six. Lorraine, Tracey, Libby, Sarah, Angie and Hannah.'

Narey shook her head wearily as she looked at the solicitor. 'That's six counts of breach of the peace. I want names and places and a signed confession. And he'll voluntarily sign an

ASBO that bars him from entering any of those salons. You need to buy yourself a hair trimmer, Mr Brown.'

Brown's mouth formed a protest but he opened and closed it without saying anything.

'Mr Brown, in your time in Hannah's salon or when you were hanging around outside it, did you ever see anyone else acting oddly, perhaps keeping an eye on Hannah?'

The man looked up rather indignantly, as if peeved that some other perv might also have had designs on Hannah. 'No. No one.'

'That's a pity, Mr Brown. You might have been able to do something useful rather than just being a waste of DNA.'

Chapter 36

Friday morning

Maybe arranging to meet in the Botanic Gardens in April wasn't the best idea Danny had ever had but the rain was holding off for now and Chloe said it was fine by her. He'd been encouraged by the cheerfulness in her voice when she'd phoned, and allowed himself the luxury of thinking she was actually looking forward to it as much as he was.

He was hoping to find a parking spot somewhere on Queen Margaret Drive; she was going to meet him there. Danny had always had a bit of a soft spot for the junction immediately outside the gates to the Botanics – if you could ever have such a thing as a favourite set of traffic lights, then this was his. With the converted church of Oran Mor on the left, the Victorian gatehouses at the entrance to the park on the right and the tree-lined splendour of Great Western Road up ahead, it made for an agreeable place to be stopped.

He particularly liked it in summer, when the lights at the crossroads all turned to red and a mass of humanity suddenly, if briefly, reclaimed the streets on their way to sunbathe in the gardens or to shop and sup on Byres Road. There was also the Maggie, the world's best burger van, permanently parked outside the Botanics and serving up grub till three in the morning at weekends.

Car safely parked, he walked over to the entrance gates and stood there, rather fretfully, looking left and right. Danny wasn't a man usually given to butterflies in his stomach while waiting for someone to appear but he was trying to net an entire kaleidoscope of them at that moment. Their previous meeting had gone okay but he was beginning to doubt that he could be that lucky twice.

Looking at his watch, he saw that he was almost ten minutes early, shaking his head at himself for being so obviously determined to make a good impression. He was fairly sure that Chloe would be coming up Byres Road from Hillhead subway station, so concentrated most of his anxious watch in that direction. With still five minutes before they were due to meet, he saw her in the distance, a couple of hundred yards away on Byres Road, her flame-red hair making her an easy spot even among the crowds. She spotted him, too, just before she reached Oran Mor, and waved happily.

He'd been thinking how he'd greet her when she arrived and still hadn't quite made his mind up by the time she was crossing at the lights. If Chloe had the same doubts, then she hid them well, slipping an arm round him and kissing him on the cheek.

'Hi, Papa.'

'Hi, Chloe. Good to see you again.'

'You too. Glad you didn't thank me for coming this time.'

Danny blushed slightly, hardly believing that he did so. Chloe laughed and took his arm, guiding them into the gardens between the West Lodge on one side and the East Lodge on the other. At the fork in the path where you could go right to the glass dome of the Kibble Palace or left deeper into the gardens, she chose left. They sauntered on, past the large expanse of lawn in front of the Palm House which on rare warm summer days would be packed with people determined to redden their pale northern bodies.

'Were you working last night, Papa?'

The use of the name tugged him in different directions, the newness of it still being slightly odd but warming him inside.

'Yeah. Finished about three. Quiet night, though. Only about half a dozen proper maniacs, and only two of those tried to punch me.'

'I hope you tried to punch them back.'

'Ha. I'm not allowed to do that. Not supposed to, anyway. And, like I said, they *tried* to punch me; they didn't manage to do it.'

She looked at him curiously, a twinkle of mischief in her eyes. 'I bet you can look after yourself, Papa. If I was a guy I don't think I'd want to mess with you.'

Danny shrugged off the awkward compliment, not sure if he wanted his granddaughter thinking of him as some kind of hard man. The fact that he could handle himself wasn't a necessary part of running the taxi lines but it did prove useful on a regular basis even if only as a deterrent to drunken misbehaviour. Plenty of guys saw an old man until they got up close and changed their minds.

'Tell me more about your uni course. You still enjoying it?'

She giggled. 'Yes I'm *still* enjoying it. Haven't changed my mind since Tuesday, Papa. Sorry, I'm teasing you.'

'It's okay. Stupid question. I just want to get to know you better. Well ... I want to get to know you.'

She pulled him tighter, clutching his arm. 'Then don't ask about my course. Ask about me if you want.'

The suggestion stumped him a bit. He wasn't exactly used to asking people about themselves and it was a long time since he'd had the chance to ask Chloe's mother anything at all.

'Okay, um, why do you like your course?'

Chloe laughed. 'Good question, Papa. I like it because I'm into words and expressing myself and I'm fascinated by how other people are able to do it so well in books, plays and films. I'm interested in the world, I guess. And the journalism ... well it sounds kinda corny but I believe in truth and justice. Actually, it sounds *very* corny.'

'Doesn't sound corny at all. If you don't believe in truth and justice at your age then you never will. Although how much of that you will find in journalism is anyone's guess.'

'So cynical, Papa.'

'Yeah. And if I don't get to be cynical at my age then I never will.'

'True enough. Okay, ask me something else.'

'Boyfriend?'

'Oh, killer question right out of the box. No, not at the moment. I had been seeing someone but it ended a couple of months ago. Actually, my mum didn't even know about him. There you go, Papa, you know something she doesn't.'

An answer to that sprang to mind, but he left it unsaid and went for the banal instead.

'What kind of movies do you like?'

'Really? It's like one of those pop quizzes you get in celeb magazines. Next you'll be asking me what my favourite colour is or whether I'm in Team Edward or Team Jacob.'

'What?'

'It's a *Twilight* thing. And I don't like those films, before you ask. I like comedies, preferably intelligent ones. Action thrillers, too. None of that chick-flick stuff. I like Italian food, maybe Chinese if I'm in the mood. I prefer cats to dogs. I like clubbing. Ed Sheeran, Emeli Sandé and Take That but don't tell anyone. My favourite colour is blue. Usually. Sometimes I spend all day in my pyjamas and I still have a doll from when I was about three. And I cannot stand beetroot. Yuk.'

She twisted her mouth over to one side in thought but shrugged, not thinking of anything else. 'I think that covers the vox-pop stuff. Did I miss anything?'

'Um . . . no.'

'Okay. My turn. Why do you and Mum not talk to each other?'

He almost stopped in his tracks but forced himself on again mid-stride, wishing that he'd never started this whole question nonsense in the first place. As he struggled for an answer, they both felt the first drops of rain splashing down on them through the overhanging branches of the trees. They looked up and saw the clouds, dark and threatening overhead. Even as they stared up, the drops became heavier and fell more quickly. They looked at each other and came up with the same response.

'Kibble Palace. Run.'

'I'll run as fast as I can but you go on without me if you want.'

'No way, Papa, We're in this together. But hurry!'

They hustled back along the path, the Kibble's domes in sight but the rain splattering down. He laughed and she giggled as they ran.

Chloe reached the door of the Palace first, pulling it back wide, and they both dashed inside, shaking themselves dry and immediately feeling the blast of warmth from the giant glasshouse.

She was looking around wide-eyed and Danny couldn't resist laughing. 'You never been in here before?'

'I think I was, when I was a kid, but I don't really remember it. It's incredible. It's like a jungle in here.'

The Kibble was a forest of ferns, every shade of green under the sun, and many of them reaching as high as the Palace's large domed roof. Some had thick, prickly-looking trunks, the fronds springing improbably from the top of them. Others were black or burnt orange, tall and slender with light-green fronds hanging down to say hello or stretching to the sky. There were new otherworldly ferns with stems that rolled up at the end like a wizard's walking stick, strange Catherine wheels of botanical wonder. As they walked they came upon an oasis of space centred on a brilliantly white marble statue of Eve, her near-naked form on a tall plinth with a semicircle of vividly scarlet flowers lined up at its base and beyond.

'This place is amazing. I can't believe all I've ever done is sunbathe outside it.'

'It used to be a conservatory at a private house over on Loch Long on the west coast,' Danny explained.

'You winding me up, Papa?'

'No. Kibble donated it to the city and they dismantled the whole thing and brought it up the Clyde by barge and cart in the 1870s. It's been here ever since.'

'How come you know so much?'

'I'm old. You live long enough, you learn things.'

'So you'll know why you and Mum don't talk to each other, then?'

He'd thought he was too old to fall into traps but maybe you're never too old for that. His first reaction was to say nothing, his second was to lie. Both crumbled when he looked at her; hope and expectancy all over her face.

'I did something I shouldn't have done and your mother can't forgive me for it. I don't blame her. I just wish she'd change her mind.'

She studied him, fierce and inquisitive, and he saw her mother's eyes. He blinked twice but they were still there when he looked again. Maybe not as accusing as Barbara's but still too close for comfort.

'Is that all I'm getting? I'm the one that's grown up without a granddad because of whatever it was.' She laughed quietly. 'I'm the victim here.'

He laughed too, despite himself. 'We're all victims, kid. Everybody loses. And, yes, it's all you're getting. For now at least. I did something I wasn't proud of and I've spent the rest of my life trying to make up for it.'

'That's not good enough, Papa. Not good enough at all.'

'I know.'

*

As they emerged through the main gates, the lights changed at the crossing, and pedestrians began to flood across in every direction. Chloe looked at them for a second before grabbing Danny close and kissing him on the cheek. In an instant she was off, dashing across the junction towards Byres Road, her long red hair flying behind her and an arm raised high waving back towards him.

He stood and watched her go, seeing her break into an impromptu skip halfway across, and laughed out loud despite the fact that he didn't know whether he was going to see her again, or when. He watched until she merged into the crowds and was swept up into their mass. Even when she was just another shapeless form in the moving human river, he stood with his hands thrust into his pockets and looked at where she had been.

He must have stood there for a minute or two, the consequences of age-old actions sinking in yet again, when the hand stuck in his right pocket was tickled by the vibration of his mobile phone. He pulled it out and saw her name at the top of the display, causing the flutter of butterflies to be released in his stomach again.

Lv u papa. Cu agn v soon xxx

Bloody text-speak. Is that really what they were teaching them at university? If he was speaking to her mother, he'd have a word about this. Instead he typed.

Lv u 2 darling. Cu v v soon xxx

There wasn't all that much that Danny loved about the so-called modern world. In fact that very phrase was one that made him scowl. It had been a modern world when he was twenty and it would be one again when he was pushing up daisies. But he did love the fact that, despite his and Chloe's separation by forty-odd years in age and a few hundred yards in distance, they could communicate instantly. It made him happy.

He would have been far less happy if he'd known that, in the river of people that was flowing along Byres Road, one was paddling rather than being swept along with the current. Twenty yards behind Chloe, unseen, unknown, a pair of eager eyes never let Danny's granddaughter out of their sight.

Chapter 37

Friday noon

Okay, so you know what you're going to do?'

'No.'

'Are you ready for this?'

'No.'

'C'mon, Tony. We've been through it a hundred times.'

'Yeah, we have but it doesn't mean that I'm prepared for it. I'm the one that's going to have to go in there. On my own with a killer. Funnily enough, I'm a bit worried about it.'

'You'll be fine.' Addison sounded more hopeful than believing and Winter got the distinct impression the words were meant as much for Alex Shirley's ears as his. The gang were all there: Addison, Shirley, Kelbie, Narey and Danny, plus the governor of Blackridge, Tom Walton, and his deputy. None of them, Addison included, seemed happy with the idea of it all being in Winter's hands, and he was even less keen on the idea than they were. But it was the only game that Atto would play, and it was his rules.

They'd hauled in a trained negotiator, a man used to dealing with potential jumpers or hostage situations, and he'd
talked Winter through conversation and negotiation strate-
gies. How and when to push it and when not to, how to
understand motivational factors and how to keep Atto onside
but not to let him have complete control. Or at least not to let
him *think* he had. It all sounded fine in theory, but the negotiator had never met Atto. Winter had, and he wasn't filled
with hope.

They all kept looking at him, individually and collectively,
full on or out the corners of their eyes, every glance and every
stare causing the pressure to crank up another notch. Their
lack of faith in his ability to pull it off was multiplied by the
need for answers and his own doubts. The interview, to be
attended by only one prison officer and Walton, the prison
governor, was to go unrecorded and would begin in under
three minutes. They'd all got to Blackridge too early and the
wait wasn't helping. He watched the clock tick slowly towards
start time. They watched him watch it.

Danny pushed his way out of the herd and took Winter
protectively by the arm, edging him away from the others. 'I
know you're nervous, son. But that's a good thing. It'll keep
you on your toes. You can do this. You've got good instincts
and you're smart. And you've got other advantages working
for you that give you the edge on Atto.'

Winter looked doubtful.

'You have. He's taken a liking to you and I know that's
probably freaking you out, but it's an edge you've got to use.
But, most of all, Atto *wants* to tell us. He wants the headlines
and he wants to deliver them through you. Work him.

Squeeze him dry. Remember, you're in charge because you have what he wants.'

Winter smiled uneasily. 'Nice speech, Dan, but *he* also has what *we* want, and I don't think he's going to give it up easily.'

'That's my boy: glass half full. Go get him. Do it for me.'

'Do my best, Dan. Do my best.'

'Okay, Winter. Let's get going.' Alex Shirley sounded nervous, his arse on the line along with everyone else's. 'It's almost time. Mr Walton, you ready?'

The governor, a no-nonsense man in his mid-fifties wearing what looked suspiciously like a wig, nodded curtly. He and Winter positioned themselves in front of the sliding door, each taking a deep breath. The prison boss was to be merely an observer, Winter's usual position and one that he begrudged giving up.

The door slowly slid back and the two men walked in, Winter taking up the chair in front of the broad wooden table and the governor retreating to the side, where he stood against the wall. Moments later, a hiss of air signalled that the door on the far wall was sliding open and Atto emerged into the room, his eyes seeking the other side of the desk and bobbing his head in approval when he saw Winter sitting there. At his back was the prison guard with the shaved head whom he and Danny had encountered on their first visit. The officer gave a respectful nod towards his boss, then assumed a position against the wall with his eyes focused on Atto.

'Thank you for coming, Anthony. It's good to see you again.'

Winter couldn't offer the same sentiment in return. How could it be in any way good to meet a man who had killed all those women? How could he possibly make conversational small talk with him. He wouldn't.

'Time is against us, Mr Atto. We need to know what's going on and we need to know it quickly.'

Atto's face fell in disappointment. 'Straight to business, is that it, Anthony? No pleasantries, no "How are you?" Okay, if that's how you wish to play it. But it's not the best way for you to get the most out of the game. Surely at least we can get beyond using "Mr Atto". No?'

The negotiator had told Winter to engage with the man, to call him by his first name if he could, but to be wary of using shorthand familiars, such as Archie or Arch in case it offended. It was all so by the book but, when push came to shove, it stuck in Winter's throat to make as if he were remotely pally with this monster. But he'd do it.

'Okay. Archibald. We can do that. You need to forgive me if I'm businesslike because this is serious. Two young women have been murdered. You say you know what's going on. Your DNA is found at the scene where one of them was abducted. You can see that it's serious.'

'I can see that it's serious for you, Anthony. And for all the policemen that are no doubt on the other side of that wall. But it's not serious for me. Why would it be? I don't know those women and probably wouldn't care about them even if I did. And it's not as if I can be locked up for any longer than I already am. Serious? I don't think so.'

'You don't think murder is serious? I saw those women. I saw how their bodies were left laid out in the cemeteries after they'd been killed. Left lying there like—'

Winter saw the light that went on in Atto's eyes and realised his mistake too late. The man was feasting on the image that he'd help serve up for him. He wanted to see what Winter had seen and was intent on tapping into his memory bank of film.

'Don't stop, Anthony. Please, go on.'

'No. There's nothing to be gained by that. If you're telling the truth, then you already know what was done. And why. Is that right?'

Atto pouted slightly, disappointed at Winter's not playing along. 'Yes, that's right. I know the who and the why.'

The bombshell landed softly in the table between them, as if disarmed by the unexpectedness of it. Winter was aware of the governor and the guard lifting their heads sharply to make sure they had heard what they thought they had. His own heart beat a little faster and he deliberately hesitated before replying, knowing that he couldn't win the game they were playing with one remark, but he could lose it. Don't ask who, he told himself. Don't ask who, not yet. Not now.

'How do you know?' Appeal to his vanity, he thought to himself, remembering the negotiator's advice. 'How can you know when you're locked up in here?'

Atto's mouth curled up at one side, smugly pleased at the question. 'I'm only locked up by walls, Anthony. This is the age of wireless technology and stone walls do not a prison make.' He gave a little chuckle, clearly amused by his own wit.

Tom Walton, the governor, wasn't so happy with Atto's answer. Winter saw him push off the wall before managing to stop himself, remembering his role of observer. If what Atto was insinuating was true, then Walton's arse was joining a long list of arses that were precariously on the line.

'Okay ...' Winter began warily. 'So you can contact the outside world. Presumably by some device that you shouldn't have. Not unknown in prisons, I suppose. And you're saying it in front of Mr Walton, so therefore confident that it will not be discovered.'

Atto gave another self-satisfied half-smile that cried out to be wiped from his face but, in the circumstances, had to be left to fester, and Winter continued.

'So now we know how you can know what's happened. And if you are in contact—'

'*Happening*,' Atto interrupted. 'Not *happened*, *happening*. This is still going on. It isn't over.'

The words stole their way into Winter's ribcage, punching his heart hard and begging a question he didn't want to ask but knew he had to.

'The killings haven't finished?'

'No.'

'How many more?'

Atto gave a little unconvincing shrug of his shoulders. The gesture didn't say that he didn't know: it said that he wasn't telling. Danny's words about Winter's being in charge because he had what Atto wanted came drifting back, and sounded even more hollow than they had first time around. He probably couldn't feel less in charge than he did at that moment.

'You know more than you're saying, Archibald.'

'Oh, yes, very much so.'

'And you know who is doing it and you know how your DNA was found at the crime scene.'

'Yes.'

'How?'

Atto sighed. 'Both of those things are explained by one simple piece of information that I will pass on to you – before you leave today but when I'm ready. But you need to indulge me first. Do you know why I said I would only speak to you, Anthony? Have you wondered about that at all?'

Of course he had. He'd thought about little else. He wasn't giving Atto the satisfaction of that, though. Instead he mimicked the unconvincing shoulder shrug. Atto laughed as if he wasn't buying it in the slightest.

'It's because of death, Anthony. It's your job and you spend your days seeing what I saw. What so few people get to see. And I can see that it fascinates you the same way that it fascinates me.'

'Not the same way. Not the same way at all.'

Atto tilted his head and pushed his lower lip beyond the upper, signifying that he'd concede the point even if he didn't agree.

'Okay, perhaps not. Maybe we're two sides of the same coin. Coming at the same prey from different angles. Like the poacher and the gamekeeper. Whatever, it's there, and I can see it. Photographing those dead girls, it gives you a buzz. A buzz that few people could understand because they've never been there.'

Winter's skin crawled as if Atto were running his fingers over it, playing him like a harp. It crawled because of how close he was getting to an unpalatable truth that he was forced to deny using a half-truth.

'No, it's not like that at all. Maybe once but not now. It's a job, nothing more.'

Atto looked at him silently for an age. 'The gentleman doth protest too much, methinks. *Hamlet*, Act Three, Scene Two. Apart from being regularly misquoted, that line is also misunderstood. We assume protest to mean "object" or "deny", but it didn't mean that in Shakespeare's time. It meant almost the opposite: to "affirm" or "vow". Just as you confirm my suggestion as much by what you don't say as by what you do.'

The harp strings crawled over Winter again, Atto working them expertly, making them sing an ugly song with a haunting melody. He had to change the tune.

'So why do you kill?'

Atto smiled, both corners of his mouth turning up in amused satisfaction. This was his kind of conversation.

'Do you know how few people have asked me that question? They want to know the obvious things: who, where and when. They want to know where the bodies are buried. They ask me for facts rather than for why, the big why. They might, *might*, ask me why I murdered this one or that one. But they rarely ask me why I choose to do it. You know why they don't? Because they're afraid of the answer. Aren't you afraid, Anthony?'

'No. And why should I be? You haven't answered it. You just asked another question of your own.'

Atto chuckled. 'Fair point, Anthony. Fair point. But in many ways you're right. Every answer I give you as to why I kill will just raise another question. Some of them I don't know the answer to. For example, I kill because I enjoy it. Why do I enjoy it? It gives me a thrill. Why? I'm not sure I know. Do I like the feeling of empowerment? Yes. Why? I don't know. Do I like hurting them? Yes. Why?'

He slowly spread his arms wide to show that he couldn't possibly explain. Winter said nothing. Atto continued.

'Do I feel guilty about the things I've done? No. Why is that? I don't know. Do I feel sorry for the girls I killed all those years ago? No. Do I feel sorry for those girls killed last week? No. Why? Because I have no such feelings. Why? I don't know. Why don't I know?'

Despite himself, Winter felt the urge to ask those questions and more. He didn't want to be in the man's head and he sure as hell didn't want Atto in his. But the itch to know was crawling over him too. And Atto knew it.

'Do you think you were born that way?'

'Probably.'

'And do you think of yourself as evil?'

Atto's eyes flashed, dark and angry, fleeting but visible, his mouth twitching at the edges. He swallowed deep before answering, and Winter sensed that he'd just won a point at last.

'No. I don't. I do know that I've probably done evil things. But I can't seem to feel bad about having done them, so how can it be so wrong? Who the fuck are you to judge me, anyway?'

A second point and so quick after the first. Atto spat out the last question as an afterthought. One that he couldn't stop himself from making. Maybe Winter had more control in this game than he'd thought he had.

'I'm not judging you. I just asked you a question. You're not afraid of the answer, are you, Archibald?'

Atto laughed sourly and turned towards Tom Walton. 'How long have we got left?'

The governor snapped to attention at the question being directed at him and looked at his watch. 'Ten minutes. Although you can have longer if you want it.'

'No, it will be long enough. Mr Winter can come back if he doesn't get everything he wants in his time today.'

Winter thought back to the negotiator's counsel on when to push it and when not to. If he remembered correctly, then this moment was right on the wire. Push.

'How can you be so sure that there will be more killings?'

'He told me so. As simple as that. He will kill as many as Red Silk did.'

'Four? And you are Red Silk?' Big push, big risk.

Atto just stared back at him, finally letting his eyelids slowly but briefly close over and give the merest upward motion of his shoulders. It wasn't a yes or a no; it was barely a maybe.

'You've forgotten the big question of the game, Anthony. The one that we started with when we discussed why men kill. Do you remember what it was?'

Winter hesitated, thinking. 'Whether people are born to kill or whether something makes them that way. Nature or nurture.'

Atto nodded. 'Yes. Nature or nurture. It's simplistic but it takes us to the heart of the matter. You'll remember then that I told you how it was much more relevant to what's happening than you might think?'

'Yes.'

'Good. Our time is almost up but there's so much more we have to discuss. However, that's for another day, I think, Anthony. You will need to come back too because there will be so much more that you'll want to know. And that your police friends out there will want to know too. It's like I said before: every answer I give you will just raise another question.'

Atto was teasing him again, drip-feeding him half-clues to keep him hanging on. Push it, damn it. Push it and ask the question.

'Okay, so what's the nature-and-nurture stuff? And why will your answer just lead to more questions?'

Atto leaned as close as the table between them would allow.

'The person who has been contacting me … he killed those girls. Why he is contacting me and why my DNA was at your crime scene is the same answer. He is my son.'

Chapter 38

'So you see, nature or nurture *is* the key argument. They say that the apple never falls far from the tree, Anthony. Looks like it's certainly true in this case. What do you think?'

Think? Winter's thoughts were racing at warp speed and spinning in all directions. Ahead of him and to his side, he saw the prison officer's jaw drop and the governor step forward, then fall back to the wall as if he'd been shoved there by his own incredulity. Atto's expression hadn't changed; he might as well have pointed out what day of the week it was.

'I think ... that's an interesting development.'

Atto preened again as if it hadn't previously occurred to him that anyone would find this interesting.

'How did he make contact with you?'

'By email. You were right: I've got a device that allows me to pick up such things and talk to the world. I'm not alone. A lot of the guests here have computers and all it needs is a small, easily hidden attachment and it becomes a passport to the rest of the world. God, it's a different place to when I came in here. Very different. The email came out of the blue.

Like a message from another planet. Like a message from the 1980s.'

'What did he say?'

'The gist of it was that he was my child. Well, "your spawn" was the exact phrase used. A bit unnecessary, I thought. Spawn has all those connotations of the Devil. Devil's spawn, spawn of evil. All that rubbish. Still, I can understand it, he was upset. Just talking emotionally. I don't hold it against him.'

Time to push it again. Ask the big question while he's in the mood. Push.

'Who is he?'

Atto's face screwed up into mild confusion, not quite understanding why the question was asked. 'I don't know. He's never said what his name is. Not even his mother's name, and, well, that wouldn't have been much help, anyway.'

'You don't know who the mother could be?'

He laughed. The high-pitched giggle that sat so at odds with everything else he did or said. Atto obviously found that question particularly hilarious.

'No. Of course I don't. I must have. Briefly. But I don't know her or remember her. Let me explain, Anthony. My child – my "spawn" – says that his mother had cancer. It was only when she was on her deathbed that she told him who his father really was. Me. I suppose it must have been a bit of a shock. People know who I am and they have ... an opinion of me. The boy had always thought some other person was his father but the mother told him just before she died that it wasn't this bloke: it was me. I think it kind of ... disturbed him.'

This was all way too much. Winter hadn't signed up to psychoanalyse the relationship between a killer and his illegitimate son. Christ, between a killer and his son, a killer. He had to deal with this and explain it to everyone waiting on the other side of the door.

'So how can you not remember who his mother was?'

Atto shook his head in disappointment the way a teacher might do at a kid who can't get simple arithmetic.

'The mother told the child that I'd raped her. She was married to some bloke and let him think that the kid was his, but she knew better. It was me.'

The bile that was in Winter's throat was pure acid and threatened to erupt over the wooden table. He couldn't stomach much more of this.

'So did you? Did you rape her? Surely you know who she was?'

Atto smiled, one of those rare ones where both sides of his mouth turned skywards at once, and held his arms wide.

'Who knows, Anthony? I didn't always stop to ask their names. Even if I did, I'd have forgotten.'

When Winter went into that room at first, he'd wished that Danny had been by his side. His confidence at being able to get the job done would have been so much higher if he'd been with him. That notion slowly disappeared when Atto boasted and taunted, knowing the rage that Danny would have flown into. Now, though ... now, he knew that Danny would have launched himself over the table and tried to strangle Atto with his bare hands. And he couldn't quite make up his mind whether he wanted that to have happened or not. He swallowed back the disgust that was climbing up his throat and pushed on.

'Do you still have these emails?'

No. Of course not. I read them, answered them, memorised them, deleted them.'

'So what did he tell you that he was going to do?'

'To kill. The way that Red Silk did. And as often as Red Silk did. To be honest, I think the shock of discovering who he is has sent him a little bit . . . nuts. So there's your nurture as well as your nature, Anthony. A trigger as well as a predisposition. A lethal combination. Oh, and I have to tell you: your time is running out.'

'How long is it since you heard from him? Before or after these girls were murdered?'

Atto gave him a strange look, a sly near-smile, before slowly turning his head towards the prison governor. 'How long?'

'I don't . . . how could I know?' Walton stuttered.

'How long do we have left in the interview session?'

'Oh.' Walton looked at his watch. 'The time's up but we can—'

'No, we can't. An hour was what was agreed. Anthony will come back. Won't you, Anthony?'

'Yes. You know I will.'

'Good. Tomorrow, then. Same time. And Anthony, when you go out and tell this story to your little friends out there, I'd suggest you tell them not to go too crazy trying to find how I get online. This goes for you, too, Mr Walton. For a start, I don't think you'll find it. But are you sure you want to? If you manage to trace it and remove it then the boy won't be able to contact me again and the only lead you have will be gone.'

When the door slid back to let Winter and Walton back into the outer room, it must have sent a spark of electricity among the waiting group, because they all snapped to attention and were staring at the door as the two men emerged. Winter was trying, but largely failing, to keep his face expressionless, while the governor looked shell-shocked.

It was Alex Shirley who took a step ahead of the pack. 'Well? What happened?' he demanded, the unease clear for all to see and hear.

Winter's eyes closed over and he blew out hard, his knees ready to give way beneath him as he lost the adrenalin that had been holding him up. He fell back into the nearest empty chair and took the time to compose himself before giving them what they wanted.

'C'mon, son.' Danny was as anxious as the rest.

'Aye, okay, Danny. Give me a minute. That wasn't easy in there.'

It was Rachel who came over to him, a glass of water in her hand. She let her fingers brush against his as she handed it over, and it felt good. A hug would have been better, but he'd settle for that and wonder just what it meant.

'Okay,' he sighed, long, deep and weary. 'The bottom line is that the person who killed Kirsty McAndrew and Hannah Healey is Atto's son.'

None of them said anything. Shirley, Addison, Kelbie, Rachel and Danny all stood and looked back, not trusting their own ears. After a few seconds, Kelbie spun on the spot, turning himself away from the news; Addison's hands came to his head; Shirley stood stock still in something approaching shock; and Danny nodded soberly at the confirmation that he'd been right. Rachel looked at him as if wondering what he'd been through.

Then they all had questions at once, bombarding him from every angle, tripping over each other, each more desperate than the others to get an answer. How does he know? Who is he? Where is he? Is Atto going to help?

'Enough!' Shirley declared. 'Just shut up and let me speak. Okay, Winter, tell us what he said. And tell us how sure you are that he's telling the truth. Christ, this is going to have the press going ballistic if they find out.'

'Atto has something, probably a dongle or the like, which allows him to connect a computer to the Internet. He was contacted by someone saying they're his child. His "spawn" was how he put it. He says the mother was a rape victim of Atto's and only told him on her deathbed. Now the kid is following in the father's footsteps and copying the Red Silk killings. Which means he isn't finished. There are two more to come. And our time is running out.'

'Shit, shit, shit!' Shirley looked ready to burst. 'We're going to have to go public with this. We can't take the risk of people not being warned about what he's planning to do. We'll rightly get crucified if another two girls get murdered.'

'They won't. Not if I have anything to do with it.' Addison was the defiant one. 'What else did he say? You need to be as precise as you can, Tony.'

'I can't be because Atto wasn't. He says he deleted the

emails as soon as he'd replied to them. They'll all be recoverable somewhere in the cloud but it's going to take time you don't have. Atto says the son's never revealed his name, never said where in Glasgow he is, who his mother was. Atto says he's raped so many that he couldn't think who she might be.'

'Well, that bastard might not be able to remember, but the police national computer can. Its memory isn't so conveniently forgetful.'

'That might not help. I got the impression from Atto that it wasn't reported.'

'Yeah, well, impression isn't good enough and I can't take the chance you're wrong. Rachel, tell Andy Teven I want him to go through every rape case that was linked to Atto, every rape case that fitted his method, every rape where there was an attempted strangulation. Get him to cross-check the victims against recent deaths, say in the last year to eighteen months. Get him to chase them down and tell him if he wants to moan about it then he should come and see me.'

'Now hang on,' Kelbie interrupted, trying to assert some authority. 'I think we should—'

'And we're going to need to pull every file on the Red Silk cases,' Addison said, riding right over him. 'Lay it all out, separate the myth from the truth and look at it from scratch. Whoever did the two cemetery killings knows this case inside out and we have to make sure we know at least as much about it as he does. Sir . . .' Addison turned to Alex Shirley. 'I want Danny Neilson on the inside on this. He knows stuff the case files won't hold because he was there first time around. We need him.'

'Agreed. Mr Neilson, you'll help us?'

'Yeah. I will. You better believe it. I want to catch this guy as much as anyone does.'

'Okay, Danny, good. Sorry for doubting you.' Addison got a nod in return, cop to cop, no more needed to be said. 'Now, Tony, we need more from Atto. Much more. Is he still communicating with this psycho? Never mind wondering how the hell he was able to do it in the first place.'

Tom Walton blanched at the barb but Addison wasn't expecting any kind of excuse or apology. There wasn't time for that.

'Yeah, he is. But he's going to wring as much out of this as he can. He's already hinting that there's more he can tell us. We've set up another interview for the same time tomorrow. And he's also said to send a not-very-subtle message about the dongle. Basically he says you won't find it and, even if you do, you'd be better leaving it where it is or else he won't be able to keep in touch with the son.'

'Oh, does he? Well, that wanker's got another think coming. Can I suggest that DCI Kelbie gets IT all over this? I don't know how the hell it works but Atto must need some kind of Internet service provider to do this and there has to be a way of monitoring these emails. Doesn't GCHQ do this sort of thing? It needs someone of the DCI's rank to get people's arses into gear.'

Kelbie regarded him suspiciously, lips curling back. 'You throwing me a bone, Addison?'

'Yeah, there's a good dog. Fetch.'

'Addison!'

'Sorry, sir. That was uncalled for. But may I suggest that

DCI Kelbie does that and does it fast? If this kid is copying his father, then my money would be on him trying again this weekend. Tonight or tomorrow, maybe both. That would fit with the 1972 killings, wouldn't it, Danny?'

'Yeah. That would be my guess, too.'

'Okay, that means we've got around twelve hours before this bastard intends to kill again. But we're going to stop him.'

Chapter 39

August 1972

The undercover job at Klass had gone on for three weeks now. Whether it had been successful or not rather depended on how you looked at it. They hadn't caught the man the papers were calling Red Silk but, then, he hadn't killed again, either.

The long, endless nights were taking their toll on him and, although he'd see it through to the end, whatever the end might be, it had better come soon. Every shift was becoming more difficult than the last, both in the disco and at home.

He'd told Jean, his wife. In the end he'd had no choice even though he knew full well that she'd be less than pleased about it. Night after night going out dressed up to the nines – it was hardly surprising she was getting suspicious. He couldn't blame her for that.

He'd borrowed a life lesson from one of his favourite films, *The Secret of Santa Vittoria*, which he'd seen a couple of years earlier. Anthony Quinn plays a drunk called Bombolini, who becomes mayor of the town just before the Nazis move in to take all of Santa Vittoria's million bottles of wine. Bombolini persuades the townsfolk that they have to let the Germans find enough of the wine to convince them that they have it all. The message was the benefit of admitting a small lie to cover up a bigger one; the moral was to give up something small to save something greater. Both of which were fine as long as you could work out which was which.

The girl, Jenny, had been in Klass a few nights a week. Sometimes he couldn't make his mind up whether he'd rather she'd been there more than that or less. He knew that he'd started to look out for her as much as he did the man he'd been sent to catch. He was still doing his job, no less determined to get the man, but he knew his mind wasn't always where it should be.

He thought maybe others had noticed that too. Billy Moffat and Geordie Taylor had started giving him knowing glances, sly little smiles that said, I know, and you *know* I know. Liz Grant had done the same and he was sure Moffat had filled her head full of gossip. That was why he'd had the three of them shifted back onto days. He'd convinced his DI that the same faces were becoming too well known and that it was time for a change in the Disco Dancing Division. He, Brian Webster and Alice McCutcheon stayed and were joined by three more: Kenny McConville, Colin Black and Sheila Mottram. The new Triple D Squad.

He'd only danced with Jenny once more since that last time. She'd been getting hassle from a wee hard nut in a black pin-stripe, the kind who wouldn't take no for an answer. He'd watched her dance with the ned once in the hope that would keep him happy. It didn't, and he kept coming back for more, and it was easy to see she was getting sick of it. He'd stepped in, knight-in-shining-armour style, and asked her to dance. The guy was far from happy and you could see he was thinking of squaring up and staking his claim, but he was giving away six inches in height and two or three stone in weight, so wisely thought better of it.

He liked to think that she'd been pleased to see him and not just because he'd scared off the pest. She'd smiled and said 'Hi' even though she knew he wouldn't hear her above the music. They danced and then danced one more just to be sure. When they were particularly close, she'd shouted and asked how he'd been. He'd said fine and asked the same of her. She'd laughed and said she was fine too. When the second song finished, she'd looked at him expectantly, but he managed only an awkward smile and a bit of a shrug before turning away off the floor. It wasn't that he hadn't wanted to.

She'd left early that night, slipping off with her pals just before the food was laid out, signalling the last hour. Maybe she wasn't hungry; maybe she had somewhere better to go. Either way, she'd left without a glance over her shoulder. The last he saw of her was her red tresses snaking through the crowds and then disappearing from sight.

That was nearly a week ago, and he'd looked out for her every night since, half glad when she hadn't shown, knowing it kept them both safe, albeit in very different ways. He'd been a grouchy, stalking presence in the disco, his mood scaring off would-be dancers even when the slow number came on at the end. Alice McCutcheon had been on duty with him twice and had sidled up to him on the pretence of chatting him up to ask what the hell was wrong with him. He'd said he was just fed up with the dancing routine and that he had been arguing with his wife. Admitting a small lie to cover up a bigger one.

The baking summer, the hottest and longest spell anyone could remember, had continued without a drop of rain or a drop in temperature. Klass continued to swelter. He'd ditched his tie that night and opened a couple of buttons on his plain, white, cotton shirt but it still didn't let in anywhere near enough air. Either the disco was having more oxygen sucked out of it with every passing night or else he'd simply been there too long.

This night was different from the others, though, and he wasn't sure how comfortable he was with it. He was standing in the queue to go upstairs and into the disco with Frances MacFarlane at his side. Brenda's sister, the one who had seen her dancing with the bloke wearing the black velvet suit with a red silk handkerchief in the top pocket, was shaking. If it hadn't been so hot or you hadn't known what she'd gone through, you'd swear she was shivering because she was cold. She'd agreed to go back to Klass for the first time since her sister was murdered, but it was clear she was thinking better of it. The girl was terrified.

He put his arm round her, not certain how she would react to it, but they were there on the pretence of being boyfriend and girlfriend, so at least it would look natural to anyone watching. His first touch seemed to produce an electric shock as she nearly jumped out of her skin, but then she sank against his arm and then in close to his side. She still shook but the tremblings were beginning to subside.

Frances was a small girl, slim and barely five feet tall, with mousy brown hair and large green eyes. He guessed she'd be very pretty if she smiled, but there didn't seem to be much hope of that any time soon. When they'd spoken about her going in with him to try to identify the man who had danced with her sister, she'd done little other than sob while saying that she'd do anything they wanted, anything that might help. The poor girl was eating herself up with guilt at being the MacFarlane daughter who had walked away from the disco alive.

She'd put on a check, flared mini-dress and enough make-up to cover the tears, and had screwed up whatever courage she had left, making him promise that he'd never leave her side. Not that he had any intention of doing so. He hugged her slightly tighter, feeling her relax as he did so. It was for him as much as for her: he had his own guilt at being part of putting her through this.

Frances had somehow managed to evade the newspaper photographers who had wanted her picture for their front pages and had told the police that neither she nor Brenda had known many people who went to Klass, so the chances were good that she'd go unrecognised inside the disco. Whether she would recognise anyone there was the question that was keeping them all awake at night.

The bouncers gave them the nod, their eyes on Frances, who could only look at her feet, finding fascination in her platform sandals. They crossed the threshold into Klass, the stifling heat immediately a contrast to the relative cool of the stairs, yet it set off another bout of trembling, and Frances tottered into the disco supported by his arm.

Her eyes were wide, trying to take everything and everyone in at once. For a moment he thought she might back out again, but there was stern stuff inside her tiny frame, even though she announced that she needed it fortified by something else.

'I need a drink.'

He daren't leave her alone while he went to the bar, so steered her towards it while asking what she wanted. 'Anything. Rum and pep. Or martini. Anything, though. Could you ... can you get me a large one?'

He could see the benefit of the booze making her relax but he couldn't afford for her to get drunk. He leaned in towards the barman and ordered a single rum and pep in a tall glass and got it topped up with ice. Her first nervous gulp emptied a third of the glass.

They moved away from the bar and took up a position on the edge of the dance floor, Frances moving from one foot to the other, the glass never far from her mouth. She was scanning the room like a mother looking for a lost child. He put his head close to hers and made sure no one else heard.

'Okay, I know it's difficult but you have to try not to look so obviously. Just look at me for now and have a conversation. Then, when you're ready, take a look over my shoulder at guys walking past. Try not to stare. Just look naturally. Can you do that?'

She nodded, doubtful but determined.

'I know it must be hard coming back in here but you're doing great. It takes a lot of guts to do it and Brenda would be proud of you.'

There was a little involuntary gasp at her sister's name but she held it together, breathing deep and swallowing hard.

'I'd do anything, Mr Neilson. Brenda would have done

anything for me and I'll walk to hell and back if it finds the ... the ... person that hurt her. Must admit I'm a bit scared, though. Being in here it ... it's strange.'

'I know you've been asked lots of times but can you think of anything else about the man she was dancing with? Or anyone else who was paying her attention?'

Frances's eyes wandered across to the other side of the dance floor, staring at a spot between two tables. He instinctively knew she was seeing Brenda standing there.

'He wasn't particularly tall, just kind of average. I couldn't even say if he was good-looking or ugly. They were over there when I last saw them. Dancing. It was the Nilsson song, you know the one? "Without You", that's it. He had on this black velvet suit. Brenda was smiling like she fancied him. I think it was a red silk handkerchief but I can't be sure. What if I'm wrong?'

'Other people remember the red hankie too. Don't worry about it. You're doing fine.'

'You think so? I don't feel fine.'

They danced. The cop and the dead girl's sister. Moving together yet rarely looking at each other. He saw McConville and Sheila Mottram, the other two members of the Triple D who were on duty, their eyes holding momentarily. She seemed to see shadows, ghosts and memories. He occasionally saw her blink and stare as if there was a familiar face, a likely lad, but then her face would crease in disappointment and she'd move on.

Frances asked for another drink and he agreed, getting himself a second lager while he was at it, she fretting slightly as he left her by the edge of the bar area. The beer was tepid at best but it still felt good, washing away some of his doubts at letting her be there. His DI had shared his worries but said it was all they had and that the chief superintendent had pushed for it. The top brass were getting it hard because the killer hadn't been caught, although they didn't feel the hurt any more than the cops on the ground.

As well as going dancing with Frances, he'd had to visit Isobel Jardine's mother and explain how she still couldn't bury her daughter. Explain how they still hadn't caught the bastard who did it. The woman had been drinking heavily, he could see that. Couldn't blame her, though. She ranted and raved at him a bit, cried on his shoulder, too. She clutched a framed photograph of her daughter to her chest until he thought that the glass might break the way her heart had done. He'd left thinking that the odds of Mrs Jardine killing herself were better than even.

When he wasn't on disco duty, he was poring over case files, and when he wasn't doing that he was knocking on doors and interviewing potential witnesses. He was either working the case or asleep dreaming about it. Every name that appeared on any copper's notebook, every date and every possible sighting, was imprinted on his brain. He ate it, drank it, slept it. Fourteen hours a day with pay and ten without.

It wasn't about clear-up rates or promotion or avoiding bad press. It was about keeping the city safe. About making sure that wee lassies could go to discos and get home alive. About making Frances MacFarlane stop shaking. He couldn't bring her sister back but he sure as hell could catch the bastard who did it.

Then he saw her.

Jenny. Her two friends came through the door first and he recognised them, just as he recognised the missed beat at the realisation that she might be there too. She looked stunning in a maxi-length halter-neck catsuit, a brown creation covered in bright pink flowers that pulled tight at the waist and showed off her figure. The outfit floated as she walked, making him think it was airy and light and with little underneath it. Her friends were decked out in long Laura Ashley-style dresses; one of them, the brunette Cathy, now had a huge Afro perm like the singer Marsha Hunt. The three of them caused a bit of a stir as they came in, causing blokes to nudge each other and nod in their direction.

She saw him, something that he was sure was a smile beginning to spread across her face until she saw him dancing with Frances. The smile dropped slightly but she still nodded in his direction. The song finished then and he was still looking towards her as he walked off the floor with Frances, back to where their drinks sat on the table.

He could see that Frances was fidgeting nervously after the dance, no doubt mentally exhausted after processing so many faces that had spun round the room as they'd moved. She was shaking the remains of the ice chinking against the glass. He hesitated but reached out and placed a hand on her arm, calming her. Frances smiled up gratefully and nodded.

He looked up to see Jenny staring over. Her friends were nattering in her ear and leading her away towards the back of the room. They didn't get there uninterrupted, though, as a tall fair-haired guy in a beige suit stopped the three of them and gave them some chat. Whatever patter he came out with must have done the trick, because Jenny turned away from her friends and back towards the dance floor with a fleeting sideways glance in his direction.

Frances was saying something about another drink but he barely heard as he watched Jenny and Mr Beige Suit dance to a Sweet song. Then to a Johnny Nash number. She smiled at the guy as she left the floor after the second dance, but almost as quickly she was back on again, this time with a stocky, dark-haired chap in a bright-blue shirt. Blue Shirt was a good dancer, showing off his moves, and Jenny seemed to be impressed. She laughed and moved, the maxi halter-neck dress floating yet tight to her.

'... another rum and pep? I know I probably shouldn't but I'm ... finding this really difficult.'

'Yeah, I'll get you one in a minute ... Just keep looking around.'

Blue Shirt was chatting to her real close and he didn't like the look of him at all. A definite air of something suspicious about him. Maybe a bit of a resemblance to the Red Silk description too. He was going in to find out. Before he could, though, Blue Shirt headed for the bar, making hand gestures to Jenny to stay put.

'Frances, there's someone I have to speak to. She's ... a possible witness. I won't be long.'

The girl's eyes widened with worry. 'No, but I—'

'You'll be okay. There are two other officers in the room. They'll be watching you. And I really won't be long. I promise. Don't move from there.'

He didn't give her time to protest and spun on his heels to make for the part of the dance floor where Jenny stood. She saw him coming and raised her eyebrows questioningly before looking over to the back, where her pals were, shrugging at them.

'Hello, how are you?' he asked her.

'I'm fine. Should you not be with your friend?'

'My fr— She's not. She's ... my niece.'

'Your niece? She doesn't look all that much younger than you.'

'She's not. Her mother is much older than me. I'm just taking her out for a night. She's ... had a hard time of it recently and I'm looking after her.'

Jenny looked doubtful but nodded.

'That's nice of you. So are you coming on Saturday, to the big Be Red Silk night? Surely you will, you being Red Silk and all ...'

She was joking again, of course she was, but the Red Silk jokes had been coming thick and fast of late. Nothing's too much for Glasgow humour, nothing goes too far. He'd heard them down the station, too: What's red and silky on a Saturday night? A girl's thighs after a night in Klass.

He was struggling to see the funny side, though. Still, he smiled, not least because she looked so good when she said it, and he forced a half-joke back.

'Och, it would hardly be fair Red Silk entering a Red Silk Lookalike contest. Now would it? There would need to be a steward's enquiry.'

'True enough. But you will be here, won't you? For the Saturday night?'

Would he? He worked most shifts but, then, that wasn't the issue. He had to remember that she was asking him as a ... well, as a what? As a guy she'd danced with? As a guy she liked? Fancied? He didn't know the answer to any of the questions and yet he heard a reply coming out of his own mouth before he'd finished thinking.

'I'm ... not sure.'

'Should be a good night. But remember, you'll need a red silk hankie to get in. Well, don't suppose it has to be actual silk. But red, though. Unless you know the guys on the door.'

'No. I don't. Know them, that is. I might be here. Will you?'

She smiled, a mischievous twinkle in her eyes. 'I might be.' She meant yes.

'I'll maybe see you here, then.' He meant yes, too. 'Look I've got to go. I need to—'

'—look after your niece. Yes, I know. Maybe see you Saturday.'

Frances was fretting when he got back, her eyes flashing left and right, a look of near panic on her face that made him immediately guilty.

'You okay? Sorry I was so long but it was important. You see anyone that looked like it might be him?'

Frances shook her head mournfully and he turned to see Jenny's dancing partner talking to her again.

'What about that guy over there in the blue shirt? The one with the dark hair.'

She looked at him curiously but shook her head again. 'No, not him.'

'Pity.'

Chapter 40

Friday evening

Winter watched the news programme in the Station Bar, a place not normally guaranteed to have the telly at full volume unless there was a football match on the box. However the words 'cemetery killings: breaking news' and the look on the presenter's face had the regulars shouting at the barmaid to turn the sound up. In moments, the entire pub was glued to the screen.

They cut from the studio to a live broadcast on the doorstep of Stewart Street, a grim-looking Alex Shirley reluctantly holding court to a forest of microphones. The station was just a few hundred yards away from the pub and a couple of smart guys slipped out the side door, intent on seeing it for themselves.

Winter knew pretty much what Shirley was about to say but he still felt strangely nervous waiting to hear the words and the reaction they'd cause. If there were pigeons, this was about to put the cat among them. There was definitely a fan, and the shit was about to hit it.

The Station Bar televisions were up high, causing necks to strain and mouths to drop in equal measure as the punters heard what Shirley had to say.

'Ladies and gentlemen, thank you for attending this press conference. As you are all aware, we are continuing to investigate the killings of Kirsty McAndrew and Hannah Healey. There has been a significant development in the case and I wish to share some of that with you this evening. I hope you will understand that there is some information that I cannot pass on for operational reasons. However, I will tell you all that I can.

'We have reason to believe that the person who murdered Kirsty and Hannah intends to kill again. I do not propose to discuss the nature of our information on this, but I can assure you that we are confident of it and that we take this threat seriously. We are doing everything we can to apprehend the person responsible and we will place extra officers on the streets of Glasgow to ensure public safety.

'However, we are making an urgent appeal this evening for people, particularly young women, to consider their actions if they are planning to go out tonight. It is our belief that the murderer of Kirsty and Hannah will try to strike again this weekend. If the pattern of the previous attacks is to be repeated, the killer will look to target young women on their own. It is our firm advice that, wherever possible, the city centre should be avoided tonight and tomorrow. Under no circumstances should young women be there on their own. If you must go out, do not go alone. Stay with a friend, preferably more than one, and do not separate.

'I realise that this is a Friday night at the beginning of a holiday weekend but there will be many other weekends to be enjoyed, as long as this one is negotiated safely. I cannot stress enough how grave this situation is. We are dealing with a highly dangerous individual and public safety is paramount. Please consider staying at home until this is resolved. It is not our intention to cause panic and we would not request this lightly.'

Shirley paused for breath and the Station Bar customers jumped into the breach.

'Stay in on a Friday night? Aye, that'll be shining bright. Who's he think he's kidding? It's Friday night! Careful girls, the bogeyman's gonna get ye.'

Winter looked round the room and saw that the bravado was mainly coming from the men. The women, particularly the younger ones, looked at each other and shared their fears, all furrowed brows and slack jaws. A couple of them huddled closer together, feeling the need of the contact of their friends.

As the Temple began to wind up his press conference and reiterate his plea for young women to stay at home, a loud voice shouted at him from out of the crowd of reporters, cutting through the jabbering ranks and demanding an answer from the senior officer.

'Detective Superintendent Shirley, can you confirm that the cemetery killings and the threat of further killings are directly related to Archibald Atto?'

Alex Shirley might as well have been hit over the head with a blunt object. He was caught like the proverbial rabbit in the headlights, his shock clear for all to see. He took far too long to compose himself, and everything he then said in a blustering attempt to deflect the question was doomed to failure. The intervening silence was tantamount to a yes.

'I don't know where you got your information from but … there is nothing I can say to confirm or deny your question. For operational reasons …'

He had faltered and the pack pounced, scenting blood.

'Is this right, Detective Superintendent?' 'How is Atto involved?' 'Is he still locked up?' 'Has Atto escaped?' 'Has Atto killed again?' 'Why hasn't the public been told about this?'

Shirley's reluctant attempts to answer the torrent of questions were cut off as his impromptu interrogation continued unabated. The irony of asking him something but not allowing him to answer because he was being asked something else was lost on his inquisitors in the rush to ask the killer question.

'Did Atto kill the cemetery girls?' 'How long have you known that he was involved?' 'Will you resign?' 'Has Red Silk returned?' 'Do you think you should resign, Detective Superintendent?'

The crowd in the Station Bar had become as rowdy as the reporters and were shouting their own questions at the television screen and at each other. Archibald Atto? How can that be? Winter watched Alex Shirley's face glow red with anger and frustration as he had to yell to be heard at all.

'We are talking to Archibald Atto in the process of our investigation. That is all I can tell you for now. And, yes, he is still in prison. That is all. No! I cannot comment further. This press conference is at a close.'

Shirley stormed off stage left, his face thunderous and the

questions continuing to hammer at his back as he walked away.

Archibald Atto was the name that resonated through the pub and far beyond. The faces that had been scared were now terrified.

Chapter 41

Friday night

It was her first visit to Glasgow and it hadn't been anywhere near the nightmare that she'd been told to expect. Sure, everyone spoke an almost unintelligible form of English and the weather was crap, but that hadn't exactly come as a surprise. Once she'd got over the idea that everyone seemed to be starting an argument every time they opened their mouth and it was just them being friendly in their own way, then she'd learned to enjoy herself.

Everyone thinks that travel PR is all global chic; making do with five-star hotels if there aren't any six-star ones available; constant sunshine and complimentary cocktails; chauffeur service and endless luxury.

And, hey, you know what? That's pretty much the way it was and that's why she loved it. Sometimes, though, a girl had to do the hard yards as well. Like conferences. Like conferences in Glasgow. Funnily enough, the prospect hadn't got her pulse racing quite in the same way as a trip to Vietnam or Dubai, but it had to be done.

She'd been in the travel game for fourteen years and the lifestyle suited her. It had its downsides, like leaving her two miniature Yorkshire terriers, Buster-Bear and Bailey-Boo, behind as she jetted off hither and thither in search of new places for the rich and famous to lay their suntanned heads.

She'd had a couple of hours to herself before the slog began and had ventured out onto Buchanan Street and had been pleasantly surprised by the range and quality of the shops. The travel blurb had said the city had the best shopping in Britain outside London, but she'd doubted it until she saw it for herself. Lots of her favourite designer names were there and she'd duly indulged. Glasgow glamour! Who'd have thought it?

Sadly, it was then down to business, and she went through the same old dance of listening, explaining, nodding and smiling, all in the correct order and with boundless enthusiasm in the name of the client. Eventually, thankfully, it was job done and she had the evening to herself. Some of the others were going for dinner in the West End and a sleazy middle-aged sort in a too-tight suit had suggested she join them, but he alone was enough to have put her off the idea. This was Glasgow and she decided she wanted to go out for a taste of it. Sitting in a trattoria with a bunch of travel executives was something she could do any night of the week back home in London.

She'd asked at the hotel reception for recommendations for somewhere to go for a drink. The man behind the desk had looked her up and down, seeing the designer clothes, the expensive bag and the polished Chanel Rouge fingernails, and asked if she wanted to go to a proper pub or a wine bar. There was almost a challenge in the way he'd said it, so she'd answered with 'proper pub' before she knew it. 'Try the Horseshoe on Drury Street,' the old boy had said with a definite glint in his eye that made her want and wary at the same time, a feeling she was entirely used to. She went.

It was a proper pub all right, perhaps the most proper she'd ever been in. The sign outside said it had been there since 1884 and it didn't look as if too much had changed. It had tiled floors of intricate mosaics, deep cornices, huge mirrors and decorative friezes, horses everywhere including a large mahogany one on top of the central bar. There were horseshoe designs on the fireplaces, the columns above the gantry and even the slate chimneypieces. There was brass and red leather but not in an English-country-pub kind of way, very much in a city-centre Glasgow kind of way. Most striking of all was the huge island bar in the shape of a horseshoe, naturally enough. The longest bar in the UK, a guy told her. At least she thought that was what he'd said.

Actually, the locals weren't even that hard to understand after a while. You kind of tuned into their wavelength and got used to the ochs and the arrs and it all made some sort of sense. The drink helped. A lot. Once she'd established that they didn't do cocktails, unless you counted a maraschino cherry or a slice of lemon in your vodka, she settled for a glass of Pinot Grigio. Happily, every glass made the good-looking barman not just more good-looking but magically more coherent as well. And whatever he said sounded a hell of a lot more sexy in that lilt and burr than it would have done otherwise. The drink must have slowed down his speech or speeded up her brain; either way, they were at the same pace, and she liked that. She wondered what he wore under his kilt. Not that he was wearing one, of course, but a girl could dream.

The Horseshoe was packed, proper Friday-night packed, and everyone seemed utterly determined to have a good time or die trying. There were men in suits who had obviously come straight from work and would go home the same way, assuming they went home at all. Younger guys who had come off building sites. Girls done up for nightclubs with the shortest skirts she'd ever seen. It was diverse and rowdy, lively and buzzing, and just threatening enough to make it interesting.

There was no room to sit despite the place being rather large, so she took up elbow room at the bar, quietly pleased with herself for braving the wilds of Friday night Glasgow on her own. Most people, male and female, who stood next to her said hello, after a fashion. 'Awrite?' or 'You being served, hen?' being the most common. When they heard her accent, they all wanted to talk. 'First time in Glasgow?' Yes, she told them. 'Mental, innit?' they asked back. 'Whitsyur name?' 'Ashleigh Fleming,' she told them. 'Good Scottish name,' they told her.

She even had a pie. Everyone in the Horseshoe told her it was the pub speciality – a pie and a pint. It seemed rude to say no, particularly when she hadn't actually eaten in hours, so she had a steak pie and a pint of eighty shilling, whatever that was. The pie was, well, not exactly to her taste. So she had just one more bite and said she was full. After the brief diversion with the pint, she went back to the Pinot Grigio, which had been a bit disappointing at first as well, but was improving with every glass. They weren't getting her drunk, though. Well, maybe a little.

A girl heard her voice and dragged her upstairs to the karaoke. The Horseshoe karaoke was legendary, according to her new friend, a petite, dark-haired girl who duly knocked out Joy Division's 'Love Will Tear Us Apart' to rapturous applause. She sat flicking through the song choices for her own turn but couldn't take her eyes off the performers: what they lacked in talent, they more than made up for in enthusiasm. Some of them must have spent all week perfecting their routines and the audience went crazy for their dedication to their art. She was going to choose Rihanna's 'We Found Love' but was firmly informed that it was Big Alice's song and 'she'd batter you' if it was sung. She eventually settled on Emeli Sandé's 'Where I Sleep', as no one had laid claim to it, and warbled her way through to big applause for not being good enough to make anyone else look bad.

You know what? This city wasn't as bad as it liked to make out. It was just a big, fuzzy, tiddly bear and she wasn't scared of it.

She had to go to the loo and unfortunately was forced to squeeze real tight past a tall, blond-haired guy coming the other way, which was a shame. Not. She looked for him on the way back from the toilets but he seemed to have been swept up in the crowd. On the plus side, there was a guy in skinny jeans and a white shirt who kept looking at her and he had a fab smile. Glasgow was great. Why hadn't she come here before? The guy in the white shirt had headed downstairs towards the front door, maybe for a cigarette, and on impulse she followed him out.

She eased her way through the crowd, feeling a rush of excitement and wondering what she'd say to the guy when she got out there. Not that it would matter, as long as she said something, then things would go from there. Ah, bollocks! Where the hell was he? Whoa! The fresh air up here must be really fresh. She felt light-headed and the narrow confines of Drury Street spun before her.

Was that him at the end of the street? A white blur walking away under the yellow flame of the street light. Where do you think you're going, mister? She lurched unsteadily left in the direction he'd gone, wondering why her legs seemed so unreliable but too concerned with the chase to care. At the corner, she emerged onto a street that stretched way up the hill as far as the eye could see and also to the left, where it seemed to turn into a junction with red traffic lights staring back at her. Fuzzy people were nearby, loud, laughing and lairy, argumentative voices and shouts that she couldn't understand. Across the road and slightly to the left was a lane that sat between a Starbucks on one side and a shop of some kind on the other. She thought she saw the ghost of a white shirt disappearing down the lane and made after it.

A car horn blared behind her and an angry voice shouted something local that she could no longer understand. Maybe there was a tipping point where so much drink meant you could understand the accent, then any more meant that you couldn't. She crossed the road, hearing another horn beep at her and the screech of brakes on the edge of her consciousness.

She could see only so far down the gloom of the lane but there was the garish glow of neon at the far end, meaning it led to another main street, so she'd be fine. The buildings rose tall on either side, crowding in and suffocating what little light there was. A row of industrial bins were parked to her left but she staggered on by them, conscious of her feet slapping ungracefully against the concrete. There was another sound, too, but she couldn't quite place it. Like the echo of her footsteps, yet not quite right.

Maybe this wasn't such a good idea. The lane was narrower, longer and darker than she'd thought. And the lights at the end didn't seem to be getting any closer. And she wasn't walking very well. Or thinking very well. Everything was blurred and there was no sign of Mr White Shirt. She stopped, wondering whether to go back, wondering whether she'd find the pub again or her hotel. She'd stopped, but she could still hear her footsteps. How could that be? She turned round and saw the shadows move, a dance in the darkness where the gloom mixed with the murkiness.

She was blinking, trying to make sense of it, when the shadow jumped towards her and there was a hand over her mouth and behind her head. She couldn't breathe or think or fight and her head spun as she was held tighter and pulled against the wall and into an even darker space. She could hear people laughing, a whole group of them at one end of the lane or the other. She tried to shout, but nothing came out and the cry for help stayed deep inside her. She'd been dizzy and tired but now even more so, sinking, slipping, drowning. She could hear the shadow talking but couldn't make out the words, just somehow knowing that they weren't meant for her.

The lane was a river now, a lazy, swirling stream that eddied before her eyes, bathed in the nearing street-light yellow. Nearing. It was getting closer and she looked down to see that she was walking. No, not walking: being half-carried towards the end of the lane, held up by the shadow's shoulder. She'd been wrong and the shadow was helping her, taking her back to her hotel or to the police. She tried to say thanks but her tongue was made of wool and only lolled around uselessly in her mouth.

She raised her head enough to see that the yellow was close, and more voices were near, too, some of them singing. In her head she sang back but she made no sound. She swayed a little, held up by the shadow as large white faces passed by, laughing at her. There was a new noise, distant but near, emerging through the fog in her head. A roar, then a slam.

They moved forward quickly, she and her shadow, towards something big and white. A van. The door was open. It was her knight's white charger, come to take her home. There was a push and she went through the open door into the darkness of the van, hitting the floor with her face and nestling there, feeling it cold and comforting against her hot skin. The floor moved beneath her and she could hear her heartbeat as she slipped deeper into the darkness until it was all around her, wrapping her up and smothering her. All she could hear was the roar of blood in her ears and a little voice in her head telling her that the shadow wasn't taking her home at all. And she knew that her beautiful red coat was going to get dirty lying on the floor of this van.

Chapter 42

Saturday morning

The morning after the Friday night before is usually a time for sore heads and self-recrimination, never-again promises that will never be kept and muddied memories of things that shouldn't have been said or done. This Saturday morning was different. The first waking thought of those lucky enough to have managed sleep was whether Glasgow was one soul lighter.

It was certainly the question that immediately went through Winter's mind as he lifted his watch from the bedside cabinet and saw that it was just 6.30. He hadn't set his alarm, sure that he wouldn't need one as fitful sleep was always its own wake-up call. Next he grabbed his mobile, but there were no unread texts, no missed calls, just as he knew there wouldn't be. The first buzz of either, and he'd have been wide awake.

He hit the shower, any thought of going back to sleep easily banished by the not knowing. Still, he was sure he'd have got the call to arrive with his camera if there had been another victim, Alex Shirley having reluctantly lifted his suspension when asking him to speak to Atto. He was back on the inside as well as the outside of this case.

Head raised to the jets that blasted his face, he let the water roll over him and wash away the last vestiges of half-sleep, steeling himself for whatever was out there. No call didn't mean no body: it meant no body had been found yet. Atto had been certain that the spawn would try again, although even he couldn't be sure that—

The ringtone from his mobile pierced the shower cabinet and the water flow, causing him to stop and think twice whether he was actually hearing it. He reached up and turned off the water, pushing through the shower door in the same movement and picking up the phone where he'd left it in easy reach on an adjoining shelf. It was Addison.

'Yeah?'

'Another one.'

'Shit!'

'The Western Necropolis. Uniform found it on a sweep of the cemetery at first light.'

'What? I thought it was being—'

'Don't you fucking start. Just get yourself over there. The place is huge and it's in a city full of bloody cemeteries. Just shift your arse.'

Addison was gone, the phone left silent in Winter's dripping hand. He dropped it back onto the shelf and snatched a towel from the rail, rubbing himself dry as quickly as he could before jumping into the first set of clean clothes that he could find. His heart was pounding and he told himself over and over to stay calm and get a grip. Just get moving, just be professional.

He was due to meet with Atto again in just a couple of hours, and his mind was flash-filled with the thought of the man sitting there with that superior, told-you-so look on his face. Winter's stomach clenched at the image, dreading being there and forced to indulge Atto in his sick self-satisfaction.

The Western Necropolis was up off Maryhill Road near Gilshochill railway station and no more than a ten-minute drive at that time of the morning. Winter pushed the accelerator as far to the floor as he dared, worried less about the certainty of cop cars flying to the scene than he was about his own concentration. Driving with a head full of an unknown young woman, probably strangled, probably raped, didn't exactly improve his chances of keeping the car on the road.

He wrenched his Civic left just after Jaconelli's onto Lochburn Road, winding his way past cars coming in the other direction with barely enough room to pass, dipping under the low bridge and racing on into the wilds of Lambhill. Swinging onto Cadder Road and climbing the hill, he punched on the radio and searched for news but got nothing. A couple of minutes later, driving straight across the mini-roundabout onto Tresta Road without thinking, he saw that the news had found him.

As he passed the primary school on his left and the flats on his right, he saw the road ahead packed with the familiar yellow and blue that rarely meant good news. He parked up on the nearest available bit of pavement, throwing the door closed behind him and barely paused to fire the remote to lock the car, running the rest of the way to the cemetery gates with his camera bag banging against his back.

The two cops on duty recognised him and there was no need to bother with the hassle of fishing out his ID, as he rushed straight by them with no more than a nod. He saw more cops up ahead, their garish yellow vests visible in the half-light, and he charged in their direction, wondering if he could have simply driven in but now too late to take the option. The bag weighed heavier with every step, not least because he knew what it was going to be used for.

Christ, this place was huge: grey granite rows on either side as far as the eye could see, field after field; whole orchards of trees and endless messages to the dead; acre after acre of statues, crosses, angels and obelisks. It was Billy Connolly who said, 'Glasgow's a bit like Nashville, Tennessee: it doesn't care much for the living, but it really looks after the dead.' He had a point.

Winter ran, eyes left, right and straight ahead, his senses peppered by the fields of death, some sparse with irregular headstones, others busy in neat, ordered rows. They pushed him on towards the lights and chatter that grew nearer and louder and yet darker and more grim. Panting, sweat clammy on his brow, he arrived among them, the hi-vis vests parting to allow him into the inner sanctum where he recognised the back view of Addison and Narey standing side by side in front of three large winged angels perched atop tall, adjoining, granite headstones. The sight of Rachel standing there jolted him into a new reality: her presence was hardly unexpected yet still caused his heart to drop into his stomach.

He walked to Addison's side and knew that all three stone

angels had seen evil that night, even if they hadn't heard it or spoken it. The proof lay at their feet: a bloodied streak across the grey face of the central headstone leading down to the sitting form of a blonde woman whose head was slumped on her chest as if sleeping. It was the longest sleep she'd ever have.

Addison didn't turn to look at Winter, just staring at the girl and knowing instinctively that it was he who was standing there.

'Her name's Ashleigh Fleming according to the cards in her bag. She worked in PR for a London hotel. London phone number, too, so she was only up here visiting. Take her pictures, wee man. I want to get her out of here as soon as we can.'

Winter nodded and moved forward, sensing and sharing Addison's uncustomary sensitivity but also gripped by the task in front of him. He remembered and repeated his earlier urge to himself to stay calm, to be professional. He pulled his camera from the bag at his shoulder and, in the very movement of doing so, he felt something switch inside him. The only thing he was unsure of was whether it had switched on or off.

He framed the girl *in situ*, an inevitably macabre scene-setter with grim-faced cops unwittingly bookending the towering headstones that she sat against. He grabbed a tighter shot, too, expelling the police from the picture and taking in the curious gaze of the angels instead, seeing them stare down with pity and disapproval.

The girl's legs, long and bare, were crossed in front of her in a position that might have suggested she'd been reading a book, propped against a tree on a summer's day. There was no book, though, and instead her arms were spread wide in a plea for mercy that would never come. Her blonde hair was dappled darkly wet with dew and blood, sparkling coldly in the early light and acting as a curtain to her face, hiding her reaction to whatever horrors she had seen.

The black cashmere dress that was rucked high on her thighs exposed dark dots moving slowly across her greying flesh: beetles crawling over a fetid feast. Winter's instinct was to wave his hand above her leg and send them scurrying off but a deeper impulse first made him fire off a shot from his camera, freezing the tiny skin vultures for ever on the dead girl's skin.

Checking for evidence of footprints at her side, he dropped to the ground so that he could photograph her face without disturbing the body, feeling the damp grass immediately seep into his clothing and begin to eat away at his threads. Raising his camera, he saw her. Young, pretty and confused, her mouth slackly open. Her eyes seemed questioning rather than afraid despite the physical evidence, a car crash of blues and purples on her neck that screamed brutal strangulation.

Her skin was smooth and still lightly tanned, despite the lifeblood draining away behind the outer mask. Her lips, swathed in nude gloss, formed a perfect pout of disappointment and her sculpted eyebrows arched in surprise. A girl in the wrong place at the wrong time and a long way from home.

He focused in on her neck, slim and taut yet made into an ugly canvas by the violent swathes of colour that disfigured it. The attack had been vicious and prolonged – he'd seen more than enough cases to know that – throttling her to the point of death and beyond. Tell-tale purple spots were almost certainly petechiae, caused by broken capillary blood vessels and a probable sign of asphyxiation. His lens had also picked them out in the whites of her eyes.

Winter pulled away reluctantly, easing himself up off the grass and turning his camera to the dark crimson splash above the girl's head that streaked like a vein across the headstone and partly concealed the family name etched there: THOMSON. The source of the blood was all too obvious and strangulation clearly had not been enough for the murderer. The girl's hair was thickly matted and her skull broken, much as Hannah Healey's had been, where her head had been battered against the monument that she'd rested against.

Moving down, his lens picked out a thin trail of blood on the girl's dress by her right-hand side, a rusty track against the cashmere that seemed unlikely, given its position, to have come from the wound to her skull. There was some spatter too on the grass nearby, vivid droplets of blood that stained the ground. Winter positioned his camera under her right hand, so that he could shoot up towards it without the need to move her, and fired the shutter.

Withdrawing the camera, he studied the image he'd taken, seeing immediately that he'd found the source of the blood. He stood, taking a succession of images of the girl's arm, securing the position it and the hand were in, before turning to Addison.

'You'll want to turn her hand round and look at it. It's odd and a bit nasty.'

Addison looked at him questioningly, knowing full well Winter's idea of what constituted nasty. He moved forward and as he did so, Tony and Rachel found themselves staring into each other's eyes, a shared look that went on moments longer than it needed to.

Addison bent down and took the girl's pale wrist in his gloved hand, turning it as gently as he could given the effects of rigor. The back of her hand was darkly purple with lividity but the most striking detail was her middle finger. While the other four nails were neatly manicured and painted bright red, the middle fingernail had been ripped out, leaving the exposed nail bed a raw and bloody mess.

Addison sighed heavily. 'What kind of sick bastard would do that? And where the hell is the fingernail?'

'He's got it.' Narey crouched down and ran her own finger above the line of the girl's violated digit.

'Okay.' Addison accepted it reluctantly. 'But why?'

'A trophy of some sort. Same as Kirsty McAndrew's shoes and Hannah Healey's bag. Find them and we find our killer. And I'm also wondering why she hasn't got a coat on.'

'And you've some idea of why he's taken what he has?'

Narey nodded. 'I think so. Give me a couple of hours? It might be complete guesswork and I'd rather check it out.'

Addison rubbed at his eyes and exhaled. 'Okay. But not any longer than that. We've got enough problems without you going all Nancy Drew on me.'

Narey narrowed her eyes at him. 'I'm going to start making a list of every time you use Nancy Drew, Juliet Bravo, Miss Marple or Jessica bloody Fletcher from now on. As soon as you hit ten, you'll be up in front of a tribunal.'

'Aye, okay, Sarah Lund. Add that to your list. Time of the month, is it?'

'You're a prick, sir.'

'I know. Now let's get on with this. Tony, you done?'

Winter nodded to Addison: he was finished.

The DI moved in, his face set firm in readiness for a task he wasn't looking forward to. On his knees next to the girl, he reached out towards her, then stopped, rethinking the situation. 'Rachel,' he called out to her. 'Come on, I need your help with this.'

Knowing what he needed, Narey moved to the girl's other side and knelt on the ground. She looked at him to signal she was ready.

'Okay, support her back, then we'll slide the dress up.' Addison looked up to see uniforms, detectives and forensics all watching them intently – and it pissed him off. 'This isn't a fucking peepshow. Go and find something to do. I think you'll find there's plenty. Tony, you stay there. The rest of you piss off.'

The cops and SOCOs dropped their heads in embarrassment, some muttering about Addison but not daring to let it be heard, turning away to busy themselves with some task or other.

'On three . . . lift.'

They eased Ashleigh's body from the ground, feeling her cold and damp even through the nitrile gloves. With their spare hands, they took hold of the black dress and began to work it up her thighs until they were completely exposed, revealing a tiny pair of black panties and a small daisy tattoo on her right hip, and finally pulling enough material beyond her midriff until it too was indelicately on show.

They'd seen it as soon as they'd lifted the dress above her navel, the first glimpse of lipstick and they'd known. There had been no doubts in either mind about what would be revealed, about what would be daubed there.

SIN

The word was carved on her flesh in artless stabs of wax, branding her and disfiguring her, if in name only. Sticks and stones will break my bones, Winter thought. As Addison and Narey turned towards him in an unspoken request to photograph the girl's stomach, he quickly shot a couple of frames and captured them crouched grimly either side of her exposed midriff. In the same movement, he stepped forward and filled his lens with the word, stealing it from her skin.

'Enough,' Addison told him, nodding at Narey to ease the girl's dress back down over her body.

Winter began to move away again but stopped, a thought occurring to him. 'I think I might know what it means.'

'Go on.'

'Sin. It's the sins of the father.'

'From the Bible?'

'Shakespeare. *Merchant of Venice*. The sins of the father are to be laid upon the children.'

Chapter 43

Saturday morning

The rain came suddenly to the Western Necropolis, crashing down onto the turf and paths and graves, forcing forensics to hurriedly erect a tent over the crime scene before any evidence was washed away. Ashleigh Fleming's body, broken and slumped in front of the memorial stone, quickly had a river washing at her feet.

Narey and Addison took up shelter in the bowels of the red-bricked crematorium at her suggestion, a hurriedly convened counsel of war that Winter was excluded from. Shaking excess water from their already soaking clothes, they descended marble stairs into a small room that at first glance Addison thought was a library. It was of sorts: a library for the dead.

Large marble stands stood in the middle of the room, polished russet grained with white. Instead of books, the heavyweight stands had spaces designed to hold wooden caskets, each adorned with a brass plaque and containing the ashes of the departed; sixteen caskets on either side and four on each end. The walls, too, were lined with the same marble shelving, identical spaces floor to ceiling and wall to wall, each opening filled with a casket. Some were in teak, oak or ebony but the majority of those on the walls, particularly the older ones, were in white marble, neatly stacked away for eternity.

A white frieze lined the lower half of one wall, its pale marble grained with grey and the words IN LOVING MEMORY etched upon its skin. Above it, soft light drifted into the room through the reds, blues and yellows of a stained-glass window.

'Cheery place,' Addison grouched.

'It's dry and we won't be overheard. Not by the people in here, anyway. And maybe it'll help concentrate the mind.'

'I think the body of that girl out there is enough to do that, don't you? This stops today, Rachel. I am not fu—' Addison stopped, the solemnity of the place curbing his natural instinct to swear. 'I'm not having this. We get this guy today.'

'So where are we?'

'Apart from knee deep in it?' Addison's hands went to his head, rubbing wearily at his eyes as he put his thoughts in order. 'Okay, we assume that Atto is telling us the truth and that his devil spawn intends to kill again. Tonight. We can't take anything he says as gospel but it's what we have to work with. Agreed?'

'Yes.'

'So he's murdered three women, all aged within a few years of each other, all out on their own at night. All three fitting the same generic profile as the Red Silk victims of 1972. We've got to assume he's working to the same template. He's left his victims in the Necropolis and then the Southern and the Western Necropolis. Obviously, there's four necropolises in

Glasgow and that leaves one. The Eastern Necropolis at Parkhead – Janefield Cemetery.'

'You think that's his plan?' Narey asked. 'To dump a fourth body there? Surely he knows that we'll be expecting that.'

'Of course he does, but he's playing with us, pissing us about. This is some kind of game to him. If he'd just wanted to kill and get away with it, then he'd have stopped after one. Or two. It's about more than doing it and not getting caught.'

'Like what?'

'I don't bloody know. Like making his daddy proud of him. Like carrying on a family tradition. We're obviously dealing with someone who's a few gravestones short of a cemetery.'

Narey wandered round the room, distractedly examining the names on the old, white-marble caskets, her mind ticking furiously, her fingers running lightly over inscriptions of names long forgotten.

'If he is the son of Archibald Atto, then maybe that explains why he has a preoccupation with death, and I suppose that might explain the cemeteries. But I can't help feeling that, if we can work out why he's so intent on leaving the bodies at the four necropolises, then maybe we'll be nearer to working out who he is. Don't we need to get more out of Atto? Go in there and press him hard till we get some answers?'

Addison shook his head. 'No. We leave that to Tony and to that tube Kelbie. It's not our job. We catch the killer. That's what we do. And we make sure that, if he's intending to leave a corpse in the Eastern Necropolis, he doesn't get within a hundred yards of the place.'

Narey's eyes widened in a show of surprise. 'What? He kills

another young woman but at least we stop him from depositing the body in the cemetery of his choice? That your idea of success?'

'That's not what I mean and you bloody well know it. Our first job is to make sure he doesn't kill again, of course it is. We flood the streets with cops; we warn everyone who remotely fits the profile to stay out of the city centre; we hit every door that we think might have a suspect behind it; we make sure Tony gets whatever he can out of Atto. We do all that and anything else we can think of. But we also take away the option of him finishing this the way he wants. If he knows he can't dump the fourth body in the Eastern, then maybe, just maybe, he won't even try to take that body in the first place.'

'You really think that?'

'I've got to. It looks like he's had some crazy plan all along and, if he knows that he can't see the plan through to the end, then we throw him off course. We put a ring of steel round the Eastern. We protect it like it's Fort bloody Knox.'

Narey sighed and scratched at her head. 'Okay, I get that. It's just . . . I want to nail this bastard. We should have done it before last night. We must do it before tonight.'

'What a good idea. Okay, so what have you got? You were hinting at something back at the scene.'

'It's just a half-arsed theory and it's going to sound stupid if it's wrong. Let me go chase it. I won't give it too long and I'll be back in not much more than an hour.'

Addison held her gaze for a bit, deliberating whether to ask the obvious question but deciding to give her her head.

'Okay, go. Get Toshney and take him with you.'

'Oh for fu– Why are you so intent on me having to take that halfwit everywhere with me?'

Addison grinned. 'He's Lacey to your Cagney.'

'Aye, very funny. Count that as Strike One.'

'Whatever. Anyway, having that annoying prick with you should ensure you don't piss around too long on whatever this wild-goose chase is.'

'And what are you going to do? Sir.'

'Some old-fashioned police work. Maxwell's been working her way through the 1972 files, looking for any link to the recent killings. Tony's Uncle Danny has copies, too. Rico Giannandrea's been doing the same with the names that Teven got from Atto's case files of rapes down south. We're going to cross-check those, knock on doors and even – God bless the Tories – get bobbies on the beat asking stupid bloody questions. Find me as soon as you're done, okay?'

'Will do. You got a plan for sealing off the Eastern? It's a big place.'

'I'm going to get Shirley on the case. I hear he went mental when he heard about this one this morning. He's with the chief constable and that's why he isn't down here. There's going to be outright panic as soon as this hits the papers.'

'There is. And that's probably the only bit of good news we've got going for us. A bit of panic is probably the only thing that's going to keep girls indoors and out of harm's way.'

'And us. This guy won't be able to kill anyone because I intend to have him locked up.'

Chapter 44

Later

Winter closed the car door behind him, the wind almost whipping it out of his hand, and girded his loins for yet another visit inside Blackridge. Both times he'd sat down with Atto, he'd felt a layer of resistance being stripped away from him and he wasn't sure how many more of these chats he could handle. It wasn't just Atto's apparent ability to see inside Winter's head that was bothering him: it was also the extent that Atto was revealing himself, every disclosure darker than the one before.

A gale blew across the exposed terrain of the prison car park, causing puddles to scurry east and all noise to be eaten up. Winter couldn't hear his own footsteps on the tarmac and he seemed to be taking one pace sideways for each one he took forward. The flags in front of the gatehouse looked fit to rip from their poles and rain was coming at him horizontally.

It was because of the wind that he couldn't hear the words coming from the two figures standing in front of the gatehouse, being buffeted by the gale, their voices stolen as soon as they gave them up. When he lifted his chin from its pro-tected position huddled against his chest, he could see them looking at him enquiringly. They said something to each other, obvious only by the opening and closing of their mouths, and then the taller of the two, a slight grey-haired woman in her sixties, tried to call out to him again. The sound didn't get within yards of him and the woman tried again, anxiety written all over her face.

Winter pushed his way through the invisible barrier until he was under the eaves of the gatehouse and standing next to the women. Behind them and through the glass door, he could see Denny Kelbie and the Blackridge governor Tom Walton waiting impatiently for him. The tail of an already spoken sentence drifted weakly to him on the wind.

'. . . for asking, but we need to know. We don't mean to bother you.'

The accent was English, south coast somewhere, and the voice was so fragile that it would have faced a losing battle against even a gentle breeze. The woman's face was lined and old before her time, her eyes wet and nervous.

The other woman was of a similar vintage, dark-hair flecked grey with time and a stocky build that looked capable of with-standing the best efforts of the wind to shift her, yet beaten and vulnerable for all that. She stood at the shoulder of her companion looking out for her and seemingly set to pounce if Winter didn't agree to whatever it was that he hadn't heard.

'Sorry? I couldn't hear you.'

The woman's face fell slightly at the realisation she was going to have to go through it all again.

'Oh. Sorry. I didn't . . . Are you Mr Winter?'

He immediately felt himself go on the defensive. Who the hell were these women and how could they know who he was?

'Um yes, I am. How did you ...?'

The woman brightened, a tired smile lighting up her face and forcing the rigid lines to make an uncommon upward turn.

'Oh. Good. We've been waiting for you. We drove through the night to get here. This is really important. We need your help, Mr Winter.'

'How do you know who I am? And how can I ...? Sorry I don't understand and I'm in a bit of a hurry.'

The woman, took half a step towards him so that she didn't have to shout to be heard.

'You're going to see him, aren't you? Atto. You're visiting Archibald Atto. We can't say who told us you were coming to see him today but we know you are.'

Winter felt ambushed. The idea had been that no one, not press or public, was supposed to know about this.

'I can't really say. Look I'm sorry but I have to—'

The smaller woman took a step forward. She was no more than five foot two but something about the certainty of her manner intimidated Winter enough that he thought she was going to have a swing at him. She got close enough that she was within inches and he could smell cigarettes and perfume on her. She spoke for the first time, her Midlands accent stronger and cracklier than the other woman's southern tones, vulnerability masked by the rumble of a smoker's croak.

'We're ... I'm Eleanor Holt. This is Marjorie Shillington. Archibald Atto murdered our daughters.'

The taller woman nodded almost apologetically, confirming that she was who her friend said she was. She edged forward till she was shoulder to shoulder with the other, both looking up hopefully at Winter for a response.

'I don't ... I'm not sure what to say. I'm sorry about ... I need to go. I'm expected inside.'

'To meet *him*.'

He hesitated. 'Yes.'

'We need your help, Mr Winter. Both of us. And others. Far too many others. Atto knows where ...' The woman's face fell, her eyes dropping to the ground, where she must have found the courage to finish her sentence. '... where our girls are. And *we* need to know.'

Shit. This day was bad enough without this. The women were right next to him now, years of hurt etched on their faces. He felt cornered, pressurised, trapped. He had to run.

He moved towards the door but Eleanor Holt instinctively moved with him, barring his path with her stout frame. Marjorie Shillington moved swiftly alongside her, finding her frail voice again.

'We need you to talk to him, Mr Winter. This is our first chance in years. He sometimes talks when he thinks he can get in the papers. Please. You need to get him to talk. To tell us. To tell us where they are.'

Winter sidestepped the women. He hadn't signed up for this. It was way too much for him to deal with. He reached for the door handle but Mrs Holt had another gambit up her sleeve.

'I've got cancer, Mr Winter. Lung cancer. My own fault for smoking all these years, but cancer all the same. I might live six years; I might live six months. The doctors don't know and sometimes I think they're just making it up. Guessing, you know. I need to know … I need to know about my Melanie. I've not got the time to wait.'

Winter swallowed back the bile of imposed guilt that surged in his throat. He nodded, shrugged and shook his head in one unintelligible movement that even he didn't understand. He pulled the door wide and with a final, apologetic look, seeing hot tears run down both their cheeks, he stepped inside the prison and left them to the mercy of the wind.

The moments that he sat alone at his side of the wooden table, the governor, Walton, silent against the far wall, waiting for Atto's arrival were possibly the worst. Four bare walls and not a chink of daylight. It was oppressive and claustrophobic and reminiscent of a six-foot-deep hole in the ground. The worst thing, however, was anticipating the look on Atto's face when he sauntered into the room with the prison guard at his back. Would he be taciturn or angry, dismissive or taunting? Bad or unhelpful as all of those moods could be, the one that Winter least wanted to see was the one that he got on his last visit: Atto being *pleased* to see him.

He jumped at the sound of the now familiar hiss that meant the door was about to begin its slow slide to the right. He knew that Atto had already taken the first of the few paces that would bring him to the table, even though there was no discernible sound of anyone walking on the cushioned flooring. In a heartbeat, Atto's head appeared through the door and Winter shrank inside at the light that went on in the killer's dark eyes at the sight of him sitting there. Having a multiple murderer being elated at your visit was something guaranteed to mess with your head.

'How are you today, Anthony?' Atto began pleasantly as he slid into the chair opposite. 'I hope the traffic wasn't too bad on the way through from Glasgow. I hear it's very wet and windy out there.'

The banality of having everyday conversation with the killer freaked Winter out more than discussing murders and psychopaths. He couldn't and wouldn't do small talk. He couldn't and wouldn't stop thinking about the body he'd photographed just a few hours before. Maybe that was why Atto picked up on it almost immediately.

'He's killed again, hasn't he?'

There was a skin-crawling edge of excitement in the man's voice as he asked the question. From anyone else it might have been just morbid curiosity, but from Atto there was something verging on pride. The question was laced with hope.

In the time it took Winter to decide whether to confirm it or not, the hesitancy was its own answer.

'A chip off the old block, right enough. Who did he kill and where?'

The exhilaration in Atto's voice was palpable. He was gorging on the news and it sickened Winter, making him determined not to feed him further.

'I don't know who it was. Or where.'

'I don't believe you. Don't lie to me, Anthony. You've seen the body, haven't you? Photographed it?'

'That's not what we're here to talk about.'

Atto sneered. 'Oh, but it's *exactly* what we're here to talk about. Murder. What he did to those girls and why. It's all about why men kill, Anthony. Remember?'

'Have you had any more contact from him?'

'No.'

'Nothing at all?'

'That's what "no" means in this case. No. Did you photograph the body?'

Winter had nowhere else to go. 'Yes I did.'

Atto brightened again, a nauseating smirk playing on his lips. 'How did she die?'

'She was strangled and her head battered against a memorial headstone.'

'Another cemetery? Tut-tut. The boys in blue should *surely* have had that covered. Was she raped?'

'That's not something you need to know.'

'So she was. Was she good-looking?'

Winter wasn't giving him this. He wouldn't. He needed to shift the conversation, wrestle back even a tiny measure of control.

'Tell me about Melanie Holt and Louise Shillington.'

Atto looked at him oddly, clearly thrown by the sudden mention of the two names. His eyes narrowed in suspicion. 'Why?'

Not for the first time, Winter resented Atto's ability to second-guess his questions. 'No reason,' he lied. 'Other than the fact that you murdered them.'

A hint of an insufferably smug smile tugged at the corner of Atto's mouth. 'Did I?'

'You know you did. You already told the police that.'

'Maybe I did. I can't really remember.'

'I think you can. Can you remember where the bodies are buried?'

'Maybe. Maybe you should ask me.'

'Why, will you tell me?'

'I might. And I might tell you exactly what I did to them.'

Winter sat and looked at him, knowing Atto was playing another of his games and determined not to indulge him. Whatever Atto wanted him to do or say, he'd do the opposite. All he had to do was work out what that was.

'You can tell me that when you're ready. Do you ever think about either of those girls?'

Atto paused, searching Winter's face for clues as to where he was going and whether he wanted to be led there. 'Sometimes,' he whispered eventually.

'Do you ever think about their parents? How they must be feeling after all this time?'

Atto leaned forward. 'You want to know the truth, Anthony?'

Winter nodded.

'I don't think about the parents. Ever. How can I possibly know what they feel? And why would I care?'

'Their children were murdered. *You* killed them.'

'So you keep saying. But why would that mean that I thought about their mammies and daddies? You're thinking that I've got feelings. That I'm the same as everyone else. I'm not.'

'You're a parent yourself.'

Atto's brows knotted in confusion. 'Not really. There was some sort of biochemical accident but that was all. That doesn't make me a parent. Not one that anyone would want. I don't even know who the mother was.'

'What if someone harmed your child?'

One of his shrill chuckles popped from the side of Atto's mouth and his head bobbed forward fitfully. 'Anthony, I'd say that he's the one that's doing the harming. Wouldn't you?'

'Yeah, I would. He's left another set of parents without a child.'

Atto sighed. 'You've been talking to the parents, haven't you? The Shillingtons and the Holts. Those people just won't let it go.'

'Can you blame them? They don't even know where their daughters are buried.'

'I don't know if I can blame them or not. Let me tell you about Melanie and what I did to her.'

'I don't want to know.'

'But I want to tell you. And maybe I'll tell you where she's buried.'

Winter said nothing but felt his heart sink into his stomach.

'She was nineteen. A sweet, pretty thing. She lived near me and I saw her walking most days. Lovely long blonde hair halfway to her waist. I watched her for ages before I did anything. Watched and waited. Sometimes she smiled when she saw me. She liked me, you see. I could tell. And I liked her. A lot. I wanted to have her, Anthony. I wanted to enjoy her.'

The sound of his own name from Atto's lips made Winter want to throw up. If Atto sensed it, it did nothing to discourage him.

'Her parents were careless. Letting her walk around, never knowing where she was or who she might be seeing. They didn't deserve to have her, looking after her the way they did.

She had lovely lips; that was one of the things I liked most about her. Full lips. Very … kissable. I had to have her, Anthony. Had to. And had no reason not to.'

'How about the fact that it was wrong?'

'Wrong? It wasn't wrong for me. It was what I wanted to do.'

'It's not what *she* wanted. It was wrong. Legally and morally.'

'Those weren't my morals and I can't be responsible for anyone else's. And don't be so sure that she didn't want it, Anthony. The simple truth is that women are an inferior species and they secretly want us to be in charge of them. She wanted it. I took her because I wanted her too and to me there was nothing wrong with it. And she tasted sweet. So sweet. She felt good. It all did.'

'It felt good? How could—'

'Oh it did, Anthony. You have to have done it to know. It's like owning someone. Completely. I took her to a little place I knew where we wouldn't be disturbed. We had sex. And, as I came inside her, I put my hands on her sweet neck and tightened. The power of that is something you have to experience to truly understand. Being inside someone as they cross over from life to death. Have you ever wondered what that's like?'

'No.'

'No? You're wishing that you'd photographed her, aren't you, Anthony?'

'No. I'm not.'

'Not even a little bit? After she was found. Strangled. Her neck broken. Her eyes staring. Her mouth wide open. Can you picture her? You can, can't you?'

'Only because I've seen your son's victims.'

'There you go. That's the gift he's given you.'

'The police will catch him. And he'll be locked up for the rest of his life. Just like you.'

'Maybe. But I doubt that he's just like me. He's copying me. Anyone could do that, whether they come from my seed or not. I do it because that's who I am. He does it because that's who he wants to be. If the neuroscientists are right, then my paralimbic system is wired wrong. I find that more believable than having some kind of rogue gene that can be passed on.'

The self-satisfied prick was grating on Winter's nerves. Claiming the moral high ground among murderers.

'I'm not so sure. The chances of there being no genetic link between two cowardly murdering rapists who happen to be father and son is a bit slim, don't you think?' Atto's eyes flashed rage but Winter continued. 'You know your Shakespeare?'

'I was an English teacher. Of course I know my Shakespeare.'

'Then you'll remember the line from *The Merchant of Venice*. The sins of—'

Atto interrupted. '—the father are to be laid upon the children. Very clever. Changes nothing. I've had enough of this for today. Interview's over. Mr Walton, I want back to my cell.'

Winter had forgotten that the governor was even in the room until he was aware of him nodding at the guard to open the far door. Atto pushed his chair back, scowling at Winter as he did so. He made his way towards the open door but turned before he got there and stared at Winter before speaking.

'Anthony, when I said I'd had no further contact with him, that wasn't completely true. We did swap a couple of messages. Perhaps one thing that you should know about.'

It was the way that he said it as much as what he said: there was the implied presence of a threat and something dropped like a stone into Winter's stomach. He had to ask the question.

'What do I need to know?'

Atto's voice was sharper, words delivered with a slash and a hack.

'That he knows about you. He knows that you and ex-sergeant Neilson are on his case. It must have slipped out. Sorry about that. It seems he's a very determined young man and won't let anything stand in his way. Maybe there is something of me in him after all. I'd be careful if I were you.'

Chapter 45

Winter left the prison interview room as quickly as he could, pushing his way past the governor and into the relatively fresh air of the outer hall, his breathing fast and heavy. Kelbie leapt out his seat and began moving towards him.

'What happened?'

'Not now. I need fresh air. I'm going outside.'

'No, you're not. Tell what he said.'

'Piss off. Talk to Walton. He was in there and heard it all.'

'Winter. *Winter!*'

Kelbie was shouting at his disappearing back as Winter hurried through the hall to the connecting door at the far end, feeling desperation building in him and knowing he had to be outside to breathe. Kelbie must have given up and settled for speaking to the governor instead, as there was no sound of footsteps coming after him. He worked his way round knots of visitors in the holding hall and finally got his hands on the cold metal handles of the exterior door, pushing his way frantically through.

It was cold and pouring down with rain, but it felt good as he grabbed lungfuls of oxygen to replace the fetid air he'd accrued in the interview room.

'Mr Winter. Mr Winter.'

Christ, this was all he needed. Eleanor Holt and Marjorie Shillington were still there and were now advancing on him from their shelter under the eaves, anxious to get to him and mindless of the rain.

'What did he tell you, Mr Winter? Did he tell you where our girls are buried. Did you ask him?'

'No. I mean yes. I asked him but he didn't tell me. He did talk about Melanie but—'

As soon as the words were out of his mouth he regretted them. There was no way he could tell the woman what Atto had said about her daughter. He saw a light of hope go on in her eyes and he cursed himself.

'What? What did he say?'

Winter's brain scrambled.

'He … didn't say where she was buried. He did say …' – shit, he was digging another grave of hope for the poor woman – 'that he *might* tell me. But he likes to play games. You must know that. I have no idea if he was being truthful and whether he will.'

'Oh, Mr Winter, you can't know how much that would mean to me. It would … it would be everything I could hope for.'

'Mrs Holt, I don't … I can't be sure he will tell me. You know how often he's strung people along before, promising details, then changing his mind. I don't want you to get your hopes up. This could mean nothing.'

Eleanor Holt nodded vigorously but he could see that she wasn't buying any of his attempts to downplay her expectations. Marjorie Shillington edged apologetically in front of her friend, looking up at him with a mixture of hope and fear.

'Mr Winter, did he say anything about my Louise? Did he ... did he say he might tell you where she is?'

He hesitated, the pause generated by the fact that Atto had not detailed his taking and killing of Louise. Winter's mind prompted him to tell the woman that she should be in some way glad that he hadn't said anything about her. Instead, she interpreted his indecision as a 'no', her brittle faith crushed by nothing at all, and she shrank back behind her companion again.

'No, it's not that.' He dug himself deeper. 'He just didn't talk about her. When he said he might tell me – and he only said he might – he meant both girls. Both.'

Marjorie brightened again, cautious optimism holding her up. She and Eleanor exchanged a long look, sisters of sorts after all they'd endured, before turning back to Winter.

'We can't thank you enough, Mr Winter. We've waited so long for this and we thought it might never happen. We owe you so much.'

'No ... You don't have anything to thank me for.'

'Oh, but we do. If you can get him to tell you where they are ...'

'No, but that's not what I'm—'

'Here. Take these. Please.'

Eleanor Holt thrust something towards him and forced it into his hands. Paper. No, photographs. He reluctantly turned them over to see the faces of two young girls staring back up at him, one with long blonde hair and a fair complexion, the other darker. Both gazed straight into the camera. Straight at him.

'Take them, Mr Winter. We want you to know what our

girls looked like. So you know that they were real. Not just some statistic lost in all the crimes Archibald Atto committed. They were our girls.'

Melanie Holt was in a school blazer with white blouse and striped tie loose at her neck, a broad smile on a pretty face. There was something mischievous about the way she looked at the camera, maybe as if someone else was making a joke within earshot and trying to make her laugh. She looked the kind of girl that would have a load of friends and be as popular with the girls as with the boys. A lifetime of possibilities in front of her.

Louise Shillington was also in school uniform but seemed less happy about having her picture taken. She was an attractive girl too but lacked the confidence that Melanie had, an obvious shyness holding back the smile and diffidence in her brown eyes. Winter immediately imagined her as more bookish, not necessarily through a love of studying but because it meant not having to make conversation or let people in.

How long had it been after these photographs were taken that Atto had ended their lives? Was it just a matter of months before they were committed to the shallow grave that he left them in? And where were they now?

He dragged his gaze away from the girls before he could hear their voices beginning to reach out to him, imploring him to help. He looked up and saw their eyes in their mothers'.

'Will you help us, Mr Winter?'

He heard a voice saying 'Yes' and realised that it was his.

Chapter 46

Saturday afternoon

Getting out of the lift onto the eighteenth floor of the Caledonia Road flats afforded Narey a panoramic view across the Southern Necropolis below. She could easily pick out the spot by the White Lady where Hannah Healey's mutilated body was found. How many times a day, she wondered, did the poor girl's mother have to stare out onto the same view? Would she ever be able to stop herself from doing so?

The view east over the city was as bleak as the afternoon sky. Everything wore that particular shade of grey that Glasgow dressed itself in most days. In the distance, the Campsie Fells were draped in dreary wet cloud, mourning in sympathy with the metropolis laid out before it.

She'd ignored Addison's directions and left Toshney in the car, knowing that his usual level of subtlety was not what was required in the visit she was about to make. She took a final deep breath and walked along the corridor to the door with the nameplate HEALEY on it and knocked.

The ghost that answered the door was even more ashen-faced than when Narey had interviewed her before, washed out from crying and beyond caring for the superficial support of make-up. Mary Healey hadn't even been allowed the luxury of burying her only daughter and, with the investigation far from finished, it would most probably be some time before she could.

'Mrs Healey, I'm Detective Sergeant Rachel Narey. Remember me? I wonder if I might come in and ask you a few questions.'

A weak sigh escaped from Hannah's mother, another breath of life that she'd never get back, but she nodded and softly managed, 'Yes, please come in.'

Mrs Healey offered Narey a seat with an exhausted wave of her hand and the two women dropped into chairs opposite each other.

'Mrs Healey, there was something else I hoped you could help us with.'

'Of course. If I can.'

'You know that the handbag Hannah had with her on Saturday night hasn't been found. We believe that the person who harmed her has it. It would help us if we knew what the bag looked like. I know you've been asked before and couldn't remember but I need you to try again.'

The woman just looked back, her eyes narrowing in confusion.

'We've spoken to her boyfriend but he can't remember. He's sure she had one because he remembers her taking her phone out at one point, but he doesn't know what it looked like. You know what men are like with these things.'

Mrs Healey nodded, almost attempting a faint smile at Narey's remarks but quickly giving up on the idea.

She got up and scrambled towards the hallway, almost tripping over her own feet in her anxiety to do something, anything, that might be worthwhile. 'She keeps them all in her bedroom, very particular about them.'

Mrs Healey led the way into her daughter's room, pausing for a reluctant second before she stepped inside. The room was a typically young woman's bedroom, whites and pinks and acceptably messy with a few framed photographs sitting on the wooden shelf near the bed. The neatest part of the room by far was on the left-hand wall, where two rows of handbags were neatly shelved and evenly spaced like trophies, larger ones in the middle and smaller ones to the outside. Narey had the familiar feeling of intruding on someone else's grief.

'These are her bags,' her mother explained unnecessarily. 'She only kept this many and if she got a new one then she'd force herself to give one to the charity shop or maybe to one of her friends. She used to joke that it was like giving up one of her children ...'

Mrs Healey faltered and nearly choked at the realisation of what she'd said.

'We're doing everything we can to find out who did it,' Narey reassured her. 'And we are getting closer.'

The woman nodded, perhaps unconvinced that catching the killer would make things any better. Narey thought in her case she was probably right.

'Can you tell which one isn't here? The one that she had with her that night?'

'I ... I don't know.'

'It's difficult, I know, but perhaps if you think of ones that you know she had. Favourite ones, maybe, that she used a lot. Maybe ones that you bought her for her birthday or that she treated herself to.'

'I can't ... Oh, God, I'm sorry. I can't be sure.'

'It's okay, Mrs Healey. I don't need you to be certain. Not at this stage. I'm just following up a line of enquiry. A hunch, you might say. Just something I think might help the investigation.'

The woman edged backwards until she rested against the far wall facing the two shelves of bags and stared at them, running her hands through her hair and concentrating for all she was worth. She nodded to herself a couple of times, then got up and walked over to the bags, touching one, then another, talking under her breath as if counting out loud but not wanting anyone else to hear.

Returning to the opposite wall, she looked at the bags again.

'There's one ... Her uncle got her it for Christmas. She really liked it. It's not here. Unless she ...'

Mrs Healey hurried over to the other side of the bed and looked there, then under it. 'No it's not ... and anyway she wouldn't ... Hannah was very particular with her bags. It's definitely not here. I think it must be the one.'

Narey nodded and breathed deep.

'Okay, can you describe it for me, please, Mrs Healey?'

For some reason, of the four of Kirsty McAndrew's friends she'd interviewed, Narey knew it was Lindsey Dornan she

CRAIG ROBERTSON

wanted to speak to first. Kirsty had left the Merchant City early after a row with Lindsey, a brash brunette who now blamed herself for her friend getting killed. Lindsey had been a pain in the bum but also the most likely to be able to keep a cool head and not turn into an emotional mess at the questions Narey needed to ask.

She had an address in Garnetbank for her and considered getting Toshney to drive them both over there, but thought better of it. She had a mobile number for the girl and, if her intuition was correct, it needed only a two-minute phone call. She made Toshney sit and shut up while she called. Lindsey picked up on the third ring.

'Hello?'

'Lindsey? This is DS Rachel Narey. We spoke last Sunday evening.'

'Yeah. I'm hardly likely to forget, am I?'

As charming as ever.

'No. I don't suppose you are. I need to ask you a couple of other questions. Have you got time to do that now? It won't take long.'

'Well, I've got to ... On the phone? Yes, I suppose so.'

'Okay, good. The shoes that Kirsty was wearing on your night out before she was killed, do you remember them at all?'

'Her shoes? I don't ... Yes, yes, I do remember them. They were new and she kept going on about how much she liked them.'

'What do you remember her saying?'

'Well, just how great they were. They'd cost a fortune, so she said. She kept admiring them and making us look at them too.'

'Lindsey, do you remember what colour the shoes were?'

'I don't understand. What's—'

'Lindsey, this is important. What colour were they?'

'They were red. Bright red.'

Chapter 47

Addison had rounded up Detective Sergeants Teven and Gian-nandrea plus three DCs: Galbraith, McTierney and Bryant. He'd also collared Kelbie's DS Ferry while DCI dog runt himself was returning from Atto duty at Blackridge with Winter. Narey and Toshney had been excused on account of their secret mission, a.k.a. the wild-goose chase.

'I want bodies in here,' Addison explained. 'Anyone and everyone who is on our list of suspects. I don't give a fucking monkey's for possible cause. Think of something and haul them in. And I also don't care if they've been ruled out by an alibi unless it is absolutely rock solid.'

'Who do you want, sir?' Ferry clearly hadn't quite listened.

'Every fucker,' Addison reiterated. 'If he's locked up in here then he can't be killing someone out there tonight. So you lot tell me: who have you got? Andy, you first.'

'Robert Wylde. Kirsty McAndrew's ex. I know Rachel thought he had nothing to do with it but—'

'Fine. Bring him back in. I'm taking no chances. Rico?'

'Stevo Barclay, the guy from the tattoo parlour. He did Kirsty's tattoo and has no alibi for the night she was killed other than being out of his skull in the boozer.'

'Yeah, I want him definitely. Anyone else, Rico?'

'Yeah. The other guy from the tattoo shop, Ritchie Stark.'

'What have we got on him?'

Giannandrea shrugged. 'I don't like the look of his face.'

'Good enough for me. Haul his arse in here as well. Ferry?'

The New Gorbals DS produced a piece of paper from his inside pocket. 'I've got two possibles. Both violent rapists, both with a history of attempted strangulation. Don't have anything on them other than them fitting the general MO, so we haven't done anything more than question them. Their alibis are all pretty weak.'

'Names?'

'Barry Holden. John 'Jocky' Summers.'

'I know of Summers. Complete scumbag. Bring them both in. Anyone else? Galbraith. What you got?'

The DC looked a bit embarrassed and shuffled slightly on the spot. 'I was going to say that Ritchie Stark guy as well. I was there with DS Giannandrea and there was something about him I didn't like.'

Addison sighed. 'Well, thanks for the confirmation. I'm sure Rico is delighted. It'll be like a blessing from his bishop. Right, anyone else got any other names?'

No one had.

'Okay, have them in here around one o'clock. That will allow us to hold them until one in the morning, although I can hopefully get that increased on "cause shown". Separate cells, obviously, and co-ordinate with each other so you don't arrive at the same time. I don't want any of them to know that the others are here.'

*

Narey had hoped to get Addison on his own but he'd left one meeting and was on his way to another with Shirley at Stewart Street alongside Kelbie. When she'd phoned he'd asked if she had got her half-arsed theory to check out and when she said she had, rather than ask what it was, he told her to join them. He said it was probably going to be the only positive thing to come out of the meeting.

Toshney had twice asked her what the phone call to Lindsey Dornan was all about and what the colour of the shoes had to do with anything, but she'd told him just to concentrate on the road. He drove but retaliated with intermittent whistling and attempts at inane chatter, which were both met by hostile glares on her part. When he tried sensible, case-related conversation, he fared little better.

'What's going on, Sarge? Has there been some kind of breakthrough?'

'I don't know yet. Detective Superintendent Shirley's called a meeting. That's all I know for now. DCI Kelbie and DI Addison will be there too. It must be important if they've dragged the DCI back in from Blackridge.'

'And us?'

'No, not us. Me.'

Toshney pouted at that and finally shut up, pointing the car back towards the station. He parked in the Stewart Street car park and she was out of the door and on her way inside before he'd got the keys out of the ignition. Toshney scrambled for the door and hustled across the tarmac at her heels, finally catching her just after she pulled the door back and stepped inside.

'Oh, come on, Sarge. Surely I should be—'

'No. This is a meeting for the big boys and girls. Sit. And don't play with anything you shouldn't.'

She knocked on the door of the meeting room and was greeted immediately by a barked 'Come in' that she recognised as being Shirley's stressed voice.

The three men were standing: Addison and Kelbie with their backs to the door and Shirley facing it and them. He looked over to make sure it was her and beckoned her in with a lift of his head.

'No ... of course I can't be sure,' Addison was saying. 'But everything points to it and I think we have to work on the basis of it being his most likely next move.'

'It's speculation, sir,' Kelbie argued. 'I can see where the DI is coming from but I'd suggest it would be foolish to concentrate all our resources on Janefield Cemetery when we can't know what his intentions are.'

'Nobody said anything about putting *all* our resources, there.' Addison sounded exasperated by Kelbie, as if he'd had to make this argument more than once. 'I've already made plans to bring every potential suspect on our list into custody to limit the chances of anything actually happening in the first place. But if – and I stress *if* – he strikes again, then we have to cover every bloody cemetery in the city. But the blindingly obvious place is the Eastern – Janefield.'

'Maybe it's *too* obvious,' Kelbie growled. 'He's luring mugs into thinking that's what he's going to do so he can get a free run at somewhere else like Sandymount, Tollcross or Cardonald.'

'They aren't bloody necropolises. He's left bodies at three of them and there's four in the city. The guy's a grade-A crazy but there's a method to his madness. His plan is to kill and dump his victim at the Eastern. I'd bet on it.'

'That's a big bet.'

'Okay, that's enough, Kelbie. DS Narey, what do you think?'

Oh, great, she thought. Thanks for the poisoned chalice.

'I can see the logic in DI Addison's argument. I'd say, given the little we know, that the Eastern is the most likely place he'd leave another body. Assuming, of course, that we don't stop him in the first place.'

Kelbie offered something between a sneer and a glare; Addison smiled approvingly at her but glowered slightly at her pointed remark about stopping the killer; Shirley, she was gratified to see, nodded thoughtfully.

'Okay, I agree. Derek, seeing as this is your call, what do you suggest we do?'

Addison allowed himself a mock grin towards Kelbie before answering. 'We go public. As soon as possible. We get the press boys in and we tell them that we think the killer intends to complete his set and leave a body at the Eastern. It will—'

'—cause widespread panic?' Kelbie suggested helpfully.

'No . . . It will let everyone in the city, including the bampot we're after, know that we're onto him. We let him know that there's no way he's getting anywhere near the Eastern and his game is up. We make sure it's in every newspaper, on every TV station, on every website. He's been calling all the shots on this up to now and we need to change that.'

Shirley seemed to be mulling it over, so Addison charged on.

'We need to shake him up. Force him into making a mistake. I'm not pretending I know how the hell his sick mind works but it seems obvious he's intent on copying the Red Silk murders and that Atto is his focus for that. He's had a plan; we force him to change it. We seal off the Eastern and manoeuvre him into a place he doesn't want to be.'

Shirley exhaled heavily. 'Okay ... okay. But we cannot make this look like we're giving in to the idea of him killing again. Everything has to be geared to stopping him first. Another bloody murder and we'll all be looking for a new job. Starting with me. But I agree, this might just be enough to put him off the idea of trying. Christ, it better. Stuff my job ... I don't want this on my conscience.'

An awkward silence fell between them, four minds contemplating the consequences of another murder – for the force, for them, for the victim. It didn't bear thinking about.

'Okay ...' Shirley sighed again. 'Denny, what's happening with Winter and Atto?'

Kelbie pulled himself up to his inconsiderable height, glad of the chance to finally take centre stage. 'Winter's back there now. He had some kind of spat with Atto earlier and it looked like that was that, but Atto's called him back in. The bad news is that the press are all over it after last night's media conference. There's a pack of them outside Blackridge. No doubt Atto is loving it. I don't think Winter is, though: the pressure's getting to him. I'd still rather we had someone else in there, sir. Like a proper police officer.'

Addison and Narey were both about to jump in but Shirley saw the protests coming and dismissed them with a wave of his hand. 'In many ways I agree with you, Denny, but Atto's already made it clear he won't talk to anyone else. We have to trust Winter not to make an arse of this. We need every edge we can get and any bit of info that might tell us who his child is or where he is. We go with Winter; we've no choice.'

Kelbie shrugged, obviously unimpressed. 'Yes, sir. I've primed Winter with questions that will hopefully lure Atto into letting information slip. He must know more than he's telling us about who's doing this. I've also persuaded Tom Walton, the prison governor, to wear a wire so we can hear what's going on in that interview room as it happens rather than wait till they come out.'

'What?' Addison let rip. 'Even though Atto insisted there would be no live transmission device? And even though he might be our best chance of stopping this guy? And even though it runs the risk of any evidence being inadmissible in court? And even though you didn't bother getting authorisation for this?'

'I made a decision because no one else was! And you should remember your place, *Inspector*!'

'Enough!' Shirley's face had turned a dangerous shade of red. 'Kelbie, next time, you ask me before you do something like that. Okay?'

'Yes, sir.'

'Addison, you wind your neck in. I don't want to have to tell you again. I'm not entirely happy about this, but it's done. Denny, you start worrying if it blows up in our faces. DS Narey, what's this new information you've got?'

The floor being thrown over to her came as a surprise and she'd just as rather it hadn't happened on the back of Shirley about to blow a gasket. Still, there was no going back. She just had to make it sound more convincing than she believed it to be.

'Well, you're going to have to bear with me on this, because it will probably sound a bit flimsy. Particularly to start with.'

She could see Addison blanching and she knew the git would be wondering whether he ought to have dragged her into the meeting on the basis of something she didn't seem to have much faith in. She'd have been more annoyed at him if she wasn't wondering the same thing.

'Okay ... so we know that Kirsty McAndrew's shoes were missing. So was Hannah Healey's handbag. And a fingernail was ripped off the latest victim, Ashleigh Fleming. I think they were taken by the killer as some kind of memento or trophy. But why those items and not anything else? Why not shoes from both or a bag or whatever? It's been bugging me for days but I think Atto's little bombshell yesterday has given us the connection.'

'Spit it out, then.' Shirley's patience was being tested.

'I went to see Hannah's mother this morning and she was able to work out which bag Hannah had with her the night she was killed. It was a favourite that her uncle had bought her. A red one.'

Everyone heard the sceptical snort that escaped from Kelbie's nose but no one responded to it, although Narey made a mental note to make him pay for it one day. She continued, resisting the temptation to glare in his direction.

'Kirsty had so many pairs of shoes that her parents couldn't tell us which were missing or which weren't, but I spoke to two of her friends and they confirmed she was wearing this new pair of shoes when they were all out on the night she was murdered. Ironic, really, as her friends said that she'd kept on about how much she loved those new killer heels. Bright-red killer heels.

'Ashleigh Fleming's fingernails, as we know, were bright red. Red Pearl according to the bottle in her bag. And I spoke to the desk staff at her hotel. She was wearing a red coat when she went out on Friday night.'

Alex Shirley's brows dived sceptically towards his nose. 'You're saying that's why he's killing them? Because they're wearing red?'

'No, sir. I'm not saying that's why he's killing them. I'm saying that's why he's choosing the ones that he is.'

'Christ, that's … insane. And … I suppose possible.'

'I think it's more than possible, sir. A red bag. Taken. Red shoes. Taken. A red fingernail. Ripped out. A red coat. Taken. Red lipstick daubed on the victims' stomachs. Red Silk …'

Shirley rubbed both hands across his face then pushed on upwards through his steel-grey hair. 'Yes, I can join the dots, Narey, thank you. Oh, for Christ's sake, as if last night's press conference wasn't bad enough. I'm going to look like a right bloody idiot going back on national television telling young women in Glasgow to avoid wearing red.'

'I'll do it, sir,' Kelbie butted in. 'If it's going to help ease any—'

'I'm sure you would, DCI Kelbie, but your selfless offer won't be necessary. This is my mess and I'll deal with it. Christ. One of you get me Media Services on the phone and bloody hurry up about it.'

Chapter 48

August 1972

There had been talk about forcing Klass to scrap its Be Red Silk for a Night event on the obvious grounds of bad taste, along with its equally dubious Red Silk Lookalike contest. However, the chief constable was eventually persuaded to let it go ahead on the grounds that it just might lure the killer into the open. Only Geordie Taylor suggested that the killer might actually go and try to win a competition to be the most like himself. Their leads were drying up fast, and they needed to try whatever they could.

Glasgow seemed to have become split into those who thought everything was okay because Red Silk hadn't struck for three weeks and those who were all the more terrified because he still hadn't been caught. So, ridiculous as it seemed, he was in the queue to get into the disco with a red silk handkerchief placed in the breast pocket of his light-weight fawn suit. The jacket wouldn't be on for long, though: the temperatures had picked up again and he was beginning to sweat even standing on the stairs, never mind what it would be like in the oven inside.

They all had them, every man in the queue. The snaking line of likely lads with red hankies made a bizarre sight and was causing hilarity verging on hysterics among the girls, particularly those whose nerves were being stretched by the nature of the event. It seemed as if the place had never been busier, the queue extending further down West Nile Street than he'd ever seen it and with more joining its tail all the time. There was no way that they'd all get in, and the bouncers had even more leeway than usual for refusing admittance – and there was no chance of the few blokes without red hankies getting across the door.

He turned and looked down the stairway, telling himself he was looking for someone matching the Red Silk description among a sea of pretenders but knowing that the truth was different. He saw a couple of redheads bobbing here and there but, despite the steep angle of the stairs making it difficult to tell, he didn't think she was among them. That was good, he told himself: no distractions, no interference, concentrate on the job in hand.

The whole of the Triple D squad were in Klass that night, no time off with the potential consequences of the Red Silk night. Kenny McConville and Sheila Mottram were there posing as a couple; Brian Webster, Colin Black and Alice McCutcheon were singles, working the room and mixing with the crowd. McConville and Mottram had been just a few steps above him in the queue, Kenny slipping his arm round Sheila's waist and she noticeably squirming with discomfort. Danny knew that McConville was likely to get a slap when the night was over.

Inside, the squad were dotted round the room, rarely in sight of each other because of the mass of humanity that was packed in there. The dance floor was already full and the DJ had the place buzzing even though the night had barely begun. It just contrived to make it still warmer, bodies cranking up the heat on each other, and even the walls were beginning to sweat. The DJ came in at the fade of Badfinger's 'Day by Day' and ventured to pump up the temperatures even further.

'Awrite there, people. I'm Jumping Jimmy Steele and you are in Klass, the best disco this side of New York City. Look at all youse beautiful men out there. Never seen so many red silk hankies in my puff. Also with us tonight is Mr Malcolm Scobie, the winner of last night's Red Silk Lookalike competition. Malcolm was so convincing he spent today down at the cop shop helping the polis with their enquiries, but they've let him back out for the night. Good to see you, Malky. Okay, guys, mind and keep those red hankies on show 'cos there's gonna be special prizes afore the night's out. We're Klass and it's all happening here. I'm Jumping Jimmy Steele and this ... is Argent with "Hold Your Head Up".'

The Argent track was less than halfway through when she came in. She seemed to carve a path through the crowds with her friends in her wake, effortlessly making her way to the edge of the dance floor, where she stopped and looked around. He could see her eyes sweeping in his direction and knew she would see him in seconds. He readied himself, smiling the Steve McQueen smile. She saw him and he enjoyed the way that her own smile slowly began to spread across her face. It was the moment he knew he was in trouble.

Jenny turned to her friends and said something that caused them to grin knowingly before she strode onto the dance floor, immediately picking up the rhythm of the song as she walked, her hips swaying provocatively. A voice deep inside him said go, and he was walking almost before he knew it. They met on the floor and were dancing together without a word having been spoken.

She was wearing a red miniskirt, brown calf-length boots and a white halter-neck top showing off her slim, sun-kissed shoulders. Her hair was loose and long, bouncing behind her as she moved, transfixing him. The red tresses danced as she did, bobbing in time to the music thumping out from the DJ's decks. The room and the dance floor were full of bodies, but he could see only hers.

The song changed, but he was almost unaware of it, conscious only of the way she moved and following her tempo rather than that of the music. They were dancing closer, forced together by the crowd and their instincts. The heat was rising.

Maybe the DJ was a bastard, because he put on an even faster track and the room was on fire, burning bodies moving more quickly, turning, spinning, sweltering. She simply picked up the speed and ran with it, her legs kicking, her arms high and her hips gyrating. The buzz of moving with her was a powerful thing, sizzling in the energy that electrified the room.

After the third song, they moved off the dance floor, over to the side away from where her friends were. He could feel the dampness in the middle of his back where his shirt stuck to it, and his breathing was quick, the heat making him pant like a dog despite his fitness. She seemed unfazed, coolly leaning back against a pillar, her long bare legs crossed at the ankles.

'Drink?'

'Good idea.' She grinned. 'Take it you can remember what it is?'

'One martini and lemonade with ice coming up.'

He reluctantly turned away from her and nudged his way through the crowd, tapping shoulders and edging people aside. The queue was three deep, desert-dry mouths aching for refreshment. As he stood and waited his turn, he took the opportunity to glance around, remembering why he was there in the first place. Everywhere he looked, there were red hankies, most being used to wipe perspiring foreheads. Red silk everywhere.

He finally caught the eye of the short balding barman and moments later he had a pint of lager and a tumbler of martini, the ice fighting a losing battle against the heat. Picking them up, he turned back towards the dance floor and straight into a bloke coming the other way. The guy's elbow caught his pint glass and caused lager to splash onto the floor, making the carpet even stickier than before. They looked at each other for a few moments, a typical Glasgow stand-off with no one wanting to be first to apologise. The man, dressed in a nondescript brown suit with a red hankie peeping out of the breast pocket, was an inch or two shorter than Danny and a good few stone slighter, so you would think there would be no contest if it came to a shoving match. There was an edge to the smaller fellow's dark eyes, though, something fierce in them under that fringe of mousy brown hair that put Danny on his guard. In this city you quickly learned the difference between height and size.

At once, they both muttered 'Sorry' and nodded an acceptance, each edging to the side to let the other through. Danny scooped a gulp of his lager, groaning slightly at the realisation that it had already gone warm, and took the drinks over to where Jenny was waiting. Halfway there, he spun on his heels and looked back at the bloke at the bar, seeing him turn at the same time, and they locked eyes before the barman brought a pint of heavy to the counter and called for the other guy's attention.

'Who was that?' Jenny asked.

Danny shrugged. 'Just some punter. He knocked my glass but it was my fault. No big deal.'

'He better watch himself,' she laughed. 'He doesn't know who he's dealing with. You being Red Silk and all.'

'Ha ha. Very funny. Be bad news for you if I *was* Red Silk. You'd be on dangerous ground right now.'

She was close to him now. Very close. He could smell her skin and see the faint sheen on her forehead.

'Maybe I like being on dangerous ground.' She looked him straight in the eye, daring him to doubt what she meant. 'Maybe playing dangerous games is what I do.'

This was the point and he knew it. The point where he had to back away. 'Nothing wrong with a bit of danger,' he heard himself saying.

'Talk's cheap,' she teased. 'I think you're all talk, Danny Neilson.'

'Try me.' The words that came out of his mouth were not the same ones he was trying to convince himself of in his head.

She smiled broadly, white teeth shining in the neon gloom of Klass, her red hair glossy under the glitter ball. 'Maybe I will. If you're not chicken.'

He hesitated, fighting the last round with his conscience but aware that he was hurtling downhill with the brakes off. 'Like I said, try me.'

Her nose was all but touching his, her breath hot on his cheek as she leaned in to whisper. 'It's very, very hot in here. Funny, but the coolest place in here is the ladies' toilets. Not that I can speak for the gents', obviously.'

Her lips scraped against his ear as she spoke, the feeling rocketing through his body, causing his pulse to quicken and his blood to pump furiously. 'Is that right?' was all he could manage to say.

'It is right.' Her lips were kissing the very tip of his ear, the merest touch at every syllable. The merest explosion as they did so. She pulled back enough that she could look him in the eyes, teasing, daring, challenging. He swallowed hard despite himself and she leaned in again. 'The band will be on in a minute. Very popular the Sweet are. Everyone will be standing on that dance floor watching. Probably even the bouncers.'

With that she let the wetness of her lips catch against his ear slightly more firmly before pulling back, her eyebrows raised questioningly. 'I'm going to the toilet. I'll probably still be in there when the band comes on.'

She walked backwards for a few steps, her eyes never leaving his and the teasing smile never leaving her lips until she turned and disappeared into the crowd. He stood, his heart pounding, a slight tremble in his legs. The hill that he was racing down had just become even steeper. Behind him, he could vaguely hear the booming voice of the DJ cutting through the fade of the last song.

'Awrite there, people. I'm Jumping Jimmy Steele and you are in Klass, the best and hottest disco this side of New York City. Are youse having fun? *I said are youse having fun?* That's better. Okay, here's the moment youse have all been waiting for. They've had three top-twenty singles and they're at number four in the charts this very week with "Little Willy". Their lead singer is Glasgow's very own Brian Connolly and they are here to rock the house tonight. Let's hear it for one of the best glam bands in the business. Give up a huge Klass welcome for ... the Sweet!'

The crowd went mental, stamping, clapping and whooping as the band emerged behind the DJ and onto the stage. Every eye in the place was on them, every head turned in their direction. Except his. Heart thumping, he turned and apologetically pushed his way past people who were paying him no attention. After just a few yards, he was beyond the crowd and standing in the open, but he didn't hesitate, his legs taking him forward to the dark recess that led to the toilets. The voice in his head that was telling him to turn around was being ignored.

There they were in front of him. Gents' to the left and ladies' to the right. He took a deep breath and went right. The door had another door a few feet behind it and he pushed through that, too, emerging into the light of the toilet. She was standing there, her back against a cubicle and an approving smile on her face. She beckoned with a curl of a single finger and he strode towards her, his will gone and a deeper, more basic force making all the decisions now. As he got within a couple of feet, she took a half-step forward and grabbed him by the collar of his shirt, turning to lead him into the cubicle and shut the door behind him.

His mouth was on hers in seconds, hungrily exploring her, hands all over each other, grabbing, squeezing and stroking. He turned her – or she turned him, he wasn't sure which – until her back was against the cubicle wall and one of her legs was wrapped round his waist. Her legs were soft and slick, hot to the touch under the hem of her miniskirt. Her mouth was hot and wet and eager, her tongue greedily wrestling with his. Her hands were through his hair and his through hers, pulling at each other.

Her hands pulled off his jacket, then grabbed at his shirt, feverishly undoing buttons, and he followed her lead by taking hold of her halter-neck top and pulling it over her head, exposing firm breasts underneath a flimsy white bra. He pulled her close, singed by the heat of her flesh against his, their bodies sticky, one against the other. As he reached under her red miniskirt, she began to fumble with his belt, seizing the leather and pulling it back until the clasp was free and she tackled the buttons of his trousers, her fingers tripping over each other in their desperation to free him. As she did so, he stroked her between her legs, feeling her warm and moist and waiting for him. She clutched the waistband of his trousers and underpants together, pulling them both down and releasing his hardness. She grasped it and he jumped at the heat of her hand on him, his own hand pulling her panties to the side. She looked him in the eye, her mouth open and panting hard, as she pulled him towards her, making it clear that she was in charge.

The voice in his head made one final, hopeless plea, but he was too far gone. He pushed his way inside her and the deal was sealed.

They moved together just as they had done on the dance floor, she setting the rhythm and he urgently following. The tempo was fast, pressing on and on, racing against the likelihood of getting caught. He thrust against her madly, their mouths eating each other, both her legs round his waist now, he deep and fast inside her, lost completely.

They danced on and on, pushing desperately against each other, the thumping base of the Sweet reverberating through the cubicle and setting a pulse for them to rock against. They were animals, no thought other than the mutual satisfaction of their lust.

When they came together, they forced back the screams they wanted to let loose, forcing the noise back through gritted teeth and swallowing it back down where it came from. Instead, they shook, breathing heavily, their mouths attacking each other and his hand caressing her cheek. She finally pushed him off, a lascivious smile spread wide across her pale features, perspiration dappling her brow.

She picked up her top and handed him his shirt as he pulled up his trousers from his ankles. He took it from her and slipped his arms through the sleeves, only then realising that his back was soaking with sweat, feeling the polyester of the shirt immediately drenched by the results of his labours.

They hadn't spoken since she'd walked off the dance floor and still not a word passed between them as they pulled their clothes back into some kind of order. He knew that his silence was borne out of guilt, a spectre that appeared immediately after he'd emptied himself inside her, a hair shirt that he wore under the damp polyester one that clung to his back. She sensed it, he could see that, and she resented it.

They gathered themselves in the awkward hush of strangers and she opened the cubicle door, peering out to make sure there was no one there, then beckoning him to follow. She strode purposefully across the tiled toilet floor and through the double doors back into the disco itself. No one saw them leave the toilets and no one paid them any attention as they re-joined the crowd on the edge of the dance floor, all entranced by the Sweet as they finished their set. She looked at him, opened her mouth as if to say something, then stalled, instead leaning in and kissing him damply on the cheek. He went to kiss her back but she'd already gone, heading to where her friends were waiting.

He felt as if someone had switched a light on in the room ten minutes before and he'd only just become aware of it. He scanned the dance floor urgently, wondering what he'd missed and who'd missed him. His eyes almost immediately fell upon Alice McCutcheon, who was staring at him oddly, confusion and disapproval on her face. Had she seen the kiss on his cheek?

He was still looking at her looking at him when the scream broke the silence and he was aware of movement behind him near the front door. The bouncers were on the move, hustling quickly and barrelling people out of the way. He instinctively followed them, unceremoniously shoving his way through the crowd and dumping two customers on their backsides as he did so. He forced his way to the door at the top of the stairs, seeing Brian Webster standing there, the detective constable having managed to get there before them. Webster was look-ing at him ashen-faced, his mouth hanging open. Danny pushed by him and half ran, half stumbled down the stairs towards West Nile Street, his anxiety nearly sending him crashing but just managing to keep his footing. 'Police!' he roared, any sense of being undercover having gone. He crashed to a stop on the bottom landing and followed the crowd to the alley that ran behind the building where he saw two people, one of them one of the Klass bouncers, crouched over a body. As Danny approached, they leaned back to give him a view of the stricken form.

The girl's neck was snapped to one side and her eyes stared at the wall, her neck violently red and her maxidress wrapped round her waist. The side of her skull bled slowly down her cheek and was matched by a dark patch on the wall.

Lying beside her, just inches from her head, was a red silk handkerchief.

Chapter 49

Saturday afternoon

It had been years since Danny remembered being as down as he was after the discovery of the third victim, the poor lassie's body found battered against the monument in the Western Necropolis. Perhaps it hadn't happened on his watch but it might as well have done. He was torn between anger and despair but knowing that he was as likely to fall victim to guilt as anything else. With all that in mind, there were probably better places for him to be on a damp Saturday lunchtime than walking through another graveyard, but that was where he found himself.

The text message from Chloe that morning was the only thing – apart from the arrest of the killer and Atto's complete confession – that could have put a smile on Danny's face. Once he had deciphered the text-speak, he was elated to see that she wanted to meet that day. He wasn't so happy that she wanted to meet at Jean's grave, but he was hardly in a position to say no. He texted back immediately and agreed to her suggestion of meeting at noon.

Sighthill Cemetery was a muddy green oasis that had survived the surrounding war of architectural death and regeneration. On its northern boundary the red sandstone tenements of Keppochill Road were fading to a washed-out pink and, to the east, Springburn Road had seen buildings come and go to make room for the expressway. The graveyard's eastern edge, Fountainwell Road and its rundown offshoots, had seen many of its ugly high-rises fall, but there were plenty more still standing close by, staining the skyline in shades of grey and grime.

Danny didn't visit his wife's grave maybe as much as others thought he should but it was nothing to do with a lack of thought or love. He carried his memories and hurt with him wherever he went, much as if they, and she, were tattooed on his heart. Every time he went through the front door of the home that they'd shared for so many years, he still found himself saying hello out loud. *Hi, it's me. I'm home.*

The cemetery was just a different place to say hello. He didn't think of Jean as being there, not the living, laughing, loving Jean he remembered. He wanted her place to be well tended and he liked to take down flowers when he visited. To show others, he supposed, that here was a woman who was still loved. The rest of the time, the love was just buried inside him.

Jean shared her headstone with her parents, Bill and Nancy Mitchell. Beloved daughter, sister, wife, mother. She'd died before Chloe was born, so grandmother had never been added to the list. How many roles was one person supposed to fill in one brief lifetime?

Danny crouched in front of the stone, his weight causing

half an inch of water to ooze from the grass and make an island of his shoes. He looked at Jean's name carved in granite and still found it odd, shocking even, to see it there. Being in denial, even after twenty-five years, was so much harder with a physical statement in front of you. It was probably the real reason he ventured so rarely to Sighthill. Without sight of that reminder, a part of him could always be convinced that she was in another room or visiting friends.

He shook himself, feeling the cold all of a sudden. An angry roll of clouds had gathered across the rooftops on Keppochill Road and the wind had picked up, whistling low across the cemetery, making the grass sing a dirge. Between that and the softness of the turf, he didn't hear the footsteps approaching until they were almost upon him.

'You managed to find your way here, then?'

He knew the voice instantly. Not Chloe: her mother. He turned his head and saw her glaring down at him, tired eyes under knotted brows.

'Barbara. I was—'

'Expecting my daughter. I know.'

It had been fully four years since he'd seen her. A cousin's wedding and a grudging acceptance of being in the same room as he was had not extended to anything more than a few words of overly polite conversation. Now, with her coat buttoned to the neck and her arms folded tightly across her chest, she didn't seem any keener to see him than before.

Danny pushed his hands onto the grass, feeling his fingers sink into the wet, and forced himself to his feet.

'Don't bother. I'm not staying. I'm only here to tell you that Chloe's not coming.'

'What? Is she okay?'

'She's fine.'

'Then why . . .? You told her not to come?'

'Of course I did,' Barbara spat, pulling her arms even tighter around herself. 'What do you expect? Meeting her behind my back.'

'Barbara, I'm her grandfather for God's sake.'

'In name only.'

The bitterness in her voice cut him to ribbons, slicing into his conscience like a stiletto. Three little words, slashing left, right and centre.

'That's not fair. Look, you're here now. Let's talk. How have you been?'

Barbara laughed, an incredulous snort of derision that broke free from her mouth.

'How have I been? You have the cheek to stand in front of my mother's grave and ask me that?'

'I'm asking because I care.'

'Aye? Well I've been just great, thanks for asking. Bringing up Chloe on my own thanks to a cheating shit of an ex-husband who buggered off with a younger model. Slaving away at a job I hate. And now my daughter is lying to me too by meeting you.'

It was her eyes as much as her words. What a person says isn't always what they mean, but their eyes – that's where the truth is. Barbara's eyes burned rage.

Danny exhaled hard, wondering not for the first time how the hell it had come to this. She had been his world from the first moment she'd been placed in his arms screaming her little lungs out. He knew right there and then that he would do anything for her; yet forty years later, all she wanted him to do was drop dead.

It was her mother dying, he knew that. Deathbed confessions are dangerous things, dropping bombshells on people when their mind is least able to deal with it. Deathbed accusations aren't much better and Barbara had absorbed the one that was foisted upon her, locked it in her heart and promised herself she'd never forget. So it had stayed there and, naturally, it festered.

They stared at each other, a stand-off above the grave of the person who both united and separated them. His baby girl, her mouth tight and contorted with resentment at the world and all its components. One in particular.

'Look, it's been a long time,' he began again.

She released her arms long enough to thrust away strands of the strawberry-blonde hair that had been blown across her face. 'Not long enough.'

'Oh come on, Barbara, it's been nineteen years since your mum died. She forgave me. Why can't you?'

'Forgave you? Maybe, but she never forgot. Anyway, I'm not here to get drawn into this. You know how I feel about it. All I'm saying is that I don't want you to see Chloe and I expect you to respect that. Forgiveness? Is that what you want?'

Danny felt the first drops of rain as he shook his head slowly in response.

'No. I just want to talk to my daughter and get to know my granddaughter. Forgiveness is for fools. Believe me, anyone else's forgiveness isn't much use to me if I can't forgive myself. I want to move on. Put all that behind us.'

'Jesus Christ!'

The acrimony made Barbara look older than she was. Not long turned forty, but when her face screwed up, the corner of her eyes twisted tight and her mouth locked like a vault, she wore the acid features of an embittered widow.

'How can we put it behind us?' she snapped, pointing at the headstone at his back. 'You cheated on my mother and now you're skulking around meeting my daughter. You obviously can't be trusted an inch.'

Danny collapsed inside; some things just couldn't be argued against, mainly the truth. She continued the assault, all the time her finger pointing at her mother's name carved in guilt behind him.

'How do you think it made me feel? My mum dying of lung cancer, using her last breaths to tell me that? She barely had a breath in her, yet that was what she chose to use it on. To tell me what you'd done. Not to tell me that she loved me or that I'd be fine after she'd gone. To tell me that you'd cheated on her. To tell me that the man I'd always thought was the greatest guy on earth was actually a cheating piece of shit.'

It was raining more heavily now, large drops slapping against their faces, mixing with and disguising the tears of anger that had begun to run down his daughter's face. Her voice was rising, giving vent to the frustration of not being able to tell him this in so long. He took it.

Danny knew that Jean had been on heavy doses of morphine in her last hours, a vain attempt to keep the insufferable pain at bay. The drug messed with her mind a bit, not to the extent that she'd said anything that wasn't true, but Danny doubted that, without it, she'd have inflicted that parting piece of knowledge on Barbara. It would have served no purpose, particularly as they'd worked so hard to keep it from her for so many years.

They had got past it, his one sordid, never-repeated infidelity. They'd got on with their lives and become a family and loved each other. Clearly, Jean had never forgotten, though, seeing that writ large and ugly as her life passed before her. Nor had he or ever would he, the guilt at his unfaithfulness being multiplied by the consequences of his negligence. The death of a young woman and the broken heart of the woman he loved was the burden he deserved to carry with him for the rest of his life.

'You're right,' he told Barbara, his right hand pushing the rain out of his eyes. 'I am a piece of shit. Or at least I was. I'm trying to make amends.'

'Amends?' Her laugh had no humour in it. 'How are you going to do that, then? Go back in time and not shag that slapper? Bring Mum back to life? Oh, I know: you're going to spend all hours standing out in the rain at night making sure wee lassies get safely into taxis so that another one doesn't get killed and it would be your fault.'

The trouble with being slaughtered by someone who knows you as well as a daughter does is that they know exactly where to stick the knife. She'd also have been as well cutting off his tongue because he had nothing to say.

Barbara took his silence for defeat and pushed past him dismissively, all but knocking Danny out of the way as she crouched down and took her place in front of her mother's headstone. Ignoring the ever-increasing rain, she began pulling at the weeds that grew at the base of the stone, manically ripping them from the dirt and throwing them aside.

Her knees quickly became dark, wet circles of neglect, her hands reddening as she worked.

'Come away from there, Barbara,' he urged her. 'You're getting soaked.'

She ignored him and continued to tear at the weeds, seemingly seeing some that weren't there. Danny pushed his hands through his hair in frustration before rubbing his palms violently against his forehead and finally finding words to come back at her with.

'I made one mistake over twenty years of marriage. I've had to live with it ever since and I always will. I'm not asking for forgiveness for that. Yeah, you're right, I work the taxi rank because I feel guilty. Because I'm trying to make something right in whatever small way I can. Is that so terrible? And now I want to see my granddaughter. My own flesh and blood. I want to see her grow up and get to know her. And you know what, Barbara? She wants that too.'

Barbara's hands, which had continued to scrabble at the earth as he spoke, stopped moving and her head snapped round towards him.

'Yes, she told me that. She told me that when I found out who she was going to meet for lunch. But you know what, *Dad*? She doesn't want that any more. Not after I told her why you and I don't talk to each other. Not after I told her what you were really like.'

Chapter 50

Saturday afternoon

'What's the worst thing you've ever photographed, Anthony? Or should I say the best?'

'I don't think that's relevant.'

'Oh, don't get all huffy on me again. It must be remarkable to be able to see things like that, to be there so soon after they've happened and be able to photograph them. It must be like making them eternal. It's special, isn't it?'

'We're not talking about me: we're talking about you.'

'But I'd *like* to talk about you, Anthony. I'd really like to know if that buzz you get when you photograph death is anything like the feeling I get when I cause it. Do you think it is?'

'I doubt it.'

'Do you? I don't. I've seen the look in your eyes. You come alive when faced with death. Ironic, isn't it? Would you categorise it as a fascination? Or maybe an obsession?'

'Neither. It's a job.'

'A job? Ha. A job that gives so much pleasure can't truly be considered work at all. It's not just a job and we both know it. If I just wanted to kill someone because they'd enraged me or cheated me, then I suppose I could have them shot or stabbed by some thug who'd be glad of a few hundred quid. But I do it myself, not because I want them killed but because I want to kill them. I want to feel it. The same way you feel it when you photograph them.'

'It's not the same thing at all!' Winter could hear his voice rising and knew he was making it obvious that Atto was getting to him, but he was past caring. 'You cannot compare photographing death to causing it. Do I like my job too much? Yes, probably. Is it a bit sick? Yes, probably. What you do – what you did before you were caught and locked away for the rest of your miserable little life – is way beyond sick. It is abominable.'

Atto's switch flicked and Winter could see the killer appear in front of him, eyes wild and nostrils flaring. He sensed the guard and the governor tensing, ready to move, and he felt the hairs on his arm and neck stand on end. He had a sudden and unwelcome insight to what Louise Shillington, Melanie Holt and the others saw before Atto attacked.

But, instead of coming over the table after him, Atto smouldered, crossing his arms and slumping into his chair in a sulk.

Addison, Narey, Teven and Toshney were in the operations room, poring over maps, files, witness statements and computer searches, doggedly working their way through every bit of information available to them.

The pungent smell of canteen coffee filled the air, endless

cups of the stuff to fortify the various members of the case team who had been in and out of the room most of the day. The java also had to count as lunch for all but the lucky few who had time to grab a disgusting vending-machine sandwich or a melted chocolate bar.

Addison worked differently from the rest of them in the room. While they were diligent and constant in everything they did, bees buzzing from one task to the next, the DI would regularly break away and sit in a chair by himself, balling up sheets of paper and lobbing them into a bin from eight feet away. Alternatively, he would pace the room talking quietly to himself, only the occasional expletive being audible, or stand in front of the large wall map and scratch his head.

If and when the thinking time paid off, he'd dash to a computer or a case file and look for whatever he thought might back up his hunch or inspiration. Stop, start, swear; stop, start, swear. Sometimes he just threw random questions at whoever happened to be there.

'What's with the fucking cemeteries? Eh? There was nothing in the Red Silk case that connected with the necropolises. One of the victims was buried in the Eastern but that was it. So what the hell is this bastard up to?'

No one was ever sure if the outbursts demanded a response or not and, as a rule, there was never a right answer. The questions that got a reply usually turned out to have been rhetorical and those that didn't were followed by furious roars that Addison had asked something and wanted a bloody answer. After a while, only Narey dared to reply to him with more than a 'dunno, sir'.

'My thinking is that he's grandstanding,' she suggested

now. 'Just wanting more attention by making it all Gothic and ghoulish. Murder victims found in cemeteries are guaranteed headline grabbers. I think that's what he wants.'

'Well, he's bloody well got plenty of headlines all right, hasn't he?'

'Yes, sir,' Toshney replied from his place in front of the map.

'I fucking know he has, you fuckwit. I wasn't talking to you and it was a bloody rhetorical question anyway! Understand?'

Toshney's eyes narrowed in search of an answer but he didn't get beyond confusion and said nothing.

'Jesus suffering!' Addison exploded. 'Am I fucking talking to myself round here or what?'

The light outside was already beginning to fade despite its being only mid-afternoon, and Danny groaned as he levered himself out of the chair and got up to switch a light on in the Stewart Street operations room. Peering at forty-year-old case files in dim light was guaranteed to knacker his eyes. Actually, just reading them at all was likely to knacker his soul. Still, after the meeting with Barbara, he felt that a knackered soul was about all he deserved.

What there was to read, he'd seen before. All of it in 1972 and for the two years he worked the case. In the years since, he had dipped into it a few times but this was the first time in a long time that he had immersed himself completely in the horror of it. Handwritten and often barely legible notes triggered butterfly memories of names that had wandered to the far reaches of his mind: Billy Moffat and Geordie Taylor. Billy had died in the mid-eighties of a heart attack and Geordie had emigrated to New Zealand in 1990. Faces of witnesses came back as other names appeared on the yellowing pages, chattering ghouls that hadn't visited him in years. Addresses immediately had him back standing outside closes in the East End or chapping on doors from Partick to Possil. They were times he wanted to go back to and also the last place he'd rather be. He was walking with ghosts, including his own.

Some of the information couldn't be read at all because technology had outstripped itself to the extent that there was simply no equipment still existing to render it useful. Later parts of the investigation had been put onto microfiche but no one had thought to keep the reader to view them on. Some later files had been copied onto five-and-a-quarter-inch floppy disks, then the original notes discarded, yet of course modern computers didn't support the old disks.

The problem with the parts of the old files that could be read was that too much of the information was familiar, making him worry he couldn't see the wood for the trees. The new stuff was different. The case notes from Operation Oslo, the national investigation into Atto's movements both north and south of the border, was full of information he'd never seen and went way beyond what was released through the media. Every nugget of it assaulted his thought processes, threatening overload and challenging him to keep up. The details of the confirmed murders were as brutal as the list of potential killings was extensive. The minutiae in between – a catalogue of lesser horrors so frequent that they ran the risk of becoming commonplace as they filled page after page – made Danny want to throw up.

The further he dug, the deeper his desperation grew.

*

CRAIG ROBERTSON

'So, Anthony, do you think I'm ill or evil?'

'I don't know. Maybe you're both.'

'That's not playing the game properly. Ill or evil?'

'I'm not sure I believe in evil.'

'Ha!' Atto's eyes lit up, delighted at this new turn of events. 'Why not?'

Those were the moments Winter hated most: when Atto took delight in anything he said or did, when he gave him something to play with. He was in the game now, though, whether he liked it or not.

'I just don't believe that people are intrinsically evil.'

Atto smiled pleasantly as if he'd received some kind of compliment, possibly the nicest thing anyone had said, or at least implied, about him in a long time. Winter hadn't finished, though.

'They are, however, capable of committing evil acts. You've clearly shown that.'

Atto frowned, disappointed, but he had obviously been called worse and quickly got over it. 'So evil acts rather than evil people? But are even the acts evil if the person who does them is ill?'

'Yes. Let's forget for a minute about whether you are ill or not. If you kill someone's daughter, then that to them is a grossly evil act. They suffer from that evil whether you are ill or not. That parent will suffer for the rest of their lives because of what you did. The state of your mental health won't change that.'

'You keep talking about parents,' Atto complained. 'I'm not interested in the parents.'

'Perhaps you should be.'

'Why?'

418

'Because you're a parent too. You killed someone's child and now your child kills another person's child. You can't escape it. The sins of the father, remember?'

'What he's doing is nothing to do with me.'

'Rubbish. He's doing it *because* of you. Do you know what he's planning to do tonight?'

'No. Not exactly.'

'Or where?'

'No. So I couldn't tell you even if I wanted to. And I don't.'

'But you do want to tell me something, though, don't you? That's why you've got me in here. To tell me about your boy. Proud daddy, are you?'

'You're trying to wind me up, Anthony,' Atto hissed. 'To make me say something I'd regret. But it's not working.'

'No, of course it isn't. You're much too smart for that. Even if you do think your brain isn't wired up properly.'

Atto laughed scornfully. 'It's wired up correctly enough for that. Either you didn't listen or it's another lame attempt at provoking me. Any defects in my paralimbic system would affect only my ability for remorse or empathy. It doesn't make me liable to be duped by an emotionally damaged cretin who presses a camera button for a living.'

'A cretin? Maybe I am. I'd have to be a bit daft to be sitting in here listening to you talking but not actually telling me anything. But maybe I was just wrong about you wanting to tell me something. You've got nothing.'

'He talks to me.'

'And why would he do that? To boast? To check that he's doing it right?'

'Oh, he's doing it just fine. And he loves it. He's feeling it just the way I did. He's owning them, tasting them. And he's going to do it again tonight.'

'Who and where?'

'I don't know. But I do know that you're wrong about him doing it because of me. It isn't me, or at least not only me. He says he's marking them all with his mother.'

'What? For his mother?'

'No. That's not what I said. He said he's marking them *with* his mother.'

Winter's mind flash-filled with a series of photographs taken in the half-light of three gloomy cemeteries. Photographs of three exposed stomachs and messages scrawled on cold, pale flesh.

'The lipstick. He's writing on them with his mother's lipstick.'

Stevo Barclay didn't look or sound very happy. His face was contorted into a snarl and every second sentence he uttered contained the word 'lawyer'. He was demanding his immediately and refused to be fobbed off by any excuses.

He sat and bristled in shaven-headed indignation, his fingers rapping the table in front of him, his mouth working its way into a frenzy of chewing at the inside of his cheek. Addison stuck his head inside the door with a cheery grin on his face.

'Mr Stevo, how are you today?'

'Pissed off. What the hell am I doing in here?'

'Helping the police with our enquiries. Has no one told you that already? I do apologise.'

'I don't see how I can help you. We've been through all this before. I've asked for a lawyer and I want to know why I haven't got one yet.'

Addison pulled back a chair on his side of the table and sat down, an exaggerated look of concern on his face.

'You asked for a lawyer? And no one's arranged one yet? Let me get onto that once we've finished having a quick chat. This is just informal. I'm just trying to get you out of here as fast as we can. But tell me, though, are you worried?'

'Worried? Worried about what?'

'You tell me. I'm guessing that, if you've told us everything you know about what happened to Kirsty McAndrew, then you'd have nothing to worry about.'

'No. I mean yes. I told you everything. So I'm not worried.'

'So why are you so desperate to get a lawyer, then? I don't understand, Stevo.'

'Because I shouldn't be in here.'

'Don't you want to help us? That bothers me a bit, Stevo. You met Kirsty. You got intimate with her. Surely you'd want to help us catch the guy that did it.'

Barclay's eyes jumped wide. 'Intimate? What the hell are you saying?'

Addison leaned in, looking perplexed, seemingly not able to believe his ears.

'You're kidding me, right? You had your hands all over her back. Beautiful young girl. She must have been, what, half naked? Hey, if that's not intimate I've been doing something wrong all these years.'

Barclay angrily pushed both hands into the table edge, forcing his seat to edge back. 'It's not like that. I want a lawyer. I'm not saying anything till I get a lawyer.'

Addison remained calm, replaying his puzzled look. 'There you go with the lawyer stuff again, Stevo. We'll get you one but I'm really not sure why you can't just tell me that you touched Kirsty.'

'Aye, when I inked her! That was all.'

'Must have been quite nice, though, eh?' Addison offered a knowing wink in Barclay's direction. 'Nice young thing like that. Must be worse jobs.'

'Okay, so I fancied her. So what? Doesn't mean anything!'

Addison blinked at him. 'It doesn't? Really? Tell you what, Stevo: I think I need to go and get you that lawyer you've been banging on about. It doesn't mean anything? Really?'

'Yes, really! I didn't kill that girl!'

'Now you're talking about killing Kirsty? No, enough's enough, Stevo. I'm away to see where that lawyer's got to. It's for your own good.'

Addison got to his feet and pushed the chair back, further pushing Barclay's buttons as he turned to the door.

'No! Wait, wait! Look, I ... I ...'

'Have you got something to tell me, Stevo?'

Barclay looked lost, searching for an answer before admitting defeat. 'No. I've got nothing.'

'That's what I thought. See you later, Stevo.'

The photographs in both the 1972 files and the later Operation Oslo stuff had Danny in trouble. The ones that he'd seen before were dragging up memories that had been buried under a thousand regrets; the ones that he hadn't were turning his stomach.

The long, vertical neon sign that hung outside Klass was

like a signpost to his conscience, looking tackier and cheaper than he'd remembered. Much of West Nile Street that surrounded it was long gone just like the sign, torn down and thrown away to make room for something newer. Some things couldn't be got rid of so easily, though, no matter how hard you tried.

The photographs of Brenda MacFarlane, Isobel Jardine, Mary Gillespie and Christine Cormack were images that he was never likely to forget. He'd mocked Tony often enough for his fascination with photographing the dead, and he'd meant it, but these images would have been his nephew's rebuttal if he'd known how familiar Danny was with them. Stark black-and-white shots of the four victims, not from a hundred and one angles, as Tony did these days, but just two or three of each.

The lack of colour in the photographs made him feel old and the events seem even longer ago than they were. His memories were all in colour, though, and his brain was pinning the monochrome horror of Isobel Jardine's bulging eyes onto a Technicolor recollection of the green of Govanhill Park and the red brick of the bandstand wall. Past and present wrapped up in a bow. The grey tones of Mary Gillespie, exposed by the ripping of the short skirt she'd worn, were similarly fastened onto the reds and oranges of an alley wall and the clear blue sky of a July morning long ago.

Being visited by the dead that you'd known was no more peculiar than welcoming the new dead. Beverley Collins and Emma Rutherford were strangers united in garish, inglorious colour. Beverley wore the gaudy hues of a blue-and-green dress on the white of her bones while Emma was dressed in the bloody reds and earthy browns of the recently buried. The forest greens of their shallow graves were peopled by the blues, yellows and whites of attending officers.

There were pictures of Atto, too – not just the familiar post-arrest photographs that had adorned so many newspaper and television features, but also rare casual snaps that had been found in his flat. Of him posing, sickeningly, with a teenager who might have been a neighbour or a student, a smiling, wide-eyed girl. There was no accompanying note to the photograph to say whether she was a victim or had a lucky escape. Long after it was too late to change anything, Danny still found himself praying it was the latter.

Atto didn't look too different from the way he did now. Same unremarkable features and middling brown hair, a smile that might have been taken for shy if you didn't know better and dark, soulless eyes that hid secrets. He wore a bland brown jumper whose dull tones were enlivened only by a badge of some sort over his black heart. Mr Anonymous, dressed to be forgotten.

In another, Atto was pictured in the back garden of a house, the semi-detached visible in the background as he and a woman sat raising glasses to the camera on a summer's day. Atto, dressed in a light-blue shirt and jeans, was smiling more broadly than usual. Danny had no idea whether the woman was smiling or even how old she was, as her face had been scrubbed over in black biro, seemingly obliterated by a furious hand.

There were also images from inside Atto's flat, taken by the team who had finally arrested him. It was a disconcertingly ordinary home, painstakingly tidy for a single man and no hints of the devil's lair that it had been. Maybe that was what made it so disturbing: photographs of glasses lined up on a kitchen shelf, a toothbrush still damp in its mug holder and a newspaper neatly folded on a coffee table in front of the television. The message was that it could have been any man's home; it could have been anyone who did what Atto did.

For Danny though, most haunting of all were the images of Atto's collection. Officers had found a drawer full of jewellery, twenty-six items in all, including brooches, ladies' watches, pendants and necklaces. They clearly weren't his, nor were they claimed by any of the former girlfriends who had reluctantly come forward to admit they'd been in a relationship with the monster. Piece after piece spoke of a former owner from whom it had been taken: bracelets that had been worn on unknown wrists; rings that had been slipped on unidentified fingers; trophies that had been stripped from the dead.

Some of the pieces could have come from more than one victim; others could have been stolen from someone fortunate enough to have survived. That was the straw to be grasped at, the lingering hope that the collection didn't mean quite all that it seemed. If each piece represented a dead girl, then the world was lost and the Devil had won.

Ritchie Stark was much calmer than his boss. Whereas Barclay ranted and raved and demanded a lawyer, Stark sat quietly and seemingly patiently. He wasn't best pleased about having to spend a Saturday in the cop shop but he didn't moan and instead just asked when he'd be interviewed. Narey explained that they had something else to attend to but that they'd get to him as soon as they could. Stark just shrugged resignedly and said nothing.

They left him on his own for as long as they could, occasionally watching unseen as he sat listlessly, until Narey reckoned she couldn't leave him much longer before he too would begin demanding legal counsel. She and Toshney entered the interview room, Stark looking up expectantly as they did so.

'Mr Stark, thank you for being so patient. As I explained, it's been a busy day. Three murders tend to increase the workload. We've got a lot to get through and I'm sure you're as anxious to get on with it as we are. Are you happy to chat or would you like us to get you a lawyer? That may take some time.'

'No. It's fine. I'll talk to you.'

'Great.' She turned to Toshney and nodded, he turning on the recording equipment at her signal.

'I am DS Rachel Narey and also present is DC Fraser Toshney. We are conducting an interview with Ritchie Stark. This interview is being recorded in video and audio. Mr Stark has indicated that he is happy for this interview to proceed without the presence of a lawyer. Is that correct, Mr Stark?'

Stark coughed and announced loudly, 'Yes.'

'Thank you for attending Stewart Street police station, Mr Stark. We'll try to keep this brief as I'm sure you are in a hurry to get out of here.'

Stark looked curious. 'A hurry? Well, I'll gladly get out as soon as I can but I'm not in a hurry as such. I just need to get back to the shop.'

'And what are your plans for tonight?'

'Um, I'm seeing Faith, my girlfriend. We're going out. Cinema, I think.'

'What are you going to see?'

'I ... I don't know. We'll just see what's on when we get there. Probably some vampire thing if it's left to her.'

'Yeah? You not so keen?'

'Not really. Not my kind of thing.'

'You not into all that biting and blood?'

'No. Guess not.'

'Is she?'

'She likes the films, that's all.'

'I see. Why do you think you're in here, Mr Stark?'

He looked confused, maybe thinking that she should be telling him that.

'Um, I don't know. Because the girl had her tattoo done at our place, I suppose. I thought I'd told you all I knew, but if there's anything else ...'

Narey nodded thoughtfully, looking at him for an age and waiting for a reaction. All she got was more confusion. She picked up her notes and made a show of reading them, even though she knew everything that was written there.

'So you didn't do her tattoo and you weren't in the shop when she had it done. Is that correct?'

'Yes.'

'And you're sure you didn't see her in the shop at any other time?'

'No. I mean yes, I'm sure.'

'What about when she came in to book her appointment and choose her design?'

'I didn't see her.'

'But you might have been there?'

'I guess I might but I didn't see her.'

'How can you be so sure?'

'Well, maybe I'm not. But I don't remember ever seeing her.'

Narey pursed her lips, running her hand through her hair. 'So it was just Mr Barclay alone with Kirsty, then, you think. Tell me, did he talk about her after she was in? Maybe after he tattooed her?'

Stark took his time, weighing up his answer, obviously deciding whether or not to say something. 'Yeah, he may have done. I think he might have mentioned that she was attractive.'

'May have done or he did?'

'I think he did. We get a lot of clients. I couldn't be sure.'

'Suddenly you can't be sure about very much, Mr Stark. Was it your impression, from memory, that Mr Barclay was interested in Kirsty McAndrew?'

Stark's eyes slid over and he breathed out hard. 'Yes. I think so, yes.'

'Okay, thank you. I understand from my colleagues that Mr Barclay has a bit of a temper. Is that right?'

Stark looked as if he'd been placed somewhere he didn't want to be. 'Sometimes,' he gave up reluctantly. 'But so do a lot of people. He wouldn't have hurt that girl. Any of them. He's not like that.'

'Hmm. So he fancied Kirsty McAndrew. He has a violent temper. And on the night she was killed he admits he was blind drunk. Doesn't look good for him, does it, Mr Stark?'

Stark's mouth opened and closed again. He said nothing.

'And yet Mr Barclay has an alibi for the night of the second killing. He says he was with you and your girlfriend when Hannah Healey was killed. And you confirmed that, didn't you?'

Stark's head fell forward and he stared at the table in front of him.

'Didn't you?' Narey repeated.

'Yes.'

'And was he with you?'

Stark didn't look up but he shook his head.

'Could you speak please, Mr Stark? For the benefit of the tape.'

Stark stared contemplatively at the table for an age before clearing his throat. 'Stevo wasn't with us. He came to me and asked if I'd say he was. He was just worried that you'd think it was him. He said he was out on the booze again and couldn't remember what pub he was in at what time. Said it would be better if he just said he was with me and Faith. So I agreed.'

'You lied to the police, Mr Stark. That's a very serious offence and you may be charged.'

Stark's head slumped again before rising in half-hearted defiance. 'I still don't think he did it. He was just scared.'

Narey's face was right in his. 'He's got good reason to be scared. Now, if you'll excuse me, I have to go speak to your friend. Make yourself comfortable, Mr Stark, we may be some time.'

Chapter 51

'Right, Mr Barclay . . .' Addison swept through the door of the interview room, catching Stevo Barclay by surprise and speaking before the tattoo artist had registered that he was in the room. 'Let's talk.'

'Look, I told you I—'

'Mr Barclay, this is James McEwan, your solicitor.'

A short, tubby man clutching a briefcase followed Addison through the door and behind him was DS Andy Teven. The solicitor shook Barclay by the hand and took up a seat next to him, beginning to arrange some papers from the briefcase in front of him.

'About time,' Barclay muttered.

'DI Addison, I'd like some time alone with my client, please.'

'Yes, of course, Mr McEwan. In a bit. Let's chat first. Andy, get the tape, will you?'

'No, I'm sorry I—'

'This is DI Derek Addison. Being interviewed is Mr Steven Barclay. Also present is DS Andrew Teven and Mr James McEwan, solicitor.'

'For the record, Detective Inspector, I would like to state my dissatisfaction at the length of time my client has had to wait for legal representation. And that—'

'Duly noted, Mr McEwan. Thank you. Now, Mr Barclay, can I refer you to witness statements you gave to officers when spoken to after the murders of Kirsty McAndrew and Hannah Healey? You told them that you were drinking heavily on the night Kirsty was killed. Is that correct?'

Barclay looked at his newly appointed solicitor before answering. 'Yes, that's right.'

'And you have little or no recollection of your events of that night?'

'I know I didn't kill anyone.'

'Hmm. And regarding the murder of Hannah Healey, you told officers that on the night in question you were with your work colleague Richard Stark and his girlfriend Faith Foster at their flat. Is that correct?'

'Yes. That's right.'

'Hmm. I think we have a problem, Mr Barclay. I don't think you were with Mr Stark and Ms Foster. Are you sticking to your story that you were?'

'It's not a story. I was. Ask them.'

Addison spread his arms wide as if enjoying an epiphany. 'Ah, of course. Why didn't we think of that? Actually, we did. And do you know what Mr Stark said?'

'DI Addison, I think I ought to speak to my client at this—'

'I'll save you from guessing, Mr Barclay, because your solicitor doesn't seem to know the answer either. Mr Stark has told us that you weren't with him that night. That you asked him to lie to the police on your behalf.'

'That bastard—'

'Mr Barclay, Mr Barclay.' The tubby lawyer looked sweaty and agitated. 'I must caution you not to say anything that—'

Barclay clamped his mouth shut, but the damage had been done.

'Go on, Stevo. Tell me. Why is Ritchie Stark a bastard? For not keeping his side of the bargain? Letting a pal down?'

Barclay stopped and started, fury building in him, wriggling in his seat and impervious to his lawyer's attempts at shushing him.

'You may as well tell me, Stevo. Ritchie's made a statement. He says you told him you were blind drunk again and needed an alibi.'

'Bastard! I gave him a job as well.'

'Hardly a way to repay you, was it? So where were you that night?'

'DI Addison—'

'Where were you, Stevo?'

'I was drunk. I was out my face.'

The solicitor's head fell into his hands before he threw them up in despair. Barclay again ignored him.

'I knew you wouldn't believe me, so I asked Ritchie to cover for me.'

'You asked him to give you a false alibi. Why did you need one?'

'I didn't! I did but . . . I didn't kill her.'

'Innocent men don't need false alibis. You are in serious trouble, Stevo. Did you murder Kirsty McAndrew?'

'No.'

'Did you murder Hannah Healey?'

'No!'

'Did you murder Ashleigh Fleming?'

'Who? No!'

'I don't believe you, Stevo. You have lied to us. You have tried to cover your tracks. Did you kill those women?'

'No!' Barclay was out of his chair, roaring, his eyes wide. Addison sat calmly and watched him.

'Terrible temper you have, Mr Barclay. Terrible.'

McEwan looked very nervous, his eyes going from his client to the cop. 'DI Addison, I really must insist—'

'Of course, Mr McEwan. Why didn't you say? I think we've heard enough from Mr Barclay for the moment. A self-confessed liar who fabricated an alibi for the time of the murder. Let's take a little break, shall we? Interview suspended.'

DC Fraser Toshney had spent most of the time in the operations room at a bit of a loss, hopping from one half-completed task to the next, opening folders, pulling up spreadsheets, looking at photographs and generally trying to find something worthwhile to do. He had the distinct feeling that there was something there for him; he just didn't know what it was.

He knew what most of the team thought of him. An arse. He irritated them and they didn't rate him. He knew he was a better copper than most of them gave him credit for, but showing that to them was another matter. He'd been in the squad for less than two months, dropped straight into one of the biggest murder investigations they might ever tackle. So what was he doing? Trying too bloody hard to fit in and prove himself.

So he made stupid jokes, he played the idiot. Maybe he *was* just an idiot. He was worse with Narey, he knew that. Maybe it was just because he fancied her. Maybe it was because she so obviously couldn't stand his being there. Or because she was always so on the ball that he couldn't help but feel useless in comparison.

She'd been rattling through task after task with effortless efficiency all afternoon: checking witness statements and ordering more, calling psychologists to test her 'red' theory, running profiles from other forces and screening everyone who was on their radar.

He knew that the three necropolis locations were bugging her: she was seeing them as the centre of the investigation but not knowing why. If he could work that out, or even just give her the key that might let it happen, then surely she'd stop thinking of him as a complete waste of space.

So he spent a lot of time online, searching everything he could about the cemeteries, looking for some link, no matter how random or offbeat, that might tie to what was in front of them. What he came up with was mostly a whole load of history.

He learned that the first burial in the newly created Glasgow Necropolis in 1832 was that of a Jew, Joseph Levi. The first Christian burial was a year later, Elizabeth Myles, the stepmother of the park's superintendent, George Mylne. He knew that 50,000 burials had taken place and that most of the 3,500 tombs were up to 14 feet deep. The tombs at the top had been blasted out of the rock face and there were monuments built by the likes of Alexander 'Greek' Thomson and Charles Rennie Mackintosh.

He could tell you that the Southern Necropolis was a rectangle laid out in three sections, those built in 1840, 1846 and 1850. It held the remains of 250,000 people across 21 acres, including Thomas Lipton, the tea man; Agnes Harkness, the heroine of Matagorda; and Greek Thomson the architect. The Western held Sir William Smith, the founder of the Boys' Brigade, and Will Fyffe, the music-hall entertainer. The Glasgow Necropolis was the final resting place of generations of the Tennent brewing family, all having to be buried facing the Wellpark Brewery at the rear of the cemetery.

He discovered that 'necropolis' came from the Greek. *Nekros* meaning death and *polis* meaning city. In Glasgow, of course, polis meant police. The plural of 'necropolis' wasn't 'necropoli', as Rico Giannandrea tried to tell him, but 'necropoleis', as Google told him – although most people opted for the more obvious 'necropolises'. He even found out that the Southern's interment records included the burials of legs. Just legs.

What he didn't learn was what the connection was between the necropoleis and their killer, and it was driving him to distraction.

The large map that took centre stage in the room had the Necropolis, the Southern and Western pegged out in red and the Eastern in green – not because the Eastern had Celtic Football Club as its immediate neighbour but because it, as yet, anyway, hadn't earned the red for death. Other old cemeteries around the city were pinned in yellow: Sighthill, Calton, St Kentigern's, St Peter's at Dalbeth, Cathcart, Jocelyn Square and St David's at Ramshorn Kirk. Toshney stood and stared at them in the hope that the answer would somehow reach out to him from beyond the graves.

He mentally discarded those marked in yellow: the answer was in the necropoleis, he was sure of it. The Necropolis at the Cathedral, the Southern and Eastern were relatively close to each other, easily within walking distance, even though the Southern at Caledonia Road was over the river. The Western on the other hand was five miles away, a good bit further north and obviously west from the others.

He stared, trying to work out the relationship between them. The shape bothered him somehow, the pinned locations reminding him of something. The Plough, that was it. If he joined the points up like the stars, they made a similar shape to the constellation. A triangle of points at the bottom then a long line up and left to the final position. Except that the bottom part of the Plough had four points rather than the perfect triangle that the three necropoleis formed.

Shit. That was it, they formed a perfect triangle. He hurried back to the first free computer terminal and brought up a search engine. 'Glasgow', 'Necropolis', 'Triangle'. Nothing. He tried 'Necropoleis'. Nothing. 'Equilateral'. Nothing.

He scrabbled about in a desk drawer until he found a ruler and returned to the map, aware that Narey and Giannandrea were looking at him oddly and that they were probably making faces behind his back. Never mind. He wasn't going to say anything, though, because this was going to sound as stupid as anything he had said so far.

He placed the clear plastic ruler on the map from the Southern to the Eastern and measured, doing the same on all three sides of his newly unearthed triangle. He carefully placed three other pins, blue ones this time, within the corners of each of the three cemeteries and measured again. They were exactly the same distance apart. They formed a perfect equilateral triangle, all three sides the same length.

Toshney retreated to a desk and sat down, unsure what to make of his discovery and unsure whether to voice it. Did it even mean anything? The last thing he needed was to draw further mockery or even just to be a pain in the butt for wasting their time by mentioning it. He got to his feet and went back to the map, staring at the triangle, deep into its heart, wishing its secret to reveal itself. He got his ruler again, fully aware he was being stared at, and traced lines from each point to the far side of the triangle, creating a point at its very centre. When he saw the product of that, he sat down again, fretting.

'What the bloody hell is it, Fraser?' Narey could take no more of the pantomime.

Toshney curled inside, dreading the words coming out, sure that he would make some stupid joke to cover his doubts. Maybe she'd just ignore him.

'Toshney!'

'It's probably nothing, Sarge.'

She sighed. 'I don't have much time today. Spit it out.'

'This is probably going to sound a bit stupid.'

'Yes, probably.'

'Well, I was looking at the map, and the necropoleis – well, three of them at any rate – form a triangle. Well, obviously it's three of them, as it's a triangle but … anyway … it's an equilateral.'

'What?'

Toshney got to his feet and pointed at his newly placed blue pins. Narey and Giannandrea following him sceptically.

'They're exactly the same distance apart. I measured them.'

'Okay . . . And . . .?'

'Well, that's what I thought, too, Sarge, and then I looked again. This is probably the stupid bit. But our man has a thing for the necropoleis, right? And we're pretty sure he lives close enough that he can get to them easily. And everything he does has been planned from the start. Well . . .'

Toshney hesitated again and Narey's frustration went over the top.

'Well what? Tell me now or get to . . . Whatever it is, tell me.'

'Well, say he wanted to stay in a place right at the middle of these three. I drew lines and the middle of them is right here.' Toshney jabbed at the map with his forefinger. 'Tobago Street.'

Narey and Giannandrea looked at each other.

'It's where Ritchie Stark lives. Remember we interviewed him there and I asked why the hell anyone would move into a street like that if they came up from Nottingham? You think that might be our link? It's only a thought, probably a bit of a stupid—'

'Fraser, the only stupid question is the one that you don't ask. The only sensible question is the one that you already know the answer to. You understand?'

'Um, no. Not really . . .'

Narey sighed. 'Think about it. In the meantime, get your jacket. We're going to Tobago Street.'

Chapter 52

Addison could have phoned, of course he could, but he'd chosen not to. He could have sent someone else to do what was basically message-boy stuff, but he hadn't wanted to. The reason was transparent, at least to him, but he hoped that it wouldn't be quite as obvious to her.

His fist was drawn back, just about to knock on the door of the lab, when he stopped on seeing her through the glass pane. She had her back to him, unfeasibly long legs slightly apart as she bent over a desk examining something. He stood there for far longer than a man investigating a triple murder should have done. She began to stand up and in an instant of panic he rapped on the door much harder than was necessary.

Sam Guthrie turned, quizzical and annoyed, wondering who felt the need to batter on her door in such a manner. Seeing Addison seemed to explain it all and she let her eyebrows rise in mild despair before beckoning him in.

'DI Addison, how nice to see you again. Have you not settled on a shade of lipstick you prefer yet?'

Just in the door and the woman was busting his balls already. Maybe he should have just phoned.

'No, not this time. Same case but different tack. I need

some DNA profiling done and I need to know how quickly you could do it.'

Guthrie tilted her head to the side and smiled knowingly. 'How quickly *I* can do it? I'm not sure why you think I'd be the person responsible. Should you not have approached Campbell Baxter in the first instance? Or could you not simply have telephoned to ask?'

He decided to brazen it out.

'Yes, I could have done either of those things but, as your lab will be responsible for carrying out the sampling, I thought you would be best placed to tell me what I need to know. And, as I will be personally asking a favour to get these delivered as soon as possible, it seemed only courteous to ask face to face rather than over the telephone.'

Guthrie nodded thoughtfully. 'Okay, DI Addison, you have my full attention. What can we do for you?'

'I have suspects in the cemetery killings investigation. I want to do a DNA profile on them and match it against the sample taken from the Caledonia Road church. And I need it done today.'

Guthrie leaned back against the desk behind her and crossed her arms.

'Suspects? Plural? To compare with a particularly poor sample? And today? DI Addison, are you confusing us with those television programmes, where the difficult is done immediately and the impossible merely takes a little longer? How many suspects do you have?'

Addison sighed, knowing the reaction he was going to get. 'Five.'

'Ha. Five? Seriously? DI Addison, is this some new

approach to police work where you just bring in everyone you can think of who has a certain letter in their name?'

'Look, Miss Guthrie—'

'Don't Miss Guthrie me, Detective Inspector. Five DNA profiles cannot and will not be done in any accelerated manner. When were you hoping this would be done by?'

He swallowed, almost beaten. 'Ten hours.'

She laughed in his face. 'Try again.'

'Sam, this guy has killed three young women. He's planning to kill another one tonight. Yes, I'm desperate. And, yes, I'm clutching at straws. But I need help with this.'

'Okay, I don't appreciate the emotional blackmail of being told there are women's lives on the line. I'll help, we'll help, all we can. But there is only so much we can do. Five samples in that time is not physically possible. If we put everything else on hold, if we put everyone we have on it and if we work flat out, we can do two profiles in that time. That's my best offer.'

'Okay, I'll take it.'

'You can choose between the five?'

'Yes, if I need to.'

'You do. And if you can make the choice then perhaps you shouldn't have five of them in custody, or helping with your enquiries or however else you are putting it. If I were representing any of them, then that's what I'd be telling you.'

'Then I'm glad you're not duty solicitor for any of them. When can we get started?'

She looked at her watch, a silver band on her slim wrist. 'Now. Let me get my kit. Who are your two suspects?'

'Stevo Barclay. He runs the tattoo parlour where Kirsty McAndrew was inked and he did the job. He's admitted fabricating an alibi for the night of the second killing. And Ritchie Stark, the other tattooist. He provided the fake alibi, and Rachel Narey and one of the DCs are off to his place with some nutty theory about his flat being in the middle of some triangle.'

'What?'

'Don't ask.'

'You obviously know that, unless they volunteer a sample, you don't have a right to swab them unless they've been arrested.'

'Obviously I do know that. Which is why I'm going to arrest them. Ready? Let's go.'

Chapter 53

Every minute spent talking to Atto felt like a lifetime. Even the scraps that Atto threw his way were laced with poisonous prices that had to be paid.

The little information that he was prepared to part with about Melanie Holt or Louise Shillington was of the double-edged-sword variety. The obvious relish with which he told of their murders was as loathsome as the details themselves. He spoke of the softness of their flesh and the brittleness of their neck bones, casually mixing perverse sensuality with psychotic brutality as if they were one and the same. He told of the noises they made, luxuriating in the memory.

He forced Winter and the watching prison governor to listen to how he had raped Louise Shillington under the pretence of giving clues to where she was buried. Atto's delusional insistence that she enjoyed the atrocity committed upon her was spiked with references to a wood outside Ipswich with a stream running through the centre of it. The hints as to the location were the bait; the sickening details were the trap.

Winter's principal task was to get him to talk about the son, but Atto insisted that the price to be paid for that was a foul indulgence. If Winter also wanted dialogue about the whereabouts of the lost girls, then Atto would make sure he would be charged for that too.

'Tell me more about the wood with the stream where you took Louise. Is it far from the main road?'

'Far enough. It has to be, you see. When you know that they are likely to try to scream, then you don't want that to be overheard. Louise tried to scream but it's difficult to do when you have two strong thumbs pressing against your windpipe, two hands clasped round your pale, slender neck. Louise was so fair-skinned and she bruised so easily. The moment my hands were on her neck, I could see it begin to change colour. Her face too. It was so red, like it was on fire. Of course' – and here Atto looked at him and sneered – 'none of this might be true.'

'Did you kill her near the stream?'

'Did I? I really can't remember. Let me try and picture it. She is underneath me, naked from the waist down. Her pretty brown eyes looking up at me, wanting more. I can smell sex and a sweet perfume. I know my hands are going to go round her neck again. This time will be the last time and she will be gone. You know, I can hear the stream, Anthony. Not too far away, off to my right. It must be close.'

'Was she your favourite?'

Atto looked up, surprised at the question but intrigued by it.

'Do you have a favourite, Anthony? Of all the dead creatures you've photographed, do you have one that you prefer over the others?'

Winter sank inside, forced by his own game to reveal more

of himself to the man opposite. His mind flashed to the wall in the second bedroom of his flat in Berkeley Street, twenty photographs in five obsessively neat rows of four; each framed in black ash, each representing a moment of death. These were his favourites, his chosen few.

'I have one or two, I suppose.'

'One or two. Like being asked to choose between your children, isn't it? But all parents have favourites, whether they admit it or not. Who is yours, Anthony?'

Winter had the answer ready but still had to steel himself to give it, knowing he was about to soil something by sharing it with Atto.

'Her name was Avril Duncanson. She went head first through the windscreen of a Renault Clio. I photographed her lying in a shroud of glass, the top of her skull smashed and her ribcage caved in. The remarkable thing was that her face was almost completely unmarked, spared by the way she'd ducked her head just before the point of collision.'

'And why is she your favourite?'

'She was my first.'

Atto smiled happily and broadly, his dark eyes full of approval.

'Yes. Yes, that's it. You never forget your first, do you? Your first kiss, your first love, your first lover.'

'Your first kill?'

Atto shrugged, more defensive now. Winter sensed it but wasn't for stopping.

'Is your favourite the first one? It is, isn't it? She was more special because it was your first taste of it. Do you remember her more than the rest?'

'I don't want to talk about it.'

Winter had hit the nerve he'd hoped for. He'd always said that Danny Neilson was the smartest man he'd ever known and he had no reason to change his mind.

'Why not, Archibald? You are usually very keen to talk about them. Why is that?'

'I just don't want to.'

Winter pushed. 'Well, *I* want to. I want to hear about your first.'

Atto responded the way he usually did when challenged or offended: like a petulant child, either hiding away from the perceived insult or lashing out.

'You don't get to hear about it unless I want you to. I try to talk to you, man to man, Anthony. Like two people who understand each other. But you're abusing that privilege.'

'Well, maybe I'll just have to take that chance.'

Atto's eyes darkened and his lip rose in a snarl. Winter saw it again, the look on the monster's face that must have been the last thing seen by so many.

'You're already taking too many chances. You *and* your uncle. I'd be very, very careful about taking any more. You are both on extremely dangerous ground.'

'Is that a threat? If so, it's not from you. You're in here.'

Atto laughed coldly. '*Fishing*, Anthony? There's no need. I'll tell you. My newfound child has been watching you and your uncle. He knows where you both live. He knows where you go, what you do.'

Danny had already dismissed Atto's talk of the son knowing that he and Winter were on his case as an empty threat, not believing that he would target them rather than the police who were also after him. He'd told Tony it was just Atto trying to be in control despite being behind bars.

'You doubt me, Anthony? If I was to tell you that I know you drink in a pub called the Station Bar, would that help change your mind? Or that I know your uncle lives in a flat in Grovepark Street?'

Winter wasn't sure if his heart slowed, stopped or quickened. Atto savoured the effect.

'Do you doubt me, Anthony?'

'No, I don't doubt you.'

Atto gave a lopsided smile and softened. 'Good. I like you, Anthony. I feel we've got to know each other and have a lot in common. For that reason, I want to help you. Will you let me help you?'

Winter hated the hold that he felt the man putting on him but couldn't break it.

'I think I might have to.'

Atto's mouth turned up at both sides. 'I want your mobile phone number.'

'What? No way.'

Atto's eyes furrowed in irritated disappointment. 'I'm trying to help you, Anthony. To let me do that, you must trust me. I wouldn't want my child to hurt you. Your uncle I don't care about. You ... you, I want to talk to more. When he gets in touch again, I may have information that I can pass on. Information that won't wait.'

Winter felt the hold tighten, squeezing more firmly round his throat so that he could barely breathe. He gave Atto his number.

Chapter 54

Saturday evening

Addison was driving towards the Eastern Necropolis, or Janefield Cemetery, as it was also known, thinking that there was no more he could have done in terms of preventing something happening on the city streets that night. They had the entire place on full alert and there had been cops in and around the Eastern since mid-afternoon. Every cop who had a uniform and those detectives who didn't were patrolling either the city centre or the cemeteries; and the Eastern was the graveyard of choice for most.

Every television news bulletin and every radio station, both local and national, and every news website had carried the story the way they wanted it: the killer was intending to strike again; the killer was intending to dump victim number four at the Eastern; the cops had it surrounded; don't bother wasting your time.

As he made his way along the Gallowgate, the cemetery only a quarter mile or so away, he became aware of increasing footfall on the pavements and what seemed to be crowds up ahead.

The closer he got, the thicker the throng became. By the time he was a couple of hundred yards away, he could clearly see the turning on the right into Holywell Street leading to the scrub-ground car park on Janefield Street where he'd sometimes parked for the football. It was thick with people, cops in hi-vis dotted among many more in plain clothes.

'Holy shit,' he muttered out loud. 'What the hell ...'

Some of the crowd went into Holywell Street and others continued down the Gallowgate side of the cemetery. Addison pulled over onto the pavement and parked there, waving his ID at an eager-beaver constable who came running over to tell him to move.

'I'm parking there, so don't waste your breath. And keep a bloody eye on it. You see anyone go near it you arrest them on the spot.'

'Yes, sir.'

'What the hell's going on here?'

'I'm not sure, sir. They all just started turning up. There's ... hundreds of them. Say they're not going anywhere and that they will stay out here all night if they have to.'

'What? How long have they been here?'

'Some of them arrived about an hour ago. But there's been more and more of them arriving all the time. I think it's to do with the news, sir. About the cemetery killer going to put a body in the Eastern.'

'It's the Gorbals fucking Vampire all over again,' Addison realised.

'The what, sir? A vampire. I don't—'

'Never mind, Constable. Just you keep an eye on my car. What's your name?'

'McArra, sir. PC John McArra.'

'Very good, McArra. If there's a single bloody scratch on that car then you're in trouble. Understood?'

Addison began to march along the Gallowgate, not needing to look back to know that the constable would be saying yes.

There were indeed hundreds of them. Men mostly, which made sense given the nature of the beast that they were guarding against, patrolling the perimeter of the cemetery, some sitting on the head-high wall that ran the length of the Necropolis along that part of the Gallowgate. It was an incredible sight: grim-faced vigilantes stalking an invisible prey under a threatening sky, clouds heavy with rain hanging ominously over the top of the Celtic Park stand that loomed behind the acres of graves.

Those who sat on the wall were just a couple of feet from time-toppled headstones or monuments to the departed, framed with trees bent by generations of wind. They were flinty-eyed guardians of the graveyard, looking left and right even though they couldn't have known what they were looking for.

Others were milling one way and then the other, rebels in search of a cause. People determined to do the right thing even if they didn't know what that involved. There were local neds, teenagers in their best tracksuits, older guys wearing anoraks and student types smoking roll-ups. The crowd seemed to be multiplying with every passing moment, a human ring round the old cemetery.

Addison went up to a couple of those on foot, two broad and bulky guys with close cropped hair who could have been on their night off from bouncer duty in a city nightclub. They eyed him suspiciously as he approached and moved together as if to block his path. For once, the production of his warrant card made members of the public relax their antagonism towards him.

'All right, guys? Listen, I don't have a problem with you being out here but I'd like to ask you a couple of questions. Okay?'

They both nodded – an instinctive reticence to talk to the cops.

'What's going on here? Is this something organised?'

The two guys looked at each other and made some unspoken deal about who would talk to him. The shorter of the two fired a look in both directions before leaning in and whispering hoarsely.

'We're kinda guarding the place. We all saw what was said on the telly an' that. How the bastard was going to kill another girl an' that. Dump her body here. Well, we were like, "No way, man." It could be my wee sister or something.'

'Couldnae just sit in the hoose and dae nothing, could we?' his pal added.

'So is someone organising this?'

'Naw, naw. Well, aye, a wee bit, like. We were coming doon anyways after seeing the telly but we've heard that there's loads of talk aboot it on Facebook and that Twitter. You know, like telling guys to come here and make sure nae cunt gets in.'

'No that we're saying the polis cannae dae their job but you cannae be everywhere at once like.'

'But is there anyone down here in charge? Someone maybe talking to the polis about what's happening?'

'Naw. Well aye. There's a guy roon on Janefield Street near the stadium. Dinnae ken his name but he was telling folk to go here and there like he wis somebody. Wisnae polis, like, just wan o' us.'

Addison frowned but nodded his thanks to the two of them. 'All right, lads, you're doing a good thing, but watch yourselves, eh? There's a proper nutcase out there. And make sure you don't get yourselves arrested. The polis tell you to move, you move.'

The bouncer boys didn't look too impressed at being told what to do but they shrugged a tacit agreement and resumed their watch duties as Addison turned and hurried back to the Holywell Street junction on his way to Janefield Street on the other side of the cemetery. As he hustled along, he pulled out his mobile and called Superintendent Jason Williams, the senior officer charged with overseeing the uniformed presence round the Necropolis.

'Superintendent Williams? It's DI Addison. I'm on the Gallowgate side of the cemetery, sir. I see we've got a fair bit of unexpected back-up.'

'Yes, we have. I can't believe how many of them there are. I'm trying to clear them from this side first but they're arriving quicker than we can get rid of them.'

'I wouldn't do that if I was you, sir. If you don't mind me saying.'

'Not get rid of them? Addison, how am I expected to protect the cemetery when there are so many members of the public milling around? It's chaos out here.'

'Then let's organise the chaos, sir. We've been worried all day that we don't have enough cops to protect a place of this size, so now we have all the bodies we need. And it might just be enough to make sure that we don't get one body extra, if you see what I mean. Let's get them on our side. Anyway, if you try to clear them out of the area you might end up with a riot on your hands, and that's hardly going to help.'

There was silence on the other end of the line as Williams digested what had been said. Addison didn't wait for a reply.

'I'm on my way over to you now. I understand there's someone claiming to be acting on behalf of the people that have turned up?'

Williams sighed. 'Yes, there's some self-appointed leader of men who thinks he's liaising with us. He's getting right on my tits, to be honest.'

'I'll be there in two minutes. Can you get one of your guys to keep a hold of him for me?'

'Will do. I have to say I don't like this, Addison. I don't feel we've got control of the situation.'

'I know the feeling, sir.'

The crowd was sparser on Holywell Street because it didn't border the cemetery, but there were still plenty of bodies walking along, presumably heading for a vantage point on Janefield Street. The familiar red railings that ran along the left-hand side of the road reminded Addison of so many walks along there en route to Celtic Park, the stadium large in the near distance. He'd gone that way as a kid with his old man and then later with his pals, taking up a spot on the terracing known as the Jungle before it was replaced by the towering North Stand.

Memories flooded back of dodgy pies from the stall in the

top corner near the Celtic end, everybody smoking, cans of McEwan's Export and finding yourself twenty yards away from your mates after a goal was scored. And the noise. Jesus, he remembered the noise. So much of that died when they knocked the Jungle down.

The rear of the North Stand and the border wall of Janefield Cemetery stood back to back, so much so that the top eleven rows of the stand were cantilevered over the cemetery. This led to the bizarre situation of Celtic having to buy the air over the graveyard from the council after locals complained about the shadow cast over the Necropolis. It cost the club £10,000 in compensation because those buried there had the right to free air space 'from the centre of the earth to the sky'. Only in Glasgow.

The left turn into Janefield Street was always the one that gave him goosebumps when he was a kid, the sight of the stadium and the massed ranks in green and white outside. This time it was slightly different. There wasn't a Celtic scarf in sight. Instead there was a mass of grey humanity, a well-meaning mob. He made his way along to the centre of the crowd, seeing them lined up along the low cemetery wall on the scrubland to his left, the sprawling green expanse of the graveyard beyond.

He couldn't see Williams but grabbed the first cop he came across and asked where the superintendent was. The constable looked and pointed and Addison saw Williams's tall frame about forty yards away through the failing light, a couple of other officers at his side. It would be dark within twenty minutes and at that point the natives were likely to get increasingly restless.

'Addison.' Cruikshanks sounded weary and wary. 'Good of you to join us. Tell me again why it's a good idea for us to have all these mentalists running round the place.'

'Look, I know it's not ideal, sir, but they can do a job for us. Have you seen the size of that cemetery and how much boundary there is to cover? And you've got how many officers?'

'Not enough. I know that and it's been bugging me all day. You've been nearer to this than I have – you seriously think this guy will try and leave a body in there? He'd have to be off his head?'

'I generally find that's the case with most psychotic serial killers, sir. But, yes, I do think he's going to try to do that. This rent-a-mob might be our best chance of stopping him.'

Cruikshanks shook his head despairingly. 'Okay, tell me what you want and I'll get it done.'

'There's a bunch of them sitting on the wall on the Gallowgate side and we need to get them down and keep them down. If they protect the perimeter, then fine, but if they infiltrate it then they become a threat. We also need to make sure none of them is a wolf in sheep's clothing. Your guys need to keep an eye on them, big time. They will also need to cover the end next to the creamery building on Holywell Street, as that's the only bit of boundary wall that can't be accessed from the road. No one is getting in here unless they parachute off the roof of the fucking stadium.'

Williams and Addison turned and looked up at the roof of Celtic Park as it peeked down into the cemetery below, and both wondered just for a second if that was actually a threat before shaking their heads at each other and returning to the equally ridiculous situation in front of them.

'Where's this seeker of truth and justice that reckons he's speaking on behalf of the mob?'

Williams pointed. 'The guy over there with the ponytail. His name's Callum McGann and he's a pain in the neck.'

'Well you know what they say. Under every ponytail, there's a horse's arse. I don't suppose that goes for schoolgirls but it sure as hell goes for guys old enough to know better. I'm going to speak to him.'

Mr Ponytail had a uniformed cop either side of him but it didn't stop him from directing human traffic this way and that, lording it with personal bodyguards courtesy of the Force. He was about five foot ten, lean and wiry, dressed in blue jeans and a brown leather jacket. The ponytail itself was black with a hint that it might have been dyed. The guy was in his early to mid-forties without a hint of grey.

'Mr McGann? I'm Detective Inspector Addison. Can I have a word?'

The guy looked pained at the interruption, the way Michelangelo must have done when he was trying to paint the Sistine Chapel and people kept asking for his autograph. 'Can't it wait? This is important.'

'Right ... it will only be important if you continue to be allowed to do it. And the decision on that is down to me.'

McGann stopped waving his arms and looked at Addison, trying to suss him out. 'You do realise that there's a life at stake here?' he argued. 'We're all here to stop anyone getting in that graveyard. I'm organising them.'

'Yeah, they all look very organised,' Addison offered with more than a hint of sarcasm. 'And what about you, Mr McGann. What's your interest in this?'

The man seemed taken aback at the question, surprised that someone could question his motives.

'I just . . . I'm a concerned citizen.'

Addison laughed, not caring if it offended and largely hoping that it would.

'That's what we need more of, Mr McGann. Concerned citizens. If there were more people like you then there really wouldn't be a need for people like me, and I could go get a job as David Cameron's butler.'

'Are you . . .? Do you think this is some kind of joke?'

Addison could see real anger rising behind the man's indignation and toyed with the idea of pushing his buttons further before deciding that he didn't have time. 'No, Mr McGann. No joke at all. Tell me, what do you do for a living?'

'I don't see what that's got to do with anything, but I'm a geography teacher. I work at Whitehill Secondary.'

'Uh huh. And were you involved in encouraging people to come down here?'

'Yes, I put a message out on Facebook and Twitter and asked people to pass it on. Are you saying I shouldn't have?'

Addison just shrugged. 'I'm not sure that too many of the people here are on Facebook. I think they came because of word of mouth. The community rallying to the cause and all that.'

McGann pouted a bit. 'Maybe. But some of them are. And I've been round the rest. They're listening to me. I have guys at various points round the Necropolis waiting for my word.'

'Really? Mr McGann, you want to help and you're organising people. That's good. But I need you to organise them a bit differently. Can you do that?'

'Of course.' The man seemed eager to help. 'What do you want me to do?'

'I want you to get them to hold hands.'

'What?'

'Hold hands. I want them in a ring round the cemetery, arm's length apart. No gaps. No one on the walls or next to it. Form a human ring round the place and no one breaks it. Can you sort that?'

'Um, yes. I don't know how many guys will be keen on holding hands, though.'

'Tell them to get over it. And I want you to form part of the ring.'

'What? Would I not be better going round and—'

'No. I'd like everyone that's down here to help to form the ring. No exceptions. It's either that or you go home.'

'No . . . I'll organise it.'

'Good. Leave me your mobile number before you go, will you? Just in case I need to get in touch with you.'

'Um . . . okay.'

Phone number handed over, McGann looked to Addison expecting some thanks for the endeavours of his concerned citizenship, but it wasn't forthcoming. He backed off before turning towards the crowds, melting into them and the gloom. Addison waited until he couldn't see the man any more and leaned back till his head was staring up at the parapet of the stadium above him and spoke to it.

'What can you see from up there, auld yin? Can you see what's going to happen? See if you can, gonnae tell me because I'd really like to know.'

Chapter 55

The light was falling by the time Narey and Toshney got to Tobago Street, Narey parking her Megane under the pseudo-safety of the lamppost outside the remnants of John's Bar. Looking up, she saw a light on in Stark's flat, presumably meaning that his girlfriend, Faith Foster, was in there.

At the door entrance on Stevenson Street, rather than push the intercom button for Stark's flat, Narey hit three others and one of them duly obliged by releasing the entry catch without bothering to ask who was there. They climbed the gloomy concrete stairwell to Stark's flat in silence, not pausing when they passed a door that creaked open just long enough for a shadow to check them out then close again.

At Stark's door, Narey stood for a few moments, listening for movement inside or the sounds of a television. There was nothing. She rapped on the door, not too loudly and trying not to pull off the practised authoritative knock of a police officer. There was no response, so she chapped again, louder this time.

Another door creaked at the other end of the corridor, throwing a shard of light into the hall as someone else wanted to know who the visitors were. Narey held out her warrant card and it was evidently recognised even from the length of the corridor, as the other door promptly closed again. As Narey knocked the door for the third time, Toshney dropped down to crouch by the door. He dipped his finger on the landing and brought it up to his face to examine what he'd found.

'It's blood, Sarge.'

'Great. Kick that door open, Fraser.'

'We don't have a warrant, Sarge.'

'That blood means we're in hot pursuit and have reason to believe a life is in danger. Kick the bloody thing open.'

It took Toshney three attempts, twice ramming the heel of his shoe against the lock before finally crashing his shoulder into the door and it gave way. It fell back against the far wall and Narey and Toshney walked into the narrow hallway before pushing the door over behind them again, seeing dots of blood on the beige carpet.

'Miss Foster?' Narey called out. 'Faith? It's the police. If you are there, please come out and show yourself.'

She didn't particularly expect an answer but had to go through the process. She followed the trail of blood to the end of the hall, where they knew the living room was, opening the door and seeing the light on but no other sign of life. The black leather sofa sat unoccupied in front of the window looking onto Tobago Street, and the television was switched off.

'Check out the other rooms, Fraser. I'm going to look round here.'

The blood came to an end in a pool below one of the

framed posters on the wall, a replica of a Nirvana gig in New York in 1994. Whatever caused the bloodstains had started here and led to the front door and presumably down the stairs, even though they'd missed it in the gloom.

'Sarge!' Toshney's voice signalled urgency and alarm.

Narey went into the hallway, seeing the second of the other two doors being wide open, and followed him in.

'Jesus Christ!'

The walls of what was obviously a bedroom were outlandishly, wildly, maniacally decorated. They were daubed in garish Gothic swirls of red and black like some lunatic, nightmare vision of Hell.

One wall was blood red adorned with paintings of gravestones and crosses, plus the scrawled letters of 'RIP' and 'Memento Mori'. Lines had been drawn linking the painted headstones into triangles.

A second wall was dominated by a tall, slim figure in a white gown, a human form but with a ram's head and cloven hooves, the background streaked in Satanic reds and blacks. The third wall was a hellish montage that included suffering, screaming angels caught up in an intricate spider's web; blood and bones resting below the salivating mouth of some devilish creature; and babies, four of them, sitting blank-eyed and staring straight into the room.

On the final wall, there was a single image. In broad strokes, someone had painted the full-length form of a woman, seemingly ordinary compared with the abominations around her, dressed as if ready for a trip to the shops or to take a child to school. Except that where her eyes ought to have been were opal pools of jet black and at her feet was a pool of blood that could be seen to have run down her leg from somewhere under her black dress.

'Jesus Christ,' Narey repeated.

'What the hell is this, Sarge?'

'What Hell is this, you mean? Someone's crazy idea of it. Check out the other rooms but try to avoid touching anything you don't have to. This is likely to be a crime scene.'

Narey put her hand inside her coat pocket and grabbed hold of the handles to the tall, black-pine wardrobe and opened it up. It was split left to right with male clothes, then female. Stark's side had shirts and jeans, while his girlfriend's half contained mainly dresses, all in either red or black or a combination of the two.

She edged back drawers to find T-shirts, socks and knickers belonging to Stark, then one containing skimpy thongs and matching bras, all inevitably in red or black. Another drawer was half full with various sex toys that made her glad that Toshney had left the room: vibrators, a cock ring, handcuffs, a strap-on dildo and wrist restraints.

As Toshney came back into the room, Narey slid the drawer shut with her knee. 'Find anything?' she asked him.

'The cooker's not been used for a while, television is stone cold. I'd say the blood was spilt quite a while ago, hours at least.'

'And Stark has been in custody since noon.'

Narey pulled out her phone and called the operations room. Rico Giannandrea answered within a few rings.

'Hi, Rico, is Addison there?'

'No, Rach, he's at the Eastern. He's still convinced our

man's going to try to dump a body there. How did you get on at Stark's place? The girlfriend in?'

'No, she's not here. But there's a trail of blood from the living room and out the front door. Check with Andy if he's around. Was the girl here when he picked Stark up?'

Rico relayed the question to Teven, who answered that, no, there had been no sign of her.

'Okay. Ta. What's Stark saying?'

'Not a word. He hasn't said a thing since we took the DNA swab.'

'Yeah? Well, I'm coming back in and I've got plenty to say to him. Make sure he goes nowhere. And send a squad car over to Tobago Street. I need them to secure the place because the door's been kicked open.'

'Us or them?'

'Us. We were in hot pursuit.'

'Of course you were. I'll get someone sent over right away.'

Narey and Toshney closed the door to the flat the best they could, jamming it pretty lamely against the broken hinge. As they did so, the neighbour's door at the end of the landing opened again.

'Excuse me!' The door had closed again before Narey could get the words out but, undeterred, she marched over and rapped firmly on it. She had to knock again before the door finally edged back, half a face hiding behind it. Narey again held up her ID card.

'DS Narey. Can I ask your name, please?'

The lone eye visible beyond the door blinked furiously. 'Sweeney,' squeaked a thin female voice.

'I'd like to ask you some quick questions, Ms Sweeney, if that's all right.'

'I'd rather no'.'

'Would you rather I sent officers back with a search warrant for your flat? There's a car already on its way.'

The door opened wide enough for the stick-thin woman to step out from behind it, her cheeks drawn and her eyes hollow. She was mid-twenties going on dead.

'Do you know your neighbours well, Ms Sweeney?'

'No' really. Keep masel' to masel'. They seem awrite though.'

'What kind of people are they?'

'How'd you mean, like?'

'Are they noisy? Do they socialise with the neighbours? Do they have many people going in and out of the flat? That kind of thing.'

'They can be noisy sometimes. At night. Enjoying themselves if you ken what I mean. But don't see them much. Never seen anyone else going in there, though. Except you.'

'And when did you last see either of them today?'

'Polis were here this morning. Lunchtime mibbe. Took the fella away but he wisnae cuffed or anything. Just walkin'.'

'And have you seen his girlfriend today? Either before that or after it.'

'Naw. No' seen her at all.'

'Okay. Thank you. We're going now but, as I said, there's a police car on its way. Should be here any minute. If they find anyone in that flat, they're under my instructions to arrest them. You understand?'

The woman frowned. 'Aye. Ah widnae go in onyway.'

'Good.'

Toshney's flashlight picked out bloodstains all the way down the stairs, sporadic spots a few feet apart. They continued through the front door and onto the pavement, a few circular drops visible in the light of the shopfront, running until the edge of the kerb where they promptly disappeared.

Chapter 56

Saturday night

Darkness came quickly to the Eastern Necropolis but nothing else did. Not unless you counted tension, frustration, anxiety and the ever-increasing edginess of the assorted nutters and do-gooders who had assembled round the perimeter in the misplaced hope of keeping Glasgow safe.

They worried Addison almost as much as the killer did. At least he had a fair idea of what that bastard was going to do.

As nothing happened and continued not to happen, the hordes were stuck between being glad at that and restless in their expectations. He knew them well enough to know that they'd rather the killer tried to take them on. They'd love it if he turned up – the bogeyman appearing out of the gloom with a body over his shoulder, trying to leap the wall into the graveyard. As one they would rise up and try to headbutt him. They'd certainly rather it be that than stand waiting and not knowing, and they'd rather have it before last orders were called at their local boozer. None of which Addison would disagree with.

He was getting regular reports of nothingness through from the operations rooms. An entire city with crime undoubtedly taking place in various parts of it, yet the word was no news. He'd worked the streets long enough to know that some silly wee sod had surely stabbed another silly wee sod, that an off-licence somewhere between Burnside and Bearsden had been robbed and that there had been a rammy between two groups of kids who thought they were angry about race or religion but were actually just pissed off with their crappy lives. No news should have been good news but he still wanted to hear it, wanted to know that the only bit of news they were all interested in had happened or not.

He knew he was in danger of losing the accidental vigilantes to the call of the pub or their wives and girlfriends, their instincts for good being eroded by boredom and overtaken by much more basic feelings. It was a long night when the bogeyman had until daybreak to do his worst. The Gorbals Vampire free to strut the earth until the sun turned him to dust; his adversaries staying out to challenge him until their mammies called them in for their dinner.

An hour passed, then another. Jason Williams questioned whether they were wasting their time; so did Denny Kelbie on the telephone. His gut still told him this was the most likely place. His heart still hoped they were wasting their time simply because they had the suspect locked up in an interview room in Stewart Street or that they had scared him off from making his move. A deeper, darker part of him, a part of him that he hated and would never admit to a soul, hoped that he was right and that the killer would try it on, try to carry out his crazy plan. He knew what that meant and the saner part of him could never countenance it but ... Shit, he wanted to catch this bastard. He really wanted it.

'DI Addison?'

The voice dragged him back from his wonderings, saving him from moral quandaries about what he might or might not settle for happening to achieve what was needed. It was a uniformed cop, his face familiar but the name out of reach.

'DI Addison? Superintendent Williams wants to know if you still require the full complement of officers here. He says that—'

'Yes. Tell him we need all the officers that are here. And tell him that if he wishes to discuss it further then he should get his fat arse over here and discuss it with me himself. Feel free to translate that any way you want, Constable.'

Later, no one seemed sure when the white van arrived or even which direction it had come from or left in. All that anyone seemed sure of was confusion. Some had seen it and thought nothing of it, others just watched and stared and were helpless to move. There were those who would tell you there was no van at all and that the red dress appeared out of thin air and fluttered down onto the Gallowgate from an upside-down version of Hell.

The reality, as well as Addison could gather, was all of that and none of it. Officers reported having seen the van turn onto the Gallowgate at the Biggar Street roundabout at the Forge, but no one paid it much attention, particularly with rain just starting to fall. With hindsight, they claimed it was driving slowly but they'd put that down to whoever was at the wheel rubbernecking at the crowds ringed round the cemetery. The van made its way along the length of the border wall, gliding past crowds and cops, nothing unusual at all until it reached the farthest reaches of the graveyard opposite the cinema.

The van was said to have slowed almost to a stop and the window wound down. The few cops and crowd who noticed thought that someone was about to ask what was going on. Instead, something was launched out of the window and all hell broke loose. No one claimed to have known what it was until it landed on the pavement, but hours of nothing became a moment of utter something. They all knew. They knew everything and nothing.

It was like someone opening a window and sound pouring in, an avalanche into a vacuum, copper pennies finally dropping onto a steel tray.

A red dress was thrown at the cemetery wall before the van slowly accelerated away and ghosted down Tollcross Road towards the motorway. Everyone turned and the game was on.

Addison was at the other side of the cemetery, sheltering under the eaves of the stadium from the rain, but he heard the uproar from a few hundred yards away. Moments later, his radio buzzed and his phone rang and people began running.

'What the fuck is going on?'

'Addison, it's Williams. We think someone in a van threw a dress towards the cemetery.'

'A what? Why the fu— What colour was it?'

'What?'

'What colour was the fucking dress?'

'Red.'

'Jesus Christ.'

Addison began running, Jason Williams continuing to shout in his ear. 'Derek, what the hell is happening?'

'I don't know but it is happening right now. The dress is either a sign or a diversion. Get as much light on the cemetery grounds as you've got, we need to see what's going on. If you see that clown McGann before I do tell him to get the people round the cemetery to hold hands and make sure no one breaks the ring. We need all the help we can get.'

Addison's feet nearly gave way underneath him on the wet ground, skidding on before he regained his footing. The rain was lashing down now and he was getting soaked, although barely aware of it. The radio buzzed again and Williams's voice roared into the darkness.

'Derek, they've had another look at that dress and there's something written on it. They couldn't make it out at first because it's red written on red.'

Addison knew what was coming before it was said.

'The word "sin" is written in large letters over the front of the dress. We think it's in lipstick.'

Shit. Shit. Shit.

There were cops dotted all over the sodden cemetery grass now, their hi-vis jackets picked out easily in the spotlights that were being turned on the Necropolis. Trees and statues and headstones, granite and green, all pale shadows in the yellow light. Beyond the wall, Addison could see the human ring of volunteers standing fast in the rain, cops beyond them and inside. Surely to hell he couldn't think he'd get through that.

There were cop cars and riot vans beyond the far wall; there were dogs straining at leashes, their senses picking up on the anxiety around them; there were almost as many people in and around that graveyard as there were bodies buried inside it.

Surely to hell he couldn't think he'd get through that, he thought again. Unless he already had ...

Addison started running again, back towards Janefield Street, his fingers furiously punching the buttons on his radio, the rain lashing down and his light-grey suit streaked with dark.

'Williams? Come in.'

'Addison?'

'There's a cadaver dog among the pack of them that's here, right? We did ask for one just in case.'

'Yes, there is. It's still in the van, near the creamery. Why? Oh Jesus ... How could ...?'

'Just get the van over here and get the dog out, sir. I'm hoping I'm wrong.'

He dashed across the turf, dodging headstones and monuments, mud beginning to spatter his trousers and cake his shoes, pushing his wet hair back on his head. Even as he ran he could see the lights of the dog unit van on the move towards where Williams was on Janefield Street. By the time he got to the wall, a dog and a female handler were halfway towards him. In their wake were Williams and two other figures: Tony Winter and DS Andy Teven.

'What's your name?' he demanded of the blonde-haired dog handler who had a black-and-white Border collie restless at her side.

471

'PC Jackie McNally, sir. And this is Davie.'

'Okay, Jackie. I can't be sure but I think we have a body in the cemetery. One that shouldn't be there. Can Davie find it?'

'Yes, sir. It's not exactly the easiest place for him – a graveyard makes for a real needle-in-a-haystack job – but, if it's recent enough that the body's still decomposing, then he should be able to pick up that scent and separate it from the rest. I think he might even have something already. He's anxious.'

'Oh, the one we're looking for is recent all right. Come on, then, let's go. Andy, you as well. Tony you stay here.'

Winter argued immediately. 'That doesn't make sense. If you find what you're looking for then you need me to photograph it.'

'Fuck's sake, I don't have time to argue. Stay where you are. *If* we find something, then you'll get to do your job. Superintendent Williams, I need you to keep everyone else as they are in case I'm wrong and that nutter is still trying to get in there.'

McNally and the dog led the way, haring towards the cemetery wall and over it, Addison and Teven making sure they kept behind them, the rain torrential now. Once in the grounds of the Necropolis, the group moved on a hundred yards or so until they paused under the relative shelter of a huge beech tree circled by hundred-year-old headstones. The dog kept sniffing at the air, distant strains of something definitely interesting him, but the swirling wind was adding confusion.

'It's a huge area, sir.' McNally was surveying the cemetery, just as her dog was. 'I'd rather just let Davie off his lead and we do our best to follow him. If I keep hold of him it could take all night.'

Addison shrugged. 'Whatever. You know what you're doing, so let's just do it.'

McNally crouched in front of the dog, holding him on either side of the face and making him look directly at her, setting out a familiar regime before he went to work. She held the pose for maybe ten seconds then gave the single command 'Search', simultaneously releasing her hands from Davie's face.

The collie immediately bounded away in pursuit of the wind, dashing west towards the creamery for forty yards or so before coming to a halt and veering left and south, back towards the Janefield Street wall. Davie stopped and sniffed at the ground before moving off at a pace again. His pursuers had barely made it to his first port of call when he was off again towards his third. The dog could move at some speed and was inevitably much less inconvenienced by the wet and increasingly muddy ground than those following him.

He chased towards a white marble monument and snuffled his way round its base before taking off east, his nose low, then high, as he ran. He stopped, seemingly confused, as if he had lost the scent altogether, standing almost on his hind legs as he sought to place his twitching nostrils as high into the wind as he could. He circled for a while, giving time for McNally and the two cops to almost catch him up, but before they could draw breath he was running, further east this time and at full pace.

Still the dog had to change his route, but he was more frenetic now, something driving him almost to distraction. He stopped and spun, his tail wagging furiously behind him, his nose moving constantly but unsure where to go. McNally caught up with him and knelt down, repeating the process of staring into the dog's eyes with a hand either side of his head, calming him and resetting him to go again.

Reassured, Davie trotted off and quickly settled onto the paths that ran almost due south towards the football stadium. He was so quick over the tarmac that those behind him couldn't hope to keep up. He bounded over what was almost an island roundabout in the road with a large tree at its heart and several headstones ringing its perimeter. Davie raced on as far as the end of the path, in the shadow of Celtic Park itself, pausing only once or twice to check his bearings or being distracted by conflicting smells. Just before the path's end he abruptly veered left, back onto the grass. McNally, Addison and Teven lost sight of his tail as he did so but soon knew where he was as the dog began barking furiously.

'He's got it,' McNally announced.

As they charged up to join the dog, they found him standing stock still, his head high, continuing to roar his findings. With no light in that corner of the cemetery, the length of the north stand away from where Williams and Addison had previously been standing, at first they couldn't see anything to confirm or deny Davie's success. McNally reached into the deep pockets of her flak jacket and produced a heavy-duty torch, which she shone at the dog's feet. In the artificial light of its beam, they could see the contours of the ground slightly raised and loose earth to its side.

Teven crouched by the gravestone at the head of the defined area and ran his fingers over its surface, McNally obliging by shining her torch on the granite.

'James Henderson,' Teven announced. 'Died August eighth, 1932. Seems to have taken a while for the earth to settle.'

Addison sighed heavily as he reached for his radio. 'I'm usually happier than this when it turns out I'm right. Superintendent Williams? I need at least two men over in the south-eastern corner with spades. We need lights as well, and get forensics here with a tent ... Yes ... Yes I think so. I think we've got a body.'

Chapter 57

According to Rico Giannandrea, Ritchie Stark had continued to stay silent since the moment he had a swab taken from him to be profiled for DNA. He hadn't been a happy bunny at all at having the sample taken, and had struggled, forcing them to hold him tight and his jaw open until they could wipe his gums with the cotton stick.

When Narey went into the interview room with Giannandrea, she found Stark stripped to the waist and staring at the far wall. She hadn't particularly expected that, and nor, once she had walked round to face him, had she remotely expected to see his torso to be emblazoned with a large, thick, red triangle.

She raised her eyebrows accusingly at Giannandrea, pointedly saying, Thanks for the warning, Rico.

Stark continued to stare ahead. His skinny white arms – the one heavily tattooed with the spider's web and captured angels like the wall of his bedroom, the other unblemished – were crossed over his triangled chest. His eyes were focused and grim.

'Good evening, Mr Stark.'

Not a flicker.

'Do you wish a lawyer present, Mr Stark?'

Nothing.

'We'll take that as a no, then, shall we?' Still nothing.

'You're in a bit of trouble, Mr Stark. You do know that, don't you? This is not looking good for you at all. You could spend the rest of your life in a room no bigger than this. Let out once a day to take your chances in the showers with men twice your size.'

Stark persisted in staring through the wall in front of him.

'I would seriously suggest that you speak, because, if you do not state your case, then you cannot defend yourself. And you will need to do that. You said that you didn't meet Kirsty McAndrew when she had a tattoo done at your shop. Is that correct?'

Still nothing. Narey needed a reaction. She got close, standing inches away from his naked and inked torso, the spiders and angels clinging to his arm and the triangle decorating his chest like a warning signal.

'Interesting tattoos, Mr Stark. Just like the ones on your bedroom wall . . .'

The man's eyes widened then tightened but he didn't move or speak.

'Who did your tattoo, Mr Stark?' Rico asked. 'Because when I first interviewed you you told me that most tattoo artists don't ink themselves. Don't get the same quality of work, you told me. Did your friend Mr Barclay do that for you? The friend that you lied for and gave a false alibi for murder. If so, I think we might need to have another word with him.'

Stark said nothing.

*

'What do you make of him, Rico?' Narey asked when they were safely on the other side of the door.

'Do I think he's a killer? Maybe. He ticks a lot of boxes, that's for sure.'

'He certainly does. I better phone Addison. He's going to love this.'

'You think? Stark's playing us, Rachel. He thinks he's in control of what's going on simply by sitting there saying nothing. It's like Archibald Atto. Behind bars but still pulling all our strings. *We* should be in charge of this game, not him.'

Chapter 58

The hastily assembled spotlights inside the forensics' pop-up tent flooded the ruptured turf in Janefield Cemetery and left the shape of the recently dug grave easily defined. Under the white treated canvas, Williams, Addison, Teven, Narey and the crime-scene manager, Campbell Baxter, stood back and watched while two forensics officers carefully began to dig into the sodden ground. Narey had arrived in tow with the rest of the scenes-of-crime officers who were outside, waiting their turn.

The only other person to work was Winter. He shot frame after frame while the SOCOs dug, one of them giving reproachful sideways glances at being photographed but unable to say anything with the senior officers present. Winter's lens almost resented the flash lighting that they had installed, preferring to have done the job itself but grudgingly grateful for the vivid green tones of the grass, the dark browns of the freshly turned earth and the reddened glow of the cop's cheek.

Williams and Addison were grim-faced, their jaws set firm, perhaps in an attempt to convince themselves that they were hardened professionals able to deal with this. Rachel didn't feel the same need to make some macho statement and her emotions were there for all to see: fearful, caring, tired. She twisted strands of hair between finger and thumb, a sure sign of anxiety or annoyance, her eyes rarely leaving the bump of earth that was being slowly stripped before them. If they did move, it was to the scarlet dress that had been laid out on sheeting at the side of the tent as if ready to be worn to a prom or a wedding.

The spotlights gave it a surreal, wholly incongruous air of glamour, memories of Hollywood starlets and red-carpet chic. Rachel's couture critique was that it was made up of a bodice, laced at the front, then tumbling into a wide, full-length ball-gown style. Size 10, good label, reasonably expensive, not the kind of thing you'd wear for any old night out. It lay just a yard or two from a body-shaped bruise in the earth of similar dimensions.

The two forensics had been digging tentatively, unsure of how deep down anything was and fearful of slicing steel blades through flesh or bone. After removing perhaps six inches of soil, they paused to look at each other and nodded, an unspoken decision made. They put the spades aside and knelt down to begin clawing at the loose earth with their gloved hands.

It turned out to be a sound decision for, just moments later, Winter's lens caught the first glimpse of porcelain white against the dark grains of brown. He immediately zoomed and focused, aware of one of the forensics stopping as if he'd been stung. The flesh that filled his lens, an inch or two of ankle, was barely grubby as the other officer's hand instinctively reached out to brush dirt from it.

He looked up and saw Rachel's eyes on his. A silent conversation passed between them, seeking confirmation that the other was okay. The forensics worked on swiftly but carefully, taking handfuls of earth at a time and revealing bare feet and legs, working their way from toe to top. It quickly became obvious that the body was both female and naked as they exposed pale, white thighs, then hips, the officers briefly leaving a mound of dirt over and around her vagina out of misplaced sensitivity until Addison softly reminded them that there wasn't room for such niceties. The taller of the two brushed away the earth with as much sensitivity as the situation and Addison would allow.

It revealed bruising at the very top of her thighs, tell-tale red and blue marks that meant the injuries had been inflicted before death rather than during whatever manipulation it took to place her where she now was.

They continued to undress her, stripping her of an ill-fitting gown of dirt. Her waist and stomach emerged, the word 'SIN' inevitably and sickeningly scrawled there in a familiar hue. Her ribs and breasts emerged, dappled with dried blood that trailed from her neckline and splashed across to slim shoulders, the heaped earth being inexorably replaced with undue humiliation.

The men gently fingered soil away from neck and jaw, then, using the kind of brush they might employ to dust a surface for fingerprints, they inch by inch uncovered an open mouth, lipstick peppered with dirt, a slim nose and high cheekbones. The two officers, one tall and broad, the other heavy-set, whispered against her skin as if it were a butterfly's wing, easing her free of her unwanted earthen mask. Winter caught the sensitivity and the hint of a tear on the stockier of the two, knowing right away that he had a photograph to keep and swallowing the pang of guilt at doing so.

They feathered away the earth from her eyes, clear blue orbs open and staring up at them accusingly. Light-blue eyes like an early morning in May. They were lifeless but still angry, furiously glaring at the person who had been there and hurt her but who had now stolen into the night.

They blew the soil from her forehead, revealing it high and lightly mottled with freckles, as were her cheeks, strands of brown hair straying onto her temples, but the rest swept behind her, still encased in a shallow tomb of cemetery earth.

Feeling suitably mortified, Winter took a final round of frames of the girl's now fully naked body. Earth to earth, ashes to ashes, dust to dust; in sure and certain hope of the resurrection into eternal life. Winter remembered the words but had long since lost the capacity to believe in them. He looked at the girl and hoped he was wrong.

Winter stood and slunk back from the girl, leaving others to work and sensing their urgency to do so. He had feasted on the corpse and duly hated himself for it.

'Your turn, Mr Baxter,' he heard Addison mutter bitterly. 'Get us everything you can. But she wasn't murdered tonight, was she? That poor cow was killed last night and buried in here before we even got the chance to work it out.'

Baxter, his heavy grey beard and plunging jowls making his face suitably mournful, offered a deepening grimace. 'You know I won't say anything remotely official until I fully carry out the necessary tests, Detective Inspector, but, yes, my initial assessment is that you are quite right. This young lady died around twenty-four hours ago. I will of course deny that evaluation if questioned.'

Addison nodded curtly, expecting no more or less, and turned to Narey.

'Rachel, you may as well get ready to add another strike to that list of sexist behaviour. As the resident woman in this tent, would you say that red dress over there belonged to her? Would it fit her?'

Narey didn't need to look at the red dress again: she'd been unable to stop herself from mentally fitting it to the girl's body as every successive inch of it appeared.

'It would fit her like a glove. It's just not who I expected it to fit.'

Chapter 59

'You thought it would be Faith Foster?'

'I thought it might be.'

'So where is she?'

'I have no idea. Maybe there's another body in here somewhere. Apart from the old ones, before you say it. I think we need to talk to Stark again. You got my message about his flat? The crazy murals and the triangles?'

'Yeah. Puts him right in the frame. We've had him locked up all day but this was done last night. He's been one fucking step ahead of us. But, if he is, then he's not on his own. Someone threw that dress out of a van while he was in Stewart Street.'

Addison fished his mobile from his pocket and punched in an address from the contact book. It rang for an age before finally being answered.

'Sam? I was hoping you'd still be up ... Yes, I know it's my fault that you're still working. Have you— No, I know what you— Right, okay, okay.'

The DI ended the call and looked up to see barely concealed amusement on the faces of those around him.

'You people not got jobs to do?'

*

Addison's phone rang again, just a minute or two after Sam Guthrie had aborted the last conversation. It was her. Fearing he was going to get his bollocks chewed off in public for a second time, he moved off away from the other cops into a quiet patch of ground under the stadium roof and steeled himself.

'Addison.'

'I don't like being rushed and I particularly don't like being rushed in the middle of something that is already a rush job. Some things deserve to be taken slowly and being fast isn't always good. Don't you agree?'

She had a way of making him think that he was always hearing innuendo in whatever she said. And, although he was thinking it, he was pretty sure she was making him think it. He just didn't know how.

'Um, yes. I do agree. What about this particular job? When might it be finished without any extra rush on your part?'

The noise on her end of the line might have been a sigh or a laugh at his expense; as usual, he couldn't be sure.

'Well, if I were needing to finish both profiles to get a positive match from either of them, then it would probably take me a further two hours. As it is, I can give you an unofficial but assured response right now. Unless you want to wait the extra two hours, of course.'

'Yes. I mean no. I don't want to wait. What do you mean if you needed to get a positive match? Surely that's what we want.'

It was definitely a sigh this time.

'Yes, Detective Inspector. I am sure that's what you want. But, you know, you can't always get what you want. Neither

DNA sample is a match to that found at Caledonia Road. Neither Stark nor Barclay.'

'Shit! You sure?'

'I did say it was unofficial but assured, didn't I? Look, as I'm sure you know, we target ten specific parts within the DNA known as short tandem repeats. If we get a match on all ten points then the odds of it not being the same person is one in more than one billion. I've been through seven of the STRs and can tell you already that neither of them match. Stark isn't Atto's son and neither is Barclay.'

'Shit, shit, shit. Okay, thanks. Um ... why couldn't you have just told me this in the first place?'

He thought he could hear her smiling on the other end of the phone.

'Sometimes, Detective Inspector, the longer you have to wait for something, the more you want it and the more worthwhile it is. Don't you think?'

'How well do you know Ritchie Stark, Mr Barclay?'

'Reasonably well. We work together. We're pals.'

'Well enough that you can ask him to provide you with an alibi for a murder and he will oblige?'

'Sergeant Giannandrea! My client has already explained his reasons for asking Mr Stark and Ms Foster to cover for him.'

'Indeed he has, Mr McEwan. And that has got him into serious trouble. It is up to him if he is able to get himself out of it. Answering my questions might allow him to do that. Can we continue?'

The solicitor nodded grudgingly towards his client.

Barclay had lost much of his earlier fury and was now looking scared.

'Mr Barclay, I'll ask again. How well do you know Ritchie
and Faith?'

'We go out for a drink now and again. Maybe listen to
music together. That sort of thing.'

'You trusted them. You must have done to put something
like that in their hands.'

Barclay scowled. 'Yeah. I did.'

'You went to their flat in Tobago Street, didn't you?'

'I've told you. Yes, a couple of times. Why?'

'Just curious. You ever been in the bedroom?'

'What? We weren't close like that! What are you suggesting?'

'Nothing at all. Wouldn't be that odd, would it? Anyway,
have you ever been in the bedroom?'

'No. Never.'

Giannandrea paced round the room a bit, hands in his
pockets, thinking.

'Strange place to live, though, don't you think? If you move
up to Glasgow from Nottingham and choose to live in that bit
of the East End. Not particularly close to your shop – must be
a mile and half away.'

'I suppose.'

'You suppose … Did Ritchie ever tell you why he wanted
to live in that particular street? Was it significant in any
way?'

Barclay's eyes furrowed in confusion. 'Significant? No. It
was just a flat. He didn't particularly like it but it did him
okay. Anyway, it kept Faith happy, so he went along with it.'

'What do you mean it kept Faith happy?'

'It was her idea. She told Ritchie that it would be a great place to live. That she'd always wanted to stay there.'

'You're sure about this?'

'Positive. Remember thinking that it was a bit odd. Hang on ... where are you going? Mr McEwan, where's he going?'

Giannandrea's phone call to Narey ended almost at the same time as Guthrie's to Addison. She walked over to find him looking ready to spit nails, Winter following on behind her.

'It isn't Stark,' he told her as she got nearer. 'That's the DNA results back and Stark isn't Atto's son. It isn't Barclay, either. We're back at square one.'

'Not quite. I think we've been looking at this wrong the whole time. Tony, think back to what Atto told you when he said he'd been emailed by his child. Can you remember exactly what he said?'

Winter puffed out his cheeks, trying to remember as accurately as possible.

'Atto said that he'd received the email out of the blue. He said, "The gist of it was that he was my child." And then he said, "Well, 'your spawn' was the exact phrase used." He said the son had never said what his name was, or the mother's name.'

'What's your point, Rachel?' Addison asked.

'The point is that the child didn't say he was Atto's son. Atto assumed that. We all assumed that. In the email the person simply said they were Atto's spawn. That was Rico on the phone. He's interviewed Barclay again and asked him if he knew why Stark chose the flat in Tobago Street. He says that

Stark didn't pick it: his girlfriend did. Faith Foster was the one that wanted to live there.'

Addison's eyes widened. 'You're fucking kidding me!'

'No, I'm not. I think Faith Foster is our killer.'

Addison sighed as he hit the buttons on his phone. Sam Guthrie picked up immediately.

'You just can't stay away, Detective Inspector, can you?'

'Seems that way. Sam, you said that the sample from Caledonia Road was very poor quality, right?'

'Yes but not so poor that I can't be certain it isn't Stark or . . .'

'Yeah, yeah. I get that,' Addison interrupted. 'But was it so poor that a gender test couldn't be done?'

Guthrie hesitated, thinking. 'I wasn't involved at that stage but yes, looking at the case notes, they weren't able to establish that. Given the circumstances, I think perhaps some assumptions were made or at least uncertainty not flagged up.'

'Jesus. Thanks, Sam.'

'Derek?'

'Later.'

Addison nodded at Narey, confirmation that she was right. Winter stole a glance at her, a sudden need to hug her. A sense of pride that he wasn't entitled to any more. Addison, however, had more questions.

'Wait a minute, Miss Marple. That's all very well but those girls were raped. I'm not sure if you remember your school biology lessons but—'

'That's strike number three. And, yes, I know. That had occurred to me. But I do remember seeing a strap-on sex toy in a drawer in Stark's flat. That would have been enough to simulate it. If it was covered in a condom, tests wouldn't have shown any difference.'

'Jesus. So what's Stark saying?'

'Not a thing. He just sits there and blanks anything said to him.'

'So he must know it's her that's been doing this.'

'More than that I'd say. We always felt getting the girls into a vehicle and moving them to the cemeteries was more likely to have taken two people. And Foster's small. I think Stark must have helped her.'

'And he could have raped them. I know you're keen on your strap-on – as a theory – but it could have been Stark.'

'Yes, it could. Doesn't matter for now. The point is, where the hell is Faith Foster?'

The three of them stood in the rain-sodden gloom of Janefield Cemetery, water cascading noisily off the roof of the football stadium just yards away, and realised they didn't have an answer between them. The Tobago Street flat had been secured by uniformed cops all day and the white van seen racing down Tollcross Road turned out to have false number plates. Funny little Faith, with her goth make-up masking much of her real face, could be anywhere in the city.

All three of them jumped when Winter's mobile rang, the

blare of the ringtone cutting through their shared thoughts. He took the phone out of his jacket pocket and studied the display. Number blocked. Normally he wouldn't even consider answering a call from a withheld number but this wasn't a normal night. He hit Receive.

'Hello?'

'Hello, Anthony.'

The self-satisfied tones crept through the line and Winter could feel the hairs on the back of his neck standing on end.

'Mr Atto,' the use of his name was more for Narey and Addison's benefit than his. The look of confusion and concern on their faces was immediate. 'How are you?'

'Oh, I'm very well, Anthony. Good of you to be so polite to ask when you must be worried about what I might have to say to you. Are you at the Eastern Necropolis, by any chance?'

Atto was playing with him, taking every chance to show off his knowledge at what was going on. Play him back at his own game, Winter thought, play up to his arrogance.

'Yes I am. What's going on, Archibald? You're the one that seems to know everything.'

Atto couldn't help but let loose a high-pitched squeal of delight that he quickly turned into a haughty laugh.

'Maybe not everything, Anthony. But enough. The prodigal son contacted me to say that his latest would be found at the Eastern but that it would be there before you expected it. He also said that it was simply a diversion.'

'A diversion?' Winter repeated it loudly enough to alert Narey and Addison.

'Yes. He said it would give him the time he needed to go after his final target. I did say he'd been keeping a close eye on you and Mr Neilson, didn't I? That's why I'm calling you, Anthony. To say that I can't help you after all.'

'Please, Archibald.' Using the man's first name was sticking in his throat but so was the tang of fear. 'If you know what's going on then please tell us. You said you didn't want any harm to come to us.'

'No, I said that I didn't want anything to happen to *you*, Anthony. I didn't say the same about ex-Sergeant Neilson. I don't like him. Never have done. What happens to him or his is none of my concern.'

'Him or his? What do you mean?'

'Well, it seems it has all become rather personal. My child has targeted the child of Mr Neilson's child. So you were right after all, Anthony. The sins of the father will be visited upon the children.'

Atto laughed again, clearly pleased with himself.

Winter's mind raced. Chloe. Danny had told him that he'd been seeing Chloe. Chloe with her bright-red hair.

'Don't do this. If you know anything, then for God's sake tell me.'

'I don't think so, Anthony. It would be interfering with natural selection. How can I stand in the way of my boy following in his father's footsteps?'

Winter knew it was a gamble but it was all he had.

'But it's not your boy. It's not a boy at all.'

The silence on the other end of the line seemed to last an age before Atto finally blurted out a response.

'What do you mean? What are you saying?'

'It isn't your son that has been doing these killings. It's your *daughter*. Your spawn all right, but not your son.'

'That's impossible. He said—'

'*She* let you think that. Just a girl, Atto. What was it you said? The inferior species, secretly grateful for men to be in charge of them? Doesn't seem that way now.'

Atto screamed with frustration. 'No. *Noooo*. That can't be true. You're lying to me.'

'I'm not. Think. Did your child ever, even once, say "son"? Or did she say "child", "spawn", anything other than "son"?'

'He's lied to me. He . . . she's . . . not my child. Just a mistake, a bastard born from a whore. Not mine.'

'So tell me where to find her. She's lied to you, like you said. Just a girl outdoing what you did. Why would you protect her now?'

'Don't try to trick me. I know what you're trying to do. I'll decide. I'm in charge here.' Seconds passed. Winter could hear him breathing hard, almost hear him thinking. Atto was manic. Addison and Narey stared at him, all sorts of questions written on their faces.

'It's not my child,' Atto concluded, his voice cold now. 'There's no reason for me to help it. I don't know exactly where that thing is going to take the girl but I know it's some-where she was with Neilson. It said it had watched Neilson there with the girl. That the girl had looked so happy there that it would be a good place for her to die.'

He picked up after a few rings.

'Danny, it's Tony. Shut up and listen.'

Chapter 60

Danny was in his car within two minutes of Tony's call. His heart was pounding, hurling itself at his ribcage despite his mental efforts to calm it. The thought that he couldn't get rid of, and didn't want to, was that it was all his fault.

He spun out of Hopehill Road onto Maryhill Road, immediately flattening the accelerator, mouth dry and eyes strained, speeding past the shops on his left-hand side. On Napiershall Street, he should have given way to traffic at the mini-roundabout but he didn't: he put his foot down even harder and flew straight through, causing a black Astra to jump on its brake, then sound its horn furiously.

On Great Western Road, he ploughed through a set of traffic lights showing red, forcing pedestrians and other cars to take evasive action. At Lansdowne Church, he forced himself onto the other side of the road and across the front of cars turning right into Park Road. Up and over the hill towards Hillhead he charged, the steeple of Oran Mor towering above everything else in the distance. Cars filled both lanes at the junction to Byres Road and the Botanics, and there was no way past. Instead, he swung across the face of the traffic, the wrong way onto the slip road by the side of Buckingham

Terrace, and mounted the pavement on Queen Margaret Drive. He was out of the car and running without a thought of locking it.

Breathing hard, he ran as fast as his heavy frame would let him through the gates of the Botanics and into the park. He headed straight for the Kibble Palace, seeing it up ahead, its dome strikingly lit and resembling an alien spaceship about to return home.

As he got nearer, he slowed, just as anxious to get to her as soon as he could but aware of the need to regain his breath and make as little noise as possible. His breathing was so loud, his heart pounding even louder.

The door to the Palace was open and he slipped inside as quietly as he could, stopping to listen for any sounds inside. The place was hauntingly lit, spotlights shining high towards the dome and giving the giant ferns an unearthly look and a warm orange glow to the curve of the ceiling.

There was something – a noise off to his right. He couldn't place what it was, couldn't distinguish even whether it was a voice or a step, but it was something. The noise was gone as quickly as it had appeared. He started in the direction that it came from, feet flat but moving quickly, adrenalin pumping feverishly.

The noise again. Someone talking. A girl's voice. Chattering.

He slowed, crept, fearful, a forest of giant ferns between him and his prey. And *her* prey.

The voice was louder now, intermittent as if the speaker was waiting for an unheard reply, more talk, then silence. He pushed past more trees and there in front of him, before he expected it, was a figure prone in the clearing by the white marble statue of Eve. His throat seized as he saw it was Chloe lying flat and unmoving on her back, her flame-red hair set vividly against the virgin white of the statue's base.

He felt something cold yet hot at his neck, followed immediately by a blow that made his knees collapse, his hand flailing helplessly towards the point between collar bone and ear where the pain was. As he sank he saw his fingers and they were wet and red, thick with the blood that poured from the wound in his neck. As blackness came, he realised the knife was still plunged into him.

He woke on his back, looking up to the dome and the heavens beyond it, ferns peering down at him in wonder. He reached to his neck and felt his skin part and nerves tingle. There was no knife there any more.

He sat up on his elbows, seeing Chloe still by the statue's base. Crouching by her side was a diminutive figure, all in black. He knew from what Tony had told him that it must be Faith Foster and that the knife must have been hers.

His head spun and his limbs ached. He'd rarely felt so weak, but he thought he could stand, slowly and quietly pushing himself to his feet, finally upright but swaying. Foster didn't look up or turn around, but simply raised her voice.

'I can hear you, big, fat man. Very surprised you're on your feet so quickly. That's impressive but don't come any closer. You'd regret it.'

The girl's voice was neutral, almost playful. And all the more threatening because of it. Danny strained to see how Chloe was but he couldn't tell much from where he stood. His brain tried to process the warning from the girl half his size: the threat had to be to Chloe rather than him, which surely had to mean she was still alive.

Foster turned and looked at him, her face pale and impassive, her eyes lined in black and a black lipsticked bow forming a quizzical centre to her features. She didn't appear remotely fazed by his being there, and that worried him. The girl was only about five feet tall once the bulky platform shoes were discounted, yet she was eerily calm.

'I might regret it if I get closer,' Danny admitted. 'But I'll definitely regret it if I don't.'

The girl shrugged slightly, the merest movement of slim shoulders, and reached into the crushed folds of her long black dress. Still showing no emotion on her blanched face, she produced a long-bladed knife that glinted in the Palace's artificial light and ran red with the rivulets of Danny's own blood.

'You will definitely regret it if you do, old man.'

Danny took one ill-advised lurching step forward and Foster calmly laid the blade across the soft white of Chloe's neck, stopping him immediately in his tracks. She kept her eyes firmly on his and drew the blade back and forth, just missing skin and jugular by tiny margins.

'Don't do that,' Danny half ordered, half implored. 'There's been enough killing. If you were trying to make a point, you've made it.'

Foster smiled sweetly, her head tilted to the side wearing a powdered face-mask of innocence, the truth being revealed only when it morphed into a lascivious, black-lipped smile.

'You think I've made my point? How could you possibly know, old man? You don't know me. You don't know what made me. The only point you need to worry about is on the tip of this knife and what it will do to your grandbaby's pretty little neck.'

Danny knew he didn't have much left. He must have lost a lot of blood and most of his energy.

'She's done nothing. If it's your father you're trying to take this out on, then it's got nothing to do with Chloe.'

'Are you actually trying to psychoanalyse me, you stupid old bastard? This isn't about taking anything out on my father. He's about the only one that hasn't tried to change me. It's about the rest of the world. At least Daddy did something. My mother just took it. Took it and hid it and infected me with it. Bad enough that she gave it to me but then she had to tell me all about it before she died. Who wants to hear something like that, eh?'

'What, you think you got genes from Atto like you caught some kind of disease?'

The girl shrugged again. 'I don't know. I just know people always told me I was weird. All my life. I thought it was them that were weird but then they all seemed to be the same. So I stayed on my own a lot and maybe I got weirder – or they did. I always liked things that were different from what they liked.'

'Like death? Cemeteries?'

'Yeah. What's wrong with that? My dad and my gran were buried in Cardonald Cemetery. At least I *thought* he was my dad. I'd go up there to visit them and it was all right. But the Necropolis was so much better and I'd go there and imagine that's where they were buried. I had graves there that I'd picked out for both of them and I'd go there and talk to them. Then I started going to all the old ones, looking for graves that were a wee bit special and choosing them for my dad and my gran. I got really into them.'

'This was before you knew about who your real father was?'

'Yeah. The old whore told me about it when she was dying. I'd always hated her. Always. And she'd always hated me. It was her last revenge, I think. Telling me as if it explained how I was. So maybe I decided to prove her right.'

'Prove her right? You murdered people, innocent girls not much older than yourself.'

'They weren't innocent. They were part of the people that made me different. Those kind of girls always hated me, so I hated them. Like her ...' She pointed the blade of the knife at Chloe's throat. 'She's one of them. Normal, pretty, popular. So I hate her.'

'She's never done anything to you. Please, let her go. I'm begging you.'

'Beg all you want. My dad used to make the girls he killed beg. I read all about him. Everything that had ever been written about him. He's pretty famous, you know. So beg, old man. I'm going to kill her, anyway, but beg me not to. She might even be dead already from the amount of Rohypnol I gave, but the knife will make sure. It's your fault she'll get stabbed. All yours. If you hadn't turned up I'd have just strangled her.'

Danny inched closer, dragging his body forward, desperately trying not to be seen, desperately trying to move the twisted conversation away from any mention of the knife.

'How did you get your boyfriend to help you with this?'

Foster shrugged. 'He's a bit weird, too, I suppose. But he'd do anything for me. You want to know why? I give great sex.

Really great sex.' She smiled at him and licked her black lips. 'You want some?'

'No, thanks.'

'You sure? If you're fit for it and fuck me good, I might kill her fast so that she doesn't suffer.'

Danny was aware of the blue lights that were tingeing the glass curves of the Kibble, strobing above their heads as they sped past. The girl didn't seem to have noticed but the lights were followed by sirens, the noise filtering through glass and steel and closing in on them.

Foster swung her head towards the gates where the sirens were blaring and Danny took another tired step. The girl turned back, saw he was closer and licked her lips.

'No time for anything but this, then. Say bye-bye.'

She drew the knife back and Danny just threw himself at it. He didn't have the strength or coordination to wrestle her for it, so he aimed his bulk at the knife itself, intent on stopping it or taking it for himself. All he could do was hope.

As he landed, he felt his knees crash into the ground and a pain rip through the wound on his neck. Foster's head snapped back as his weight hit her and crashed against the concrete floor. All at once he felt the slice of cold deep inside him as the knife penetrated his soft flesh and sought his internal organs. He tried to lift his head to look at Chloe but darkness swallowed him up and he dived into a whirlpool of oblivion.

That was the way they were when Addison, Narey and Winter led the charge of cops through the doors of the Kibble. Danny lying on top of Foster. Chloe to their side. All three unconscious.

Chapter 61

Monday morning

It was to be his last visit to Blackridge Prison, a grudging thanks to Atto for the information that led the police to Kibble Palace. A final opportunity, in Atto's mind at least, to let him boast about the appalling acts he'd committed. For Winter, it was his last chance to get the man to tell the truth.

There was a sense of an ending and maybe of something starting anew. He doubted his ability to cope with it and even whether there was enough available space in his head, given all that had happened on the night after the final body was found. Raw emotion, death and failure – an impulsive, reckless mix.

He and Rachel had gone back to her flat, hand in hand, clinging to the safety of the truth inside each other. Waiting wordlessly for news from the hospital, letting their bodies speak, moving together in echoes of old times and not thinking what the morning would bring.

He'd held her and watched her sleep, fighting off slumber of his own so that the moment wouldn't end and be replaced

CRAIG ROBERTSON

by an awkward reality. He didn't know much but he knew he couldn't let her go again.

When she was finally wakened by the straws of spring leaking through the bedroom window, he caught the look of uncertainty on her face, silencing her with a finger placed gently across her lips. He'd had her mobile phone in his hand, a number already on the display, ready to be called. She'd smiled and nodded. He'd pressed the call button and had left her alone to talk to her dad while he made their first breakfast in far too long.

To go from that to this ...

Atto was in full flow in front of him, discussing murder as if it were an electrical appliance like a toaster or a microwave. 'If I am what I am because of the wiring in my brain, then how can I be held responsible for my actions? How can I continue to be locked up if it's not my fault?'

Winter, weary after the opening sentence, had heard the same pointless arguments from him again and again.

'Well, if you are the way you are because of your brain, then that's why you have to be locked up. Because you're incapable of not doing it again. Society needs to be protected from you.'

'That's not the point, though,' Atto yelled. 'I am ill. You wouldn't lock someone up for being ill. You would treat them.'

'You cannot be treated.'

'Not yet maybe. But one day. They will be able to treat all illnesses one day and I will be ready to be set free.'

Winter couldn't take much more. 'But you don't want to be treated, not really. You enjoyed it. You took pleasure in what you did.'

Atto smiled, almost shyly. 'Yes. Yes I did.'

'And that's why you can never be released. And why what you did was monstrously wrong.'

He used the word deliberately, knowing it would rile Atto. Being called a monster was something he couldn't abide. Winter saw the anger in the man's eyes and enjoyed it.

'I am not a monster,' Atto seethed quietly, the lower register of voice a sure sign that he was on the point of fury. 'I am ill. It is the fault of my brain.'

'No, you're a monster. You did terrible things to innocent girls. You can never get away from that. You took everything from those girls, yet you claim you feel nothing. No regret, no remorse, no guilt.'

'I took their lives, nothing else.'

'That's not true. You took their future, their innocence, their dignity. And you stole from them too. You took your grubby little mementoes, the jewellery. What were they, trophies?'

Atto shrugged dismissively. 'Perhaps. They're not important.'

'Of course they're important or you'd never have taken them. What was it, something to remind you of them? Taking a bit of those girls with you so you could play with yourself later while looking at their brooches or necklaces?'

'No.'

'Then what?'

They loved me. They'd have wanted me to have something of theirs to remember them by. To be close to them.'

Winter recoiled at the sentiment, revolted by Atto's pathological self-serving. He caught the look on Tom Walton's face and the prison governor obviously felt the same.

'You believe that they liked you?'

'Loved me. Yes.'

'And that's why you took items from them? The watches, bracelets and the rest.'

'That's between me and the girls. It's personal. Nothing to do with you or the rest of them.'

'I guess I can understand that. I've loved people and lost them. Having something of theirs makes them feel closer, like they're still a part of you.'

Atto looked at him warily but nodded, some of the anger seeping away. 'Yes. You still have things of people that died?'

'I have a necklace and a bracelet that belonged to my mother. And a watch that was my dad's. I don't look at them all that often but I like to know that they're there if I want to.'

'Yes. That's it. I knew you'd understand, Anthony.'

Winter's skin itched but he continued to push.

'Most people wouldn't, I suppose. But it makes sense, really. It means, in a sense, that you'll always have them.'

'Exactly.'

'Do you have a favourite piece?'

Atto shrugged coyly. 'I like them all. Or I did until they were taken away from me.'

'That must have been hard. The police taking the jewellery away like that. Must have been like having a little part of you cut away.'

Atto looked at Winter strangely, surprised that anyone could understand but still wary that he did. He edged closer in his seat, speaking softly, seeking a kindred spirit.

'I hated it when they took it all away. It was, it really was, like losing part of me. Those things were mine, not theirs.

They meant something to me but they were completely meaningless to them. They only took them out of spite.'

'There was no need for that. Come on, tell me. What was your favourite? Was it the silver fish brooch?'

Atto opened his mouth and Winter could see the word 'Yes' forming on his lips before he stopped and clamped it shut. It was enough.

'I've seen the photograph of you wearing it. My Uncle Danny found it in the Operation Oslo files. You wearing a brown jumper and posing next to a teenage girl. We also got hold of a photograph of Christine Cormack on her twenty-first birthday in which she was wearing the same brooch. My Uncle Danny remembered that too.'

Atto said nothing but Winter could see the anger gradually stoking flames in his eyes.

'Do you remember when we first met, Mr Atto? You told me that you were grateful that the police didn't have such sophisticated techniques forty years ago? Well, we do have them now. I have very sophisticated equipment in my lab that allowed me to take both of those photographs and isolate the brooch, enlarging them to many times their original size without losing any quality. There's no doubt at all. It's the same brooch.'

Atto said nothing but just sat and glared at Winter like a petulant child, eyes open but rocking back and forth from his waist, his mouth tightly pursed. Winter enjoyed his discomfort but couldn't afford to let the man slip into a sulky silence.

'Was it your favourite? We know you had it, there's no point in denying that. Share it with me. Was it your favourite?'

Atto looked as if he couldn't choose between anger and a

desire to talk about it. His deep, bleak eyes troubled and searching Winter's own.

'Yes. It was my favourite.'

'Because she was your first?'

'Yes. She . . .'

Atto faltered, realising what he'd said, and closed his mouth, his eyes beginning to close over and his head to rock forward rhythmically. Winter pressed on.

'You told me that you never forget. First kiss, first love, first lover, first kill. Was Christine Cormack all of those?'

Atto continued to rock, eyes locked shut and emitting a low humming sound from tightly pursed lips.

'She was your first but supposedly Red Silk's fourth. Wasn't she?'

'Hummm. Hummm.' Atto tried to block out the world the way a child would. Not listening, I'm not listening.

'You didn't keep anything from the first three Klass killings because you didn't do them, did you? Christine was your first. And, because she was, you kept that brooch, kept it beside you, even more precious than all the other bits of jewellery that you stole from those other poor girls. My guess is that you always kept it on you, somewhere secret and safe. So that when you were arrested you were able to keep it from the police.'

The obsessive rocking got faster and the humming got louder.

'I'm guessing that it was so special that you kept that brooch pinned inside your clothing. Had it on you when you were arrested and kept it ever since in your civilian bundle that is locked away awaiting you if you're let out. And you thought you would get out if you could ever get someone to believe your fabricated theory about your brain being wired wrongly. Isn't that right?'

Atto's eyes had screwed tighter than ever at the mention of the clothes he wore on admission and that were held by the prison. By the time Winter finished, he could stand it no longer and his eyes opened wide and frenzied.

'You better not go near my things!' he screamed.

'Too late.' Winter didn't take his eyes off Atto but shouted behind him. 'Danny!'

The door at Winter's back slid open and in walked Danny Neilson, a swathe of dressing at his neck and the signs of considerable padding below his ribcage. In his gloved hand, something small and silver was glinting.

'Recognise this?'

'That's mine,' Atto shrieked, quickly on his feet and his face turning purple with fury. He moved towards Danny and the guard behind him smartly moved off the wall and wrapped his arms around him. Atto shrugged him off, surprisingly easily throwing the officer back and reaching behind to throw his chair out of the way, his eyes an inferno. He got within two feet of Danny, who stood stock still, welcoming the threat despite his injuries and ready for the struggle, before the guard recovered and threw himself at Atto, knocking him to the floor and this time pinning him securely.

Atto lay on the floor, the beefy prison officer on top of him, his legs kicking furiously but helplessly. Danny stood over them, looking down at the little man, squashed and full of impotent rage.

'You really think this is yours?' Danny held the brooch out so that Atto could see it from his position of humiliation on the floor, taunting him with it, intent on making him angrier and angrier. 'This isn't yours. This is Christine Cormack's.'

'It's mine!' he screamed. 'You have no right.'

'Oh, and you have a right because you killed her? You really think so?'

'She was mine. It's mine! You had no right to go through my things. No right at all.'

Danny shuffled closer so that his feet were by Atto's face, his boots just an inch or two from the snarling contortion of hate that disfigured the man's bland features. The temptation to swing his boot back and then violently forward was enormous, and he had no doubt how satisfying it would be. Instead, he crouched down as well as the wound in his stomach would allow, holding the brooch between gloved fingers and sliding it past Atto's nose.

'Christine's brooch. Not yours. Hers. And we will find her DNA on it.'

'It's mine, you fucking bastard. Mine. I earned it. It's mine. Give me it!'

'Earned it? Jesus Christ. Your brain being wired wrongly would only explain half of it. And, yes, we heard every word. All recorded too, thanks to the nice governor here.'

Atto squealed and flapped, a fish out of water and knowing it was out of time.

Danny inched closer. 'We met once before, didn't we? Before Tony and I ever came to Blackridge. You were in Klass on the night of the Red Silk for a Night contest. And you took it way too far.'

Atto recovered a sliver of his bravado, sneering up and looking more deranged than ever before.'

'That's right. You spilled my drink, ex-Sergeant Neilson. Spilled my drink and couldn't do your job.'

'I've done my job now, though, Atto. Maybe it's forty years too late but I've still done it. You will be arrested and charged with the murder of Christine Cormack in July 1972.'

Atto laughed, manic but hollow. 'You think I care about that?'

'Maybe not but I do. The law does. Christine Cormack's family does. Oh, and I know you care that people think you were Red Silk. You get off on that like the sick bastard you are. But you weren't Red Silk, were you? You were a pretender. You were only Red Silk for a night.'

'You can't prove that I didn't kill those first three girls.'

Danny threw his head back and laughed loud and long, causing pain to rip through his stomach wound but not caring in the slightest. When he'd finished, his sight settled on Atto, a huge grin on his face.

'You pathetic little prick. Are you really that stupid? We don't have to prove that you didn't kill them. We only have to know that you didn't. If you want to claim them as more notches on your bedpost then you are the one that has to prove you killed them. And you can't, can you? You can't prove it because you didn't kill them. You're a fraud, Atto. Red Silk? Red face more like. You're nothing.'

Atto put his face to the floor so that Danny couldn't see it, hiding from him and the truth. But he could do nothing to stop his ears from being filled with Danny's laughter as he left the interview room, the sound of the last laugh echoing even after the door slid closed behind him.

Winter waited till the door was fully in its lock before he

walked over and took Danny's place crouching beside Atto's head, a knowing look up at the prison governor as he did so.

'It's not nice, is it, Archibald? The humiliation. The loss of face. The loss of legend. All those sordid little trophies will have to be handed back.'

Atto squirmed, his face still firmly to the floor. Winter hesitated.

'Okay, Archibald. Maybe there is another way. I've got a proposition for you.'

Chapter 62

Epilogue

Friday night, Saturday morning. It all rolled into one in Glasgow. Just as you couldn't tell where the gloom of the night met the darkness of a city street, you couldn't always tell where the night before became the morning after. No one could see the joins and no one had seen the horizon in a long time.

This night the rain was stoating off the slick, grey surface of Gordon Street in front of Central Station and blurring the distinctions even further. A sodden conga of the barely dressed and the fretful waited in boisterous turn for the taxis that would ferry them out of the city centre towards home. The rain dampened only their clothes and hair; their spirits, whether good or bad, were protected by an umbrella of booze.

It was ever thus and would ever be so. Danny Neilson had spent more time than he cared to remember on this damp bit of pavement. Long after he was gone, there would still be different versions of the same angry little men and daughters of the same leggy teenagers, singing party tunes and eating chips and cheese, waiting on a black hack to Cardonald or Anniesland.

Taxi o'clock, Chloe had called it, but it was time that stood still. On Friday and Saturday nights, he and the other marshals were on until five in the morning when the last of the clubs shook the stragglers out of the doors and onto the streets. Weary, beery and occasionally cheery, they still wanted to be driven home to their mammies or their jammies. It was his job to make sure they got there.

The hi-vis yellow tunic that was pulled over his jacket said, Look at me and listen to me. I'm the man who will get you home. I can't sleep until you do. Can't sleep until I know you're in safe.

They all demanded that of him. Even the arseholes. Daft boys with a bigger thirst for beer than they had a head for sense. One of them tried his luck, edging in from the side of the queue with the gallus bravado of the unashamedly blootered. He was met with the flat palm of Danny's hand in his chest, looking from the hand to the man behind it and doing a quick bit of mental maths and coming up with the wrong answer.

'C'mon, granddad.' He glared. 'It's late and I want to get hame. Get oot my way and there'll be no bother.'

Danny shook his head wearily. Here we go again.

'Don't worry, son, there won't be any bother. Listen, if you're really in a hurry then the ambulances are pretty quick at this time of the night. You want to get in one of those?'

The guy focused and took a closer look at Danny. 'Um, nah.'

'Didn't think so. Get to the back of the queue and wait your turn like everyone else.'

The boy gave a skew-whiff grin. 'Worth a try, big man. Eh?'

'Sure, son. Now away out my road.'

These nights in the rain were seeping into his bones, washing away at the marrow of him. He wouldn't, couldn't, do it any other way, though. It was him.

Just as he couldn't stop watching the news coverage of the digs near Ipswich and Coventry. It seemed that every minute he wasn't on the street was spent in front of the television. The cameras were kept at a discreet distance but they still spent long hours showing shots of large white tents, the comings and goings of grim-faced coppers and forensics and endless shots of presenters talking into the screen.

Eleanor Holt did most of the TV interviews, telling of her feelings as the digs proceeded. Marjorie Shillington consented to one or two but she remained, outwardly at least, much more frail than her friend and shied away from the spotlight. The TV stations couldn't get enough of them – the first two parents finally, after years of heartbreak and not knowing, to discover the potential for some peace. The story was that Archibald Atto had found a conscience and had given police the locations of the two shallow graves where Melanie and Louise were buried. He had also promised that, once they had been recovered and given proper and long overdue funerals, he would divulge the sites where his other victims could be found.

It stung Danny's soul to hear presenters give credit to a serial killer for finally doing the right thing. To be fair, the acknowledgement was made grudgingly and each time couched with a reminder of his atrocities, beginning they always said, with the four infamous Red Silk murders in Glasgow in the early 1970s.

Mrs Holt and Mrs Shillington had both sent him expensive bouquets of flowers as thanks for the little he had done. Even if he was fond of flowers, which he wasn't, his conscience wouldn't have been able to bide the sight of them. Instead, they were being watered from the heavens, propped up on Jean's grave in Sighthill Cemetery.

He did appreciate the gesture, though, and the display of emotion behind it. But, more than that, he'd appreciated the sight of tears of happiness on the faces of the two women. The recovery of the bodies meant confirmation of something they hoped would never be but that they desperately wanted. Their babies were home again.

There is a price to be paid for everything and the ticket for the women's peace of mind was that Atto got to glory in murder. Including murders that he didn't commit. Then there was the tax on top of it: that the real killer of the three girls from Klass had never been caught and now probably never would be because the world thought it was Atto. Death and taxes are the two certain things, so they say.

He knew he would have to carry around with him the knowledge that Foster and Stark hunted victims because of the red connection, Foster thinking her father had killed those four girls. Kirsty McAndrew, Hannah Healey, Ashleigh Fleming and finally a student named Beth Owen who had been on her way to a party in a new red dress: all died because of that. He would be haunted by the irony that they killed

Kirsty just because she wore red shoes and had no idea that she had had a tattoo done by Stark's boss. What he couldn't be sure of was how much of that would be put right by the fact that Atto had finally been charged with Christine Cormack's murder. It was a selfish little victory, a sticking plaster on a torn conscience, and he struggled to take any pleasure in it.

Barbara was talking to him, though, and that was something he could be satisfied with. It was a talking of sorts, a start of something rather than an end. She still couldn't make up her mind whether to blame him for Chloe being at risk or thank him for saving her life. He'd have settled for either as an alternative to distance and silence. She was his own lost girl. The others were finally going home to their parents, and maybe she would too.

And then there was Tony. Tony and his deal with the Devil. Even the suggestion of it had been enough to turn Danny's stomach. A means to an end that was against everything he'd tried to do for forty years. Atto would give up the sites of nine graves, starting with Melanie and Louise. The drip of information would be spaced out in order that the finds got maximum and prolonged television exposure. And so, of course, would Atto.

In return, Tony wouldn't tell the world that Atto was not and never had been Red Silk. He was to be allowed to continue in his twisted charade, luxuriating in a renewed status as multiple killer with a social conscience, the peace of mind of others within his gift.

Atto revelled in it every bit as much as it sickened Danny to watch him do so. He tried to call Tony every day from prison, anxious to discuss the latest developments and share his memories of the locations that appeared on television.

Sometimes Tony would take the call and sometimes he wouldn't. According to prison staff, this would alternately enrage Atto or amuse him as he declared that Tony couldn't handle having him burrow into his mind.

However, Atto was wrong.

No matter how much he had tried to get inside Tony's head, he had failed to learn enough about him.

It wasn't until the police had confirmed that the two shallow graves in England did indeed contain the remains of Louise and Melanie that Tony shared the truth of his plan with Danny. He would play along, he'd let Atto talk and boast. He would indulge the killer's vile need to share. Then, as soon as the last of those lost girls was returned to her parents, he would contact every news station, every newspaper and every website in the country and tell them that Atto was a liar.

Atto had entered into the agreement blindly, bound by the need to trust Tony to maintain the façade he had carefully cultivated for so long. Ultimately, he would be undone by his own arrogance. He wasn't the Devil: the Devil was in the detail of Winter's deal.

Atto would surely rage and he would threaten all manner of revenge that he couldn't deliver. He would sulk and lie but he couldn't prove he was something he wasn't. The certainty of death and the tax on Danny's conscience could be reduced by one.

The real killer of the three girls from Klass would never be known only if everyone stopped looking for him. Brenda

MacFarlane, Isobel Jardine and Mary Gillespie didn't deserve that, and Danny would keep looking, even if no one else did.

He surveyed the girls among the late-night, early-morning revellers in the lashing rain outside Central Station, thinking them a world away from the young women in the summer heat of Klass, yet knowing they were exactly the same.

Danny knew he couldn't save them all, but that didn't mean he couldn't try. He stretched a restraining arm in front of two tall mid-twenties wide boys whose eyes were looking west but seeing east as they were about to get into the front taxi. Instead, he beckoned forward a teary-looking teenage girl from further down the queue whose tottering heels were barely holding her up. 'In you go, hen. Make sure she gets in her front door, Sammy? Good man.'

There, he'd saved one.

Acknowledgements

I owe a vote of thanks to everyone at Simon & Schuster, in particular my editor Maxine Hitchcock for her unstinting support and enthusiasm but also to Emma Lowth, Florence Partridge and a host of others.

To my agent Mark "Stan" Stanton" I offer my apologies that this book is not named Necropolis and also my gratitude for his grey-bearded wisdom.

While much of this story comes simply from the dark recesses of my own imagination, I needed the technical know-how of reality to stitch those thoughts together. To that end, I am grateful to the following.

To Professor Jim Fraser, director of the Centre for Forensic Science at the University of Strathclyde for helping me out of the DNA hole that I'd dug for myself. To retired Detective Inspector Bryan McLaughlin, former head of Criminal Intelligence at Strathclyde Police, for his invaluable knowledge of 1972 policing methods.

To David Hamilton of the Scottish Government for his

insight into the formation of the new Police Service of Scotland. To staff at the Scottish Prison Service for their help in the creation of the entirely fictional Blackridge Prison.

And finally, to my stunt-double and fellow crime writer Michael J. Malone for the story of the boy that saved the starfish.

To the ghosts who inspired this book, I wish them peace.

The Faroe Islands.

Forty-nine thousand people.

Seventy thousand sheep. Eighteen islands.

Nineteen connecting tunnels. Three traffic lights.

One murder in twenty-five years.

Until now.

Turn the page for an exclusive extract from
Craig Robertson's brand new thriller
coming soon in Summer 2014

Hardback ISBN 978-1-47112-773-1

Ebook ISBN 978-1-47112-776-2

Nogle stukke med lange spyd,
Og andre med knive skare;
Inver mand gjorde sin dont med fryd,
Slet ingen ænsede fare.

Some were stabbing with long spears
And others were cutting with knives
Everyman joyously performed his task
Nobody noticed danger.

Grindevisen, Faroese Whaling Ballad verse 47

Chapter 1

There comes a moment in the wrestle for life where the distinction between opposing sides is blurred to the point of blindness. Did I start this fight or did he? Am I on top or being forced back down? Am I winning or losing? Have I won or already lost? My blood or his blood?

I can see the blood, taste it, smell it. I can feel it lick my skin and hear its rush in my ears. Blood means life but it also means death. My senses are suffocated, drowning in shades of red. All I can do is fight.

Would-be killer and would-be victim, rolling and grappling; life fighting death fighting life.

If he doesn't die, I can't live. If I die, he has won.

The blood's in my nostrils now, not just the scent of it but the liquid reality of it. My bones ache and my lungs burn. Life and living is on the line.

I feel a tiredness that I know I can't afford. The life thief thrashes at me, sending pain surging through my body. It rings in my wrists and my chest, my knees. Then three violent knocks in quick succession against my ankles, an orchestra of pain, all my joints singing from the same hymn sheet.

I'm losing. I'm lost.

My eyes snapped open, seeing the world through a bloodshot veil. They slid closed again, reluctant to see whatever the orange half-light had to offer. The final, familiar chords of a tune were still playing in the back of my mind but out of reach.

I moved a hand beneath me, groping blindly for clues. Wet. Smooth. Cold. Whatever I was lying on was as hard, sleek and unforgiving as marble. It explained the brutal ache in my joints and the throbbing in my back. But they were nothing compared to the pain echoing through my skull.

I tentatively moved one leg then the other, trying to shift from the foetal curl I was locked in, my muscles protesting at the call to action. My right eye edged open again and I saw that it rested half an inch above a pillow of dark grey stone, my cheek flat to its rain-dappled surface.

So cold. At the realisation of the raw chill, a shiver squirmed through my body and didn't stop until it rattled my teeth. My bones were as cold as my limbs were stiff. Every little movement was slow and painful. I withdrew back into my curl, wrapping my arms around myself hoping for warmth and salvation. Neither came.

I lay there, disorientated on my unknown bed of stone, drifting back towards sleep. A voice deep inside told me I had to move.

My head was so heavy and the world spun as I lifted it. My brain tumbled inside my skull like a ship cut loose from its moorings in a storm.

I managed to push myself up onto my elbows and looked around. My surroundings were a blur. It was dark, or at least what passed for dark here. Still dark or newly dark? I couldn't be sure. What light there was glowed amber from up above.

Shop fronts and vaguely familiar facades slowly came into focus. It was the colours of them that made some sense: red, then mustard yellow, white, then pale blue. I was on Tórshavn's western harbour, at Undir Bryggjubakka.

On the breeze of that realisation, came the smells of the sea – salt and seaweed and a faint whiff of oil – and I slowly turned to see it lapping blackly behind me, white boats bobbing obliviously to whatever plight I faced.

I looked below me, stupidly, a realisation slowly dawning. My black stone bed was one of four great slabs on the harbour where the fishing catch was laid out daily. Slate beds for fish and shellfish. Not for drunks.

The canopy above the slab had kept me reasonably dry. Maybe that's why it had seemed like a good idea at the time. I couldn't stay here now though, too cold and the fleet might be due in. I had to move.

I edged forward, inch by aching inch until my shoes dangled over the side of the slab. I pushed myself to my feet and immediately wished I hadn't, oxygen surging and balance gone. I half sat, half fell back onto the stone, my hands reaching up to massage my temples. I pushed again and staggered onto the empty street, veering left because of a homing instinct rather than any real sense of direction or purpose. I walked, head low, arms out, weaving my way up Torsgøta, turning my head away from the disapproving glower of the cathedral high to my right, and climbed towards the hills.

The wind had picked up from nowhere and was taunting my ears, whistling cold round them but helping to keep me on the right side of sleep. The pavements were black wet beneath my feet, the road even steeper than normal and it made for hard work. I took a stumbling turn left and just minutes later, another freezing gust came at me off the sea, making me shiver and forcing me to abandon the use of my hands as balancing aids, driving them into my jacket pockets in search of warmth.

'Shit!'

A sharp pain flashed through my right hand and I tore both of them back out of the pockets as if I'd been electrocuted. Underneath the streetlight, I could see that my right palm was stung with blood.

Cautiously, I reached back into the pocket and pulled out a short, stubby knife. Even in my muddled state, I knew what it was, this wooden-handled dagger with its thick blade. All adult males on the islands had one. It was a *grindaknívur*. A knife for cutting whale meat at the dinner table.

But this one had been used for something else. Its blade was coated with blood. Blood that was dry enough that it hadn't come from the cut to my hand.

I patted myself randomly: hands, arms, head, stomach. I pulled up my shirt, examined the visible flesh. There was no blood and no cut other than the one I'd just made. The blood on the blade wasn't mine.

I stared at the knife, wishing it away. Wishing I could remember where it had come from. What it had been used for.

The street, Dalavegur, seemed more exposed than it had moments before. Standing there with a bloodied knife in my hands, I could only wonder how many curtains were twitching at the sound of footsteps in the middle of the night.

I slipped the *grindaknívur* back in my jacket pocket, turned up my collar, bowed my head and walked on, hoping I was no more than a ghost, unheard and unseen.

The little knife weighed a tonne though, dragging my pocket down with doubt. Hard as I tried I could remember almost nothing. Drinks in the Café Natúr. Then waking up on the fish slab in the rain. Blackness in between.

She'd been there, I remembered that much. Laughter. Drinks. Maybe an argument. Then nothingness.

I crossed the intersection and up a narrow path. The houses were further apart now, the lush green of the hills carved into generous sections by the coloured, timber frames of traditional homes. The wind hurled itself at my unsteady frame, spinning me and forcing me to turn and look at Tórshavn laid out below me, its odd shapes pushing through the mist. Roofs of turf and rainbow hues, the cathedral spire and swathes of green. All tumbling down towards the sea. Always to the sea.

I don't know whether I was driven by instinct or guilt but I took a few steps off the path and knelt down, the blood flowing to my heavy head and making me feel I might throw up or pass out. I grabbed the sharpest stone I could find and began digging at the earth, howking out dirt until there was a hole big enough to contain the little knife.

I pulled my shirt free of my waistband and used the bottom of it to wipe the handle of the *grindaknívur* before dropping it into the newly-dug hole. Earth to earth, ashes to ashes. I kicked the dirt back over the knife, filling the hole and stamping it down. Picking up three similarly sized stones, I used them to both mark and conceal the hole. With a final look around, I pushed on up the path to the shack that passed for my home.

*

It was three hours later, when I'd somehow managed to rouse myself from my brief second sleep and get myself in to work, that I heard. Everyone there was talking about it. No doubt all of Tórshavn and the rest of the Faroes were talking about it too.

The stabbing.

The murder.

Chapter 2

Three months earlier. June.

I was blown into the Faroe Islands on the wind. Picked up by a squall that dumped me on the first bit of dry land that held fast between the sea and the sky. Due north of where I started. Both zero and 360 degrees north of the place I'd left behind.

It was 180 miles from Scotland, 360 west of Norway and 270 south of Iceland. It could have been the definition of the middle of nowhere. It could have been anywhere. Just as long as it wasn't where I'd come from.

Emerging from the front door of the tiny airport, I stood and looked. And saw nothing. It wasn't just that the concrete concourse was enveloped in mist and drizzle, it was that there was nothing to be seen.

There was the bus which would take an hour or so to Tórshavn. That apart, there were just the ghostly outlines of a handful of cars scattered around and beyond them what might have been the vertical shadows of telegraph poles.

My bags stowed in the belly of the bus, I found myself a seat next to the window, huddling myself against it and staring out into the summer gloom until the vehicle rumbled to life and moved off.

A few of my fellow passengers fell into conversation and, despite myself, I tuned into their chat – not the words which were incomprehensible to me, but the sound. The accent sang, like the Gaelic. It was like listening to fishermen from Galway on Ireland's west coast or crofters from Lewis. It had a lilt and a rhythm that smiled through the murky evening.

On the connecting flight from Copenhagen, I'd heard the song loudly and constantly. It had been the last flight of the day and more than a few of my fellow passengers had fortified themselves for the journey by downing plenty of beer or wine. The plane's aisle heaved with so many cheery, ruddy-cheeked Faroese it looked like we were flying to a farmer's convention. The boozing didn't stop there either. The cabin crew were worked off their feet trying to satisfy the demand as free alcohol flowed freely indeed.

Perhaps that was what explained the apparent sang-froid when the weather came calling. Despite our flimsy piece of flying aluminium being pitched and tossed left, right, up and down as we flew through a storm, the locals didn't bat an eyelid other than calling for fresh drinks.

I watched the wings of the plane flutter like a girl's eyelashes, at times just yards from lush green mountain tops that emerged suddenly and threateningly through the clouds. As we neared the Faroes and circled them, trying to find a way to land, the rugged crags appeared nearer and more often, looming up from the angry sea that was occasionally visible through breaks in the porridge-thick fog.

The skyline changed constantly, unnatural angles being

created and the sea far too close. The wind roared as it buffeted against the side of the plane, slapping it like wet towels against bare legs and hinting at what it could do if it had a mind to. The good slaps sent it sideways, the bad ones caused it to drop alarmingly, leaving stomachs behind.

Tall, improbably balanced rock stacks reached up to us from below. Islands flashed by. If I'd cared about it, I might have seen my life passing by before my eyes.

A middle-aged woman across the aisle feverishly fingered a cross round her neck and mumbled a prayer to her god, tears streaming down her cheeks. She, like me, must have been a visitor. The rest had seen it all before or were viewing it through the bottom of a glass. I watched a man in a business suit turn to his companion and shrug, a grin on his weathered face.

Then it got worse.

We must have caught the edge of the jet stream because the plane tipped almost on its side and glasses and cups flew through the cabin as we dropped further and faster than before. In the long seven seconds that we went into free-fall, I found time for three thoughts. One, that maybe there was such a thing as karma and that payback would definitely be a bitch. Two, that I wished I'd drunk the last of that whisky before the glass went flying on its own. Three, that I was going to die.

There is something comforting in that moment. Particularly when your own survival isn't something that concerns you too much. Seven seconds to contemplate mistakes and weigh up regrets. At the end of the day they don't amount to a damn thing.

We hit the bottom of whatever it was we had fallen into and the pilot had the thing going forward again, even if only straight to hell. The woman opposite was in hysterics but the islanders merely laughed, if they bothered to react at all. Most had skilfully managed to hold onto their glasses of booze and little tin soldiers of reinforcements. A man in a grey suit, his tie at a crooked angle, signalled to a strapped-in stewardess that he'd like a refill of his vodka. She said no and he shrugged in equal measures of acceptance and disappointment.

I lacked their confidence in it all working out all right but I cared as little as they seemed to.

Instead, I found myself mulling over the relative benefits of death or beer. It wouldn't be my choice to make but it passed the time while fate and the wind decided the matter for us. Death or beer? Die on that flight or get to the Faroes where the beer was said to be particularly good. Both had their attractions although death was a cop-out and I could hardly choose it without taking a planeload of presumably innocent people with me. I'd never been one for praying and although this was probably a good time to start, beer struck me as a pretty frivolous cause for divine intervention. But it didn't matter as I didn't believe. In anything.

Make a choice, I told myself, shades of *Trainspotting* coming back to me. Choose life. Choose beer. Choose death. Choose to close your eyes and let your whole shitty little existence be chewed up by your conscience till you choke on it. Choose.

As it happened, I didn't have to. An excuse for a runway appeared through the soup and, on the third pass, the wind accommodatingly presented us at a suitable angle and the pilot successfully defied improbability and kept us in line with the landing strip.

The ground rushed at us. Tyres hit tarmac with a couple of bumps and a banshee screech. A lone voice triumphantly roared 'Føroyar!' before a smattering of polite applause rippled through the cabin, reminiscent of and yet a world away from the drunken clapping that accompanied the landing of a Costa flight out of Glasgow.

They were home and I was here. It was probably a bad time to start wondering why.

The road from Vágar to Tórshavn wound its way through green countryside. Rain washed down the windows of the bus. Every so often, hamlets of no more than a dozen or so homes would appear without warning. The square, weather-beaten houses, most made grimy by the elements, all faced the sea. All the better, I supposed, to see the next wave of weather that would come to torment them.

There were no people. Not one single soul on or by the road. I saw sheep though, plenty of them. I saw seabirds. I saw horses. I even saw the brown flash of a mountain hare scampering across the lower slopes of a grassy hill. I just didn't see any people.

Suddenly, the road dipped and the bus sailed down a steep incline into the black mouth of a tunnel. I'd read online that many of the archipelago's eighteen islands were connected by undersea channels but it still took me by surprise. In seconds we were under the Atlantic in a passageway carved out of solid rock. It burrowed its way straight and long as far as the eye could see, like travelling through the stomach of a giant serpent. The concept of a tunnel with no light at the end of it was depressingly familiar.

Finally, slowly, we began to rise then turn until we emerged gasping from the serpent's mouth onto another island.

The process was repeated a number of times, some of the islands only being traversed for a few minutes before the sea swallowed us up again, leaving us underwater for miles at a time. We didn't island hop; we burrowed.

Above ground, the terrain was a moving feast of greens and browns with russet highlights through the gloom. Hillsides were studded with grey rock and cut through with lazy streams running from top to bottom. Regularly, the misty showers were pierced by the sight of brilliantly white waterfalls tumbling down from the higher mountain tops, seeking a return to the sea. The landscape was a battlefield for opposing forces; earth and water collided with casualties of war everywhere you looked. There was barely a piece of hillside that didn't carry the scar where rain and river had left its mark.

We ran parallel to fjords, verdant hills menacingly looking back at us from the other side, dark clouds low above their tops. When the mist cleared, you could see hill behind hill, peak beyond peak, an endless rolling maul of volcanic eruption now covered in green. Wherever the fjords or the sea made natural bays, there were houses dotted by its shore, communities formed out of opportunity.

Against that backdrop, the first hints of a near-urban sprawl came rudely: a garage, a shop, a forest of direction signs, houses packed together in rows, the floodlights of a football stadium, industrial units, zebra crossings and offices. The bus careered round a ring road, spun off a roundabout and turned left before dropping us onto a concrete canvas upon which was painted the drizzly shadows of a ferry port. *Welcome to Tórshavn*.

I stood on the tarmac, two bags at my side, the rain in my face, and shivered slightly in the chill of what was supposed to be a summer's night. My fellow passengers trooped off to waiting cars or taxis and within seconds I was standing alone. I had wanted remote; I had no right to start complaining.

It took less than five minutes to walk into the centre of town and find the Hotel Tórshavn, a tall, red building sitting at the bottom of a steep hill and just yards from another section of the port. It was to be home until I found somewhere to live.

Inside, I shook the rain from my jacket and dropped my bags by the front desk. The receptionist, a slim young man with dark hair, smiled politely and asked if he could help me. I told him I had a single room booked and he began to thumb through his reservations.

'Your name, please?'

'It's Callum. John Callum.'

'Ah yes, I see it. Are you in Tórshavn for holiday or business, Mr Callum?'

'Neither. I'm here to live.'

The desk clerk's head rose from his paperwork and he regarded me oddly. 'Really?'

The room was tiny but functional. A three-quarter bed was pushed up against one wall yet floundering halfway along it with no head rest behind. The door of the narrow wardrobe banged against the wall-mounted television and everything was in touching distance of everything else. The windows ran the length of the far wall – a somewhat insignificant feat given the size of the room – and light poured through them despite it being so late. I closed the blackout curtains, making pretence of it being night despite the lack of darkness, and poured myself a generous glass of the malt I'd bought in passing through the airport. After a movie on television and several revisits to the bottle of whisky, I found some sleep, my six foot two frame cramped into the inadequate space.

I woke what seemed like five minutes later, snapped from sleep by the sound of banging on the wall from the room next door. As my eyes searched around me, trying to work out where the hell I was, the angry greeting from the neighbouring room stopped. The noise that I'd so obviously been making had ended with my sleep and my nightmare. I realised I was soaked in sweat and disorientated, my breathing heavy and my system in shock. I lay there, recovering.

Getting to my feet, I pulled back the curtains and was dismayed to see the day had already begun. It was going to be a long one.

I tumbled into the shower, enduring the jagged needles of hot water, then put on some clothes and left the room. The receptionist looked up, bemused, as I walked through the automatic doors onto the streets of Tórshavn.

I walked where the wind took me. Up one deserted street and down another, daylight and drizzle on my shoulder, in search of something but not knowing what I was looking for. There was an eerie sense of solitude about the place, disturbed by neither cars nor people, that only increased my sense of confusion.

I stopped to look in the window of a shop that sold

local-made knitwear and, above a range of chunky-knit sweaters, I saw a large white clock hanging on the wall. It was 2.30am.

My heart sank but at least my legs were strong. I started walking again.